The Blissful Omegaverse

THE COMPLETE SERIES

KATE KING & JESSA WILDER

Copyright © 2022 by KATE KING & JESSA WILDER
All rights reserved.
First published in 2022
King, Kate, Wilder, Jessa
The Blissful Omegaverse: Complete Collection
No part of this book may be reproduced in any form or by any electronic or mechanical means, including information storage and retrieval systems, without written permission from the author, except for the use of brief quotations in a book review.
All characters in this publication are fictitious and any resemblance to real persons, living or dead, is purely coincidental.
Editing: One Love Editing
Cover Design: Kate King

Authors' Note

We want to thank you so much for coming along on this ride with us and finishing this series. We loved writing Bliss's story, and watching her grow into the best version of herself. We hope you love reading it.

For everyone who has read our Gentlemen series, you know that we like to leave some plot lines open-ended to allow room for the possibility of further books within the same world.

This is the last book for Bliss. She and her alphas will 100% get their Happily Ever After.

For certain other characters…this isn't their story.

Trigger Warning

Pack Bound:

If you are a seasoned dark romance reader, or even a casual dark romance reader, this book likely won't phase you. Much of the story is light in tone and would fall in the realm of sweet omegaverse. However, please be aware that the underlying world and themes of this story are dark. They will remain dark throughout, and the subject matter may be upsetting for some.

CW: Dub-con, Sex Trafficking, Non-Consensual Drug Use, Multiple references to violent sexual assault and physical abuse by a domestic partner (not within the harem), Kidnapping and Imprisonment, PTSD, Depression, Violence, Murder. One of the characters cuts their own arm. We are including this as a potential trigger for self harm.

Tags: Omegaverse, Reverse Harem, Rejected Mates, Childhood Friends, MMFMM, M/M, Knotting, DVP, Stretching, Heat shenanigans, Touch Her and Literally Die.

Pack Bliss:

CW: Sex Trafficking, Kidnapping and Imprisonment, Multiple references to violent sexual assault and physical abuse by a domestic partner (not within the harem), PTSD (Descriptive), graphic violence, dub-con.

Tags: Omegaverse, Reverse Harem, Breeding Kink, MMFMM, M/M, Knotting, Stretching, Heat shenanigans, DVP, Orgasm denial.

What is Omegaverse

The Omegaverse (or A/B/O dynamics) is a speculative alternate reality where humans live in a wolf-like hierarchical social system, and take on some lycan traits such as scenting pheromones, mating for life and forming packs. People are unsure of their designation until they transition to either an alpha, beta, or omega.

The alphas tend to be larger, more athletic and more aggressive than regular humans. They have the most prominent animal instincts, and are the elite of society. Omegas are rare and physically delicate. They are the perfect biological mates to alphas, and the only ones who can have alpha or omega children. Betas are the most common designation and are essentially average humans.

There is no magic in this book. While the alphas, betas and omegas may have some animalistic instincts and practices, they are not shifters or werewolves.

Pack Origin

For Emily.

Our biggest supporter, most honest critic, and third member of the Baby Desert Eagles Club.

PACK ORIGIN

A BLISSFUL OMEGAVERSE PREQUEL NOVELLA

INTERNATIONAL BESTSELLING AUTHORS

KATE KING   JESSA WILDER

CHAPTER 1
Rafe

Ares' fist slammed into the man's nose with a wet crack, and blood sprayed across the pavement, splattering on my shoes. I stepped back slightly out of the line of fire. I'd planned to help, but clearly there was no need. One punch and the beta was out cold.

My best friend and I stared at each other.

"Shit," Ares spat, echoing my thoughts. "I didn't mean to do that. Now we have to wait for him to wake up."

He let the bleeding beta drop onto the filthy ground, and I nudged the guy with the toe of my worn-out boots. I grimaced. "I don't know, man. I feel like we're going to be waiting awhile…if he wakes up at all."

Ares groaned, running one hand through his white-blond hair. The blood on his fingers turned it pinkish in the front, like some kind of boy-band idol. He frowned and wiped the rest of the blood on the inside of his leather jacket. "Dammit."

I hid half a smile. It wasn't supposed to be funny, and it

wasn't really, but if he'd paused for ten seconds to think, Ares would have realized this would happen. Betas didn't bounce back from a hit like that like an alpha would, and now we'd have to find someone else to question.

Ares bent down and rummaged in the man's pocket, unearthing a wallet, a phone, and— "Fuck, yes."

I blinked a few times, trying to focus on what he was waving in front of my face. "Car keys?"

"Yeah. How much you want to bet he left the product in his trunk?" He grinned, pale eyes flashing in the low light from the nearby streetlamp. "Come on, let's find the guys and go look for the car."

I nodded and followed Ares back through the side door into the back of the nightclub in search of our friends.

Hanging out in alleys behind clubs and beating up betas wasn't how I expected to spend my senior year of high school. Fuck, it wasn't how I expected to spend any part of my life, period. Running errands for the local gang had started as a one-off thing, but it turned out we were all pretty good at it, and the money was too good to pass up. There weren't a lot of job opportunities for teen alphas, especially foster kids. Betas tended to be afraid of us, and to be fair, that incident in the alley just now wasn't helping our case much.

My eyes darted all around the darkened club, skimming over the writhing bodies and flashing lights. This wasn't my scene at all. The smell alone was too much. The air tasted like lust, anxiety, and desperation. Like salt and burnt marshmallows.

"There." I grabbed Ares' arm and pointed across the room toward where I'd just spotted Killian and Nox cutting a path through the crowd to reach us. A head taller than everyone else, they weren't exactly blending in. Nox had his gaze fixed straight ahead while Killian was gesturing animatedly, chatting in Nox's ear as they walked.

"Find anything?" Nox asked when they reached us. His red hair had turned neon under the strobe lights, giving him the appearance of a lit match.

"Yeah, sort of," I replied, throwing Ares a sideways look.

"I'll tell you outside," Ares said, already pushing his way past a group of dancing beta girls in tight dresses to reach the exit.

The exterior of the nightclub was a standard brick warehouse, like a converted storage loft. The heavy metal door slammed behind us as we stepped out onto the darkened street and turned to face each other. The bouncer stared at us, possibly wondering if we were old enough to be here, then seemed to decide not to comment. Good choice. He smelled like a beta. Taking on four alphas wasn't a good idea, even if he was at least ten years older than us.

"What now?" Killian asked. He was practically buzzing with pent-up energy, his curly hair bouncing as he spoke.

"Parking lot," Ares replied vaguely, setting off around the side of the building and expecting that we would just follow him. Of course, we did, so he wasn't wrong.

There weren't many cars in the tiny lot. Our beat-up Impala was one of only five or six. Ares scanned the stolen key fob, then popped the trunk of a newish-looking Nissan. My eyebrows rose as we peered inside.

A dozen cardboard boxes sat stacked on top of each other. The top row was open slightly, displaying the product inside. I reached into one of the cardboard boxes and pulled out a vial, turning it over between my fingers. It smelled sickly sweet, like fruit and honey. Euphoria and lust, but manufactured.

"Fuck," Killian said, his eyes growing wide. "That's more than I expected."

"Yeah," I agreed, not knowing what else to say.

The vials contained alpha and omega pheromones, sold to betas as party drugs. Betas couldn't usually sense things like that, but when they were concentrated like this, I guess they had some sort of temporary effect. This shipment belonged to the gang Alpha Lupi but had gotten mysteriously lost in transit when the beta that Ares knocked out in the alley decided he could take a cut for himself.

"Come on, let's take it and go. I want to do this fast and go home," Ares said harshly.

I rolled my eyes at him. No shit. We all wanted to go home and see Bliss. It didn't really need to be said.

Bliss was the only reason we did this shit anyway, and she didn't even know it.

"It's my turn," I said quietly as we strode across the grass toward the house. I hid my smile at the idea of getting to go upstairs to Bliss' room instead of ours.

Killian punched me lightly on the shoulder. "I'll trade you tonight for Saturday."

"Fuck no, 'cause on Saturday you'll forget and say it's your turn. I know how this goes."

He laughed. "Whatever, man. Worth a try."

"Quiet, both of you," Ares hissed, stopping short several paces from the front porch.

The hair on the back of my neck stood up as I listened for whatever sound had set him off. "I don't hear anything."

"Fine. Must be nothing. But be quiet—don't wake up the Wards," he snapped.

Dropping off the pheromones at the Alpha Lupi warehouse had taken longer than any of us would have liked, and we were cutting it way too close to curfew. The couple who ran our group home was already trying to get rid of us, and we didn't need to give them any more ammunition.

At the top of the stairs, the guys headed toward our room while I hovered in front of Bliss' door. Her room had a peeling plaque on it reading "Girls" in faded gold lettering. Sometimes she had up to three roommates in there, but right now, it was just her.

I slipped inside and shut the door quietly behind me, leaning against it for a moment and listening for any footsteps in the hallway.

"I heard Mr. and Mrs. Ward go to bed an hour ago," came Bliss's quiet voice.

My gaze snapped to hers. She lay on her back in the middle of her bed, staring up at the ceiling. Or rather, at the roof of the blanket tent she'd hung around her bed. She wore nothing but an oversized T-shirt and mismatched socks, and her blonde-and-purple hair fanned out across the comforter like a halo. I swallowed thickly. "Yeah? Good. We were kinda loud in the yard."

She snorted a laugh and sat up. "You think? I could

hear you guys through the window. You should be more careful."

I crossed the distance between us and slipped off my shoes and T-shirt before climbing onto the bed beside her. "Yeah, I know."

"What did you do tonight, anyway?"

I ran a hand through my dark hair, unsure if I should give her any details. Ares and Nox were pretty adamant that we keep Bliss out of what we were doing with the Alpha Lupi, and I tended to agree with them. "Just work."

She huffed, rolling her eyes. "You're the worst."

I leaned over and threw an arm over her waist, tugging her closer. "I know."

Bliss made a small, contented sigh, and my chest swelled with satisfaction. I yawned as the taste of Bliss' sleepy calm filled the air. Sleeping next to her when she was tired and projecting her feelings was like taking an extra-strength dose of melatonin, which was good, because otherwise it was almost impossible not to think about touching her. Sometimes I was glad Bliss was a beta, if only because she couldn't smell how much I wanted her.

It was beyond stupid that we kept sneaking in here to sleep next to her. Any romantic relationships between foster siblings were grounds for instant relocation. We were risking way too much for this. But Bliss had nightmares, and none of us could stand to smell her terror from down the hall night after night, so the risk was worth it.

"I had an idea today," she muttered into my arm.

"What?"

"I feel like when we age out of the system, we should move to California."

I barked a laugh. "Why? You've never been there."

"I don't know. I saw some propaganda thing on TV for the Omega Institute today, and that's out in California, and it just made me think it sounds warm out there. I just want to go somewhere warm."

"Sure. Warm sounds good."

She yawned and nodded, snuggling deeper under her blanket. I pulled her closer into my shoulder and made a mental note to mention this to the guys tomorrow. With all the money we were making running errands for the gang, we probably could move out to California. Or wherever.

In reality, we'd always find a way to do whatever she needed. Because every single one of us was in love with her, and every decision started and ended with Bliss.

CHAPTER 2
Bliss

Bliss: Where did you guys go last night?
My nose scrunched up as three bubbles appeared and disappeared in the group text. It was like they made a pact to keep me out of the loop.

"Bliss, can you head down to Mrs. Clark's office after class?"

I looked up from where I'd been hiding my phone under my desk and made slightly guilty eye contact with my English teacher, Mr. Williams, across the room. *Crap.* I stuffed the phone in between my knees. "Why?"

He gave me a look that told me in no uncertain terms he'd seen me texting but just sighed and waved a slip of yellow paper at me. "It doesn't say. The note just asks that you head down there ASAP."

"But I have algebra," I said feebly. You knew it was bad if I'd rather go to algebra.

Mr. Williams just shrugged and turned back to the

smart board, effectively dismissing me. I sighed. *Please kill me.*

I'd been called down to see Mrs. Clark, the ancient and holier-than-thou high school guidance counselor, at least once a month ever since my freshman year. At first I thought it was just because I was a foster kid, but there were a bunch of kids from the group home at my school, and none of them ever had to go see Mrs. Clark. Apparently, I was just lucky. Or cursed. Whatever.

My phone buzzed again, and I subtly checked it between my knees.

Killian: Miss me?

Rafe: She just saw you, Asshole.

When the bell rang, I got up, swung my backpack over my shoulder, straightened my sundress, and headed for the door. No one paid me much attention as I went. No one ever really did—except for Mrs. Clark, obviously.

"Hi, Sandra." I threw a smile at the school secretary as I entered the office.

Sandra looked up from her computer and blinked a couple of times at me. Her blonde whisper bangs fluttered as she spoke, brushing the top of her cat-eye glasses. "Hello again, Bliss. What can I do for you this time?"

I struggled not to roll my eyes. "I don't know. Mrs. Clark wanted to see me?"

She laughed lightly. "Oh. I thought it might be about those boys again."

I shook my head. In fairness to Sandra, the other reason I was often in the school office usually had to do with my four best friends. They weren't the best at staying out of trouble.

"You can wait there, dear." Sandra pointed to a black plastic chair.

I sat down, dropping my backpack and pulling out my phone again. Of course, in the last ten minutes, it had exploded with unanswered messages in the group chat.

Killian: Bonfire at the spot tonight.

Nox: K.

Ares: I have to work.

Killian: Come after.

Rafe: I'll get the booze.

Killian: B, what do you think?

Nox: Bliss, where are you?

Ares: What the hell does that mean?

Nox: She's not in algebra.

Rafe: What the fuck?

Me: I just got called into guidance. Please try not to hulk out.

The door to the guidance office opened, and I whipped my head up, instinctively flipping my phone facedown on my bare thigh.

Mrs. Clark stood in the doorway wearing a navy blue suit, her graying hair pulled into a tight ponytail. She smiled. "Sorry, Bliss. I didn't mean to startle you."

"You didn't."

"Why don't you come on in."

The office was tiny and drab, just like the rest of the school. Everything in our town had needed updating since 1985, but there wasn't any government funding to do it. As much as I didn't like Mrs. Clark, you had to respect being a high school guidance counselor in such a dismal town.

She gestured for me to take a seat in the chair in front of her desk and sat down across from me. She folded her hands and gave me a smile reminiscent of visiting a sick relative in the hospital. "How are you doing?"

"Um, fine."

"I like your hair. It's so original."

I almost laughed as my hand flew involuntarily to where I'd dyed the bottom few inches of my pale blonde hair neon purple. Her comment had a very "hello, fellow kids" vibe. "Thanks."

I tensed, knowing that whatever bizarre thing she wanted to talk to me about was right around the corner. My grades, my life at the group home, my relationship with my friends, all seemed to be fair game. Lucky me.

"So, I called you in today because I wanted to chat about what you plan to do after high school."

I blinked at her. That was at least a somewhat normal subject for a guidance counselor to bring up—unlike a month ago when she went on a weirdly obsessive rant about my friends. Still, she'd unintentionally touched on a sore subject. I was turning seventeen soon, which meant I only had a year left until I aged out of the foster care system. All my friends had already turned seventeen, so we were quickly running out of time to make money and a plan. Actually, maybe Mrs. Clark *did* know that.

"This is the time when you should apply to colleges," Mrs. Clark said. She clearly hadn't noticed my moment of reflection.

I snorted. "Ma'am, I'm sorry, but college requires money. There is no chance I can afford to go anywhere."

She smiled and pushed a stack of papers toward me. "There are lots of government grants and scholarships for betas. I know it might sometimes seem like only alphas get that kind of leg up in education, but you just need to know where to look."

I glanced down at the top brochure and frowned. It was for a betas' college in the Midwest. Well, that wasn't going to work. "Er, thanks. I'll think about it," I lied.

Mrs. Clark gave me a shrewd look. Maybe she was used to kids lying to her, or maybe she just knew me well enough by now, but I got the strong feeling she didn't believe me. "Bliss, can I offer you some advice?"

No. "Sure."

"You need to start putting your own best interests first and thinking realistically about your situation."

I blinked at her, my fingers knotting in the fabric of my skirt. "What does that mean?"

Her eyes darted to the side, like she was choosing her words carefully. "If I'm being frank, with no family and no plan, you don't have a lot of good prospects."

"I have a family," I said automatically, indignation rising in my stomach.

"Your…friends aren't going to provide a stable future for you. Packs don't form around betas."

"Um, I mean…"

"Those boys you hang around with are still young, but alphas get possessive. You could end up hurt."

My heart pounded in my ears. I'd heard this kind of thing before from my foster parents, teachers, random girls at school. People just didn't get it. They didn't understand *us.* "Ma'am, I don't know what you think is going on, but we're just friends." I forced myself to maintain a neutral expression. "We can't have any relationships like that at the group home. Nothing is going on."

She gave me a "yeah, right" look. I wished I could tell

her that, unfortunately, the second part of that was completely true. "Bliss..."

"Thanks for your advice. Was that it? I think the bell's about to ring."

She stood as well, smoothing her hair. "Yes, but please take the college brochure."

"Uh-huh." I grabbed one at random and stuffed it in my bag.

Mrs. Clark walked around her desk and swung the door open for me and then halted in her tracks. I peeked over her shoulder, and my face split into a grin.

Thank God.

The chair where I'd waited was now occupied once more, this time by one of my best friends. Killian's head popped up when the door opened, his chestnut curls bouncing, and he stood up to his full—considerable—height.

Behind him, Rafe leaned against the wall, seeming to want to blend into the shadows with his dark hair, black eyes, and all-black clothing. His tan and sharp jaw made him look like the star of some teen drama, and he absolutely knew it. He grinned at me over Mrs. Clark's shoulder, and my heart beat faster.

"Hey, B," Killian said loudly, trying to reach for me.

Mrs. Clark visibly stiffened. She, like most betas, was probably afraid of all alphas, even if they were seventeen. I didn't really blame her. Except for my guys, most alphas scared me too. Their size and strength were enough, but add in their ability to control a room with just their bark, and I saw no reason to mess with them.

"All set?" Killian asked, half to me and half to our guidance counselor.

Mrs. Clark paused, and for a minute, I thought she was going to shove me back in the office and slam the door, but then she relented. "Yes. Bliss, you can go."

Killian grinned. His height and muscle mass made him look old for his age, but his cheeks were still slightly rounded with youth, and his damn dimples made him more adorable than hardened. Even if he didn't look at least five years older than seventeen.

Rafe pushed off the wall to stand on my other side as we left the office. "What the hell was that about?"

I had to tilt my head all the way back to look up at him. It was the same with all four of the guys. It had been clear from the time they were children they would turn out to be alphas, but in the last couple of years, things had really gotten out of control in the size department. It was like I woke up and suddenly all my friends were a foot taller than me and sporting muscles on their muscles. I was still waiting to morph into the standard willowy tall beta, like I remembered my mother being. In the meantime, I'd seemed to have stalled out at 5'2".

"Nothing important," I said truthfully. I definitely would not be dwelling on that conversation if I could help it.

Killian's eyes were skeptical, but he didn't push it. "Come on, we're skipping out on last period."

I laughed as he grabbed my hand and pulled me toward the double doors to the school parking lot.

"Why?"

Killian winked. "Because we can."

———

I stood in the shadows of an overflowing dumpster in a darkened alley, my back up against the brick wall of a shabby convenience store. The low, flickering streetlamp cast the only light, and the dumpster was giving off the distinct smell of week-old food. I could honestly say I would have preferred to go to algebra than hang out here.

I took a few steps to the left to distance myself from the dumpster, the filthy water from a puddle splashing against the hem of my sundress. My heart sank. *Gross.*

Beside me, Killian laughed. "Don't tell me you're prissy all of a sudden?"

"There's 'prissy,' and then there's 'oh my God that smells disgusting.' Don't judge."

I slapped the back of my hand against his entirely too firm stomach and glared up at him. He made a satisfying oomph sound, making me smirk, even if he was faking it for my benefit.

"Come on, B. You don't gotta play that way." His homey scent overpowered me, blocking out the reeking garbage as he wrapped one of his heavy arms around me in a bear hug, lifting me off the ground away from the puddle.

I squirmed against the familiar hold, pinching his side as laughter bubbled its way out of my mouth. "Let go of me!"

"Make me." His threat was completely undermined by the laugh in his voice and the way he stood primed to attack me.

"Betas have skills too, you know," I said between gasps of laughter. His smirk took up his entire face. "Yeah? Show me."

"Listen—"

Blue and red lights reflected off the side of the building, cutting me off. Killian hauled me behind the dumpster and out of view of the street just in time for the cop car to pass. I let out a breath.

We weren't doing anything wrong…at least, not yet. Rafe was the one in the store getting the alcohol, and he wasn't back. It wasn't like the cops could give Killian and me a ticket for loitering. What they would do, though, was run our names and drag us back to the group home. The last time we got caught, our punishment was a weekend in isolation. A shiver ran through me at the thought.

Killian ran his hand up and down my arm as the lights from the cop car disappeared. He grinned down at me and shook his honey-brown hair out of his deep brown eyes, only for it to flop back in place, skimming the tops of sharp cheekbones.

"You need a haircut."

He glanced down at my hair, eyes maybe lingering for half a second longer than usual on where the ends brushed my chest in my thin dress. "Nah, never. If I need a haircut, so do you."

"Shut your mouth." I grinned, fingering the ends of my mostly blonde hair.

Killian's eyes were slow to meet mine. "I like the purple."

"Got it." Rafe jogged up the dark street, interrupting our conversation, a wicked smile across his mouth. In his all-black attire, he blended in with the night.

"Hurry up," I hissed, reaching out for the bag in his hand as I looked around.

"Chill, we're good." He handed the brown paper bag to me with a grin.

I shoved the vodka, bag and all, into my backpack. "Come on, let's go."

I wasn't being dramatic—at least, I didn't think so. There weren't any second chances at the group home, and underage drinking was definitely on the list of offenses that would get you kicked out. Fast. My gaze bounced around, looking for anything that might get us caught. The faster we got out of here, the better.

Rafe glanced down at me, taking in my rigid posture, and slipped his fingers below my jaw. "Relax. We've got this."

I frowned. I hated when the guys downplayed things. "Mmmhmm."

Rafe's skeptical gaze scanned my face, and he rubbed his thumb over the seam of my pinched brows. His voice dipped low. "There's nothing to worry about, Bliss. No one's getting caught."

I entwined my fingers with his, swinging our arms as we walked. "Whatever. The guys are waiting."

The park was only a few blocks up the road, and I followed Killian through the winding path surrounded by trees, Rafe close behind us. The crisp night air nipped at my hair and ears, and I was grateful to see the light from the fire up ahead. Either Nox or Ares—hopefully both— were already here.

Our spot wasn't anything special. A small clearing in the center of a grove of secluded trees. The previous summer, we'd built a fire pit and scrounged up a collection of old lawn chairs, logs, and one moth-eaten old couch to furnish our home away from home. It still wasn't great, but anything was better than the group home.

My footsteps crunched over twigs and dead leaves as

we approached, announcing our arrival. Nox lay stretched out on the ratty couch, like he had sprinted all the way from school just to get the best spot first. Honestly, he probably did. He glanced up as we came into view, his slightly freckled face splitting into a grin. "Hey!"

Killian flopped down on a lawn chair on the far side, a smile taking over his face. "Hey, brother."

I rolled my eyes at the theatrics as I dropped my schoolbag and sat on the arm of the sofa. I reached for the book Nox had discarded when we arrived. "What are you reading?"

"Nothing you would like."

"You don't know that." I grinned, even as I tried to look offended.

"Uh, yeah I do, but be my guest if you want to bore yourself to tears."

I raked my fingers absently through the tips of his copper-brown hair while flipping through the book with the other. "Yeah, I don't know about this." I pretended to grimace. "I'm going to leave the extra-credit English assignments to you."

He leaned into my touch like a cat, and a soft rumbling sound came from his chest. I snatched my hand away. Nox's arm wrapped around my middle and dragged me over his lap to sit beside him. He kept my legs draped over his, and I rested my head in the crook of his arm to hide my flaming face.

"It's fine, Bliss, I'm a guy. Cut me some slack."

"Mmmhmm."

That was the problem though. Lately I didn't want to cut them slack—any of them. The last year had been filled with barely there touches and not so accidental grazes, but nothing ever came of it, and it couldn't. At least, not right now.

"Where's Ares?" My gaze flicked around the clearing as if he'd suddenly appear.

Rafe stood by the fire and tossed a few hot dogs on the grate over the fire. "He's working, remember?"

"Oh, yeah." A sick feeling flipped my stomach. Lately, it seemed like one of them was always missing. They'd been showing up with money, and I knew for a fact they hadn't picked up any legitimate jobs. "I supposed you're not going to tell me where he went though?"

Nox squeezed my knee, and Rafe gave me an apologetic shrug. "No idea, actually. Sorry."

"Whatever…" I mumbled under my breath.

"I'm here." Ares' thick voice met my ears before his face became visible from the path. His pale blue eyes and white-blond hair would have made him look almost angelic if his smirk wasn't so self-satisfied. Clearly, he'd heard me. "Alright, Love?"

Relief washed through me at the sight of him, quickly followed by a tinge of anger as he slid an envelope stamped with a crescent moon—the symbol of the local gang—into the pocket of his leather jacket. I ground my teeth. "Yup."

Ares took the seat next to Killian and pulled a Sharpie out of his pocket to doodle something on his calf. "What did I miss?"

"Nothing," I said honestly.

He looked up at me, eyes almost fluorescent in the flickering light. "Why were you in guidance again?"

"Oh…" The back of my neck heated. I didn't even know why I was embarrassed; it was so damn stupid. I chuckled awkwardly, trying to make it no big deal. "Just another person sticking their nose where it doesn't need to be."

"Meaning what?" Rafe's tone was just on the edge of turning dangerous.

Killian stood up and cleared his throat, drawing my attention to him. "Scoot over." He plopped down on Nox's left, pulling my legs into his lap and running his fingers over my calves.

"Bliss, what happened with guidance?" Rafe asked again impatiently, sitting on Killian's now empty chair.

I tilted my head, searching Rafe's face across the fire. His hooded gaze branded me, making my skin heat. I licked my dry lips. He never looked at me like that…at least, not that I'd noticed. "It's not a big deal," I said, looking down. "Just wanted to remind me packs don't form around betas. We're different, so it's not worth talking about."

Ares growled, and my eyes flashed to him, as though I'd been summoned…or something. His eyes went dark, and I had a sudden, almost uncontrollable urge to stand and go over there. The air tasted different, like iron and wool.

"C'mere, Little Wolf." Nox reached for me again and picked me up easily, placing me on his lap. My back tucked in against his chest, and his chin rested on my shoulder. "Ignore her. They just don't get it."

I nodded. That was true. Our situation wasn't normal, but then again, nothing about our lives had ever been normal.

Our group home was state run, specializing in placements for teen alphas. It was hard to find permanent foster care for them because people considered them aggressive, especially after years in the system. That wasn't exactly untrue, but it was still shitty and unfair. My guys had all bounced in and out of foster care as kids, but because they all came from an alpha parent and it was clear where things were headed, none of them had ever been adopted.

I'd ended up in the group home by chance. My beta mother had dropped me off when I was five and never came back. I'd been fostered out several times but kept getting sent back to the group home. As a beta, it should've been easy for me to find a permanent home, but it never was. The longer I was away from my guys, the more miserable I became. It was a deep ache that grew each day we were apart, and no amount of pretending could hide it forever. All the foster parents eventually sent me back, trading me in like a used car for a younger, happier model.

Every time I came back, my guys were waiting for me. My family. My pack. The thought of being permanently separated from them made my heart twist in my chest. Not after all of these years and everything we'd been through. They wiped my tears when I scraped my knees, beat up school bullies, and loved me when no one else would.

We were family, and family took care of each other.

Rafe's attention focused on me, his elbows on his knees, where he sat across the fire from us beside Ares. His shoulders were stiff, and my gaze settled on a muscle that ticked in his jaw. Energy snapped between us, sizzling in the air, but he leaned back, breaking the moment. The light of the fire cast shadows over his face until all I could see was his piercing gaze. "Next week's your seventeenth birthday."

I leapt on the change of topic like a starving animal on an all-you-can-eat buffet. "We all know that's not my real birthday," I said too fast, playing it off like it didn't matter, but a twinge of pain stung my chest. My mom didn't bother to leave a birth certificate when she dropped me on the center's doorstep. The best they got out of her was I was five, and she was clearly a beta. Knowing your designation was a main staple of our lives, so at least I knew that.

Ares gave me an intense stare, and when he spoke, his voice was low and assertive. "It counts to the system, which just means we only have a year left to figure out where we're going."

"Five months." I grinned. "You're almost eighteen."

He nodded, conceding the point.

"You two are so serious." Killian leaned over the edge of the couch to grab my abandoned backpack and pull out the vodka. "We should be talking about a birthday party, not this stressful shit."

I smiled at him, holding out a hand. "Give me some of that, then."

He took a deep swig before handing it to me. The cheap liquid burned my throat, forcing me to clear it, but it warmed my stomach when it settled.

Nox did the same, then screwed the lid on and tossed it to the guys across from us. The mix of heat from the liquor pooling in my stomach and Nox pressed against my back left my body languid. I needed to get off him before I did something stupid. "Kill, move over. I need room."

He shifted until there was enough space for me to slip between them, but he grumbled something about being comfortable while doing it.

I made a high-pitched noise when they both pressed into me. Warm energy coursed through my center, and Nox's hand clamped around my thigh, holding me still. I slammed my mouth shut—*oh my God, what the hell was that?*

Killian moved closer so that his leg lined up against Nox's, but neither of them mentioned it. Sweat trickled down my neck, and I lifted my hair to expose it to the cool air. Was it hot out here? Did we really need that many logs on the fire? Except when I looked at the fire, the embers were nearly out.

Nox's soft growl rumbled against my side as his nose traced a line of my neck. "You smell good, Bliss. Almost like…I'm not sure. But I like it."

I focused on the others, and they all stared back at me with that same hungry expression. The taste of smoke and honey hit my tongue, as though it was filling the air, and my mouth started to water.

"Knock it off," I croaked out.

"Truth or dare, Bliss?" Killian asked, and an unexpected spicy taste of mischief filled my mouth. I expected the guys to protest, make a big deal about such a childish game, but they were all leaning toward me, waiting for my answer.

I swallowed hard, and a trickle of excitement ran down my spine as the full weight of their attention sank in. "Okay, fine, but I'm not going first. Someone else go."

"I'll go first. Dare," Rafe said, looking directly at me, and waited for my question.

Too nervous to ask anything I actually wanted, I bit my lip and asked, "Jump the fire."

His brow raised, his eyes rolling, and he made quick

work of it. "You're going to have to think of better dares than that."

I squirmed in my seat. The distinctive feel of his alpha bark ran up my spine. "No fair. No coercion."

He just smiled and shrugged.

Ass.

No one picked truth. Instead, each dare became increasingly riskier as the night went on and the vodka made its rounds. When Killian stripped down naked and ran through the woods, I damn near swallowed my tongue. When he got back, he took his time redressing, and I soaked up every detail, unable to look away. His chest was cut with muscles, each one forming a hill and valley. My mouth watered as his muscles flexed, and his skin pebbled under my gaze. My eyes drifted lower just in time to make out the shape of his knot before his shorts covered him. I snapped to his dark, hooded eyes, and a slow smirk formed on his lips.

The taste of honey filled my mouth again. We'd never passed this line. It was practically a cardinal in to admit that anything more developed between all of us. I knew all too well how fast the system would move you if you were caught in a relationship with another member. We couldn't risk losing each other.

Ares held my stare, ice-blue eyes mesmerizing in the dying light of the flames. "Your turn, Love."

I swallowed hard. Nerves had my stomach fluttering. "Dare."

His jaw twitched, and his eyes darted around to his friends before returning to me. He bit his bottom lip with too-sharp teeth, expression turning wicked. "Kiss Rafe."

I sucked in a sharp breath. That was crossing the line,

and we all knew it. I avoided Rafe's gaze, instead watching the other three guys for their reactions. Their eyes were hooded, and no one disagreed.

I stood from the couch and wavered on my feet. Nox reached out to steady me, his fingers practically spanning my entire waist. My heart beat out a pounding rhythm as I slowly circled the fire. I stilled, frozen in place directly in front of Rafe. His gaze was like a brand across my skin, and heat flooded through my chest. I wet my lips, and his eyes zeroed in on the movement.

When I didn't budge, he stood up and stepped closer until there was barely an inch between us. His head dipped down, black eyes searched mine, and his tongue wet his bottom lip. Heat flooded me. I wanted this. I'd wanted this for a while now.

His mouth brushed featherlight against mine. The barely there touch set me off like a Roman candle, and I stole the inches between us, opening my mouth against his, practically begging him to take it. He didn't disappoint, sliding his tongue against mine, pulling a moan from my throat. My fingers tightened on his shirt, holding him in place, then pushing him away. A liquid fiery feeling filled my limbs, and a buzz inside me begged to press harder against him. A faint scent of jasmine wrapped around me, and four deep growls filled the air.

Rafe ripped away from me, and a pained whimper escaped my lips before I could stop it. I didn't want the kiss to end. My body practically ached to continue. Rafe's hands slid across my jaw, cupping my face, and his fingers trembled as he held me. His gaze glued to me, eyes flipping back and forth between mine before he shook his head and stepped back.

I stood there, frozen, my entire body shaking. Something had shifted in the air, something big.

A tinge of worry pinched at my chest, but that was stupid. I was their beta. This was the natural progression. Just not yet.

I walked back to my spot on the couch. Neither Nox nor Killian touched me, no more hand holding or slow circles on my arm. Rafe kept his eyes on his shoes, while Ares studied me, his brows pinched together and his mouth tight.

What the hell did we just do?

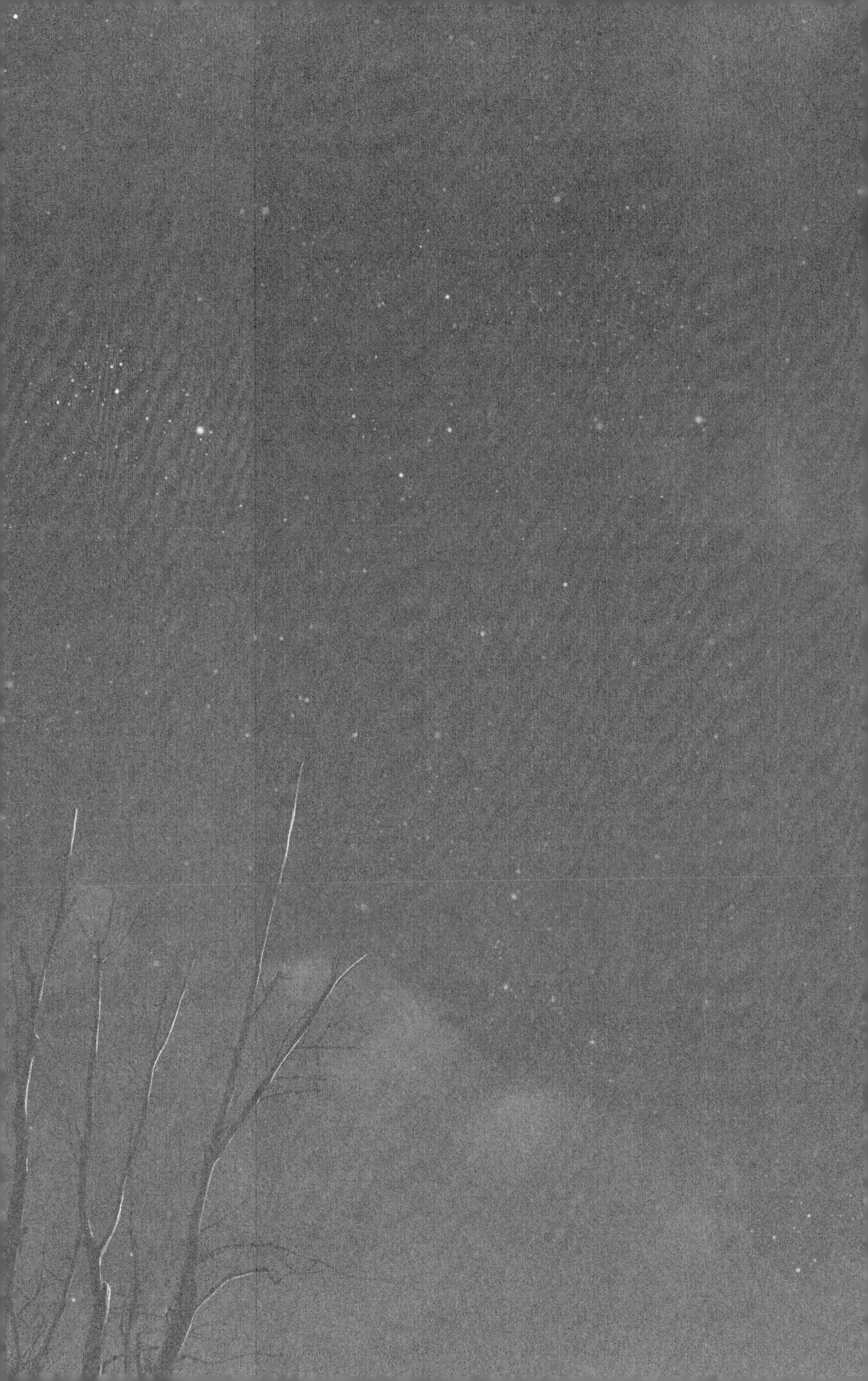

CHAPTER 3
Nox

Killian grunted as he pushed a textbook off the edge of my bed. "I don't know how you even sleep in all this."

I ignored the uneven spines of the books digging into my back. "You can always sit on your own bed."

"Nah, you wouldn't want that." Killian dropped his feet to the hardwood floor and sat up, the muscles in his back tensing under his thin, white T-shirt. He smirked. "Everyone knows I'm the only one who'll get in it with you."

I rolled my eyes. *Fuck, he's annoying.*

I jammed my foot against his back, trying to push him off, but only succeeded in knocking a few more books to the floor. I really did need a shelf. "Oh, right. 'Cause you're with a different girl every night? Can't wait to explain that to Bliss."

Killian's honey-brown eyes drained of all playfulness.

"Don't even start, man. It's been over a year, and you know it."

"Yeah, okay," I said, a sarcastic edge to my voice.

His hand whipped out, grabbing the neck of my shirt, and I laughed, twisting as I tried to break his hold on me. He was way too defensive about this. We'd all messed around, but Kill was always crawling with girls. He was right though—in the last year, he had put an end to it.

"Cut that shit out." Ares' low command pierced through me. I had half a mind to ignore him just to prove I could, but ignoring a bark took effort, and this wasn't important.

Killian dropped my shirt immediately and looked toward where Ares sat on his bed directly beside mine.

Never able to resist a smart-ass comment, Killian turned his smirk toward Ares. "Oh sorry, didn't realize you'd become a monk. Hypocrite."

Ares raised one eyebrow at Kill across the room. "You have no idea what I do. Bliss does, so shut the fuck up."

I frowned. I wasn't totally sure what that meant, but he was right. We didn't know. Unlike Killian, Ares liked to keep his rotation hidden.

About a year ago, we all started noticing Bliss making excuses to leave every time a girl was around us. Which was often. At first, we were just less obvious about our hookups, but even the idea we were hurting her had us all stopping completely. It didn't take a genius to know we were all just filling space, waiting for her.

I rubbed my palms over my eyes. It had been a long-ass night.

Rafe strode through the room and sat next to Ares. His dark hair stuck up in all directions like he'd been running his hand through it. He'd immediately taken off when we got back to the group home.

"Nice of you to show up," Ares said sardonically.

"Yeah, well, I needed to think."

"I dared her to *kiss* you." Ares punched him in the arm. Hard. "You weren't supposed to *maul* her."

Rafe grunted and narrowed his eyes at Ares. "Don't you think I know that?" He dropped his head in his hands like he needed the extra support. "I couldn't help it."

I leaned forward, setting my jaw. "Couldn't or wouldn't?"

His eyes met mine. "You think you could have her on you like that and not react?"

I looked at the ceiling and adjusted myself in my pants, trying not to picture the whole thing. "Why would you dare them to do that?" I asked Ares incredulously. "There was no world where that was going to go well."

He shrugged. "I don't know. I was drunk, and I didn't think they'd actually do it."

Lie. We could all taste the lie the moment he spoke. With our metabolism, he'd have to drink an entire handle of vodka to get drunk, and he absolutely knew Rafe would jump at the chance to kiss Bliss. Any of us would.

"Bullshit." I glared at him. "At least try to lie better."

He rolled his eyes. "No, I'm good."

"So, what is it? You're trying to push us into breaking the rules early? Well, stop. All we have to do is be patient for one more year until we get out of this shithole."

Ares' icy-blue gaze bored into mine. His voice was low and serious, as if he was proposing a bank robbery instead of dating our girl. Might as well have been. "What if we lay it out for Bliss? Just tell her now and see what happens."

Rafe's head jerked up to Ares. "Woah, wait. We haven't told her because we know damn well none of us are turning her down if she gives us the green light."

Killian's chest rumbled beside me, stealing all of our attention. "I'm in. That's exactly what I want. Fuck the plan."

I clenched my teeth, fighting back the pull to agree with him. Usually if we disagreed on anything between the four of us, it was Ares and Rafe versus me and Killian, but right now, things were split all wrong.

It was never a question of whether we wanted it. I'd kill to have her now, but I wasn't stupid enough to risk everything. I stood from the bed and pinned each one of them with a glare. "The Wards are already watching us like hawks. They'll separate us if they find a shred of proof something's going on. That sound better to you?"

I walked out of our room, my skin practically crawling with anxiety. I should leave and cool the hell off, but I couldn't ignore the magnetic pull coming from Bliss' room. No one calmed me like she did. It wasn't my turn to sleep with her tonight, but I didn't care. Whoever's turn it was was going to need to share or swap.

The girls' room was smaller than ours. They didn't stay here long. Not in a place designed for soon-to-be alphas. Instead, they used it as almost a rest stop between homes.

All except Bliss.

The way Rafe had devoured her, drawing out shallow, edible noises, made me burn with the need to press myself into them. The entire world narrowed, darkening at the edges until it was just them. It felt like years had culminated for that moment, everyone forgetting exactly why we'd never crossed that line.

We all wanted her. And we all *knew* we wanted her. She was the only one too blind to see it. But there was something different tonight. Something more.

The second their mouths parted, the overwhelming feeling that everything had changed washed over me. The realization of how far he'd gone left the air frozen. Like pressing pause on a movie right before the finale.

I slid the door closed behind me, halting momentarily when it whined. I didn't want to have to explain why I was sneaking into Bliss' room in the middle of the night. No doors opened. They never did.

The room was empty of her presence, but the window on the far wall was lifted a few inches from the sill. Cold air drifted through it.

I climbed through the window after her, my shoulders scraping the frame and the sleeves of my hoodie catching on the sides. This used to be an easy fit. The rough grit of the shingles kept my footing sure as I made my way around the side and lifted myself onto the barely angled roof. My breath came out on a sigh at the sight of Bliss' silhouette illuminated by the streetlight. Her knees were tucked to her chest, and she curled over them to rest her chin on top.

Her head jerked up at the sound of my footsteps making their way toward her. Her blonde hair was pulled into a high ponytail, the purple tips impossible to make out in the low light.

"I thought you'd be here."

Her lips tipped up in a tentative smile, and she

stretched her legs out in front of her. "You've always been the first to find me."

I lowered myself down beside her, close enough to feel her pressed against my side. The chill of her pajama pants seeped into my thigh. Her arms were covered in goosebumps, and she vibrated with a slight tremble. Fuck, she was freezing.

I pulled my hoodie off with one hand and pulled it over her head. My chest rumbled silently, pleased at the sight of her engulfed in my clothes, and wrapped my arm around her.

"How long have you been up here?" I asked, tucking her shivering body closer to my side.

She shrugged against me. "Not long."

Liar.

Bliss came up here whenever she was thinking too hard, letting worry take over. She thought she needed space from us, but her shoulders relaxed every time we found her, as if she'd been waiting for me the entire time.

I took a deep breath, debating on calling her on her bullshit. Instead, I laid us both flat and tucked her against my chest, staring up at the stars like we'd done a thousand nights before.

I pointed at a formation of three stars. "Orion's belt."

She vibrated against me with her laugh. "You always find that one. You'd think you'd start somewhere more creative."

We'd done this so often I could pick out any constellation, but I liked the way it made her laugh each time I pointed at the protective hunter.

She pointed out constellation after constellation. The

normalcy had her relaxing into me. "What's that one's story?"

I laughed. Of course she'd choose that one. I adjusted the story slightly each time I told it. "The bear. Zeus turned his girlfriend into a bear in order to protect her and hide any sign they'd been together." My skin itched, and my chest tightened as I went on. "One day when he left her, a hunter made a killing shot. When Zeus found her dead, still in bear form, he sent her to the stars to remember her forever."

She shuddered against me. "I don't like that one."

"You don't like any of them. The Greeks told miserable stories."

She snuggled deeper into my sweater and took deep breaths. Each one had her eyes drooping further.

I kept my voice low, resting my head on hers. "Why are you out here?"

She stiffened in my arms, but I didn't let her pull away. Moments passed before she answered. "I don't want anything to change."

It was my turn to stiffen. The idea that she wanted to stay friends forever didn't sit well with me, and I knew it wouldn't sit well with the guys. I pushed out my next words, knowing the guys would kill me if I screwed this up. "I think you know things are changing. You felt it, same as us."

My heart slammed into my chest with each second it took her to respond.

She tilted her head until she met my gaze. "They could separate us."

I grabbed her chin and stared down with every ounce of surety I felt. "Never."

CHAPTER 4
Bliss

The following morning, I woke to sunlight streaming through the gauzy material of the canopy I'd hung around my bed. The sun warmed my skin—hotter than it should have been. Nox and Ares' scent still clung to the sheets, and I snuggled my nose in deeper. They were gone, of course, always up and out of my room before the house woke up.

I took one last inhale before lifting my head and swiping hair out of my face. Warmth heated my body from the inside out, like I was running a fever. Or I'd been having a nightmare I'd somehow already forgotten.

Maybe I drank more than I realized last night.

I swung my legs over the side of my bed and put my bare feet on the cold, dusty floor. There were no other girls in my age group staying at the house right now, so I had my room to myself for a couple of weeks—small mercies.

Sounds already emanated from every corner of the house, despite the early hour. I could hear Rafe and Killian talking over the sound of the radio down the hall, and pots and pans banged downstairs where Mrs. Ward was no doubt cooking breakfast for some of the younger kids. That was the thing about living in a group home—no matter how hard you tried, there was no sleeping in.

At least everything seemed normal.

Images of last night came flooding back to me, and my skin seemed to heat another few degrees. That hadn't been my first kiss by any means. I wasn't even a virgin, thanks to one jealousy-induced fling I had last summer, but this was my first time kissing any of my guys. Some invisible line seemed was crossed, and I was simultaneously thrilled and terrified.

It was April, but still, for whatever reason, the weather hadn't quite decided if it was winter or spring yet. I compromised by throwing an oversized sweatshirt over cutoff shorts and slipping my feet into Converse sneakers. The blue hooded sweatshirt had either belonged to Rafe or Nox originally. I couldn't remember anymore. It was so long it covered my shorts like a dress. The fabric stuck to my flaming skin, and I strode over to the tiny mirror in the corner. I looked okay. Maybe a little better than okay—kind of...glowy, actually.

I pulled my hair over my shoulder to get it off my neck and fanned myself with the back of my hand. There was literally no chance that Mr. and Mrs. Ward would let me stay home from school even if I was running a fever, so I needed to suck it up. I opened the door to my room and took the stairs two at a time, thinking maybe the fresh air outside would help. If the guys weren't already out by the car, I'd wait for them on the porch.

Our house was shabby but relatively large. Big enough

to house up to twelve foster kids at a time, at least. Right now, we had eight—the four guys, me, and three younger kids all under the age of ten. The little kids never lasted long here, especially if they didn't look like they were going to grow up to be alphas. This group would all get sent to more permanent placement within the week. It sucked—I loved playing with the kids while they were here. It was hard not to get attached.

At the bottom of the stairs, I grabbed my backpack off the coat rack and practically sprinted out the front door.

"Bliss."

I froze in my tracks. *Shit.* Doubling back a few steps, I turned slowly. "Hey, Mr. Ward. Sorry, I didn't see you."

Mr. Ward, one half of the couple who ran our group home, sat at the kitchen counter reading the newspaper. An alpha in his late fifties, he had graying hair and lines around his eyes but otherwise looked good for his age, and he liked to make sure everyone knew it. Not that that was unusual for an alpha, but he made it seem like he was the second coming.

He lowered his paper slowly and deliberately ran his gaze up and down my body. He was already dressed for work, wearing his police uniform. My skin crawled as his eyes lingered too long on my legs and then traveled up to my chest. He took a deep breath through his nose, his eyes narrowing. "Are you heading to school?"

"Yup," I said, trying to keep my voice light. "It's Friday."

He took another deep breath, gazing at me. He was always staring at me when his wife and the guys weren't around. "You were out late last night."

"Not past curfew," I blurted. "I had to work."

"Uh-huh." He nodded and tapped his spoon on the edge of his coffee mug.

I took a step toward the door. *Okay—that wasn't too bad.*

"Wait, Bliss," he called, a bark in his voice.

I froze. *Goddamnit.*

I turned, the compulsion to obey almost impossible to ignore. "Yes?"

"How are your grades?"

"Uh, fine." I danced from foot to foot, my eyes darting around the kitchen. I needed to sit down or something. I could actually feel my skin getting warmer, though now it was accompanied by nervous nausea.

"Good. Don't want you getting distracted by those gangbangers."

Anger curled in my stomach. "That's not—"

His muscles rippled under his sweater, and it made the back of my neck crawl. I broke off. Most alphas—my guys excluded—scared me. Mr. Ward had never touched me, but I always felt like there was a "yet" at the end of that sentence. *I need to get out of here.*

The stairs creaked behind me, and both Mr. Ward and I glanced up. Ares leaned against the wall at the bottom of the stairs, black backpack slung over one shoulder, wearing a tight black T-shirt that showed off the tattoos that he'd started accumulating on his heavily muscled arms. His white-blond hair was a little long on the top and fell into bored, icy eyes.

My heart beat against my ribs, and my stomach leapt in some strange mixture of anxiety and excitement. Ares' nostrils flared, and his eyes flashed to me for half a second before darting back toward Mr. Ward. "You good, Bliss?"

I nodded slowly. It was almost weird when he used my

real name—though, of course, any nicknames in front of the Wards would be a terrible idea.

"Shouldn't you be at school?" Mr. Ward sneered.

"Yeah. We both should." Ares took a protective step toward me, and Mr. Ward's eyes flashed.

As a beta, I couldn't smell pheromones—not the way alphas and omegas could—but I could swear, even I noticed something going on here. As Ares and Mr. Ward stared each other down, the level of testosterone in the room quadrupled, I was sure of it.

I took a step further back toward Ares and grabbed him by the wrist, pulling his gaze to mine. For half a second, his eyes turned dark as he looked down at me. "Let's go. We're going to be late," I said pointedly.

To my surprise, he let me pull him out onto the porch and down to the driveway, where the other three guys waited by the car. Mr. Ward's eyes bored holes into the back of my neck as we left. I glanced back, and sure enough, he stood at the window, his gaze fixed on where I was still clutching Ares' wrist. Damnit. I dropped his hand quickly, but it made no difference as he slung an arm over my shoulders instead. I sighed, torn between telling him to back off for the sake of appearances and liking his warm scent.

"Finally," Nox called across the yard as we approached, waving at us. In the sun, his hair and scruffy stubble was particularly ginger, as opposed to their usual red brown. "I have Mr. Roberts first period, and he's always up my ass for being late."

I gave him an apologetic shrug. "Sorry."

I couldn't care less about school, but I didn't want anyone else to suffer because I was a terrible student. Nox more than any of the rest of us had a decent chance of getting into college—assuming all the guys stopped hanging around the guys from Alpha Lupi.

"So, what the fuck did I just walk in on in there?" Ares growled in my ear, not removing his arm from around my shoulders.

I tilted my head, only half-aware of the words actually spoken, as an insane urge to press my neck into his mouth hit me. "Nothing," I whined, my voice sounding foreign. "He was just asking about my grades, that's it."

Ares stepped back abruptly, just before the skin of my neck grazed his teeth. "Didn't seem like it."

I shook my head, trying to clear it. "You shouldn't challenge him like that," I muttered. "You're going to get hurt."

Ares snorted. "No, I'm not. I'm already bigger than him, and there's four of us."

"Well, forget hurt, then. You could get us kicked out."

That shut him right up.

We reached the car, and Ares unlocked it, jumping in the driver's side and starting it up. I opened the passenger side and got in while the other three guys piled in the back, just like we did every morning. The guys had done a ton of work on it, and it looked pretty good now. We were honestly just glad that the Wards hadn't sold it out from under us yet.

"Did you hear about Flora?" Killian asked as we pulled out of the driveway and headed off toward the school.

I turned around in my seat, grateful for a distraction from my burning face. "No, what about her?"

"She's gone."

I breathed a sigh of relief, then covered it as if I didn't know exactly what was going on. "What? Why?"

Flora Cabot had gone to our school ever since I'd lived at the Wards. She was popular because she came from one of the few rich families in town and had been going to senior parties since the eighth grade. I despised her.

"She's about to turn seventeen," Nox replied, as though it were obvious. "She should have been sent away long before now, but I think her parents were trying to have her finish out the school year."

"I didn't realize," I muttered.

I turned back around and sunk down in my seat, putting my face against the window's cool glass. Suddenly, I was even more insecure about her general existence. Not that it mattered. No one knew for sure she would present as an omega, and until then, she was no different from a beta, but that didn't stop her from using it to flirt with all the guys. Especially the alphas.

If she ended up presenting as a beta, the Institute would send her back. A jealous part of me wanted her to.

"How long until we know if she's coming back?" I asked, trying to sound casual.

"She won't," Rafe replied flatly.

"How do you know?" I said too fast.

I could tell from his tone he was raising an eyebrow at me. "She was tiny. She's definitely one. If we ever see her again, it will be on TV."

Killian barked a laugh, kicking the back of Ares' seat so hard the whole car shook. "Good thing you never fucked her."

My ears burned—right there was the sole reason I

despised Flora. She'd been making a play for my guys for years. Petty? Yes, but I didn't care.

"I'm not a fucking idiot," Ares snapped, giving me a sideways look. "She was always going on about how she was probably an omega. I wouldn't risk going anywhere near her. "

I didn't comment. My skin itched with irritation knowing any kind of heat from an alpha could push an omega over the edge of transition. That Flora was willing to risk it just to be with my guys had my stomach turning over. Normally, if there was even a chance that someone was an omega, they were sequestered away to a training facility to be trained for rich alphas. No celebrity alpha would want to mate an omega who had been scent bound.

Thank God for that, because there was no way I could survive losing my guys to an omega.

CHAPTER 5
Killian

We pulled into the school parking lot, and Ares parked in our usual spot right out front. No one dared take it, even if we were close to twenty minutes late to first period. As a pack of alphas, we ruled this school, and everyone knew it.

I jumped out of the car and rushed around to Bliss' door, entwining our fingers as I hauled her out with enough force that she landed against my chest. She squealed in surprise but didn't step back.

Her sweet, flowery scent wrapped around us, and I dropped my nose, unable to stop myself from breathing her in. The way she curled her fingers into my chest told me she could feel my heart slamming into my rib cage.

"Good morning." Goose bumps ran down her neck as my breath grazed her ear. We hadn't had the chance to talk yet, and the distance was killing me. I pulled my head back, meeting her violet eyes, and nearly stuttered on my words. "Missed you." I punctuated it with a playful wink.

She stepped away from me, cheeks pink, but didn't let go of my hand. "I saw you last night."

Heat shot to my dick, and I had to adjust my pants. I desperately wanted to know how she tasted.

Ares shot me a look over Bliss' shoulder. "Get her to class."

I couldn't give a shit about class, but I tugged her hand, leading her into the school anyway. If we didn't hurry, Mr. Walsh would write Bliss up, and she'd hate that.

All eyes turned on us as we walked into the school, Ares on Bliss' other side and Nox and Rafe following behind. There was a hum of whispered words as students parted for us, pressing themselves against the walls, knowing better than to get in our space. I glowered at a kid who stared at Bliss a second too long, and the tangy, bitter taste of fear filled my mouth.

Good.

We walked directly to her class before the guys split off, Ares hesitating at the door. "Stay with her."

"Hell yeah." I smirked. I hadn't planned on letting Bliss go, but it helped that he was on board.

Ares took a step toward her, and she had to tip her head all the way back to meet his gaze. "I'll see you at lunch."

She swallowed before answering, voice a little shaky. "Yup. See you then."

Her scent filled the surrounding space, and I had to work hard to suppress my groan. She always smelled good, but this was more than that. Ares' gaze met mine, his brows pulled together. I shrugged. His guess was as good as mine.

The teacher did a double take as I strode into class but

didn't say a word. Whatever. I didn't give a shit if I didn't belong here, so he shouldn't either.

Bliss walked to her spot a few rows in, where a guy took up the seat beside her. I raised an eyebrow at the beta. He fumbled picking up his things, nearly dropping his books, and shifted a seat down.

The teacher droned on about mitochondria while I tuned him out, turning my attention to Bliss. Nox's sweater practically swallowed her, so big it hid her shorts. Her smooth, tanned skin on full display had my fingers twitching to run my fingers over it. I shifted until I barely brushed my leg against her and smiled at her sharp intake of breath.

Bliss flushed, pink rising to her cheeks. She firmly ignored me, which just taunted me to do it again. She pulled her hair up into a high ponytail, the baby hair around her neck damp with sweat. My girl was hot, and not just in the sexy way. With her neck exposed, nothing prevented her sweet, addictive scent from wrapping around me, and I shifted in closer until I pressed fully into her side. Her hooded gaze met mine, lip caught between her teeth. Fuck. An electric current burned through me as her tongue wet her lips. A low rumble formed in my chest. I was going to kiss her right here. Damn the consequences.

The guy in the seat in front of us turned around and leaned on Bliss' desk. "Hey."

"Hey?" She jumped, whipping her head up to meet his eyes.

My lust morphed into anger as his fingers brushed close to her arm. I racked my brain trying to come up with the guy's name. Jason, or maybe Jake. Who cared? He wasn't going to last long enough for her to say it. He glanced my way but quickly turned his eyes down.

That didn't stop him from opening his damn mouth. "Can I borrow a pencil?"

"Oh, sure." She let out a breath, sounding almost relieved. I glared at him, my heart rate spiking. I didn't fucking like him.

She grabbed a pencil at random and tried to hand it to him without looking.

The idiot reached out, but instead of taking the pencil, he grabbed her hand, linking his fingers with hers, the pencil held awkwardly between them. A low growl of warning rumbled from my chest, and he snapped his hand back, looking a little dazed. He glanced between Bliss and me before saying, "Never mind."

The only thing stopping me from slamming his sandy-blond head into his desk was Bliss' worried gaze. *What the fuck was that?*

She looked at me, eyebrow raised. "You okay?"

I nodded. "Sure."

We moved through the morning like zombies. My irritation only got worse at the looks she was getting. Her skin had stayed flushed, and I raised my hand, rubbing my finger over her cheek. "You feeling alright?"

"Yeah, just warm." I had half a mind to tell her to take the sweater off, but then I really would bash someone's head for looking at her. She was tugging every protective instinct in me to the surface.

On the way to lunch, she sidestepped an overenthusiastic theater kid who was trying to talk to her about the upcoming show. I moved her to my other side and tucked her between me and the lockers. I swear, if one more person approached her—

"Hey, Bliss." Andrew, a guy from our history class, sidled up to her and put his arm against the closest locker, stopping her from moving forward. *Fucking dead man walking right here.*

"Er, hey." She glanced up at him as she stripped off her sweatshirt, not even caring that now her tank top underneath was sweaty enough to be sticking to her skin like a wet T-shirt contest. I groaned and pulled her back firmly into my chest, dropping my chin to the crown of her head.

My voice dipped dangerously low when his gaze dropped to her chest. "Fuck off."

He took a step back, looking at me, but returned to Bliss. "What's up?" The dead man grinned at her.

"Nothing?" Her scent turned sour with suspicion.

In the entire time we'd been here, no one dared to disobey our order to stay away from her. Hanging out with four gigantic, terrifying alphas was one hell of a deterrent.

Her voice came out firm. Good girl. "You're blocking my way."

"What are you doing later?"

This guy has no survival instincts.

"Uh…" She opened her mouth, half-shocked and half-amused.

"We could go to a movie or something?" he continued.

I wrapped my arms around her middle, and she sighed, relaxing into me. "Dude, you're two seconds away from losing your teeth." I let the growl come through my words, and he blanched.

"Uh, no, just being friendly."

"Don't be," Nox said, coming up beside us. "She has friends. Fuck off."

Bliss tipped her head back, resting it on my chest, not caring that we chased off her potential date. A low purr silently rumbled through me, and she momentarily stiffened before relaxing further into my embrace.

I smirked as Andrew turned tail and scampered back down the hallway, giving the impression of a deer lucky to have escaped an apex predator. Bliss didn't bother watching him go. Instead, she turned to Nox smiling. "That's one way to do it."

He smirked and took in her features. She was even more flushed, sweat dampening her skin. Nox took one look at me, sensing my restlessness. "How's your morning going?"

"You don't want to know," I grunted. It was now two random guys that came on to her. I clenched my teeth from the force of possessiveness I was feeling. She let her full weight lean against me, and Nox's brows pinched together. She seemed weaker than normal.

Something was off with our girl. Nox growled low, the sounds reverberating in me. I loosened my grip, letting him pull her against him, but I didn't let go of her hips.

Nox rubbed the back of his neck, looking highly conflicted. Then, the taste of smoke and honey filled my mouth, and his arm wrapped around her, pulling her tight, forcing me to let go. I smiled at the sound of his groan. The bastard was against us telling her everything and letting this play out. It was good for him to crave what he was demanding we couldn't have.

"Maybe we should bail for the rest of the day," he said, looking down at her outfit—or lack thereof.

Hell yeah, I was down for that.

She tilted her head, staring up at him with hooded violet eyes. "Are you serious? You never skip."

Nox's gaze caught on her mouth, and his chest rose and fell like he'd just run a marathon. He took a deep through his nose, and his voice came out on a groan. "Dead serious."

A huge crowd of soccer players moved past us, shouting and running. As if slapped in the face, Nox jolted away from her. His eyes narrowed slightly, and he took another deep breath through his nose. Brows pinched together, he said, "Yeah… never mind. Come on."

He kept more distance than usual between them as we walked down the hall in the cafeteria's direction. Like everything else in the school, it was about thirty years out of date and falling apart at the seams. The yellowed, round tables and chipped linoleum floor definitely didn't say "appetizing" any more than the substandard food. Still, there wasn't really anywhere else we were allowed to hang out.

We made a beeline for our usual table. As we approached, I could swear his eyes followed her more than usual, and God knew I'd been paying attention.

We'd put the word out to stay the hell away from her, and no one had crossed that line. There weren't a lot of alphas in town—at least, not teenage ones. Since omegas were dying out and alphas only came from alpha-omega parents, you just didn't see a ton of non-beta kids in low-income areas. We didn't know who our parents were, but it was a safe bet they were all either the product of infidelity or some kind of gang environment, born to parents who wouldn't or couldn't keep us.

Nox sat down at the table across from Bliss, a smile tipping his lips. "You look flushed."

I sat beside her, and she rested on my side. She yawned. "I'm burning up, but I feel fine otherwise."

Nox leaned over the table and ran a finger over her cheek. "Yeah?"

"Mmmhmmm." She purred at his touch. The sound had him practically crawling over the table before a cough nearby had him sit back down. We couldn't be seen as too friendly. People were used to our touching by now, but there were always going to be rumors about us. We were careful not to give any proof they were true.

He scanned his phone, seeming to relax. No doubt texting the rest of the crew. "Few more classes, then we can get out of here."

If he knew the half of it, he wouldn't take that bored tone.

His gaze stayed glued to his phone, even as his body turned toward her. The bastard was doing his best to stay distracted.

Bliss' soft voice caught his attention. "What are you looking at?"

He flipped his phone around to show her. It was some kind of build-a-castle game. "I'm winning, see?"

She frowned, twirling one strand of blonde-and-purple hair around her finger. "Since when do you have data for stuff like that?"

My smile turned a little forced, answering for him. "Come on, B. You know we don't want you involved in that stuff."

She tapped her fingers against the table in agitation, gaze turned away, not happy with that answer. We tried to keep this stuff away from her. Anyone with eyes could see we were a good investment from a recruiting perspective, and for all we knew, we had blood family in the life.

"Hey, Bliss."

I snapped my head up at the same time as Nox. The figure of one of the soccer players loomed behind her.

"Er, hi," she replied.

Across from me, Nox growled audibly. "Who are you?"

"Hey, man." The kid's voice got far less confident speaking to Nox, but I had to give it to him—he was ballsy. "So, um, Bliss. Is this seat taken?"

"Excuse me?" she spluttered, shocked.

Talking to her was one thing, but no one sat with us. Ever. Nox and I gaped at each other, taken aback for a full beat as the guy sat down on the other side of her.

"Yeah, it's very much taken," she said quickly, trying to scoot away from the soccer player. "Sorry."

He tried to reach for her arm. "Aw, don't be like that."

My hand shot out and grabbed the soccer player's wrist, twisting hard. "Don't touch."

The guy yelped and scrambled to his feet as rage poured through me.

"What the fuck is this?" Ares' harsh voice boomed through the cafeteria, and I jerked my head up, smirking.

'Bout fucking time.

Ares strode down the center of the room, Rafe slightly behind him. Rage rolled off them in waves to the point where everyone in the room had to feel it.

For half a second, I thought he was only talking about the guy at our table now cradling his hand, but then I saw his icy eyes were fixed on the rest of the soccer players loitering just to our right. The guys—all betas but big for their designation—were right there waiting to back up their friend, and they were all staring *right at Bliss*.

"Do you want to keep your eyes?" Ares barked at the soccer players, using the full force of the power behind that statement. It tasted like iron.

In the back of the room, a girl burst into tears, and out of the corner of my eye, I saw a beta teacher retreat into a classroom and shut the door. *At least they remember why they don't fuck with us.*

I looked around us, expecting everyone to be cowering away. Surprise filled me when I realized they were getting closer. *What the hell?*

Bliss shifted in her seat, and without thinking, I ran my nose up her neck. A groan caught in the back of my throat. Her floral smell filled my nose, and my hands gripped her waist. I burrowed my face in her neck again, my teeth aching.

"Holy shit," Rafe said, his eyes growing wide. "We need to get out of here."

Ares and Nox nodded silently at each other.

"Why?" she asked at the same time she turned her neck, exposing it fully to me. I opened my mouth, my teeth aching to graze over her soft skin. Sudden clarity hit me, and I scrambled back so fast I nearly hit the ground.

Bliss' eyes met mine, hurt and confusion filling them. "What's going on?"

There was a long pause before I answered, "Probably nothing, baby."

"I have work later," she protested.

"No, you don't," Rafe laughed darkly as we steered her toward the double doors of the school.

She dug her heels in, refusing to move. "No, wait. What the hell is going on?"

All four of us turned in unison to face her. She was framed against the sunlit entrance to the school. The sun cast a fuzzy halo around her as she stared us down, almost too perfect to be real. Her eyes turned heated, and she bit down on her bottom lip, making the softest of whimpering sounds.

Four growls tore through the silence, and I shuddered as heat drove through me, practically yelling at me to take her.

Ares ran his hands through his hair. "Fuck."

CHAPTER 6

Bliss

The tires screeched along the road as Ares turned the corner near our clearing. All four boys shouted over each other in a dull, unintelligible roar. Anxiety licked up my spine, and I shifted in my seat. What the hell was going on?

Nox's hand dashed to grab mine, running his thumb over the sensitive skin on my wrist. My gaze traced his face. A line stood out between his brows, and his hair stood straight up from where he'd repeatedly run his fingers through it. He squeezed my hand and shifted his face to look out the window. "It's okay, Bliss."

It didn't feel okay.

For once, I had been relegated to the back seat instead of the passenger seat as usual. Ares avoided my gaze in the rearview mirror as Killian beat out a frantic drumbeat on the dash beside him. While Nox seemed afraid to let me go, by contrast, Rafe had moved as far away from me as possible, keeping his nose pressed to the window.

If they didn't tell me what was going on soon, I was going to scream.

The car slammed to an abrupt halt in the tiny parking lot on the edge of the park, and my seat belt dug into my chest. I yelped when it pinched my skin.

"Fucking, Christ." Nox removed my seat belt and ran his thumb over the small purple line on my chest. A low, menacing growl emanated from his throat when his glare whipped up to Ares. "What the hell were you thinking?"

I tilted my head to the side. The mark had already disappeared. "I'm fine, calm down."

My words were lost. Ares was already up and out of the car, ripping my door open, and he hauled me out. He crowded me until my back pressed against the trunk, and his head dipped down to rest against my forehead. A too-sweet smell filled the air, and I tasted worry on my tongue, like dying flowers. Piercing blue eyes lingered on the sore spot before meeting my gaze. "I'm sorry, Bliss."

I lifted my hand to his face and ran my thumb over Ares' sharp cheekbone. "You're acting weird."

Killian slipped his hand in mine, interlacing our fingers, and pulled me from under Ares. "We just need to get to the clearing, baby, where no one can hear us. Then we can talk about everything."

I pushed past him on the trail, stomping my feet with each step. My patience ran dangerously low being kept in the dark like this. Their footsteps tore after me, the air filling with citrus and bitterness. Like unsweetened cranberry lemonade.

Crossing the clearing, I turned to glare at them. I put my hands on my hips. "Start talking."

Four boys stood in front of me. My boys.

Their eyes snapped to mine, and I had to take a step back as a tangy, bitter taste filled my mouth. Fear. It tasted like fear. My feet stumbled back as the realization hit me: I was tasting their emotions…and I'd been doing it for days. The world spun.

"But…that's crazy. Betas can't smell emotions," I said, more to myself than to them.

Rafe leapt forward and caught me, pulling me into his chest. "It's going to be okay, Bliss. I promise it's going to be okay." His arms bound tight around me, and I took gulping sips of his familiar scent, letting him soothe me with each passing breath.

My legs solidified beneath me, but I didn't pull away from the safety of Rafe's arms. My body craved his strength, and by the way his arms tightened, it didn't feel like he'd let me go. I turned my head against Rafe's chest, looking into Ares' electric-blue eyes. "What's happening?"

Ares had always been the most opinionated and dominant of our group. Now though, he looked like he would have happily passed that job to anyone else. He rubbed his palms over his eyes, then slowly met my gaze. "You know what's happening, Omega."

The world seemed to tip on its side. Rafe's powerful arms held me up, even as my knees threatened to buckle again. He whispered reassuring words I couldn't make out into my hair.

"That can't be right." I should be ecstatic to be an omega. It was every girl's dream. Instead, the same tangy, bitter taste filled the surrounding air. What did it mean for me? For us? "Have any of you ever met an omega?" I asked, almost desperately.

Killian laughed, and my gaze flew to him. He'd

perched on the arm of the threadbare sofa, his head in his hands. "It's right. I've never been more positive of anything."

"I don't understand. My mom was a beta."

Nox stepped forward, his hair more red than brown in this light. "We don't know either. We never knew who your dad was. Male omegas are even rarer than female ones, but they're out there."

I sucked in a breath. It was possible, but... "Why would an omega sleep with a beta?"

Killian's eyes met mine. "Probably to avoid asshole alphas during their heat."

The trees swirled around me as my vision blurred. Ares barked, the dominance in his voice filling the space. "Put her on the couch."

Rafe turned us so he sat down on the sofa cushion first and pulled me onto his lap with him. Something in the back of my mind fought against my helplessness, but I couldn't pull myself out of it. I kept my eyes closed, head tucked into his chest.

I was about to become an omega. A flipping omega. How the hell had no one ever noticed? How had I not known? If anyone had guessed there was even the slightest chance of this, I'd have been ripped from the home and sent to the Institute immediately, just like Flora from our high school.

Shit. The Institute.

I jolted up from Rafe's arms, and everyone stared at me. My voice sounded weak to my ears. "I don't want to go to the Institute."

Their muscles tensed like they were holding themselves back, as if my worry physically pained them. *Oh.*

Of course it's literally upsetting them because they can smell it.

Suddenly, so many things became more clear. There was a vast difference between being intellectually aware that alphas were different from betas and experiencing the difference firsthand. It had never been more clear to me that my friends and I weren't the same. *Except, actually, now we kind of are.* I was going to pass out.

No one spoke for a full minute, and tension pulled tight in the clearing. I turned toward Ares, but his head was down, supported by his hands, elbows on his knees. Dread tightened like a band over my chest. I didn't want to leave, but did they want me to? "Ares?"

His nostrils flared, and his gaze snapped to mine. "I should tell you to go. You'll mate some rich alpha and live in a giant house near a lake and never have to worry about anything ever again. You deserve that." He took a breath. I hated every word. "But I can't. I'm too fucking selfish to let you go."

My breath caught in my chest, warring with my frantically beating heart. *Oh my God.*

Ares's eyes darted around to the rest of the guys, all nodding with him. "It's got to be your decision. You've got to tell us to let you go, Bliss. We can't do it on our own."

"My decision?" A laugh escaped my mouth, but it was missing the lightness it usually held. I could hardly breathe. "Are you serious?"

"Bliss, look." Nox looked like he was going to crack a back tooth from clenching his jaw. "You should at least consider it. The Institute only mates omegas to celebrities and government officials and shit like that. You literally just won the lottery."

Pain sliced through me, and I flinched involuntarily. "Why would you even say that?"

Nox shook his head, his eyes pleading. "We're all really young. If you go to be trained now, they'd put you on blockers for a few years. None of this has to start right away."

I gazed around the circle incredulously, my vision blurring. "Why are you trying to talk me into this? They can take their fancy houses and prudish alphas and shove it. You're my pack."

The space filled with their growls, and my blood sang in my veins in response. Rafe spun me in his arms, and his hand gripped me delicately around my jaw, only hard enough to keep me in place. "We're just trying to make sure you understand. You know once you present as an omega, there's no turning back. You'll be stuck with us."

The words filled me with such relief that I collapsed against his chest. Omegas were scent bound with whoever scented their perfume when they'd fully transitioned into an omega.

Whether that be a single alpha or a pack of them. That's why it was safer for young omegas to be sent to the Institute. They'd be placed on blockers all the way until the Institute found someone "appropriate," in other words, "rich," to be mated to an omega.. Suddenly, I counted down the seconds until my perfume came in and our pack became official.

"Give her to us," Nox said, and Rafe handed me over to him.

He and Rafe must've switched places, because Nox's and Killian's scents surrounded me, merging until it became a delicious medley. Killian's hand ran up and down my legs as Nox ran circles up my back, his mouth peppering barely there kisses on my collarbone. A shiver ran through me, and warmth pooled between my thighs. I whimpered, and four matching growls responded to my call. Thick need filled the space and pulsed around us.

A new sickening smell hit my senses. I tasted the air, still new at being able to sense emotions. My chest caved, realizing what it was: sadness.

"What if we can't protect you?" Killian's voice was so low it nearly covered the fact it was shaking.

"She'll be fine," Ares growled. "Don't even talk like that."

"Come on, man," Killian said. "Have you ever heard of a teenage pack with an omega? Even a really famous one? Fuck no. It's too dangerous."

Anger stung my chest, and I made a growling noise of my own. "Well, I'm not going anywhere, so we'll have to figure it out."

Everyone moved closer to me, compelled to give an omega what she wanted. Nox was the first to speak. "We need a plan. We need to find somewhere to lie low."

"We can't go home," Ares said, his eyes glued to me.

"Why?" I whined, surprising myself with how needy my voice sounded.

My face grew hotter, the warmth traveling all the way down my body as the taste of the air shifted. All eyes snapped to me again, expressions shifting from worry to obvious hunger.

Nox groaned and shifted slightly away from me. "That's why. We can't just parade an unmarked omega out in the open. People will riot."

"I knew something was off this morning," Ares said,

more to himself than to me. "You can't go anywhere near Ward like this, even if you haven't fully presented yet. Any alpha in a five-mile radius will recognize an omega in transition."

My eyes grew wide. *Oh.*

So many things were hitting me so fast. It hadn't even registered that the guys weren't the only alphas who would be interested in me.

"Mr. Ward is mated," I pointed out.

Rafe crossed his arms, making meaningful eye contact with Ares across the circle. "Better not risk it."

"Fine. Then where are we supposed to go?"

There was an extremely long beat of silence where no one seemed to know what to say. I glanced around. I was not excited about sleeping out here, even if we were all together.

"Let's get a hotel," Killian said, shrugging.

I was about to ask if they even had the money for a hotel, but it didn't matter anyway.

"We can't," Rafe replied. "Too many people."

Ares stood and started pacing, his hands in his white hair. I'd never seen him so agitated.

"What about the warehouse downtown?" Nox sounded unenthusiastic. "Almost no one knows about it, and no one will be within scenting distance."

Rafe's head snapped up. "Nah, everyone knows about it."

I looked around. I didn't know who "everyone" was, but I was willing to bet it was the gang they weren't really supposed to be a part of. This was just another one of their secrets.

Ares' razor-sharp teeth pierced his lip as he nodded.

"I'm almost positive no one will be in there tonight. We'll have to figure something else out tomorrow."

"Where would we go?" The question was out of my mouth before I could stop it. I didn't want to put any reason out there that would change their minds.

Ares replied quickly, "Doesn't matter. We'll figure it out together."

CHAPTER 7
Bliss

The warehouse was an enormous open space. There were no walls to block the view from one end to the other, and only a few crates lined one side, but other than that, it was pretty much empty. The building was old, paint peeling from the steel walls, and the windows were covered in film, making it impossible for anyone passing by to look inside. Not that we expected any company.

"What is this place used for?" I muttered. "There's nothing in here."

"There's shit in here when there has to be," Ares said vaguely, exchanging a glance with Rafe. "We're going to grab stuff from the car. We'll be right back."

My skin prickled as I surveyed the space. My body whined. I didn't like it here. It was too big and too cold. "I liked the fire pit better, honestly."

Warm arms banded around my middle and spun me against Killian's hard chest.

His head dropped beside my head, and his soft breath fanned across my neck. "You can't sleep outside, B."

His alpha scent calmed my jittering nerves, and I leaned into him. They'd always been able to calm me, but this was different. It was on an instinctual level to let them take care of me.

"We can feel your anxiety. Tell us what you need."

My gaze shifted around the warehouse, and a shudder ran through me. Nox stepped in close to us, his heat warming my back. I relaxed, liking the feeling of being surrounded by them. His chest vibrated through me. "She needs a nest."

I gasped at his words. Like a good alpha, he was already more attuned to what I needed before I was. They slowly peeled away from me, and I made a pained sound at the back of my throat. Killian's forehead dropped to mine, but he didn't close the inches of space between us. "Let us take care of this."

I straightened. I refused to let my instincts get the better of me and took a step back. "Of course."

Ares and Rafe walked through the entry door, carrying blankets and the clearing's sofa cushions with them.

The boys dragged the crates from along the wall to one corner and boxed it off into a small room-like space with them. They used the cushions from our couch to line the floor, creating a makeshift bed. There weren't any pillows, but they'd brought all the throw blankets from the clearing. I pulled a blanket to my nose, all of their scents surrounding me, and made a distinct omega hum of satisfaction.

Nox gestured to the space, and a too-sweet taste coated my tongue. "I'm sorry it's not better."

I shook my head and focused my attention on him. "It's perfect."

Rafe walked straight to me, pulled me into his arms, and dropped to the floor, dragging me with him. His nose ran up the side of my neck as he breathed me in, growling low in his chest.

I hummed and tilted my head to the side, exposing my neck to him. He placed gentle nips there, a low rumble against my back.

Ares appeared on my other side, running his tongue along my collarbone like he did it every day. "Tomorrow, we'll slip into the group home and grab our stuff. Tonight, we'll stay here."

"Mmmhmm," I said.

I probably would have agreed to anything right now. They could have asked me to commit murder, and I would have happily gone along with it.

"Fuck, she's close to heat." Rafe's words against my skin brought me back to attention. I couldn't tell from his tone if he was excited or worried.

Ares and Rafe pulled back abruptly from either side of my neck, and I whined at the loss of contact. I snapped my mouth shut. The omega was coming closer to the surface as my presenting approached. I'd grown up thinking I was a beta. I'd never prepared for this transition. Being an omega was more primal, more wild than I expected.

Every omega went into heat as soon as they presented. Heat meant something different for omegas. Their bodies were vulnerable when it took over them. It's why the Institute took precautions to keep them safe by having them on blockers until they were mated off to rich men capable of protecting them. I didn't believe for a second protection was why those men mated. No, it was the status it brought them. Omegas were rare, and mating one meant you were above everyone else.

Killian crawled across the cushions toward us. He grabbed for me, and Ares and Rafe didn't protest—that seemed like a good sign to me. I wasn't all that familiar with omega pack dynamics. The last thing I wanted was for them to start fighting, but at least with us, that didn't seem like a concern.

Nox reached over to where Killian held me between his knees and ran his fingers across my face. "I hate to be the voice of reason here, but she needs blockers."

"Why?" I asked. Now that I'd gotten a taste of this, I didn't want to go back to being regular.

They seemed to be having some kind of silent argument with their eyes over my head. If I had any experience with reading the smell of emotions in the room, I would probably have a better sense of what was going on, but as it was, all I was getting was the heavy odor of dead lilies and pennies.

"He's right, B," Killian said finally. "You can't present right now. Not until we have a better plan and a safer place for you to stay."

Intellectually, I could understand what they meant. I was still in the transitional stage, but if I presented and went into heat, then that could last for days. The irrational, animalistic part of my brain didn't care though. I wanted them to claim me. Now.

That thought must have triggered some kind of emotional response because growls erupted around the circle. Their combined scents overtook me, and my stomach warmed.

Killian shuffled back, a low growl rumbling in the back of his throat. "Yup. We need to get those blockers fast."

I sighed, defeated. My mouth tasted sour—the guys looked as unhappy about that as I was.

A yawn took over my face, and my eyes drooped. Today was long, and tomorrow would be more of the same. I shifted up the bed until I could lie out fully. All of their eyes were on me like a weighted blanket, but they didn't move to join. I'd probably made them nervous.

"Will you sleep with me?"

That's all it took to be surrounded by them, Nox on my left, with Rafe behind him, and Killian on my right, followed by Ares. I knew they were concerned about not being able to protect me, but I'd never felt as safe as I did right now.

———

The following morning, I woke in a pile of limbs. Sun streamed through the plastic-covered windows of the warehouse, and I burrowed under someone's arm to try to shield my face from the light. I'd never thought I would miss my bed at the group home, but my canopy was pretty cozy. Wherever the guys and I ended up, we would have to get something like that.

Nox shifted against my back, and I craned my neck to look at him. He had one arm thrown over my hip, and behind him, Ares had his long arm wrapped around both of us. I smiled. I liked the closeness with all of them like this. In any of my fantasies of all of us together, I'd never imagined I'd get this lucky.

The arm covering half my face twitched, and Rafe shifted to look at me. "Are you okay?"

"Never better," I yawned.

In some ways, that was true. Yesterday was a blur. Like a scene out of someone else's life and I was just visiting. Nox had probably said it best—I'd essentially just won the genetic lottery, and now I got to share my win with all my best friends. It was almost too good to be true.

What made this so crazy was how rare omegas were. I'd heard that there used to be lots of them, but due to war, famine, and selective breeding, omegas now made up only about two percent of the population. The Omega Institute was a relatively new government program set up to combat the problem, but it was far from a perfect system.

Killian's head popped up over Rafe's shoulder, and he grinned. "I, for one, slept great."

Ares growled. "My hip hurts. We're getting an actual bed tonight."

I couldn't help grinning. I didn't care where we were—this was perfect.

A sweet, fruity smell filled the air as happiness bloomed in my chest, and everyone shifted around me. Nox twisted his fingers in the back of my hair, running his nose up the column of my neck. "We're running out of time."

I rolled over until I was half on top of Nox's chest, looking down into his green gaze. I gave him a small smile. "You keep trying to turn me off."

Ares grabbed the back of my neck with surprising strength and forced me to turn my head to look at him. He leaned close so he was speaking against my mouth. "You're lucky one of us is half-rational, Love. Be grateful."

I whined, my teeth aching to open up and bite his lip. It was right there. I didn't want to be grateful—I wanted to say screw it and just do this. Now.

The flowery smell took on a spicy taste. Like jasmine, honey, and chili peppers.

"Cut that shit out," Rafe barked at Ares, who dropped me and flopped back down against the cushions.

My spine went straight at the dominant note in Rafe's voice. "Sorry."

"Don't be sorry, baby," Killian said. "We just need to make sure we get you blockers ASAP, or we're going to have bigger problems."

"We can steal some," Nox said, keeping his eyes firmly fixed on the ceiling, as though trying not to look at me.

"Okay," Ares said, back to all business. "We'll go there and then back to the house to get our stuff."

"And then what?" I asked.

Killian reached across Rafe and ran a hand through my hair. "Dunno, baby, but we're going to take care of you no matter what."

The guys argued for a full five minutes about if it was safer to keep the windows down in the car so they could breathe or keep them closed so no one else would scent me. I watched with alarmed fascination.

This was so not my world.

Potential omegas spent years in training so they would have a good idea of the culture and what to expect. I was totally lost, guided exclusively by animal instinct.

Nox wrapped his arms around my waist, holding me

tightly to him, even as he argued with Killian about how we all needed to maintain distance from each other. The cognitive dissonance of that action told me the guys were equally rattled by this whole thing, even if they were hiding it better.

Finally, we all piled into the car and sped down Main Street in the direction of the center of town. I leaned my head against the passenger-side window, thankful for the cool glass against my burning skin. I was burning up from the inside out. "How long will it take to get those pills?"

"Not long." Rafe threw me a glance in the rearview mirror. "They always have them at the free clinic."

My eyes widened. "Do I have to go in?"

"Fuck no," Ares snapped as he skidded through a barely yellow light.

"Drop me off there," Nox said. "I'll get the stuff and meet you back at the house."

Ares nodded in silent agreement, and I sank lower in my seat, pressing my knees together. This was a lot of drama over just me. All I could hope for was that soon things would calm down and we could all be together for real.

CHAPTER 8
Ares

I held my breath as I sped down a heavily settled suburban street in the direction of the group home. Some old lady waved at me to slow down as we whipped past, and I flipped her off. *Do not test me today.*

"Please don't kill us," Bliss said from the seat beside me.

I growled involuntarily at that image and eased off the gas. The sweet taste of her satisfaction filled the car, and I forced myself not to inhale.

Rafe met my eyes in the rearview mirror, and his brows arched. I knew he was thinking the same thing I was: *This is fucking crazy.*

Two days ago, I would have done anything for Bliss—any of us would have. Today, that was still true, but it was like I didn't have a choice anymore. Not that I was complaining—it was just uncomfortable not to be in control of your own body.

I turned onto our road and slowed to a near crawl. All

we needed was for Ward to hear us and come out to investigate. I ground my teeth. "We'll run in and grab some of our stuff. You stay in the car."

Bliss looked up at me with wide, violet eyes. "I need to pack though, especially if we're not coming back."

"We've got it," Killian said from the back seat, reaching forward to twist the end of her hair around his fingers.

She huffed out an annoyed breath, and I warred with myself over giving her what she wanted and keeping her safe. Safe won out.

I pulled into the driveway, my heart beating fast with pent-up adrenaline. There weren't any other cars here, but that didn't mean anything. Someone was always hanging around the group home.

I leaned across the center console and grabbed Bliss's chin, tipping it up. "We'll be right back. Stay here, Love."

Love. I couldn't remember when I started calling her that, but it was accurate. I'd loved her since I was six years old. Beta or omega, there was never going to be anyone else.

"But—" she started to say.

I could see the exact moment she got distracted. Her pupils dilated, and the honey smell of her arousal hit me all at once. *Fuck.*

"Ares." Rafe kicked my seat. "Let's go."

I wrenched myself away and slammed the car door without another word. If Nox didn't get back soon with those blockers, this was going to fucking kill me.

"You've got to stop touching her," Rafe muttered as we jogged up the porch steps. "You're making it worse."

I barked a laugh. "You're one to talk. You set this off in the first place."

He came to an abrupt halt with his hand on the front door, and Killian slammed into his back. "Dude, what the fuck?"

Rafe ignored him. "What do you mean I set this off?"

I glanced around. *Do we really need to be talking about this now? On the fucking porch? No.* "The other night, you clearly triggered it. Now, come on."

Rafe fell too quiet as we moved up the stairs toward the room the four of us had shared for the last decade. I had no idea what his deal was. Everyone knew you had to keep potential omegas away from alphas, or it would trigger their heats. Of course, we hadn't known Bliss was an omega, but it didn't matter now anyway.

I stuffed a bunch of clothes and shit into a bag and then moved on to Bliss's room, Killian close behind me. I almost laughed. We both stood there and stared at the nest she had created around her bed. "How did we not put two and two together?"

Killian chuckled. "We're idiots—"

His words cut off abruptly, and the hair on the back of my neck lifted. Sight, sound, and smell came into focus. Killian's eyes were wide, and his muscles clenched in his jaw as he sucked in through his nose. A bitter, tangy taste turned the air acrid. Blood rushed in my ears, blocking out the words Killian was shouting as the smell of fear swelled until it burned my nose.

Bliss.

Rafe darted out of our room, thundering after me down the stairs and out the door. My heart beat against my ribs, and my blood boiled as the metallic taste of panic filled my mouth. I whipped my head around, searching for the source of the smell.

The bitter smell of Bliss's fear permeated the air all around me as I tore down the porch steps and across the yard toward her muffled screams.

No.

Ward had Bliss pressed up against the side of the car, one hand around her throat and the other trying to tear at the belt of her shorts. A red haze came over my vision, and I charged forward, a growl tearing from my throat.

Nox ran up the driveway, reaching Ward first. He grabbed Ward by the back of the neck and tore him off Bliss, throwing him to the ground with enough force that he sunk into the grass a couple of inches.

"You boys think you can keep her safe?" Ward started to get up. "You think I'll be the only alpha to figure this out? To come after her?"

Rafe slammed his fist into Ward's mouth, snapping his head back as he dropped to his ass.

The corner of Ward's lips tipped up, and he spit blood onto the ground before wiping his mouth. He looked toward where Nox and Killian held Bliss between them. "She needs men who can protect her. Not boys who want to fuck her."

I grabbed him by the collar and pulled him onto his knees. "Men like you?"

Ward shook his head. "It's only a matter of time before some sick bastard kills you all and gets his hands on her."

"We'll protect her better than you could." My fist clenched at my sides, and I did my best to block out his words. I wouldn't let him get into my head.

"Oh yeah? What happens when those thugs you hang out with find out you're hiding an omega?"

I paused, chest heaving as I stared at Ward, then

slammed my fist into his face until the asshole laid flat out on the grass.

My eyes found Bliss, shaking by the car. If I believed in omens or that kind of shit, this wasn't a good one.

We drove in silence until I spotted a rest station and pulled in, desperate to catch my breath. Ward's blood smeared my steering wheel where it had covered my hands, but no one commented. This felt like the kind of thing we wouldn't bring up again after today.

"Here, Little Wolf." Nox shoved a pill bottle at Bliss, the capsules rattling like a bass drum in the silent car.

She held them up to the light. "I need water."

I glanced back at the rest stop convenience store. It was run-down, just like everything else in this town, but it at least looked open. "Killian, go grab her a water."

"Can you see if they have a bathroom key too?" Bliss asked. "I just need a second…"

"No, you can't get out of the car," Rafe said too loudly.

Bliss snorted. "Well then, we're going to get really comfortable with each other really fast. It looks like a single-stall bathroom. I'll be fine."

I glanced at Nox, who usually had the most rational opinion on shit like…well, not like this—this was fucking crazy—but on other things. He was just rational in general.

"Just hurry," Nox said.

It was only a minute before Killian was back, and he handed the bottle of water and bathroom key to Bliss. "Take your pills."

She smirked, jumping out before we could stop her.

We got out of the car and waited. My eyes darted back and forth toward the door where Bliss had disappeared the moment she went into the bathroom. I didn't like this. "One of us should have gone with her."

Nox opened his mouth like he was going to tell me to calm down and then closed it again, clearly thinking better of it.

"Okay, so, where to?" Killian said, doing his best to keep the mood light.

For once, I had no answers. Rafe and I looked at each other, both hoping the other would come up with something. We all knew this was bad. Really fucking bad.

Rafe's gaze traveled over to the closed bathroom door and then back to me. "We need to be fucking real about this. We can't keep her with us."

An involuntary growl erupted from my chest, and I took a step forward. "What the fuck does that mean?"

Nox reached for my shoulder, trying to pull me back, but I shook him off. "Didn't you hear Ward? More alphas will be after her."

"I don't care. She's ours," I barked.

"Get your head out of your ass. You think you could protect her if someone else tried to take her?" Rafe spit the words at me.

I held up my bloody hand, waving it at Rafe and Nox. "Were you not watching just now?"

Killian stepped up behind me, seeming unsure what side of this argument he wanted to be on. I was about to lose my fucking shit on all of them—no one was making any sense.

"Ward is nothing," Rafe said. "If this happened in five years, yeah, no problem, but right now, we're going to get fucking killed, and Bliss will end up passed around Alpha Lupi or some other gang circuit for the rest of her life."

"So you're saying you wouldn't die to protect her," Killian growled at Rafe.

I stepped back to stand next to him, wholeheartedly agreeing with that statement.

"Fuck no," Nox growled back. "I'm saying she shouldn't have to watch us all die and then get taken anyway. Ward was right about one thing: we can't protect her."

My chest caved as the weight of his words sank in. We'd be picked off one by one only to eventually leave her alone with whoever managed to kill us. "Do you have a better idea? Because all I fucking care about is keeping her safe," I snapped.

I couldn't believe we were even having this conversation. What the hell else were we supposed to do? Our options narrowed to a single fixed point the moment that Bliss had started transitioning.

"We could call the Institute," Nox said quietly.

He always was the smart one. I just wished he'd figured out a better way.

"Fuck." Killian slammed his fist against the trunk.

Rafe held up his phone and met each of our gazes. "I'm calling."

My heart was being ripped out of my chest, but I forced myself to nod. We said we'd save her even if it killed us. This just wasn't the type of death I had imagined.

The door to the rest stop bathroom opened, and Bliss looked toward where Rafe paced talking on the phone, just out of hearing distance. She sniffed the air when she got to us and tucked herself into Killian's arms. He pulled her tight to his chest, and his jaw clenched as he fought an inner battle.

Bliss' gaze darted between us, and her brows pinched together. "What's going on?"

Rafe jogged up to us, saving me from having to respond. "We're waiting for someone."

It was like we were waiting for a train wreck to happen, each second ticking down closer to the inevitable crash.

Nox stepped up to her, running his nose along her neck and placing a slow kiss to her temple. Killian did the same on her other side, murmuring soft words I couldn't make out. She looked right between them, like she was meant to be there.

Not for much longer. I clenched my teeth, and a rumble of a growl escaped my throat at how fucking bullshit this all was.

Bliss' head snapped to me. She ran her thumb over my bottom lip. "Stop frowning at me like that. I'm fine. Plus, now we don't have to worry about Ward anymore. Right?"

My lip burned where she touched it, and I couldn't stop myself from running my tongue over her thumb. She tasted like jasmine and honey, and this was my last chance to kiss her. My mind went blank as instincts took over.

I closed the distance between us in half a step and crashed my mouth over hers, swallowing her whimpering sounds and sucking her air into my lungs. Blood rushed through my ears, drowning out everything else as I focused entirely on Bliss. I needed to burn this kiss into my memory to replay later when I was at my worst. When I would have turned to her, but now she would be gone.

Fuck. I didn't want to let her go, and I needed some part of her to know that.

I deepened the kiss, owning every part of her—stamping myself in her mind, begging her to remember me. Her fingers clung to my shirt, nails biting into my chest. Her soft moans turned wild as she lost control in my arms. An electric current sparked over my skin as the rich scent of her slick, jasmine and honey, filled my nose, my chest, my mind until my mind went blank except for one word. *Mine.*

Her eyes dilated, and my shoulders dropped as her scent dissipated in the air. Scent bonded.

I jerked back, shock trickling through me as she leaned in closer, chasing the broken kiss. Three need-filled groans circled around us. Their dark gazes pinned on our girl, as if they'd just discovered the secret to happiness and she was standing right in front of them.

"Jesus fucking Christ." Killian's voice was weak, barely above a whisper.

Bliss opened her eyes and smiled at us as she fully became an omega, her scent bonding us forever. My eyes met Rafe's over Bliss's shoulder, then darted to Killian and Nox. Their expressions were equally shocked as they processed the bond slamming into place.

"Fuck." Nox ripped the water bottle from Killian's hand and shoved pills at Bliss. She looked at him, and a sadness tinted the air.

Rafe's voice barked out the command. "Take it."

He wasn't asking—the alpha demand came through loud and clear, and she had no choice but to obey. But it was too fucking late…and we all knew it. No blockers in the world could fix this now.

Instant regret hit me. Fuck. "Rafe, how long until—"

I didn't get a chance to finish my question.

CHAPTER 9
Bliss

Killian's crisp smell of lemon and vanilla swirled with Nox's smooth sandalwood, Rafe's peppers and coffee beans, and Ares' cloudless night sky. An overwhelming sense of rightness sank into my bones as each of their bonds snapped broken pieces of me back into place.

Strangled voices shouted around me, but as if I was underwater, I couldn't make out the words.

I leaned toward Ares like a plant seeking sunlight, and a smile stretched across my face, so wide my cheeks hurt. I met Ares' conflicted gaze, and my smile fell as a bitter taste tainted their bonds. Before I could even try to process the torment there, pills and a water bottle were thrust into my hands.

"Take them." Nox's bark was a slap in the face.

No. I didn't want to take them. I'd lose everything I was feeling, and he knew it, but the coercion of his bark wouldn't allow for any argument.

My hand moved of its own accord, bringing the blockers to my mouth. Theoretically, I understood why I needed to hide my omega scent, but I wasn't ready. The taste of my bonded faded, and an immense sadness took their place. We stood in silence for a long moment.

"So, are we leaving?" I asked finally. The guys exchanged guilty expressions of misery that had unease crawling up my spine. "What's going on?"

I turned at the purr of a car engine behind us. Panic bled into me, turning my veins into ice as three black sedans wearing the Institute logo pulled into the parking lot. Dread dropped my stomach to the floor. How did they find us?

It doesn't matter—they're too late. We're bonded now.

I cowered behind Rafe and Ares, digging my fingers into their backs as a beta woman in her late thirties stepped out of the car. She was tall and willowy and wore a crisp white pantsuit, with her hair up in a severe bun. She was everything I wasn't.

"Hi, hon." The lady's voice was sickly sweet. "I'm so happy we found you."

I trembled as I burrowed my face into Rafe's back, taking in deep, sucking breaths, trying to chase what little of his comforting smell I could still find with the blockers working their way through my system. This woman needed to understand I couldn't go with her.

"I'm staying with them," I said into Rafe's shoulder, refusing to meet her eyes. I peeked up at my guys, instead, surprised to see agony rather than resolve. *Why aren't they saying anything?* "Tell her. We're a pack."

Rafe twisted, pushing me out in front of him. Relief

filled me. He'd keep me safe and show her that I belonged with them.

His voice was flat as it rumbled against my back. "Thanks for coming. She's ready to go."

Pain pierced through my chest. I couldn't breathe.

I turned, reaching desperately for Ares instead, fingers grasping at his arm. "What's happening?"

He took a step closer to me, and hope lifted my daze, but it froze in my lungs as he stopped just out of my reach. Confusion wrapped around me as I met his dejected eyes.

Nox broke my loose grip on Ares, and I spun to him, fighting his grip. "Nox?"

His expression was a blank wall, closed to me as he nudged me toward the strange woman, his words burning my ears. "They'll be able to take care of you, Little Wolf."

This couldn't be happening. "I don't understand. Why?"

The woman from the Omega Institute nodded, smiling with too much teeth. She seemed to agree with that statement.

I choked on my breath, and hot tears streamed down my face, as the realization of what was happening finally sank in. I met each of their gazes, searching for something familiar, but they might as well have been strangers.

"You said *you* would take care of me," I pleaded as a tremble ran through me.

Ares looked over my shoulder at Rafe. He gave a quick shake of his head, a hint of doubt there.

I turned back to Rafe, offering him a hopeful smile. *Maybe he'll change his mind?*

Rafe crossed his arms, his expression blank. "Yeah, until

we realized what that actually means." His tone was harsher than I'd ever heard it. "You're going to get us killed, Bliss. You need to go. Sorry, but we're not about to die for you."

I sucked in a breath, begging for a taste of what they were feeling. I couldn't believe it. It didn't make sense. "But—"

"Make her go," Nox hissed so low I could barely make it out.

Ares growled. "Fuck you."

I met his icy-blue gaze, a sliver of emotion breaking through the wall. I thought I saw regret there, but he'd shut it down too fast to be sure.

Killian stepped into me and dropped his head close to mine. Tears pooled in my eyes as he tucked a piece of hair behind my ear. He scanned my face, lingering for half a second too long. He took a deep breath, and his lips tipped up in the corner, but there was a wrongness to them. "It's going to be okay, baby. It's going to turn out fine."

"No." The world dropped out from under me, and I shook my head at him. My voice cracked around the vowels. "This isn't how it's supposed to be. I...I know you don't want this." I dug my fingers into his shirt and pulled myself into him, refusing to let him go. "Tell them, Kill. Tell them you're my pack."

I reached for my senses. I could've sworn I tasted hurt there, but Killian's face was completely blank. His thumb ran over my jaw one last time as his bark filled the space. "Go with them. Now."

I gasped, and betrayal wrapped around me. My trust in them splintered. They didn't want me. Tears burned my skin as his bark forced me to take a step toward the woman. I had no choice but to follow her into the black sedan. I pushed against my instincts, fighting as they shut the door after me. The click of the locks pierced the air.

The hole in my chest threatened to consume me. The same bonds that moments before had felt like coming home, anchoring themselves into every part of me, now left me hollow. Everything I thought was all a lie. Some kind of teenage fantasy of a girl desperate for boys' attention.

I sat, numb in the back of the car, and my heart tore open with every foot that separated us. I watched, hands clenching the seat, as their silhouettes disappeared when the car turned the corner.

The sharply dressed women beside me glanced my way. "It will be okay, Bliss. You'll finally be where you belong."

The echo of her words stung. I *had* a place where I belonged. Or, I thought I did.

Even missing my omega senses, my heart screamed as the newly formed bonds were nearly stretched to their breaking point. The further we drove, the more faint the tug on the tethers between us became. Tears stung my eyes as I fought to hold on to the invisible connection—the only thing I had left to my pack. Distance couldn't sever the bonds, but that didn't stop my soul from feeling their loss.

Killian was the first to fade, his joy slipping away until I almost couldn't feel him at all. Nox's calm understanding went next, followed by Rafe's protection. I gasped and had to choke down a sob as the last bond went dormant, and Ares' unconditional acceptance of me disappeared with it.

I bit my lip to hide its wobble as my heart shredded in my chest. I would never see them again. They'd let me go, knowing we would lose each other forever. Not one of them helped me as I begged them. They knew what they were doing, and none of them moved to keep me. They got rid of their needy little omega. Too much work to keep around. Too much of a burden.

The ache in my chest became unbearable.

Rejected.

That was what they called it when your pack abandoned you and left you to the wolves. Because that's what the Institute was: a bunch of wolves preparing you for your new master.

Pain burned through my chest as I closed each door to my heart, building a wall brick by brick. The bond wouldn't break no matter how many years passed, but I could protect myself from it. I would turn myself to ice and become the perfect little omega, giving the guys exactly what they wanted. The next time they saw me would be on the TV, mated to a new man. Rejecting them right back.

All I'd have to do was survive without them.

Pack Bound

To the readers who turn the page and ask "Oh…am I attracted to this? No… Am I?"

PACK BOUND

A BLISSFUL OMEGAVERSE NOVEL

INTERNATIONAL BESTSELLING AUTHORS

KATE KING   JESSA WILDER

CHAPTER 1
Bliss

The omega let out a loud moan as her alpha wrapped his hand around her throat, driving into her from behind.

I ducked my head and let my blonde hair fall in a curtain against my desk, shielding me from the show. Still, it was impossible to ignore the noise and the heavy scent of pheromones. A heady mixture of honey and wool.

I picked up my pen and doodled a heart on the corner of my notebook. My notes were awful—rushed and unfinished. I'd scribbled "Omega Heat Cycle: Practical" at the top of the page next to the date and made a few rushed bullet points before giving up.

The omega mewed, and I scratched out a couple of uneven stars around the heart.

Flora leaned over from the desk next to me, digging her long, manicured nails into my forearm. "Oh my God," she hissed, half-excited, half-horrified. "Serious question. Do you think they get paid for this?"

"I doubt it," I said through my teeth, keeping a benign smile plastered on my face in case anyone was looking. "No alpha with a mate would need the money. I assume they're just into it."

As if on cue, the alpha growled his approval of whatever the omega had just done.

Flora tossed her long, dark hair over one shoulder and glanced down at my paper. She scanned over my notes and snorted a laugh. "I thought you, of all people would be paying attention."

I shifted slightly so my back was to the instructor standing in the corner and rolled my eyes at my friend. "What, are we supposed to draw a diagram?"

It was a semi-rhetorical question. A couple of months ago, we sat through a memorable class where we *were* supposed to draw diagrams. I'd lost points on that assignment because my knot picture came out looking more like an inverted lollipop, and I hadn't been in the mood to fix it. Flora giggled, clearly thinking of the same incident.

In the corner, our instructor, Mrs. Charlemagne, coughed. *Shit.* I sat up straight again, shifting my gaze back to the couple in the center of the round lecture hall.

The alpha and omega stood in the middle of the coliseum-style classroom, lit by a single spotlight. He had her bent over a desk, her cheek pressed hard into the polished wooden surface. Even at this distance, the red bite marks on her neck stood out against her pale skin. Some new, some scarred and healed over.

The lecture hall could hold several hundred students, but there were only twenty of us here today. Every omega sitting spread out across the dim room was close to graduating and participating in the Agora Ceremony.

A girl in the row in front of us raised her hand. "Will we get pregnant every heat cycle?"

The couple didn't stop—they either couldn't hear or weren't bothered by her question.

Our teacher smiled brightly, like she'd just won the grand prize at the annual student/faculty bake-off. All the teachers loved pregnancy questions. "Likely not during your first heat, but it's possible."

Beside me, Flora pretended to gag. I shot her a warning glance. She was going to get us in so much trouble.

The alpha groaned and moved faster, completely losing control and rutting against his omega. Some of the girls in the front row picked up their pens, scribbling quick notes with clear academic interest. I sighed, crossed out my doodles, and wrote, *"Alpha rut. Brought on only by omega heat. Both parties are controlled by hormones and unable to use any cognitive reasoning until heat subsides,"* near the top of my paper. Just to look like I was doing something.

"Who do you think they are?" Flora whispered.

"I don't know."

"I don't recognize her. She must have graduated before we got here, so she's got to be at least four years older than us," she mused. "He's hot though."

"Shhh," I hissed nervously. "You're not supposed to think that."

"Right." Flora ran a hand through her hair, glancing around to see if anyone had heard her mistake. "I knew that."

The alpha pulled out of the omega, flipped her over on the desk, and thrust back in, locking inside her.

He licked her neck where some of the old bite marks

were, and my chest seized. The sex didn't bother me—we watched it all the time—but I hated this part.

"Mine," he said against her neck, as though they were the only ones in the room. "You're perfect. My good girl."

Seeing mates happy together always reminded me of how I would never truly have that. *It's not fair.*

Flora reached over and patted my thigh under the desk in a subtle show of solidarity. "Maybe it won't go on that long this time," she whispered.

I grunted, shaking my head. "When has an alpha ever knotted for less than half an hour? I bet we're not getting out of here before 4:00."

Flora muttered a noncommittal agreement as the omega moaned incoherently at her alpha. The girls in the front row hurried to copy down whatever nonsense the omega was saying. I groaned, not even bothering to hide my annoyance.

When the couple finally left and the lights turned back on, I let out a sigh of relief. At least we only had this class once a week.

Flora stood and tugged on the neck of her sweater. "God, it's hot in here."

It wasn't, but I nodded, moving to follow her out of the lecture hall.

"Omegas Bliss and Flora," Mrs. Charlemagne called after us. "Please stay."

My heart sank. What now?

I didn't dare look at Flora as we made our way to the front of the room. Mrs. Charlemagne's eyes bored a hole in me as I walked, reminding me a little of the woman who ran the group home I grew up in. Even though I was an adult now, there were always some older adults who had a way of making you feel small.

"Chatty today?" Mrs. Charlemagne asked.

"No," Flora said bluntly, at the same moment as I said, "Sorry."

I glanced at Flora. She'd thrown hair over her shoulder and was making direct eye contact with the teacher—not very omega of her. My stomach churned like I'd eaten a live snake.

"Well, since you two don't seem to need any more lessons." The teacher clicked her tongue against her teeth. "You can help guide someone else. A new girl came in this morning. She's fourteen, from Houston. She's down at the headmistress' office now."

I pursed my lips. Fourteen was young. Not unheard of, but still young to arrive at the Institute. That poor girl probably knew nothing, and now she'd be here for seven years before she got out. Not that "out" was a great alternative.

"Was she a retrieval or a rescue?" Flora asked.

Mrs. Charlemagne raised an eyebrow at the directness of Flora's question, but answered anyway. "I don't know. The sooner you go down there, the sooner you'll find out."

I sucked on my tongue, holding in a response. Asking questions in this place never got you anywhere, anyway. At least she wasn't punishing us.

Flora and I shuffled down the long, dimly lit hall toward the main office. Our footsteps echoed off the wall and vaulted ceiling, and I hugged my bag to my chest like a shield. New girls entering the Institute always brought back terrible memories.

"So, what do you think?" Flora kept her voice low. "Rescue or retrieval?"

"No idea," I whispered back. "Mrs. Charlemagne is right, I guess. We'll find out in a minute."

"Imagine not telling us. What the hell? If she's a rescue, who knows what just happened?"

I swallowed thickly. This was why I didn't like it when new girls arrived at the Institute. I'd been a rescue. Flora was a retrieval. We'd had very different experiences on our first day at the Institute. "If she's a rescue, it's fine. We'll figure it out. We have before."

We stopped in front of an oak-paneled door, and I paused to make sure my sweater was buttoned correctly—all I needed was to get a lecture from the headmistress about appropriate appearance.

Flora did the same. "I need to order new skirts," she muttered, trying to smooth her uniform in the back. "I swear to God, my ass is growing by the day."

I snorted—I appreciated her light change of topic. I bent to look at her skirt. It was a little short, but it honestly looked better that way. "Don't let them hear you say 'ass.'"

She rolled her eyes. "Right. Bend over for your government-assigned alpha, but don't say 'ass.' Fucking hypocrites, I can't."

I choked, somewhere between a laugh and a cough. She was absolutely right, of course. The system, and the Institute as a whole, was messed up. My situation was different from all the other omegas, though. No matter how much I hated the Institute, I had no choice but to make the best of the way things were. Graduating from the Institute was the only way to get revenge on the boys who'd put me here, and that was all that kept me going in the last four years.

"You can borrow my skirts if you want," I offered, bypassing Flora's comment. "I'm a twelve."

She scanned my hips, comparing us. "Yeah, alright. Thanks."

Muffled voices sounded from beyond the office door, and Flora and I glanced at each other. My stomach sank a fraction lower. "We should go, I guess."

Flora pushed her long chestnut hair behind her ears. "I'm getting too jaded for this shit." She raised her right hand and knocked softly.

"Come in."

The door creaked, brushing along the thick carpet, and we stepped inside. The room was already full. Headmistress Omega DuPont sat behind a large desk, her graying hair pulled into a severe bun. In front of her were two women.

No, I corrected myself as I leaned around Flora to get a better look. *A woman and a girl.* I'd sat in that girl's chair myself four years ago, right after my world had come crashing down around me. It felt like another life.

"Good afternoon, Omegas," said Headmistress Omega DuPont without looking up.

"Good afternoon," Flora and I replied in unison.

The headmistress was one of the few actual omegas working at the Omega Institute. Most of the staff and instructors were betas, partly because omegas were so rare, and partly because it was safer overall for unbonded Omegas to only come into contact with betas. Despite the cocktail of hormone and scent blocker we all took daily, the Institute wasn't taking any chances with our safety.

My eyes darted to the blonde beta woman sitting across from the desk. I knew her, or at least, I'd met her before. Every omega at the Institute had. Sarah Miller was in charge of rescues and retrievals.

For most omegas—the ones who had grown up with alpha and omega parents—that meant simply calling the Institute when the girl reached the age of sixteen. Sarah arrived on their doorstep and took the girl to live at the Institute until she was twenty-one, when she would be mated. For some omegas, like me, things were a little more complicated.

"Will that be all, Headmistress?" Sarah asked. "Or do you need me to stay?"

"No, Sarah, the ladies and I will take it from here."

Sarah rose and took a step toward the door, only to realize Flora and I were blocking her way. She smiled at me. "It's good to see you, Omega Bliss. It's been a long time."

"Four years," I said flatly. Flora elbowed me. I'd sounded rude. I cleared my throat. "I mean, yes. Sorry. It has been a long time. How are you?"

Sarah smiled graciously, glossing over my mistake. Would the headmistress be as gracious?

"I remember your rescue so vividly. It's one of our best success stories."

My smile was brittle. "Thank you. I agree, of course."

The new girl swiveled around in her chair, her head tilting to the side as she stared at me. She was tan, with dark curls and large, light blue eyes that made her look even younger than she already was. My heart broke for her, just like it did for all the new girls.

"We rescued Omega Bliss late in life," Sarah explained to the girl.

"Rescued late in life" was a polite way to say, "was betrayed by the boys who were supposed to love me and was sent here against my will." Granted, Sarah didn't know that. She honestly believed in what she was doing; you could see it in the zealous gleam in her eye.

"I was seventeen when I came to live here," I clarified, forcing a smile.

"Exactly, extremely late," the headmistress said as though I weren't here. "It was nearly a disaster. She didn't know she was an omega. We rescued her just before four teenage criminals forced her to mate with them. Now, thanks to the Institute, she'll have a wonderful future."

My heart pounded, and my breath came faster. No matter how much I wished otherwise, I thought about my former pack constantly. *No. Not mine. Not anymore.*

"Isn't that right, Omega Bliss?" Sarah asked.

It was impossible not to think of them, like white noise in the back of my mind at all times that occasionally got louder at times of stress. It had been that way since almost the second I was separated from them four years ago. But I could count on one hand the number of times anyone had brought them up to me. I wasn't prepared for this.

My heart screamed. A physical, stabbing sensation, like an ice pick through my chest. "Yes." I smiled through the lie. "That's exactly what happened."

———

Flora watched me out of the corner of her eye as we led the new girl around campus. Her wide brown eyes screamed, *"Are you okay? Do we need to ditch the kid and get out of here?"*

It was as though she was afraid I was going to crack and start crying right in the middle of the tour. She wasn't far off.

Seeing Sarah and having her bring up my "rescue" wasn't how I'd planned to spend my Tuesday morning. It was putting me on edge. Then again, everything was putting me on edge the closer we got to graduation.

Graduation meant taking part in the annual Agora and mating one of the country's most influential alphas. I'd always known that was the endgame of my time here—I'd even relished it. The only thing that kept me sane sometimes was knowing that the pack who hadn't wanted me would one day see me on TV or in the tabloids, mated to someone else. The closer we got though, the more real everything became.

I frowned, rubbing my chest where the incessant throbbing refused to leave me alone. It had been worse lately, like my body was turning on me. Staging a protest against my changing allegiance. *As though I have a choice.*

I ignored the throbbing and swallowed. The back of my throat tasted like lemon and pepper—a phantom sensation from across the country. That wasn't good.

"That's the library." I pointed to a large brick building surrounded by flowering trees. "And over there are some more dorms, but they're empty right now. The Institute is only at twenty-five percent capacity because there are so few omegas left in the world."

The new girl—Eden—nodded, keeping her eyes fixed on the ground. We'd started outside, showing her the dorm buildings, the pond, and the meditation gazebo. The grounds were usually less jarring for rescues. Inside, where everything was soft, dark, and silent, could be a lot.

"That's the recreation field where we do morning yoga," Flora said. "If you pretend to be sick to get out of yoga, they will make you drink this horrific root infusion, so I don't recommend it."

"They took my phone when I got here," Eden said, clearly not paying attention to us at all. "How do I call my friends?"

Flora and I glanced at each other. This culture shock was a tricky one for the new girls, especially the rescues.

Everyone in the country—the world, even—grew up knowing about the Omega Institute. Ever since the omega population started dwindling, the government had stepped in, theoretically for the omegas' protection. They brought girls to the Institute before their first heat, trained us to be good wives and mothers, then mated us to alphas who could protect us. I could see why the idea made sense to most people.

The retrievals—who knew they were likely omegas from birth—had been preparing to come to the Institute their whole lives. They had alpha and omega parents and knew what to expect. The rescues had no idea what they were until they began pre-transition. All they knew of the Institute was what they'd seen on TV, and the propaganda didn't align with reality.

"You don't," I said, probably too bluntly. "Call your friends."

Eden blinked at me with wide, horrified eyes. "What? But they won't know where I went."

"There's a landline. You can call your parents on

Sundays if you want. No cell phones, no internet, and mail is monitored."

"What, is this jail or something?" Eden grumbled, pushing her hair behind her ears.

"Yes," Flora snapped.

"No," I said quickly, stepping on Flora's foot. I tried to give the girl a soothing smile. "Eden, do you understand what's happening?"

"I'm going to be an omega," she said.

"You are an omega," Flora corrected. She looked her over and amended, "Pre-transition, probably."

Eden gave us a scathing look, like we were idiots. I almost smiled. I was just as angry my first day here, and it was surreal to see someone with normal, unsuppressed emotions. They probably hadn't gotten her on blockers yet, either because there wasn't time or because she was so young.

"Look." Flora crossed her arms. "If you'd been left alone in the wild, you would have transitioned, but you're here, so they're going to put you on blockers."

"I'm from Houston." She glanced between us, clearly unsure if we knew where that was. "It's not wild."

I coughed on a laugh. She reminded me a little of…no one. My smile slipped. "Figuratively," I said. "She means that if you hadn't been picked up by the Institute, you would have transitioned into an omega around the age of seventeen when you went into your first heat. Maybe sooner if you knew any alphas."

It was Flora's turn to step on my foot. That wasn't the kind of thing you just said out loud.

There were so few omegas left in the world that matings were hardly ever natural anymore. Back in the days when there were almost as many omegas as alphas, an omega's transition would be triggered by her pack. Now, they kept us on blockers and artificially induced heat as soon as we were mated, to ensure that packs didn't form and only wealthy alphas had children. Keep the rich, rich.

You couldn't just say that though, even if it was true. We weren't supposed to talk about teenage omegas triggering their heats with teenage alphas. That was a big no-no in the eyes of the Institute, and exactly what I'd been allegedly rescued from.

Unfortunately, Eden was clearly smart, and she was listening now. "Is what they said in the office true?"

My heartbeat sped up, and I clenched my fists in my jacket pockets. "Which part?"

"They found you about to go into heat and saved you from mating by force?"

I gritted my teeth, unable to answer. That part wasn't true. Well, I had been about to go into heat, but my mating wouldn't have been forced. They'd been my best friends.

They don't want you. They didn't want you. Don't think about them.

"All matings are forced," Flora said. "Just because the alpha is rich doesn't change the fact that you didn't choose him."

"Flora," I hissed. "You're going to freak her out. Er, sorry. *Upset her balance.* Let's go look at the vegetable garden."

I led the way past the huge brick school building and under an ivy-covered stone arch toward a vast, fenced-in garden. Eden wrinkled her nose, unimpressed. I couldn't blame her.

If she hadn't transitioned yet and wasn't on any

hormone suppressants, she wasn't any different from a beta. A fourteen-year-old beta, who had just been ripped away from her family and told she couldn't see her friends anymore. The soothing style of the Omega Institute wouldn't have any effect on her yet.

It didn't have much effect on me either, but that was a separate problem.

I forced another smile, already annoyed with myself for playing along with this ridiculous charade, and gestured toward a patch of flowers. "Why don't you try sitting in the sun? Most of the girls find it really soothing."

If I heard the word "soothing" again today, I was going to scream.

Eden stared at me, clearly trying to decide if I was joking. Finally, she shrugged and wandered away to sit in the center of a patch of flowering clover. I watched her shredding the petals with a grim satisfaction.

"You're better at this tour shit than me," Flora muttered.

"Only because you're tonguing your suppressants," I muttered, too low for Eden to hear. "Don't say 'shit.' Who knows who's out here."

Flora scoffed, pretending to be offended. She put on a high-pitched, fake Southern accent. "My word, Omega Bliss, you wound me. I would never. It is our duty to our country to stay pure and suppressed until mating."

"Yeah, yeah. Keep your voice down, Scarlett O'Hara."

Flora had been my roommate since the day I moved into the Institute. The headmistress thought it would be a good match since we were from the same town growing up. "A fortunate coincidence," she'd said. We hadn't been friends back home, but now I couldn't imagine a day without her. I would never turn her in, but we both knew she hadn't taken her hormone blockers regularly in months. Her comment about her ass growing wasn't figurative, and her emotions had come back tenfold—the other day, she had nearly sworn in front of an instructor.

"I just wanted to know what it was like for you," Flora muttered.

My blood ran cold, and I glanced around, suddenly panicked that someone would hear us. I smoothed my hands over my hips—wider than the rest of the girls here. "Mine still work, just not that well."

"I know. I know what those guys did to you was shitty, but in a way, there's a silver lining, right? At least you can think straight because you're technically bond—"

"Shut up! Don't say that word out loud," I snapped, panicked. I completely forgot not to swear. I took a deep breath. "Sorry." I threw Flora an apologetic look. "I just mean, there's nothing lucky about it. I'd rather be a mindless, hormone-suppressed zombie than have to feel them with me all the time."

"I know." She shook her head. "That was a dumb thing to say."

I grimaced. It was, but I wouldn't rub it in. Partly because I wanted to change the subject. Two mentions of the guys in one day was practically my hell on earth.

I grew up on the other side of the country in a foster home specializing in difficult placements. My four best friends and I were a pack before we had any understanding of what that meant. Rafe, Ares, Killian, and Nox were alphas, but they took care of me even when they thought I was a beta. When I was seventeen, I began my transition into an omega, and everything changed.

For a moment when I'd started my transition, I believed we were going to become a real pack. It felt like they loved me as much as I loved them, but I should have known it wasn't real. Nothing ever turned out that well in my life.

My pulse doubled, and I sucked my bottom lip into my mouth. They didn't want me. A lifetime of friendship meant nothing when faced with real-life decisions, and they called the Institute and sent me away.

At least I could thank them for wiping away the naive girl I was. Back then, my entire life—my personality, my interests, all my time—had revolved around them.

They were the whole world, and I was a satellite. Until one day, the world stopped turning.

And then, somehow, I woke up the next day and kept going.

I still didn't know why they called the Institute, but I could take a guess. It was illegal to mate an omega outside of a government-approved union. If we became a pack, we would have instantly become criminals. Our lives would have narrowed to the kind of future you have if you're always on the run—gangs and violence. We never would have gotten out of the shitty town we grew up in.

My teeth pierced my lip, and the salty tang of blood filled my mouth. It hurt less than the constant pain in my chest that still refused to go away, even after all these years.

My boys had chosen their future over me, but they hadn't done it fast enough. By the time Sarah arrived to "rescue" me, it was already too late.

We weren't fully mated because none of them had bitten me and I never went into heat, but they'd triggered my transition. Just like the omegas and their packs a hundred years ago, we were bound. I could still feel them with me sometimes, even with an entire country between us.

I glanced over to where Eden was still shredding flowers and forced a practiced smile back onto my face. "Come on," I told Flora. "If we don't go inside soon, they'll think she escaped."

"Yeah, alright." Flora still looked wary, but she changed the subject. "Who do you think they'll make do tours after we're gone?"

I shrugged. I didn't really care. As far as graduation went, I was single-minded.

I would graduate. I'd allow myself to be mated to someone new, and I would integrate into omega society. The first time my former pack saw me after all these years, it would be when my mating was announced in the press.

I smiled grimly. Next week, for the first time, I would be glad of the weird bond that forced us to share feelings sometimes. Wherever they were, whatever they were doing, I hoped that when I mated a new alpha, my former pack would feel a fraction of the rejection I'd felt when they abandoned me.

CHAPTER 2

Rafe

Air rushed from my lungs on a sharp exhale when Ares' fist collided with my kidney. Motherfucker, he was fast.

"That all you got, *boss*?" He hissed the last word out like an insult as he pulled back and circled me.

Tension tightened my skin and a rumble formed low in my chest, echoing in the warehouse we'd been living in for the last four years. I was seconds away from losing control and pounding Ares into the red makeshift MMA mat. The problem was, the sick fuck would love that.

The fighting ring, if you could call a few mats thrown together on the floor a ring, was one of the first things we set up when the four of us moved here after… I rubbed the slice of pain from my chest, pushing the intrusive thoughts down. When everything happened, we knew we'd need to blow off steam without outright killing each other. What Ares wanted was different. He didn't want to burn off energy. No, Ares fought to forget.

I pivoted, keeping him in sight, taking deep, calming breaths. His moon-white hair stuck to his forehead, and a cut on his brow leaked red down into his pale blue eye and onto his tattooed chest. The shadows on his sharp jaw stood in stark contrast, giving him a look of being carved from stone. He'd become cold, *ruthless* over the past four years. The world we lived in and the constant ache of our missing bond had changed him beyond recognition.

I dodged Ares' next attack, and his narrowed gaze met mine head-on. He growled low in his throat as he came for me again. "Stop analyzing me, asshole, and fucking fight me."

I swung out of his way. "Stop making it so easy to read you. You aren't looking for a fight."

I felt the all-too-familiar tug buried deep in my gut and stumbled, leaving myself open. A hint of jasmine and spice filled my mind, and my heart burned in its cage. *Bliss.*

It was impossible not to worry when Bliss' emotions were so high that we could feel her through our bond. Impossible not to worry what could be causing that.

Ares must have felt it too because he jerked back, eyes wide on mine, before shutting down any signs of emotion. His usually pale face reddened before he slammed a fist into my side, purposely aiming for the same kidney he'd just hit. "I'm going to fucking kill you."

The ammonia scent of his lie burned my nose before pain rioted up my side and down my hip. Anger I'd been holding back boiled over, and I slammed my fist into his jaw. The loud crack split the open warehouse.

Ares' head snapped back with the force, and he staggered a few feet before righting himself. The pupils of his cool blue eyes widened until only the very edges were rimmed with color. He grinned, teeth coated in blood. "That's better."

Fuck. This is what I get for engaging.

He lunged for my knees, trying to take me down, but I slammed my elbow into the side of his head instead. He collapsed on the mat, a red smile briefly splashed across his face, before coming at me again. He staggered to one side, unable to keep his balance as he took another throw at me.

I took a step back and held up my hands. "Enough. I'm not playing into your shit."

Ares spit blood at my feet. "Fuck you."

"Oi! Cut the shit." Killian's voice cut through the room. "Not really the time to be trying to kill each other."

Killian leaned against the doorframe, looking like an urban lumberjack wearing his usual plaid shirt over a plain T-shirt and jeans. He had a hat pulled low over his light amber eyes, and his curly hair brushed against his collar.

Ares' eyes turned on Killian. "Stay out of it."

Kill grinned. "Are you trying to fight me, too?"

Kill showing up to stop us didn't surprise me. He'd been the peacekeeper of our pack since we were in the group home together. Four young alphas living in close quarters was a recipe for disaster, but between him and Bliss, they'd managed to keep us from outright killing each other. Without Bliss, it had all fallen to him. Judging from the blood pooling down Ares' face, he wasn't doing that well on his own.

Ares didn't hesitate to take advantage of my distraction. I dropped to my knees with the force of his blow, my head ringing like a bell.

Killian crossed the warehouse in three strides and jumped between us before Ares could do anything to push things further. "Alright, you're done. Take a shower."

"You act like it doesn't fucking bother you." Ares spit the words like a weapon.

The growl that emanated from Killian filled the space as he crowded Ares, his larger frame pushing him backward. His hat covered his eyes, hiding his darkening stare as he gestured around the warehouse filled with crates of illegal goods. "Are you kidding me? As if we haven't all sold our souls to get her back?"

We'd been working our way up the Alpha Lupi ranks, finally taking over a few years ago, with the sole purpose of getting Bliss back. The shit we had to do to get where we were now would haunt the fuck out of me. Enough blood coated my hands that they'd never be clean. But we'd all do it again in a heartbeat.

We'd been a pack. Promised each other we'd stay that way, and the second she presented as an omega, we'd sold her out to the Institute under the misguided bullshit assumption we were protecting her. Not before scent binding though. No, we couldn't just leave her to live her life. We had to tie her to us forever.

Killian grabbed the back of Ares' neck and pulled his forehead to his own. The veins in his arms pulled taut, straining to keep Ares in place. "I've been on your side this entire fucking time. Regretted everything from the second the Institute car rolled up. Fuck you if you're trying to take your shit out on us when we're so close to getting her back."

Ares met Killian's gaze and then looked away, breaking his hold on him.

I cleared my throat and stepped closer. "We'll have her back in a few days."

Ares' sharp gaze bore into mine, and his lips tipped up in the corner in a sneer. "Then what? You think she's going to come running into your arms after what we've done?"

I stood silent, heart pounding against my ribs. The look of betrayal she wore as the Institute dragged her from us pierced my heart. Bond or not, Bliss had every reason not to trust us.

Ares skirted around Killian and stood so close, the toes of his black shoes touched mine. His pale blue eyes narrowed as he hissed, "And when she tells us to fuck off? Are we going to force her to stay with us?"

A growl rumbled through my chest as anger pulsed through my veins. Every instinct screamed at me that yes, that was exactly what'd we do.

We were boys when we'd let her get away. Unsure of who we were or what we could do, willing to give up the best thing to ever happen to us to keep her safe and happy. But that was all over now.

No, when we finally got her back, we'd lock her the fuck away. No chance of her escaping. She was ours to protect, possess, fucking devour.

Ares stilled, brows pinched as he scanned my face. "Maybe she's better off without us."

He grabbed his towel, wiping the blood off his face as he left, slamming the door behind him.

Killian watched Ares leave before he turned to me, lifting his hat and raking his fingers through his hair, tugging at the ends. He attempted a smile. "Ignore him. He'll get over it when Bliss gets back."

I grunted something like an agreement, but I couldn't help worrying that Ares had a point.

Bliss wasn't just going to come with us. That was why we couldn't give her a choice. Alphas weren't meant to be apart from their omegas. And no amount of money would change the fact that she was ours.

One more job and we'd have more than enough to win her back.

"Ow," I hissed at the sharp sting in my brow as Nox placed the last stitch where Ares had sucker punched me. "Hurry the fuck up."

Nox shifted the needle and thread he was holding to his other hand, tying off another stitch. "Calm down. I'm almost finished."

I sat at one of the kitchen stools, Nox hovering over me as he stitched up my face. The sleeves of his crisp white dress shirt were rolled above his elbows, and his black vest was folded on the nearby chair. His tailored appearance was offset by his shaved red hair and the black-and-silver piercings that ran up one ear.

My brows rose only to shoot more pain where the new stitches tugged. "Goddamnit!"

He pushed his thick black glasses up the bridge of his nose, rolling his eyes. "Don't be such a pussy."

"Fuck you."

Now I sounded like Ares.

I pushed Nox back and stood, steadying myself on the edge of our marble kitchen island. The warehouse had changed a lot since we took over Alpha Lupi. There was still a wide-open loading dock, where we stored and moved our product, but we'd renovated a twenty-five by one-hundred-foot section of the east side to function as an apartment.

I crossed to our double-wide industrial-sized fridge and grabbed a bottle of water, finishing it in a few sips. With four alphas over two hundred pounds each living in close quarters, our grocery bills were massive.

I turned, leaning my back against the cabinets, and tried to picture what Bliss would think when she finally got here. We'd hired an architect to eliminate the icy feeling of the warehouse, instead changing it to a calm, welcoming home. Even though it had an open-concept kitchen and living room, the long narrow structure of the apartment had the entire place feeling like a cocoon.

We'd researched the shit out of omega living preferences and decorated with neutral tones and oversize furniture to create a cozy environment. There were floor-to-ceiling windows on one side dressed with different sheerness of drapery that could darken the room to varying degrees, the last being pitch-black. From where I stood in the kitchen, I could just make out the rooms located down the hall. My eyes stilled on the door between our rooms.

Nox's burnt-copper brows pulled together. "Do you think Bliss will like it?"

I huffed out a breath—sometimes Nox was like a damn mind reader. "I fucking hope so."

Nox had always been the smartest of us all, but his foundation was shaken after we'd realized our mistake in sending Bliss away. He'd agreed the Institute was the safest place for her based on basic facts. We were young, poor alphas with no influence and no contacts. On top of that, we were tangled more than we'd like in the gang world. We had no business taking care of an omega. Especially one as precious as Bliss.

When we lost her, something broke in Nox. The guilt he felt led him to being a shell of himself.

Within minutes of the Institute driving away with our girl, we'd erupted into a fight. The ache of the distancing bond felt like it would tear me apart. I blamed them; I blamed myself. Fuck, I blamed the world for losing her.

We'd taken off in different directions and put as much space between us, not wanting the support of our pack if Bliss wasn't with us.

In the end, our scent bond dragged us back together, each of us showing up back at the warehouse where we'd been with her last.

Ares was the last to show, several months after the rest of us, looking pissed that he was even there.

Nox's face lost any remaining color it had. "We may get her back, but she'll still despise us for what we did. You have to understand that."

My jaw clenched, and it took several moments before I could answer him. "I know."

CHAPTER 3
Bliss

The Omega Institute prided itself on providing a warm and comforting environment for omegas. Our dorm rooms, unironically called "nests," were just as small, dark, and quiet as everywhere else in the Institute. It was an architectural marvel, really, to have such large buildings with such tiny rooms.

Flora and I shared a nest on the fourth floor of the only dorm building currently in use. At the moment, the Institute was home to 112 omegas from all over the United States. Now, 113 since Eden had arrived. It was a disturbingly small number when you considered that there was only one Institute in the country, and attendance was mandatory.

"You were right," Flora said, twisting in front of the mirror in the corner of our room. "Your skirt does fit better."

"Good," I said, trying to force a note of enthusiasm into my voice. I didn't want to get out of bed this morning, but as I'd learned several times over, pretending to be sick was worse than just going to class.

I rolled over on my plush bed and watched her modeling one of my sweaters. We wouldn't have to wear the uniforms much longer, anyway.

"Ow!" My fingers spasmed, pain shooting through my hand, disembodied and unbidden.

"What?" Flora spun around, her eyebrows pulled together.

"Nothing." I swung my legs out of my bed, ignoring my throbbing knuckles. I didn't want to worry her.

I pinched my leg. Hard. I hoped someone felt it.

I used the edge of my fork to push my scrambled eggs into three tiny, even piles along the edge of my plate. Each pile had to be exactly the same size, with only the round lumps showing on the top. Then, I moved on to the sausage. How even could I make the slices? I cut each link into twelve first, and if the pieces weren't even, I moved on to twenty-four.

"What the fuck are you doing?" Flora reached across the breakfast table and grabbed my fork out of my hand.

"Hey!"

"Here, eat this." She shoved a piece of buttered toast into my hand.

I rolled my eyes at her but took a bite, washing it down with a gulp of orange juice. We weren't allowed to have coffee. "I'm so sick of scrambled eggs and sausages," I told her honestly.

All our food was carefully monitored to make sure we

were getting exactly the right amount of nutrients. I would kill for a soda, or some ice cream, or hell, just anything other than eggs.

Flora assessed my plate with a raised brow. She reached for a sausage sliver and popped it into her mouth. "I feel you. Just imagine all the real food we can eat when we get out of here."

I frowned. Flora had been oddly calm about our impending graduation lately—or calm for her. I was expecting more of a tantrum, especially since she'd stopped regularly taking her hormone suppressants.

I glanced around our table to make sure that none of the other girls seated near us were paying attention to our conversation. They weren't.

The nearest girl, Omega Chelsea, wore a benign smile—an evident sign she'd just taken her morning blockers. Two tables over, Eden had a slack look on her face and was staring blankly into a full glass of milk. It was a jarring change from the girl we'd met yesterday.

I sighed. Some days I wished my blockers worked that well, but they never had.

I opened my mouth to ask Flora about her strange acceptance of our graduation but never got the chance.

The doors to the dining room opened, and Headmistress Omega DuPont entered, followed by three tall men in suits. My back stiffened. Beside me, Flora reached over and dug her nails into my thigh. The vinegar scent of her panic hit me like a freight train—I hadn't smelled any emotion so strong in years.

Men rarely entered the Institute. All the instructors were female, and we hadn't had a male omega student the entire time I'd been here. I privately thought all the male omegas were out in the world somewhere, either using blockers or illegally mated.

The only men who came to the Institute were alphas, either for classes, or—

"Excuse me, ladies," the headmistress called, making a beeline toward where Flora and I sat with the other girls in our age group. "We have some visitors this morning."

"Good morning," we all intoned, keeping our eyes down.

I peeked up through my lashes. The two alphas in the back were nearly indistinguishable from each other. That wasn't to say they looked alike—not at all, really—but their scents were similar. Mid-level aggressive and unimpressive. The one in the front, however, made the hair on the back of my neck stand on end.

He was perhaps forty with sharp bone structure and slick blond hair. His expression was cool, and he smelled like cigars and whiskey. Everything about him said "danger, stay away."

"These are the ladies who will be in New York at the end of the week for the Agora," the headmistress explained. "Girls, we are giving a tour to some of the prospective alphas today. Please be on your best behavior."

Again, there was a quick muttered response. I felt my mouth move, but no words came out. Out of the corner of my eye, the dangerous alpha stepped forward, taking in a deep breath. His eyes zeroed in on Flora and me and froze.

Alphas had an acute sense of smell, and it was geared specifically toward finding an omega. There was no chance this whole group didn't smell *something* off about us.

"They've all been here since before their transition?" the alpha asked, staring at us.

"Oh yes," the headmistress said, a little coldly. "Some as long as seven years."

"Hmmm," he said, not taking his eyes off us.

It was almost an insult, but not quite. Everyone knew omegas had to stay on blockers from the moment they transitioned until they mated. Preferably before they transitioned, just in case. No alpha would want an omega who had been scented before.

Like me.

Flora shook, her nails digging painfully into my leg, her panic palpable. *How long has she been off suppressants?*

If any of them got too close, they would know. They could tell the headmistress, or worse, it could trigger her heat. She'd be scent bound, like me.

Her fear burned my nose. This whole thing was unbearably stupid, but I'd yell at her later.

The tall, dangerous alpha strode around the table, coming to a halt right beside us. My heart beat against my ribs, and I was sure the scent of vinegar was now heavy in the air.

I threw my arm out, knocking my half-full glass of orange juice off the table. Flora shrieked in surprise as it toppled, drenching the front of her sweater and landing in her lap.

"Sorry," I said dully, keeping my eyes on the table.

The headmistress spluttered in indication. "Omega Bliss. Are you feeling alright?"

"Yes. I'm sorry, I didn't see the glass."

Flora jumped to her feet. "Excuse me."

I didn't dare watch her as she dashed from the dining

hall. The scent of berries with a hint of sour citrus filled my mouth. The alpha had watched the whole scene without comment, and now he was staring at me.

I turned around in my chair to face the alpha, keeping my eyes on his shoes.

"What's your name?" he asked.

"Bliss."

"Do you know what you smell like, Omega Bliss?"

I swallowed, still not looking up from his shoes. "Orange juice."

His large hand shot out, fingers stretching to wrap around my neck. I bit back a scream.

"Alpha Nero, please do not touch the girls," the headmistress said quickly.

My muscles went weak with relief.

"If you want Omega Bliss, you can make a note on her auction card. I'm sure the cost will be no concern."

Any relief I'd felt left me in a woosh, replaced with nausea. I couldn't breathe. I needed to get outside.

The alpha let his hand drop back to his side. I didn't have to look at him to know he was smiling. "Fine. Thank you, Headmistress Omega Dupont. I'll do that."

After dinner, I didn't return to my nest. Instead, I snuck out the side door and made my way out to the gardens and took a seat under a gnarled apple tree. The sky was clear, illuminated only by a fingernail moon and a thousand tiny stars. For the first time since breakfast, I let out a full breath.

The grounds of the Institute were beautiful, especially

at night. No matter what I thought about everything else, I really did like the gardens. For a kid who had grown up in foster care in the city, a sprawling vegetable and flower garden was basically paradise.

I was almost one hundred percent sure I wasn't allowed to be outside on my own, but in four years, no one had ever expressly told me so, and I'd never asked. Even if someone had told me no, tonight I would have risked it.

In an abstract way, mating a new alpha had always seemed like the best revenge. Now, faced with the real thing, that idea came into stark perspective.

Bonding involved sharing your soul. That was the only way to describe what it felt like to constantly feel emotions that didn't belong to me, to know that I was probably projecting my own feelings right back. To constantly feel like a piece of myself was missing and fractured into four.

I had no idea what would happen if I tried to mate another alpha on top of all of that. It was absolutely possible, since my existing bond had never been sealed, but I didn't think it would erase the first bond entirely. In all likelihood, I'd simply become overwhelmed with another person sharing my soul.

I felt fractured now, but soon I'd be lost entirely.

As if triggered by my thoughts of them, pain and frustration trickled through the bond. I screwed my eyes shut, willing the feeling away. I didn't want to feel them. It hurt too much.

I dug my fingers into the grass at my sides, like holding on to the ground would somehow make me less lost. I hated them. I hated them for leaving me and forcing me to choose between impossible options. They'd sentenced me to life without parole, and there was no way out.

My eyelids cracked open, and I found myself staring up at the Pleiades. It was always the easiest constellation to spot because it was so bright and grouped so close together. *And then, if you look just to the side of that...* My eyes found Orion's Belt, just like Nox and I used to.

Another stab of pain shot through my chest, but this time it wasn't coming from anyone else. This was all me.

As I did every day, I wished my blockers worked. That for just once, I could be numb like everyone else.

CHAPTER 4

Nox

"Hey!" Killian sat beside me on the old, tattered couch, his perpetual grin firmly in place. "I thought I'd find you here."

He crossed one leg over the other, and one of his pristine white Vans covered the rip in his jeans. He'd let his curly honey-brown hair grow out, giving him a boyish look, only undermined by his enormous size.

I'd been sitting on the warehouse roof for the last hour, attempting to settle my racing mind. There was enough riding on our job tonight to send me over the edge into a verifiable panic attack. I didn't have the time nor the energy for that shit tonight.

I side-eyed Killian and swallowed another sip of my beer, letting the bitterness linger in the back of my throat. "If you knew I'd be up here, you also know I'd prefer to be left alone."

Killian ignored that statement. *Consider me shocked.*

"Not the same without her though, is it?"

It was my turn to ignore *him*. Killian already knew my answer. Nothing had ever been the same.

I kept coming up here because it was where I felt the closest to Bliss. If I stayed perfectly still, I could almost feel the ghost of her body wrapped around mine, almost smell her jasmine and chilies scent. It was a sick form of torment I couldn't seem to resist.

"Do you think she still climbs on the roof when she's trying to think?" Killian asked.

His question stung, and a low rumble formed in my chest at the memories of all the times we'd sat on the roof of the group home, me making up bullshit stories about the stars to make her laugh.

I huffed out a breath and took another sip, the cool taste refreshing on the humid night. "After what we did to her, she probably cusses me out when she sees my favorite constellation."

Killian leaned back and took a long sip of his bottle. "Yeah, well, we were fucking idiots."

There was no arguing with that. We'd done the unthinkable. We'd rejected our bond. At least, that's what we made her believe.

"You know, there's a distinct possibility she'd prefer to be with one of the rich and famous alphas, regardless of the scent bond." I voiced something I'd been mulling over for a while.

I didn't know what would be worse: Bliss hating us for leaving or her being grateful we'd let her go. It was a choice between Scylla and Charybdis—both options equally likely to kill me.

"You're listening to Ares again." Killian tossed his empty bottle in the bin and cracked open a new one.

"You're just getting nervous because we're so close. Once we have Bliss, you better believe I'll be fighting tooth and nail to show her what she means to me. She belonged in our pack long before we knew she was an omega, and she's never stopped being ours. All the bond did was reinforce that."

I nodded, pushing my glasses back into place on my nose. I envied Killian for his eternal optimism.

Once I pulled my head out of my ass four years ago, it didn't take long for me to realize just how badly we'd fucked up by sending our girl to the Institute. Since then, we'd been driven by the single-minded focus of getting her back.

Tomorrow was Bliss' ceremony. The details of the annual Agora Gala were a well-guarded secret, and even with all the influence we now held, we couldn't figure out exactly how it worked. The only thing we knew for sure was that it required money. A lot of money.

I'd been sick for days when we found out we should expect to pay over a million to walk out of there with our omega. Apparently, the money went to the Institution to keep the program afloat and to prove you could take care of an omega. I couldn't stop the feeling something didn't add up.

It didn't matter though. We were willing to do whatever it took to get her back.

To make the money for the Agora, we took over Alpha Lupi and saved every cent from every job, stretching a dollar into hundreds of thousands by the time we were twenty. We'd taken contracts we had no business getting involved in and worked with people I wished I'd never met.

We started working with the Institute on the side, providing them with discounts on their blockers for a seat at the table. It damn near killed me not to demand answers about Bliss, but the less they knew about our connection, the better.

Anything and everything, for her.

Still, even after everything, we didn't have enough. That was why it all came down to tonight.

We'd tripled down on our usual amount of product. Once we made the switch, we'd have enough to get Bliss back.

The rooftop door slammed open, and we spun toward it, guns out. Ares glared at us from the entry, moonlight making his already white hair glow, giving him an ethereal look. He was wearing his standard uniform of black leather jacket, white T-shirt, and worn black jeans. "Good fucking God, there you are. We're headed out."

I lowered my gun and rolled my eyes as I pushed up to my feet. The idiot nearly got himself shot. Hell, that could've been his plan—it was hard to tell what he was thinking anymore.

A deep ache formed in my chest. Kill was right—Ares had been getting to me. Did he really believe that Bliss would reject us? Honestly, I believed that half the time. *Not that we ever discuss it.*

I took one more glance at the stars, then brushed by Ares in the doorway. His sleeve skimmed my arm, and I did my best to ignore the shiver sent down my back. No matter how hard we all fought it, we were just as bound to each other as we were to Bliss, both in our history and the scent bond. It just didn't feel right without her here. She was a crack through our foundation, and without her, our fall was inevitable.

All that would end soon. We'd get her back, then spend the rest of our lives proving to her we were meant for each other. That all the shit we'd said in the parking lot to get her to go with the Institute was absolute bullshit.

I took the stairs two at a time, Ares close behind me. Rafe was already in the kitchen, guns and ammunition spread out on the island. His midnight-black hair fell over his face, covering his intense dark eyes. Where I was tall and lean, Rafe had filled out in both height and muscle. His forest-green henley shirt stretched over his shoulders as he pushed his hair back. His sharp gaze met mine. "Where the hell were you?"

"Lay off." Ares snapped his ammunition clip into his gun, making a loud click sound. "We don't have fucking time for this."

I rolled my eyes. It couldn't have been more apparent that Ares didn't care; he just liked arguing with Rafe. I also didn't need his help, but that was beside the point. What we really didn't have time for was another power struggle, but pointing that out would only extend the animosity.

Rafe's brows pulled together before he ran us through the plan. "Forget the amount. Tonight's just another job."

Ares laughed under his breath, setting my teeth on edge.

Rafe placed both his hands on the island and leaned into Ares' space. "You have something to say?"

Ares just lifted one white-blond brow and went back to working on his weapons.

"That's what I thought." Rafe stood straight and holstered his guns. "The product is already at the dock. All we have to do is show up, make the exchange, and get the fuck out of there."

That didn't mean we weren't going in armed to the teeth. We couldn't trust anyone in this business. We didn't have many friends after the shit we'd done to take over, but people were forced to work with us because we had a monopoly on the hormone blocker and scent markets.

None of it mattered. It was a means to an end. If selling drugs was what it took to get Bliss back, I'd happily do it for the rest of my life. I had no problem selling my soul for her. She already owned it.

Rafe ran his hand through his hair. "In and out, just like normal. After this, we go get our girl." He looked at Ares. "Don't fuck this up."

Ares glared at Rafe. He was unpredictable on a good day, and we all knew it. "You think I don't want this as much as—"

The front door crashed open, and Wes rushed through. My stomach lurched with dread.

The beta was the only person allowed in our home aside from us, but he shouldn't be here now. He'd gone to help move the product with the rest of the crew.

The sadness on his face, mixed with the blood splattered on his clothes, stopped my heart and sent my stomach through the floor.

Ares growled and stepped around the kitchen island, pinning Wes to the wall with his forearm. "What the fuck happened?"

When he didn't immediately respond, Ares slammed him against the wall again as if to pound the information out.

Killian grabbed Ares' shoulder, pulling him off. "He can't breathe."

Ares cut him a sharp look but let the beta slump to the ground, gasping for breath.

Rafe dropped to his haunches to get on eye level with Wes. "Tell me." Rafe's bark split through the heavy air, raising goose bumps on my arms.

"We were attacked. They're clearing the warehouse." Wes dropped his eyes, voice missing its usual cockiness. He knew what this meant for us.

Oh, fuck no. Not when we're so close.

Before Rafe could say anything, I ran out the door and swung into our navy blue delivery van's driver's side. Three other doors slammed simultaneously, and I took off down the road to the drop point. *Like fucking hell they'd rob us.*

The drive to the dock was a blur. All that mattered was getting there before the product was gone. We did our trade from an old, abandoned fish market located on a long-deserted strip of the dock. Row upon row of deserted market stalls left the perfect location to discreetly move less than legal products.

I'd barely parked before the guys threw their back doors open. *Shit.* "Fuck, wait!" Tension filled the air, the iron smell of their rage burning my nose. "Just fucking wait a second. We can't rush in there. They'll kill us instantly."

Three growls rumbled through the van, their instinctive nature taking over, but no one got out.

I pointed toward the fish market blocking the view of the dock. "They aren't guarding the entrance, which means we can expect a battle once we're in. We'll have to split up and come at them from both sides."

Rafe seemed to snap out of his haze of anger first and started shooting off orders. "Nox and Ares go through the east, Killian and I will take the west. Our first prerogative is stopping the boat from taking off at the back. Clear?"

"Clear." Our voices merged as one.

Gun raised, I jumped from the van and rushed toward the east side of the market. I raced past the first few stalls and stepped in the path of a large man ten feet in front of me, gun pointed at my chest. The man's lips tipped up in a sneer before he cocked the gun. *Fuck.*

Ares' giant body crashed into mine, forcing me behind a line of crates just as the ringing sound of a shotgun filled the air. The scent of dead flowers filled my nose as Ares checked me for wounds.

"I'm fine. Get off me."

He sprung off me like he was burned and looked sharply away, a muscle ticking in his jaw. "Don't be a fucking idiot." He left me there, not glancing back, and easily shot my would-be killer.

We moved toward the back of the dock, using the old crates for coverage. A group of our men lay unconscious on the floor in the middle of the market, their hands and ankles bound together. They were all alphas. It would've taken a powerful bark to put them in this state.

A boat was tied to the back of the dock, sitting deep in the water with the weight of all our product. The driver turned and spotted us. "Hurry the fuck up," he shouted at his men.

Two men loaded a crate onto the back. We stepped out from our cover, and they took off before they could finish loading the last one, and it bobbed in the water before going under.

I fired off round after round at the thieves, managing to hit one in the chest. His hand went to his heart and came away coated in red before he collapsed overboard.

Killian rounded the corner. He would've jumped off the dock after them if it wasn't for Rafe's arms bound around him. "It's gone."

My breath stuttered at the sight. There were crushed and broken crates but no vials in sight.

I dug my fingers into my hair and pulled at the ends until the pain took over my thoughts. I couldn't process what had happened. We'd been so close, and some petty fucking gang retaliation was going to stop us from getting her back.

Fuck no. I couldn't accept that. Not after everything. Not when my every breath counted on hers.

Killian dropped to his knees, oblivious to the blood soaking through his pants. His gaze was blank as he looked over the water where the boat sped off into the night, taking any hope of the money we needed with it.

The scent of helplessness was thick in the air. Ares broke the silence, his words barely above a whisper. "No." His voice cracked around the word. "It can't end like this. Not when we were so close."

A deep rumble emanated from Rafe's chest, and when I turned to look at him, a darkness took over his face, pulling his features taut.

"We aren't fucking accepting it. If we can't play by their rules. We'll just have to steal her back."

I swallowed. We'd thought of that before, but it meant being hunted by the Institute. They had a special ops team specifically created for missing omegas. We hadn't entertained it then, but now...

I met each of their stares, knowing damn well this could get us all killed.

"Whatever it takes. We can pray she forgives us after."

CHAPTER 5
Bliss

The Omega Institute didn't fly commercial, but our private plane was still housed at the nearest major airport. I suspected it was intentional. The Institute liked to show the omegas out and about every once in a while, and there were only so many opportunities to do so. Traveling as a group, all in uniform, appropriately drugged and docile, was about as good press as they were going to get.

Well, most of us were drugged and docile. As usual, I was more alert than I should be.

I walked beside Flora, my arm looped tightly through hers. The chemical smell of the airport mixed with the scents of thousands of strangers burned at my nose and made my head swim.

"I'm excited to see New York City," she commented pleasantly.

"You've seen the city a hundred times." I grimaced. "You're from New Jersey."

"Oh." She laughed. "That's right. Where are you from?"

I rolled my eyes. "*Jersey.*"

There was no point in this conversation; I was going to make myself crazy.

Flora had taken twice the recommended dose of blockers today, for fear of discovery or accidental bonding while we were in public. The incident in the dining hall had stunned her into temporary submission. She, like all of us, would be coming off the blockers in a matter of hours anyway, but I missed talking to her in the meantime. I'd forgotten how lonely I was before she stopped taking them.

"Ladies and gentlemen, if I could have your attention," a redheaded flight attendant working one of the major airline check-in desks spoke into a microphone, her voice projecting over the loudspeaker. "We have the honor of having Omega Donnelley flying with us today. Is there anyone who would be willing to give up their seat—"

The flight attendant didn't get a chance to finish her sentence before several people rushed forward, clambering to give up their seats. As though the omega was a valiant war hero returning from battle.

I craned my neck as we passed, trying to get a look at the omega. I wasn't the only one looking, but it was impossible to see her beyond her wall of security.

There was a fair amount of people staring at us too. I caught the eye of a beta child, holding her mother's hand, and smiled. Her mouth dropped open, and she tugged on her mom's hand, pointing at me.

"Eyes down, Bliss," one of our handlers scolded from the back of the group. I nodded, returning my gaze to my black patent-leather shoes, marching in line behind the identical black shoes in front of me.

The headmistress called for us to follow her toward the boarding queue, and I steered Flora in the right direction. She made no objection, shuffling her feet along the scratchy industrial carpet of the waiting area.

The flight was five hours from gate to gate, and I spent most of it pretending to sleep. In reality, I was listening to the frantic beating of my own heart in my ears.

My body seemed to know I was on my way back to the East Coast—far closer to the site of my worst memories than I'd ever wanted to be again.

I had no way of knowing if my guys—*the guys*—lived anywhere near there anymore, but I had a feeling they did. The closer the plane got to New York, the easier I could breathe. It was like I'd spent the last four years wearing an iron corset, and it was loosening by the hour.

I refused to be grateful for that. The lack of pain was only a reminder that my pack had cursed me, and the pain was bound to be worse when it returned.

When we landed, night had fallen. It was impossible to see much beyond the window of the plane except the lights from the airport and the headlights of the vehicles on the tarmac.

"Are we going to a hotel first or something?" I asked one of the handlers as we taxied to our gate.

She narrowed her eyes, suspicious of my question. I smiled, trying to look innocent. What did it matter if I slipped up a little now anyway? They were almost done with me.

"No, we are going right to the venue."

I raised my eyebrows. I hadn't been expecting that. "Oh."

Wherever they were taking us, it wasn't far from the airport. Our limousine had no windows, and I busied myself counting to sixty over and over to try and guess the time. It was a stupid and pointless game, but it was better than nothing.

"It was thirty-seven minutes," I told Flora when our car came to a halt. "Maybe thirty-eight."

She pressed her knee against mine and smiled. "You're so good at math."

It would be a bad time to scream.

I shivered violently as I stepped out of the car and onto the pavement. The wind was biting and cut into the exposed skin of my face and forearms like a thousand tiny needles. I'd gotten so used to the California climate, the weather was shocking.

They'd parked us in a deserted alleyway with tall, nondescript buildings on either side. I turned to the headmistress, confused. I assumed the event would be held somewhere grand.

The headmistress pointed to an unmarked, black service door. "Let's go, ladies."

My confusion spiked. Where the hell were we?

The door opened to a basement maintenance hallway, lit by flickering fluorescent lights. My heart rate kicked up a notch. Neither the headmistress nor the instructors seemed concerned.

They led our whole group down the hall and into an elevator. I craned my neck to read the buttons. All I could see from where I stood pressed into the back corner were the buttons marked L, B, and P1-4, probably for parking.

Help.

"Um," I started. We weren't supposed to ask questions, but this was crazy. If Flora were lucid, she would be apoplectic. At least ten swears, probably half of which I'd never heard, would have been out of her mouth by now. I had to ask for both our sakes. "Where are we?"

If the instructors heard me, they ignored me. I'd seen a scary movie or ten as a kid. This was how we died.

The elevator dinged, and we filed out into another long hallway—this one at least was better lit. The architecture up here was more impressive—huge windows, crown molding, and stone walls. Like a college, or a museum. I itched to go over to one of the windows and try to figure out where we were, but the headmistress was already on the move again, rushing down the hall.

"In here, ladies." She swung open a door and ushered us inside.

I paused, trying to decide if I could reasonably refuse to enter. Maybe I could say I needed to go to the bathroom?

"Bliss." Flora tugged my hand. "In here."

Well, there goes that plan.

It was a conference room. Or it had been. It now looked more like a pop-up beauty parlor. At least a dozen people were crammed into the room, all moving around the various mirrors, salon chairs, and racks of clothing.

A beta woman in a black apron strode toward us, a brush in one hand and a water bottle in the other. "Hi!" she said brightly. "We're ready for you."

I stood stock-still, overwhelmed by the smell of the

chemical hair products and the bright-colored clothing, salt, and bitter cranberries. I couldn't believe I hadn't smelled it in the hall.

"Are you Bliss?" A different beta approached me.

I took a breath, tasting her resignation. "Yes."

"I'm Clarissa. Your stylist."

I tried to smile but caught my reflection in one of the many mirrors. I looked like I'd just been to the dentist and was frozen with my mouth open. "Great."

"Do you want to come over to the chair?"

Not at all. "Absolutely."

I must have blacked out while Clarissa worked, because before I knew it, she was finished. "Okay, what do you think?" she said as she spun my chair around.

I gasped. The woman looking back at me in the brightly lit mirror wasn't me. For four years, I'd worn the same clothes every day. We weren't allowed to wear makeup, and our hair had to be kept its natural color. I barely looked in the mirror, so while I knew I'd aged, my perception of it was skewed.

Anxiety bubbled in my throat, forming a lump, almost like tears. She'd lightened my hair by several shades. I was already blonde, but now it was practically white. That was the least jarring change. Whatever they'd done to my face was extreme, and not in a good way.

The stylist frowned, looking nervous. "You don't like it?"

"Er, no," I said too-fast. "It's fine."

It wasn't. I'd worn makeup before the Institute, but this was less makeup and more of a mask. I lifted one eyebrow, and my false lash hit the top of my brow bone. That was going to make me crazy.

"Oh, well, it's for the lights," she explained. "There will be bright lights on your face, and it reflects off the glass, so your features need to stand out. It will look normal from outside the box, I promise."

"Right," I agreed, not really listening as I tried to get used to my face.

I swallowed and nodded, hoping she was right. Not that it really mattered. We would all get auctioned off regardless of what we looked like, and any buyer would be just as bad as the next.

"Wait." I looked up at the stylist in the mirror, meeting her eyes fully as I processed what she had said. "What do you mean 'from outside the box'? What 'glass'?"

The stylist's eyes widened. "For the event?" Her inflection implied it was a question—like she was asking if I was sure I didn't know. "Wait here. I'm going to go get your dress."

She darted away before I could protest, disappearing into the crowd of stylists and airborne hair products.

I tipped my head back, and my curls crunched against the black plastic cape they'd thrown around my shoulders. To protect my uniform, I supposed—from what, I wasn't sure. I doubted I'd ever wear it again.

"It's going to be windows," a voice to my left said.

I turned only my neck to see who had spoken, still lying back in my chair. Something about the awkward angle was cathartic after sitting perfectly straight for four years.

My neighbor's name was Omega Blair, and we'd never really spoken outside of class. She was a retrieval who had arrived before me and therefore had never been fully lucid during my time at the Institute.

"Windows," Omega Blair hissed, the curlers in her hair bobbing as she leaned forward. "I think they're putting us behind glass."

I sat up straight again to look her in the eye. "Why? How do you know?"

"One of the handlers just mentioned it." She shook her head and reached for a half-full glass of water on the vanity in front of her, sucking down the rest of it in one gulp.

"And you remember that?" I blurted out, shocked.

"Yeah." She seemed as surprised as I was.

I turned away from Blair for a minute, searching the room for Flora. All around us, girls were blinking wide eyes and turning to talk to each other. My eyes darted to my own vanity and untouched water glass. I reached for it and sniffed. Nothing.

"Bliss!" Flora's urgent voice shrieked from somewhere across the room.

I swiveled, scanning the crowd for her shiny, dark hair. She was no where, lost in the sudden uptick in voices and activity.

"Okay, I have your dress!" The stylist appeared behind me, blocking my view with a garment bag in hand. Her eyes immediately darted to the glass in my hand. "Oh, make sure you drink that before you go put this on, hon. You want to stay hydrated."

CHAPTER 6

Killian

Ares, Nox, Rafe, and I sat in silence as our hired car inched toward the front of the gala. The museum where they held the Agora Ceremony each year had eight tall columns holding up the stone arches that worked as gateways inside. It looked like something that belonged in Ancient Greece instead of being twenty minutes outside of the city.

An opaque film covered all the windows, protecting our country's most exclusive event. It was damn close to a secret society for how under wraps they kept everything. Even with our connections, we didn't know the details of what went down on the other side of those doors. The blatant display of money grated on my nerves. We'd spent years working toward being invited into this circle, but that didn't mean we liked any of the stuck-up rich dicks.

The weight of the next few hours sat heavy in the air like a stifling blanket. Our plan to participate legally was blown to shit, and the new one was reckless at best.

"Get ready." Rafe straightened his suit jacket and adjusted his watch.

Between our size and clothing, we almost fit in, but there would always be something "other" about us. We were wolves dressed in designer clothing, and we'd come to steal our girl back.

The car came to a halt, and I followed Rafe out. The sound of paparazzi shouting hit my ears, drowning out everything else. They were desperately trying to catch the celebrities' attention to get the best shots of them.

The mix of fame, fortune, and secrecy made it the most talked about event of the year. Everyone wanted to see behind the curtain and find out what went down at these events. How exactly the beautiful omegas got mated off to the rich and famous men.

Nox and Ares came up beside me. They scanned the surrounding space with predatory gazes. Someone here was going home with our girl, and we had to let him. The thought sent anger riding up my chest, and a low growl pierced the air.

"Calm down." Nox's hand landed on my shoulder, giving it a tight squeeze. "Follow the plan, and we'll get her back. Once she's committed to an alpha, we won't have long before he mates her and we lose her for good."

Ares glared at Nox and took a step toward us. "Was that supposed to be reassuring?"

"We don't have time for this. Shut up and pay attention," Rafe bit out. His alpha bark tinged his voice. Not that it mattered—we were too evenly matched in strength for him to command now. In high school he could get away with it, but we'd all grown into our power over the last several years.

"Fuck. Okay." I straightened to my full height, and we walked up the stairs four abreast—Rafe and Ares to my left and Nox to my right.

People visibly shifted away from us. Our power was undeniable, and we weren't trying to dampen it. In this world, money made things happen, but that didn't stop the fact that biologically we were higher on the food chain. By the time we made it to the entrance, all eyes had turned toward us, and whispers followed in our wake. Who were we? Where did we come from?

A smirk tipped my lips. We didn't belong in their small circle, and I was sure it was killing them to not know who we were.

We got to the top of the stairs, and my eyes widened as the large iron doors opened. They had medieval designs carved into them and had to be fourteen feet tall. Nox took a deep breath beside me, the slight scent of dead flowers drifting off him. I let my fingers brush his, resisting the urge to entwine our fingers.

Nox stiffened and jerked his hand away.

I ignored the sting of rejection. There was no point if Bliss wasn't with us. The idea of being happy without her made me sick to my stomach.

Ares grabbed my left wrist in a nearly painful grip but didn't let go as we stepped through the doors into the dimly lit hall. The room opened up into a wide-open space, a clear path delineated with ribbon and art displays on either side. They were lit with deep blue lights, blanketing the room in a mythical feel.

I shifted closer to Ares, sucking in deep breaths of his calming scent as we followed the path, proceeding to where the event was happening. We'd be seeing Bliss for the first time in four years, and my heart was trying to jump out of its cage with anticipation.

The closer we got to her, the clearer her emotions were, and the edge of desperation had me holding my breath. There was something distinctly wrong about the feelings she was projecting.

We stalled in front of our assigned table. It had a perfect view of the stage. What we didn't expect were the levels of glass display cases filled with omegas, lit like the statues in blue light so we could just make out their silhouettes. *Jesus.* There was something almost inhumane about how everything was set up. Like they were displaying products instead of our most precious designations. The weight of the need to protect them hit me like a punch, and I sucked in a breath of the distinct taste of fear.

What the fuck. Three growls matched mine as rage tumbled out of me.

A hand landed on my shoulder, shoving me to the side. "Move out of the way." The hair on my arms stood as the alpha bark rolled over me. I turned to be met with a man in his forties with slick blond hair. Ares' grip tightened painfully on my arm, but I was too distracted by the alpha in front of me to care.

He raised a brow when we didn't budge, clearly unused to not being the most powerful man in the room. Rafe, Ares, and Nox closed ranks around me. Their very presence should've been enough to have the guy scurrying. He looked between us, sucking on his teeth before saying, "Excuse me. I'm seated there." His words were lined with anger, as if he was barely holding it in. The table he pointed toward was only two away from ours. A rumble formed in my chest. "Go around."

A muscle twitched in the man's jaw, his entire body stiff. Probably never been told what to do a day in his life. He turned away and walked the long way to his table, speaking in a low voice to the man beside him.

Ares let go of my arm, and his hands shook at his sides. I leaned in close. "We can pick them off one by one later."

Ares' gaze shot to mine, not letting up for several moments as he took in deep breaths until he finally nodded and took his seat. The rest of us followed his lead.

Our table was matte black with a tray of lit votive candles in the middle. There were no names, just corresponding numbers to our tickets. Within seconds of being seated, a server brought us glasses of champagne. I sniffed mine, the bubbles making me want to sneeze while Nox took his back in one swallow. *That's one way to start the night.*

"Good evening, Alphas, and welcome to the fifty-sixth annual Agora." A woman with graying hair pulled back into a tight bun stepped out on stage. She wore a feminine-cut dress, covering her soft curves. *Omega.* "My name is Headmistress Omega DuPont, and I will be leading tonight's events. We are so happy to have you all here to help match with your very own omega." She gestured her hands outward. "As with every year, you have all signed NDA agreements. Everything from this moment on will be held at the utmost of secrecy. Please look at the center of your table. You will find a digital pad with your information as well as the profile of each omega available tonight."

The way she said that made me uneasy. As if we were online shopping for them.

"From that device, you will input your donation amount upon the start of each girl's presentation. Once the highest donation is reached, the omega will be brought to the back for you to bring home with you." She smiled wide, clapping her hands in front of herself. "It brings the Institution the greatest joy to find the perfect match between our omegas and their alphas. We will begin momentarily, so make sure you are ready. You'll find the process moves quickly."

Rafe's growl pulled my attention to where he was staring down at the screen, the glow illuminating the snarl on his face.

The alphas at the surrounding tables flipped through their screens, eyes widening with each flick. The smell of wool and honey was thick in the air. My skin burned at the idea that they were looking at images of Bliss with lust.

Before I could do anything stupid, like smash everyone's electronic devices, an orchestra started playing from the corner of the stage, and the lights dimmed further, tipping us into near blackness. The glass cages provided the only light. The music picked up, drawing out the moment before one of the glass cases lit up with clear white light.

Holy shit. I thought this event was so the omegas could mingle with the alphas. At a minimum have some kind of veto power over who could bid on them. That was fucked-up enough, but this was so much worse.

A young omega stood inside, now fully visible. She looked familiar. I squinted and tried to make out her features. She had long dark hair and a full body, and her eyes searched the crowd. There was no way she could see us with the way the lighting was set up, but she tried.

"Holy shit. It's Flora." Rafe's hands were shaking as they held the device.

Fuck. Flora had been the only potential omega I'd ever met. She'd gone to our high school and had been relocated to the Omega Institute before she turned seventeen. I couldn't say we were friends, but my stomach still dropped seeing her up there.

Rafe flinched, then paled when tablet beeped. He dropped it on the table as if it burned him before searching the other glass cases. Noise from the alphas around us rose rapidly. Sounds of excitement, disappointment, and anger almost overpowered the music.

I watched the screen as the dollar amount climbed over two million dollars. It flashed three times before the light in Flora's case went dark, and I could see a sliver of light as a small door cracked open at the back as they escorted her out. That was it. They'd sold her.

Four tables away, an alpha who looked to be at least sixty stood from his table, a wide, tooth-filled grin on his face. He looked punchable. The only thing that stopped me from starting a riot was knowing that Bliss was in one of those cases.

The next three omegas went fast, the rumble of the crowd growing louder as the odds shifted out of their favor. My fine-cuisine supper sat untouched in front of me. Even the idea of taking a bite made me want to puke. The last hour had been a horror fest of young omegas being sold off to sneering men, none of whom looked a day under fifty.

The electronic pad beeped and flashed with the image of the next girl. My stomach dropped through the floor at the sight of her. Her hair was lighter, and she'd grown more curvaceous and lost the softness of adolescence, but there was no denying she was our Bliss.

Ares' growl rumbled the table. "I can't fucking do this—"

Nox glared, cutting him off. "You better learn how because this is how we're getting her back. I didn't hear any better ideas."

Power surged between them, and my gut twisted. Nox never confronted Ares. They had their own fucked-up codependent relationship that neither would own up to. Tonight, Nox's eyes were narrowed in challenge, daring Ares to say anything.

Ares broke away first. I couldn't blame him. My instincts wanted to riot at the idea we were letting Bliss go through this. We should be the ones bidding, not some fucking rich asshole. My neck ached and my muscles tensed in anticipation of seeing her. I almost wish we wouldn't. Not like this, not in some fucked-up glass cage.

Bliss' white light flipped on, and I sucked in a breath. No matter how many times I dreamed of her, nothing could prepare me for this moment. The picture on the screen didn't do her justice. She was all curves, big doe eyes, and long blonde hair. The quintessential omega.

My heart bounded against my chest as blood flooded my ears. She was everything I remembered but so much more. *Please, babe, look at me.*

A craving rose in me, so strong I couldn't swallow it down. She was ours, and the alpha side of me was taking over all rational thinking. I tugged on the bond between us, and her face snapped toward our table. I knew she couldn't see us with the light so bright in her room, but she fucking knew we were there. I tugged again, and the guys around me all jerked as a tangle of her emotions slammed into my chest.

I couldn't tell if she was happy or not, but she damn well knew we were here. I was so fixated on her, I didn't notice the bidding had begun and ended until the crowd erupted in a roar. It looked like every remaining alpha had his eyes on her.

Of course, it was the asshole from earlier who stood up two tables in front of us wearing a familiar smile. There was nothing soft in his eyes. He'd gone hunting and caught the kill he'd wanted.

A growl climbed up my throat, and I stood, shaking with the effort to hold myself back.

The asshole smiled at me. "Sorry, did you want that one?"

"She's ours." Ares jumped from his seat, and Nox barely caught him around the waist before he managed to reach this rich dick.

The man looked at him, taking in his suit and watch. "We aren't on the same level. There was no world you were walking out of here with her on your arm. You have power, but I have both money and power."

Rafe walked up to us and shook the man's hand and placed his hand on his shoulder in a reassuring pat. "Ignore him. He can't handle his hormones."

Ares practically roared, and Nox looked like he would turn purple from the force it took to hold him back. Ares was damn near feral at this point. What the hell was Rafe doing?

The asshole gave him a curt nod and followed a guide around backstage.

We all spun on Rafe the second he was out of hearing distance. "What the fuck."

A smile slowly grew on his face as he ignored us, looking down at his phone.

Nox, as always, was the first to catch on. "Did you get the trace?"

Rafe held up his phone. There was a map with a small red circle that was moving slowly away from us.

I smiled. *Let's go hunting.*

CHAPTER 7
Bliss

"Do you remember me?"

I swallowed the lump rising in my throat as I practically jogged to keep up with the alpha walking two paces ahead of me, wobbling on my too-tall heels. His legs were nearly twice as long as mine, and the evening gown the stylist had squeezed me into made every movement difficult. My thighs rubbed together with every step, and the train kept getting caught underfoot, forcing me to pause and detangle myself.

The alpha stopped short, whirling to face me. "I said, do you remember me?" he barked, pushing power into his voice.

My head snapped up, and I dropped the train of my dress. "Yes."

He was, if possible, even taller than I remembered him from that day at the Institute. His blond hair was slicked back in the same perfect coif, and he wore a tailored tuxedo, but other than that, he looked a bit like the bust of a Roman emperor come to life. His piercing, black eyes assessed me. They held no warmth, only triumph. That, I supposed, made sense. He'd just secured his place as one of the most powerful men on earth. Having an omega was the ultimate status symbol, and after tonight, no one could take that away from him.

Well, almost no one, but he didn't know that.

He started walking again. "Answer me when I speak to you, and we'll get along fine."

"Yes, Alpha."

I hoped he was right and we would get along fine. The Omega Institute promised all omegas that once mated, we would love our alphas no matter who they were. It was biology. The same chemical response that put us into a mindless heat would make us love them, honor them, and obey them for the rest of our lives.

A small voice at the back of my head screamed that there might be something off about that idea. Maybe it was propaganda, just like everything else I'd come across so far.

Or maybe it was true, just not for me.

We reached a door to a staircase, and he pushed it open, taking the stairs two at a time. Finally, we stepped out onto an open-air roof. I gasped. The city lights were mesmerizing, almost like stars. The noise of traffic and the wind engulfed me, and I spun, wanting to see everything at once.

The alpha stepped into me until he was mere inches away, blocking my view. He breathed in deeply. "I can't smell you yet, but no matter. Your blockers must not have worn off. That's fine—they will by the time we get to my home. We'll be taking my helicopter. I want to make this as fast as possible."

I nodded, noting the use of "my home," as opposed to "home." It didn't matter. Once I went into heat, hopefully that would be enough of a bond that he wouldn't notice.

"What's your name?" I asked, trying to make conversation.

He looked down his nose at me and waited a full beat before answering. "Nero," he said finally. "But you may call me Alpha or sir."

I stared at him. Oh, he was expecting a response. "Yes, sir."

He smiled, but it didn't reach his eyes.

Alpha Nero had several homes—or so he told me over the deafening noise of the helicopter. We were going to his summer residence, where we were least likely to be disturbed.

"Thank you," I said. That seemed like the right response.

My mind drifted to Flora. It was too much to hope Flora and I would end up in the same city, but maybe we would both be in the country and could see each other at social events. This couldn't be all bad. It had been hard to hear or see anything going on in the other booths from where I sat on the stage, but I hoped she had ended up with someone who would be kind to her.

The smell in that room was one I'd never forget. The testosterone and excitement, mingled with the panic of the omegas—now clearheaded for the first time since we'd entered the Institute. And somewhere, under every other smell in the room, lemon, coffee, peppers, and rain. My boys were in that room, and for a second time, they'd let me be taken away.

I forced the thought down. Soon, my former pack would see my mating announcements in the press, and I wouldn't care. This was the last time I would ever dwell on it. The last time I could ever dwell on it.

In a shorter time than I would have expected, the helicopter landed in the center of a huge lawn. The only lights came from a house as large as the Institute. It was surrounded by a wraparound porch to the right and an expansive garden to the left that, from what I could see, probably hid a pool. The house had several balconies and a tower on either side that really said "castle" more than "house." I glanced around for any other houses in the area, wondering if this was common.

"Do you have neighbors?" I asked.

Alpha Nero ignored me. Instead, he opened his door and leapt out onto the lawn, tugging me along after him.

The front door opened onto a vast entrance hall with a double staircase that led to the upper floors. I had no time to take in much of the house before Alpha Nero was ushering me up one of those staircases.

"Take them off," he said as I stumbled over my dress and shoes.

I looked up at him quizzically, unsure if he meant the shoes or everything. The scent of his frustration was evident—like bitter dandelions—and I ducked my head, kicking off my shoes.

He practically shoved me along an upstairs hall. There

was no art on the walls, no personal touches or distinguishing features to be seen.

Like what little I'd seen of the house so far, the bedroom was large but without personal touches. The room had high ceilings and large windows without curtains. There was a king-size bed with a white comforter and an empty bedside table on either side. I wrapped my arms around myself the moment we entered, feeling a chill.

"Is there a nesting room?" I asked tentatively.

"Next week, you can decorate your own room however you like."

My mouth became a thin line. *Oh.*

"Sit." He pointed to the bed.

I sat on my hands, watching him. He crossed the room, opened the drawer of his bedside table, and pulled something out, his back to me. "I was assured you would be cleared of blockers by now. Who the fuck do they think they are?"

I reached up, twirling a tendril of hair around my finger. I was sure he could smell my worry and hoped he would take that for concern that we hadn't yet bonded and not guilt over the knowledge that we never would.

He spun around, and my gaze zeroed in on what he was holding. My pulse sped up. "What is that?"

It was a rhetorical question—it was a syringe. A more appropriate question would have been "What's in that?" or "What are you doing with that?"

"Shhh," he said in what might have been a soothing voice. "Speeding things up a bit. If your blockers had worn off, this might not be necessary, but it doesn't matter. Some alphas do this regardless."

My eyes widened, my heart hammering against my chest. Of course.

I suddenly saw a gaping hole in my survival strategy—I wouldn't go into heat naturally without the bond. We wouldn't mate without my heat. If we never mated…well, that wasn't really an option, so it wasn't worth thinking about.

Conveniently, Alpha Nero was right. Many alphas did artificially induce heat—it made it last longer and hit harder, apparently—but if he did that, I had no idea how lucid I would be. A normal heat took away all cognitive reasoning. This was—

"Come here," he barked.

I stood, unable to resist the pull of an alpha bark, and stood in front of him, tilting my neck to the side. The top of my head barely reached the middle of his chest. "Shhh."

Nero held the needle to my neck. Every muscle in my body screamed, fully aware that I was actively going against my existing bond. My heart constricted painfully, like it was trying to stop itself rather than let this happen.

"Relax."

The needle pricked my skin, and the effect was immediate. My eyes rolled into my head as boiling water filled my veins.

I stumbled backward, the backs of my knees hitting the bed again as I struggled to stay upright. Every smell was suddenly too much. Too heightened. Not only emotions, but everything—the fibers in the bedspread, the plants outside, the sweat of the beta helicopter driver smoking a cigarette in the driveway.

"I'm told it takes a few minutes to kick in," Nero said

casually. He tossed the syringe on the nightstand and shrugged off his jacket.

I looked this way and that, feeling like I had just gotten off the Tilt-A-Whirl at the county fair and landed in a pool of lava. I took a few deep breaths, then regretted it as Nero's scent filled my nose.

I covered my face with my hands. I needed to lie down, but the bed hurt and smelled like whiskey and cigars. I took another deep breath, willing myself not to cry.

A new smell filled my mouth, wrapping around me. It was indescribable and better than anything—like lemon tart and freshly brewed coffee on a rainy morning. It was the scent of a hot bath and an old book and stargazing in the summer. I turned, looking for the source. It was essential—like breathing. I needed it. Now.

My heart swelled as I faced the door, and then confusion hit me.

Oh my God, I'm hallucinating.

I had to be hallucinating, because what I was seeing wasn't possible. My former pack could not be standing in the doorway.

I let out a hysterical laugh, unable to hold it in, and all eyes turned to me. My body burned under their gaze, and a wave of mind-numbing heat and arousal hit me, as painful as it was exciting.

Come to me. I need you.

They aren't really here, I tried to remind myself, fighting to keep the haze out of my brain. This was just my mind unable to reconcile the pack bond with my new mate. That was it.

Fire burned through me, and my head was too heavy, like it had been weighed down with sand. That smell got stronger. I wanted it everywhere—to bathe in it. I wanted to know what that smell tasted like.

The last time I'd seen my boys, we'd been barely seventeen, but my brain had conjured how they'd look now. My brain was very generous.

Rafe stood in front, black hair longer than it had been, but his black eyes were the same. Like all of them, he'd gained about a foot of height and fifty pounds of muscle, but I knew it was a hallucination because Rafe would never lead the group. That was Ares' job.

My eyes found Ares, and I laughed again. Still bleach blond, tattooed, and wearing that stupid leather jacket—although it fit him now—but he would never stand in the back behind Nox like that.

Nox was the most obvious change. He'd shaved his bright red hair close to the scalp and no longer resembled the slightly nerdy kid he'd been.

And Killian, whose curls and smile used to make him look boyish, now looked menacing as he glared at something over my shoulder.

I tried to look at what he was seeing, and my eyes rolled into the back of my head. The bed bounced under me, a disembodied crash sounding from somewhere to the right.

"What the fuck?" someone growled. "What are you doing here?"

"What the fuck are *you* doing? What's wrong with her?"

The fire burning through my body was too hot, physically eating me from the inside out. I couldn't focus—couldn't make out the cacophony of voices suddenly filling the room.

That smell got stronger. Closer. I wanted to reach out and grab it. Run my tongue all over whatever it was and mark it as mine.

"Bliss."

I blinked down, and tattooed arms were reaching for me. Where was I?

I laughed, maybe. I might have moaned. Needles pricked every part of my body like one million poisonous stings. I reached out blindly. "Help me."

CHAPTER 8
Ares

"Alpha," her voice came out on a whine.

Rage pumped through my veins as I ran over the threshold and out of the mansion. Bliss was deadweight in my arms, her eyes rolling back into her head. Something was wrong. Her heat shouldn't have hit her this fast.

My blood roared. We'd almost been too late. We were dangerously close to losing her forever.

I stumbled over the bottom porch step and clutched Bliss tighter to my chest. She keened in pain and lifted her head slightly, burying her face in my shoulder. "It's so hot, Alpha. I'm so hot."

A growl pushed itself out of my chest as instinct tried to take over. *Protect, fuck, claim.* I couldn't fucking think straight. My body screamed at me to go back inside and kill that fucker for touching our omega, but that was in direct conflict with the overwhelming need to stop right here and claim her against a wall.

Not safe here.

Her pupils nearly drowned out the violet in her eyes as she looked at me pleadingly. Jasmine, chili, and the seductive smell of honey overtook my senses, and a wave of lust slammed into me. She wiggled in my arms, and her grasp twisted my shirt. I shook my head and kept running, trying to force myself to stay alert. This wasn't just any omega—it was Bliss. *This is Bliss.*

I reached the van, and Nox threw the back door open violently. His eyes were near black, and his breath came in heavy pants as he ran a hand over his shaved head. I smirked at the blood on his knuckles. Good. I hoped he killed the bastard.

He held his arms out, his jaw tight. "Give her to me."

Mine. Mine. Mine, my head chanted at me, and I couldn't differentiate how much was instinct and how much was me. "I got it. Fucking move."

Bliss moaned, and the smell of vinegar filled my nose. He stepped out of the way. "Fine."

Nothing else mattered but our omega.

I clambered into the van and laid Bliss across the back seats. She whined, reaching for me the moment I let her go. She pulled at her dress, but she couldn't reach the zipper. "Help me, Alpha."

A pulse of lust pounded against my brain, and I grunted with the effort to rip off her dress and claim her. My hands shook as I held her face in my palms and traced her cheekbones with my thumbs. "You're okay. You're okay. We'll figure it out together."

Her head snapped back, and she truly looked at me for the first time. Her eyes were clear, shocked—like she was seeing a ghost. Tears pooled in her lashes. "Ares?"

Fuck. The realization she'd been calling me alpha this entire time ripped at my chest, pulling me out of the drugging haze her heat held me under. She hadn't known—*didn't know*—who I was. She just needed to be touched by her alpha. I dropped my forehead to hers, taking deep breaths. I was a fucking asshole for touching her. "I'm sorry. Bliss. I'm so sorry."

Another wave of her scent hit me, and all recognition vanished from her face. She pushed up on her knees and dug her fingers into my chest, chasing my mouth with hers. "Alpha..."

Shit. No.

She whimpered in pain when I shifted back toward the van doors before she could touch me. This was wrong. So fucking wrong. I didn't deserve her.

She cried out, and her fingers wrapped around my neck, trying to pull me forward, her back arching in an attempt to erase the space I'd put between us.

Mine.

Fuck. No.

This whole fucking thing was my fault. I'd set everything off years ago. It was me that had dared Rafe to kiss Bliss and set off her initial transition. It was me that pushed her over the edge and created the bond before she got sent away, and it was me that was supposed to be in charge but didn't stop her from being sent to the Institute.

Maybe we shouldn't have come back for her. This wasn't how this was supposed to go—any of it. For all we fucking knew, she was happy with that asshole in the mansion, and now we'd never know because she wasn't lucid to tell us. I wanted her to be happy. I locked down any visible emotion and untangled her hands, leaning out of her reach.

"What the fuck are you doing?" Rafe's alpha bark rumbled from the front seat of the van.

My head snapped up. I hadn't registered Rafe or Killian arriving. Killian scrambled into the seat behind us while Nox came down next to me.

Rafe turned the key in the ignition. "She's in pain. Touch her, or get the hell out of the way."

"You want to trade places?" I barked back as Bliss reached for me again.

Rafe's expression in the rearview mirror was conflicted. He did, that was obvious, but he knew what I was getting at. Bliss was lost to her omega instincts and would hate us when this was over.

"Alpha, please." Bliss' voice breaking around her words was my undoing.

I'd never been able to say no to her. Ever. Not when I was sixteen and thought she was a beta, and sure as fuck not now when I was barely in control of my own body. I'd loved Bliss since before I could remember, long before any hormonal bonding or fucking biological mind control.

I hated that she'd turned out to be an omega. I hated what we did to her. I hated the fucking Institute. I hated myself, but I'd always love her.

I leaned over her small frame and covered her mouth with mine. She opened for me, and her sweet taste of chilies and honey coated my tongue. Lust filled my veins, taking over every coherent thought. I growled and pushed my body against hers. "Yes, Omega."

My cock hardened painfully with the need to bury deep inside her. I rocked against her, but her dress kept me from giving her the pressure she desperately craved. She whimpered, writhing against me, practically begging me to ease her pain.

She keened, and her kiss turned desperate. Lust pulsed in the air, and three alpha roars returned her call. Omegas were perfectly designed to please their alphas, and we were perfectly designed to give her everything she needed in return.

I growled, tearing at the skirt of her dress. "Get it off."

Nox pulled out a knife and cut the beautiful fabric from the hem up to her bust. He took meticulous care not to nick our omega. I peeled it to the side, exposing her black lace matching bra and panties. Her slick had soaked through her dress and covered her thighs. A deep roar rumbled up my chest. "Mine."

The sentiment echoed from my pack.

Killian reached over the seat and slid his hands down her neck and chest. She moaned when his fingers dipped into the see-through cups of her bra. I watched, mesmerized, as she responded to his touch. He rolled her nipples between his fingers, and her hips ground against my painfully hard cock.

Nox crowded my back and caught her mouth in his, eating her delicious cries. Another wave of lust plowed into me. The overwhelming scent of jasmine, peppers, wool, and honey overtook every sense.

The van swerved as Rafe growled. "Fuck." His gaze snapped away from the rearview mirror and focused to the front. *Hold it together, Rafe.*

I drove my jeans-clad cock against her slick core, and she made a pleased sound. The world swirled around me as every instinct I had screamed at me to take her. To knot her and make her mine. She was already mine. Or ours. All I had to do was sink my teeth into her smooth neck and she'd be mine forever.

She'll hate you. She already hates you.

I was losing what little grip I still had on rational thought. She was everything to us, and when her heat finally lifted, she'd hate me even more for forcing her while she was in this state.

I met Nox's gaze. There was no way we were knotting Bliss in the van no matter how desperately she called for it, but there were other ways to lessen the heat for our omega.

I slid off the seat and dropped to my knees on the floor. Bliss cried out, fingers clawing to bring me back. I worked the thin black lace down her thighs and calves, exposing her perfect pink core.

I slid my fingers up her legs, marveling at how her soft skin felt against my calloused hands. Her muscles twitched under my touch, and she moaned into Nox's neck. Her tongue stroked over his mating glands, marking herself all over him. His chest rumbled, and his head tipped back, eyes closed, giving her better access.

Killian rose from the back seat and crashed his mouth against Nox's. My eyes widened in interest. It had been years since they'd touched each other with any kind of affection, but Bliss' heat broke down the walls we'd built between us. She hummed and licked up Killian's neck, marking him too.

Fuck. They look good.

I licked up Bliss' inner thigh and groaned when her hips jerked up. My eyes rolled back as I ran my tongue through her core. Her sweet slick ran over my face and down my throat. Omegas were practically drenched for the duration of their heat, and it was the hottest thing I'd ever seen.

I sucked, licked, and stroked my tongue over her, grunting as my dick ached against my pants. Her whimper drew my attention. As she watched Nox put his cock in Kill's mouth, her eyes were wide with interest. Her hips ground against my mouth. She liked that. *So do I.*

I slid three fingers into her, and I grunted as her core sucked them deeper. My brain splintered at the thought of burying myself in her. I worked her with my fingers and ran my teeth over her clit. The honey scent of her lust slammed into us, driving us into a rut. I slid my cock out of my pants, cum already leaking from the tip, and covered it in her slick before pumping it mercilessly. Nox grunted, holding Killian's head still as he emptied himself. *Fuck, I'm close.*

Bliss made a needy, keening sound that drove everything higher. Killian tilted her head up and dripped Nox's cum into her mouth. She cried out as she sucked his tongue and clamped down around my fingers. Her orgasm rippled through the air, and Killian and I both groaned with our releases.

I laid my head on her thigh, still breathing in her sweet slick, and ran my cum-soaked fingers over her sensitive core. My chest thrummed as our scents mixed, and I had to clamp down on my jaw to stop myself from biting her. *Fuck.*

The heat broke enough to think again, and I glanced around, disoriented. Rafe's tan knuckles were white on the steering wheel. I yanked my shirt off and pulled it over Bliss' head, taking care to pull her hair from the collar.

She reached her arms around my neck, and I lifted her, switching our positions until I sat on the bench and she folded herself up over my chest. Her eyes were glassy and unfocused. She probably still had no idea what was going on—heats lasted days, and omegas were often out of it for the majority of the time.

Killian reached around the seat to take her from me, and I growled deep in my throat. "Fuck off."

"Bro—"

"I'm not going to stay for the rest. You can have her then."

Killian furrowed his brow but didn't argue. It physically hurt to say, but I wouldn't let myself take part in the rest of her heat, not knowing what she must think of me. I tightened my arms around her as she drifted off against my chest.

My Bliss curled into me, wearing my clothes as I stroked her back. These would be the seconds that I'd take out and remember. They'd have to last me, because her heat was the only reason she wanted this, and I wouldn't force myself on her again.

We pulled up to the warehouse, and Nox and Killian jumped out, yelling something I didn't care to listen to. I placed a soft kiss against her hair. "Please, don't hate me. Fucking please, Bliss."

She mumbled and rubbed her face against my chest, her skin heating again as the next wave of her heat came on. It was time for me to let go.

CHAPTER 9
Bliss

An all-consuming gnawing pain radiated every inch of me, like I was on the verge of being incinerated from within.

I squeezed my eyes shut against the world spinning around me. Deep breaths of the soothing scent of peppers and coffee beans were the only thing anchoring me to this world. I snuggled into the hot chest pressed against my cheek, and thick arms banded across my back and under my thighs hard enough it felt like we would meld together. It wasn't enough.

My fingers dug into strong shoulders as I pulled myself closer, burying my face in a warm neck as he carried me. I licked up the column of taut muscle, finding his mating glands. A sense of rightness solidified in my center as our scents combined.

His chest reverberated with a growl, and we jerked as he stumbled.

"Don't fucking drop her." The rough timber of another alpha's voice sang to me.

I whimpered as scalding heat pooled between my legs. I wanted to touch him, feel him, please him.

"I've got you. It's okay. It's okay. It's okay."

The chest under mine rumbled with each promise, and my heart slowed. Alphas. They would take care of me. They'd make this stop.

"Please." I sucked on the tender spot.

"Fuck. Nox, get the door."

Lights burned my eyes as my alpha carried me across the threshold, and I tucked my face deeper into his neck.

"Turn off the lights." A new voice to my right eased over me, and we were instantly plunged into darkness. There were three alphas. A trickle of a memory tightened my chest. Something was off. Where was my other alpha?

Strong hands tightened on my waist as we jostled up stairs. The friction of my clothes tore at my sensitive skin as he rushed. I didn't know or care where he was taking me, so long as he made this stop. "It's so hot. It hurts. *Please*," I begged, praying they could fix it.

A door opened, and the mix of sandalwood, coffee, lemons, and fresh night air flooded me. A different kind of warmth filled my chest. I knew these scents. *Bonded.*

Their scents burned my lungs and coursed through my veins, stoking the fire that ignited inside of me. My skin itched, my core ached—everything was too much and not enough. "Please."

My alpha lowered me to the mattress and groaned into my neck. "Breathe. We're going to make it better. Breathe, Bliss."

Three sets of hands roamed over me, digging into my

hair, gliding over my breasts, and dragging up my legs. I couldn't tell their touches apart, and I didn't care. The only thing that mattered was the small voice whispering in my mind: *Mine.*

A smooth tongue licked my lips and explored my mouth. He grunted when I sucked on it. *Yes.*

I worked to pull off his shirt but refused to let go of his mouth for it to be removed. His lips smiled against mine. "I missed you, Little Wolf."

The name danced around my head, and a swirl of giddiness bubbled through my chest. I liked that nickname. Hot lips ran up the other side of my neck, grazing my ear. "It's my turn to taste that sweet mouth of yours."

Lips broke away from mine, only to be replaced with hungry kisses as I gripped his hair at the base of his head. A wave of heat rolled through me, sending sparks down my arms into my fingers.

It wasn't enough. I felt so empty. I needed to be full. I needed them.

Hands grazed my sides, over my hips, and rested on my thighs. An alpha's large body moved between my feet and gripped my knees, spreading them wide for him. My scent flooded the room.

Teeth clashed with mine as the kiss turned bruising. The room filled with need, want, lust. He bit my lip, and the coppery taste of blood hit my senses. Then he sucked it into his mouth, groaning his approval. That groan had my body on fire. This was what I needed.

The alpha between my legs kissed a trail up my sensitive skin on the inside of my thigh. "We're going to take care of you, baby."

Large shoulders pushed my legs wider as if to prove

his point. My hips bucked, and my back arched as he ran his tongue through my wetness. He groaned and licked and sucked until my toes were curling. My core grasped around nothing, and I cried out. I was so empty. "Please."

He pushed thick fingers into me, making an indecent sound. I rocked against his hand, core clutching him as he brought them in harder. *Please, yes, yes, please.*

Lips trailed over my chest, and a hot, flat tongue ran over my nipple and stroked it in time with my other alpha's fingers. An alpha pulled my hair back, tilting my head, and devoured my mouth. The three of them consumed my senses, and tension built, tightening, heating, burning until it exploded through my veins with the force of my orgasm.

Before I could collapse back, I was pulled over a large, naked chest. I licked across his nipple, running my teeth over the edge. His chuckle vibrated under me. "Careful, it's sensitive."

His voice was soft, soothing, a deep familiarity to it. I peeled my eyes open, and pitch-black eyes met mine. *Rafe.*

His eyes searched mine, the corners rimming red. "Bliss." His voice was reverent as he cupped my face, thumbs drawing soothing circles.

"You're here." My breath hitched, throat closing around my next inhale. "How are you here?"

Fingers slid my hair back from my face and cupped my chin, turning it to the side. My gaze broke from startling black to honey brown, and a cry broke free. "Killian."

I didn't look away from him as soft lips kissed up my spine and marked my neck with his scent. "Little Wolf."

My heart clenched, and tears burned my eyes. *Nox.*

I'd missed them so much. A voice cried from far within

me. I wasn't supposed to want them here. I should tell them to leave. But that didn't make any sense. They'd take care of me. My heat seemed to agree because the room became stifling. I shifted over Rafe, needing the friction my body craved and pried to his belt off.

The heat became painful with each second my alphas weren't inside me. Tears pooled in my eyes as I met Nox's gaze. "I need you."

"We're here." Rafe stroked his thumb over my cheek and took a deep breath. His eyes searched mine tentatively. "We can make it stop, but you need to be knotted." He clenched his jaw and let out an unsteady breath. "This wasn't supposed to happen like this, but let us take care of you."

"Please." Fire burned away my coherent thought, and my slick soaked between my legs. Yes, that's exactly what I needed. "Yes, Alpha, please."

He flipped me over to lie beneath him, and he positioned himself at my entrance. Black eyes pierced mine. He hesitated, brows pinched together as they searched mine, a flash of panic visible.

I used my heel to force him forward, and my mouth opened as he slid inside me. I stretched around him inch by inch. I whimpered as he moved deeper. So full. Too full.

My slick drenched us, and my alpha slid to his hilt, dropping his lips to my ear. "That's a good girl. You were made to take us."

He sat back on his knees, only to have another mouth capture mine. Fingers dug into my jaw, holding it open as he thrust his tongue deep, nearly choking me. I rolled my hips, and bruising fingers dug into my skin. Soothing words turned to growls as each touch turned sharper, uncontrolled.

Wet open-mouth kisses trailed from my breast to my stomach. "Let me taste her."

He lifted my hips high off the bed, my eyes rolling back as my alpha pounded into me while a soft mouth captured my clit. Three alphas claimed me. I moaned into the mouth still covering mine. They thrust, licked, sucked until I was a writhing mess, my slick a pool under me.

Mine, mine, mine, chanted through my brain as he moved again, washing away everything else but the feel of them.

He grunted, becoming painfully bigger, pushing deeper within me. His knot locked on as he lost himself to the rut. My orgasm came on hard, detonating as my alpha's hot liquid filled me.

I floated in and out of myself, sometimes aware, sometimes seeing only in scent and color. Hands and teeth and tongues covered my body, and I focused on that—trying desperately to cling to anything tactile.

My blood boiled until everything that was me burned away and only instinct remained. I rocked my hips as my core stretched around my alpha. *Yes, please, yes.*

They were the only thing that gave me any peace.

I tilted my head, exposing my neck as a tongue lapped my mating glands. I wanted his teeth to break my skin, to own me in all ways. Something held back my plea, fighting the fog of heat to stop me from begging him for it.

As if sensing what I craved, he sucked hard on my

flesh. A knot stretched me wide, and pleasure pulsed through my core, ricocheting up my body with my release. The tension seeped out of me, and I went limp against the mattress. A soft hum of satisfaction settled in. Brilliant green eyes met mine, and he brushed damp hair off my face, his cock still twitching inside me. Some of the haze lifted, and my eyes widened.

Was I hallucinating? If I was, I didn't want to stop. Nox laid his chest against mine, holding most of his weight on his forearms, and I hummed at the contact.

"She's more lucid than last time."

I turned my head, and Killian's lips tipped up, drawing my own smile. His brows furrowed, a sadness taking the place of joy. Why was he sad? We were together.

He kissed my forehead and lifted from beside me. I reached out for him but settled when he came back with a glass of water. Nox sat up, carefully positioning me so I straddled him, and moaned as he sank in further. It would take time for his knot to go down enough for him to let go.

I took a sip from the glass, blinking away the fog. "Is this the second time?" Confusion pushed forward. Something was missing. "Was Rafe here?"

Nox kissed up my neck. "He had to leave, but he'll be back. It's been days, Little Wolf."

Days? That couldn't be. How could any of this be real? My boys, my pack. How was this possible? I pressed my face into Nox's chest. "Are you real?" My breath caught. "I need you to be real."

A growl rippled through him, and his hands bound around my waist. "We're real. Please remember this. Please don't hate us."

That didn't make sense. Why would I hate them?

Heat rose in my chest in a wave, and I shifted on him. I was so warm.

Fingers smoothed up my back. "Don't worry, babe. We'll take care of you. For as long as you need." He kissed my neck. "For as long as you want us."

CHAPTER 10
Rafe

I shut the door to the nest and leaned against it, closing my eyes. My skin crawled as I tried to breathe through my mouth to lessen the scent still coming from the room. Bliss was still in her heat, and it was torture to walk away from her—even temporarily.

Wes walked backward down the hall, a cocky smile spread wide across his face. He wore his usual black biker T-shirt and ripped jeans, with his long dirty-blond hair pulled back in a man bun we never ceased to give him shit about. With his leather vest on, he looked like that guy from *Sons of Anarchy*. "That good, huh?"

A growl ripped from my chest, and red seeped through my vision. The haze of Bliss' heat still clung to me. "What the fuck did you just say?"

Wes' smile dropped as I took a step forward. He raised his hands in front of him and muttered, as if trying to calm a charging animal. "Easy there, killer. I was just joking around."

I stilled, taking deep breaths. I knew damn well I was out of control, but this fucker should've known better. He had called my cell enough times in the last few hours that eventually the ring broke through to me. The functioning part of my brain knew whatever he wanted, it must be important, because the guy wasn't suicidal. "Well, don't. What are you doing here?"

Wes moved his fingers over his mouth in a zipper motion, but he couldn't hide the smirk from his eyes. I reminded myself that he was nearly family, and therefore I shouldn't kill him. Although, at the moment, I couldn't think of a single reason we let him hang around.

Wes cleared his throat. "Calm down. We got another order, and after the shit that went down at the dock, we don't have enough supply."

The muscles in my back tensed, every instinct screaming at me to go back to Bliss. "Can't. I'm not done taking care of something."

Wes let out a breath, and his brows pinched in the middle. "Fuck, man. You think I'd be asking you if it wasn't an emergency?" He raked his fingers through his hair and cradled the back of his head, arms winged out at the sides as he looked at the roof. "Listen, if I could do it myself, I would, but we both know my beta blood is useless. So you're going to have to break the heat spell and leave your girl in the very capable hands of your pack." Wes met my gaze and bit his lip as he looked me over. He must've been able to see the "fuck off" written on my face, because his next word sealed the deal for him. "Please."

I huffed out a breath and glanced back at the closed door. Bliss was in there, and it went against everything in my nature to walk away, but Wes wouldn't be asking if he thought there was any way around it. Our position and our jobs were precarious. The Institute didn't fuck around—if we didn't come through, they'd find someone else, and then where would we be? Back to not being able to take care of our omega? Not a chance.

I cracked my neck from side to side. "Let's get Ares and go."

Wes' eyes widened. "He's not in there?"

The smell of decaying flowers filled my nose. You didn't need to be an alpha to know one didn't just leave their omega in heat unless they absolutely had to. Ares had his own demons that he had to work through. "No, but if you want to keep that pretty face of yours, I wouldn't mention anything to him about it."

Wes grimaced. He knew I wasn't joking.

The hall opened up to the kitchen and living room. Ares sat in the corner armchair with a half-drunk bottle of vodka in his hand. Strands of white hair fell into his eyes as he completely ignored us. It was a good thing blood alcohol levels didn't affect the product. "Get up. We've got another order."

Ares' ice-blue eyes narrowed on me before he looked away and took another swig of the bottle. A muscle ticked in his jaw, and his knuckles were white where he clenched his hand in a fist. Any other day, I'd leave him alone, but the sooner we got this done, the sooner I got back to Bliss.

"Listen, you can wallow in your bullshit another time. The others have to stay with Bliss. Which leaves you and me."

Wes looked between us, his fingers drumming on the counter. "I don't get it, guys. I thought you'd be ecstatic getting her back. You know, because it's the only thing you've cared about for the last four fucking years."

Ares stood and crowded Wes. "Yeah, we're selfish bastards. I'm just seeing that clearly now."

Anger radiated off Ares, and I stepped between them in case he took out his anger on our favorite beta. "Let's go."

Ares glared at me before grabbing his leather jacket from the back of the lounge chair and walking out the door.

I shook my head. "Well, that went well."

Twenty minutes later, Wes pulled into an old research labs parking lot we'd rented out as soon as we could afford it. The building looked completely on the up and up, with the name MediLife Research Lab glowing in big letters on the sign overhead. The main reason we'd chosen this lab over the other ones was the lack of windows. We couldn't have average people seeing what we were up to. The Institute might buy from us, but if shit went down, they wouldn't do shit. We were on our own.

The development and sale of hormonal enhancements was completely illegal. You weren't supposed to fuck around with nature, which was exactly why it was such a lucrative business.

Ares trailed behind me as I walked through the doors. We'd been here every week like clockwork for the last couple of years. The Alpha Lupi had always dealt hormones, but it wasn't until we'd figured out how to use our own blood that the game really changed. Prior to that, everything was synthetic, but we had the genuine stuff. We could make a regular beta irresistible at a club or completely neutralize an omega. We had the top product in the market, and how we did it was under lock and key.

There were only two people that knew the secret outside of our pack: Wes and Dr. Lewinsky.

Wes got to work, disabling the alarm and unlocking the door, holding it open for Ares and me. A chime rang as we walked in, announcing our presence. The doctor came around the corner, a hand tucked behind his back. He placed his gun on the counter and huffed out a breath. "Jesus Christ, I wasn't expecting you."

He was an older man in his late fifties with dyed brown hair and a fake tan to hide his age. Not that it mattered. All we cared about was he was the best at what he did. When we found him, he'd just been busted for making synthetic blockers for one of our rival gangs. He was a disgrace in the medical field, and losing both his lab and practice had crippled him. Which made him perfect for us. At the time, he was making a more potent product and was desperate enough to switch sides. Once he was in, we gave him a cut and knew he'd be loyal to us from that point on.

Lewinsky straightened, pulling his shit together. "Last-minute order? I thought what you had would last you a month."

It fucking should have.

Ares strode through the reception area into the back, where the lab was located. "You asking questions now? I thought you worked for us."

The doctor paled, chasing after him. I rolled my eyes. I wondered if Wes and the doctor could smell the vodka leaking out of his pores or if that was just me.

The lab was small but well-kept. We set four gurneys up with blood donation stations on each side. Not that we were in the business of giving away blood. Ares laid out on his gurney, his jacket off and his eyes closed. He gave off a *don't fucking talk to me* vibe that was backed up by the scent of ginger wafting off him. I collapsed in my usual spot, kicking my feet up. Anxiety was riding high with the overwhelming need to get back to our girl. She was close to the end of her heat, and I didn't want to miss the last of it.

"Just make it quick," I grumbled. "We've got shit to do."

Dr. Lewinsky slid a needle into one of the large veins in my arm. He was practiced, and within seconds, the bag to my right was filling with blood. If we weren't alphas, our veins would've collapsed like drug addicts by now, but luckily, we healed fast.

Lewinsky switched out the bag on my arm and brought the full one to his steel worktable. We'd set him up with every high-tech piece of equipment he needed. The key to our success was quality product fast, and enormous quantities. That was how we undercut the market and ran everyone else out of town. The doctor used a syringe to place a few drops into each vial before setting it on a device that spun them at rapid speed. I didn't know how it all worked, but I knew we had the best.

Blockers convinced an omega's body that they'd just come out of a heat cycle. Their body stopped producing scent for the following couple of days, making it possible for them to recover without their alpha being all over them. Which made it the perfect solution for unmated omegas.

We'd been selling the Institute a steady stream of product for years now. They weren't who we were selling to the other night. In our attempt to make enough money to get Bliss back, we tried a new client, and that shit blew up in our faces.

The doctor's magnifying glasses dropped to the table, and a smile widened on his face. "Well, this was unexpected."

Ares sat up. "What are you going on about?"

The doctor looked at us. "What aren't you telling me? Your blood has four times the pheromones it normally does. You could put an omega to sleep for a week with this blend."

Wes cleared his throat but wisely stayed quiet. There was no need to inform Dr. Lewinsky about Bliss.

Ares must have thought the same because he yanked the needle from his arm without flinching. "We're out."

The doctor looked up from where he was typing on his laptop. He was a beta, so he couldn't scent the shift in mood, but he was smart enough to feel it. "Alright, with this higher potency, I can clear your quota for the month."

"We'll check in later. This product needs to move tomorrow."

I pulled my needle out with significantly more care than Ares had. My skin itched with the need to get back home because, for the first time in four years, Bliss was waiting for me there. If she would forgive us was still up for debate.

"I'm gonna drop you guys here," Wes said, stopping the van a good hundred yards from the warehouse. "Don't want to get too close to your girl's nest again."

Ares grunted something that sounded like "catchya"

and jumped out, seeming to not notice or care that Wes hadn't driven all the way up to our front door. I shook my head, staring after him as he disappeared into the darkness. "I need to do something about that. He's gonna end up killing someone."

Wes let out a low whistle. "Good luck with that."

"What the fuck does that mean?" I barked, pushing more power into my voice than I'd intended.

Wes' hair blew back, and he looked a bit shell-shocked. "Easy, man."

"Sorry." I meant it. "I'm on edge."

"Clearly." He shook his head. "I just meant I wouldn't want to deal with Ares on a good day."

I grumbled in agreement. To his credit, Wes hadn't been around when Ares had good days. I'd expected that Bliss being back would make a difference, but so far, not so much. Stubborn prick.

"I gotta go." I reached for the door handle. "There better not be any more emergencies. If anything else happens, don't call."

Wes laughed. "Right. Thanks for doing this."

"I'm not kidding. If you call again, someone better be fucking dead." I hopped out of the van and slammed the door.

Re-entering the warehouse was almost painful. Bliss' scent overwhelmed me—fucking captivating after being away from it, even for an hour. I tore down the hall toward the nest with single-minded focus. Easing the door open, I scanned the darkened room.

Nox lifted his head and squinted hard at me over where Bliss lay draped across his chest. It was dark enough that without his glasses, he probably couldn't see me that well, and the smell in here was probably muddling my scent.

"All set," I said, more to identify my voice than anything else.

He relaxed. "Shut the door. They're asleep."

I nodded, glancing at Killian passed out on Nox's right side, using his tattooed arm as a pillow. I raised an eyebrow. "You're not?"

"'Course not."

It didn't actually surprise me all that much. Nox was a perpetual insomniac—an overthinker by nature. Still, if there was ever a time to sleep, this was it.

I stepped up to the bed and pulled off my T-shirt with one hand, then paused before taking off my jeans too—trying to decide if that was weird since Bliss was currently resting.

Nox snorted and shifted Bliss slightly, rearranging her hair. "Fuck, man, don't get modest on us now."

I rolled my eyes and kicked off my jeans too. "Shut up." Crawling into the nest on Nox's other side, I stared up at the ceiling. "Do you think it's almost over?"

He glanced down at her. "Yeah. She was mostly lucid the last time, I think."

My chest ached at the knowledge that I'd missed that, but there was nothing I could do about it now. "She recognized you?"

"Yeah. You have no idea how hard it was not to claim her." He didn't sound happy about it, mostly just resigned.

A growl ripped from my chest, and my eyes flew to her neck. "You didn't."

"No."

We fell silent. We didn't need to finish the conversation;

I could smell his anxiety. Even though it went against every instinct we all possessed, none of us were going to just claim Bliss while she probably had no agency. At least not before we'd spoken to her. She was already going to be livid, and a mating couldn't be taken back. Neither could bonding, but that had been completely out of our control.

"Do you think that all her heats will be like this, or is it the drugs?" I said after a long beat.

He shook his head. "I don't know. Little column a, little column b, probably."

The problem was that information about omegas was kept very secret and passed down mostly in families. There were rumors, sure, but it was impossible to tell what was real. It wasn't like any of us had ever spent any time with omegas or even knew any other alphas who were mated to one. There was only one in our state that we knew of, and she was well into her forties. Her daughter, Flora, had gone to school with us.

"What if she's never fully lucid during it?" I voiced a concern that had been rattling around my head for the last few hours. "Then what?"

Nox barked a sarcastic laugh. "I'm not even thinking that far ahead. I want to get through a conversation first. One step at a time."

"Fair enough."

He shifted Bliss again, and she stirred, mumbling something in her sleep. We both froze, watching her.

As if alerted by Bliss' voice, Killian cracked an eye open and sat up. "What's going on?"

"Shhh," I hissed, knowing I sounded like a goddamn hypocrite. "Don't wake her up."

Killian sniffed the air and glanced down at my arm. It

had healed over, but dried blood still stuck to the skin. No doubt, that was what he was smelling. "When did you get back?"

"Ten minutes ago."

"Did you take Ares with you?"

I nodded but didn't answer, not wanting to get into it again. "There's enough product to keep the Institute off our asses for a few weeks, which is good timing…"

I trailed off, and they both watched me, eyes resigned. We'd handled this badly. I wouldn't change anything about what we'd done, but we'd still fucked up. We now had an angry alpha on our hands who thought he had a claim to our girl. We'd protect her regardless, but it was going to be a lot more difficult while she remained unmated, and our pack was fractured.

"We need a plan," I said unnecessarily.

"A stratagem," Nox muttered.

"Sure." I wasn't really listening.

We needed to talk—all five of us—but that couldn't happen until Bliss woke up. A lot had changed in the last four years, but in other ways, nothing had. Every single one of us was still in love with her, and every decision still started and ended with Bliss.

CHAPTER 11
Bliss

I drifted in that warm place between sleep and waking, cozy and unwilling to open my eyes. My cheek pressed into something warm and solid, and fingers tangled in the back of my hair, stroking lightly. Who was that?

Whoever it was, I never wanted them to stop. I sighed, pressing my nose deeper into the scent of lemon and sandalwood, and shifted, giving better access to the nape of my neck. It had been years since anyone had touched me like that. Not since...

My eyes popped open and met warm brown ones, and I reeled back, confusion crashing over me in waves.

I choked, a noise somewhere between a laugh and a scream coming out of the back of my throat as Killian and I stared at each other. His hand hung in the air, as though he'd forgotten what to do with it. He seemed to realize at the same moment I did, and he put it back down on the bed.

"Bliss? It's okay."

Killian's voice didn't sound exactly the same as I remembered. It was deeper and warmer now. He gave me a nervous smile, like I was a wild animal he was afraid was about to bite him.

"I—" I peeled my face off the chest of my former friend and jumped to my feet, becoming all too aware that I wasn't wearing anything. My heart started to pound out of control in my ears. "I—where am I?"

Nest, my muddled brain chanted. *Nest. Mine. Safe. You remember this. Put the pieces back together.*

I was standing on a bed in the middle of a small, dimly lit room. There were no windows, and the bed took up almost all the limited floor space. The room smelled of sex—so strong that it was incredible that I hadn't immediately noticed. I wobbled on legs that felt like Jell-O, toppling sideways on the unsteady mattress.

A second set of strong arms circled me, the scent of sandalwood suddenly filling my nose. "Little Wolf? Take a second. Don't panic."

I swiveled around and almost laughed as I came face-to-face with another old friend—the comedy of errors was too much. "You shaved your hair," I blurted out, sounding idiotic.

The corner of Nox's lip twitched as he nudged me back to standing on my own. "Yeah. A few years ago."

He ran his hand over the back of his shaved head, looking sheepish, and my anxiety spiked. It was a familiar expression on a face that was far older and more angular than I remembered. Like trying to trace back the plot of a book you read as a child or the words to a song you only heard once.

"I'm not panicking," I said bluntly, as much for my benefit as theirs. "I'm…"

Confused wasn't really the right word. Fuzzy.

"Disoriented," Nox supplied.

"Sure."

I made awkward eye contact with him—I didn't have to see his expression to know he was disappointed and nervous. I could smell it. Like dead flowers. Scrambling off the bed, I scanned the floor for something to wear.

"Here."

I looked up into dark eyes, and my brain detonated. "Not you too."

I winced as I heard the words pop out of my mouth. That hadn't come out right.

Rafe's face fell as he held out a black T-shirt to me. He looked the most similar to how he had four years ago, at least compared to Nox and Killian, who had both clearly undergone some kind of second puberty, but he was still older, taller, and more angular. His tan was more pronounced, like he was spending the majority of his time outside these days, and there was a fresh cut above his right eye. That must have been deep to not have healed over yet, even with alpha genes.

I straightened, taking the T-shirt and slipping it over my head. The spicy scent of chili peppers surrounded me as the fabric fell to my mid-thigh. I spun on my heel, searching for a door.

"B, wait," Killian called. "Where are you trying to go?"

"Uh…" I blanched at the sound of my familiar childhood nickname. I wasn't sure where I was going; I just needed to get out of this room.

"Let's just take this slow." Nox put his hands up like he was under arrest. "We'll explain everything, I promise."

My mouth opened and shut. What was wrong with me? It was like my brain was moving, but my voice couldn't keep up. The tension ticked up a notch in the room. The scent of their collective anxiety mingled with my own, making the air smell salty and oppressive.

"Shower," Rafe said after a long moment. It wasn't a question.

I stared at him and huffed a laugh—a real one. "Okay, bossy."

His eyebrows shot up in clear alarm, and for some reason, that made me laugh harder.

If seventeen-year-old me could see me now.

I spent over an hour in the shower, and slowly the fog clouding my brain cleared.

It was like coming out of sleep paralysis, or waking up after a very high fever. Which, I suppose, made sense. I'd never experienced heat, but I knew first heats were always the most intense. Combine that with the drugs I'd been given, and no wonder I was addled.

I remembered getting into Alpha Nero's helicopter. Arriving at his house. Then things got a little hazy, but they picked up again a few days later. I remembered parts of my heat, sort of, but it was like everything was covered in a film. Maybe this was how the girls had felt on blockers.

As the memory of Alpha Nero stabbing the needle into

my neck resurfaced, rage pooled in my stomach, and I dug my nails into my palms.

I willed myself not to scream—undoubtedly the guys were feeling the full effects of my anger right now, wherever they were. If I started yelling someone would come barging in here. I doubted they would have a choice—alphas, like omegas, had little control over their instincts. Alpha Nero had a choice, though. I wasn't his mate yet—he knew what he was doing.

In every revenge fantasy, and pain fueled fever dream I'd had over the last four years, I'd never imagined this possibility. Maybe if I'd had a better understanding of the Agora... but no, not even then.

I was grateful not to be mated to Alpha Nero right now. I needed to focus on that, and not how potentially messed up my situation was about to become.

When I was done in the shower, I stood in front of the mirror and tilted my head to the side, examining my unblemished skin. None of my mating glands had been so much as bruised. No bite marks. No claiming. No mates.

I was lucky, if not a little confused. It was almost impossible for an alpha to go through an entire heat cycle and not claim an omega, especially when bonded. I'd never even heard of it.

So, why? Why would they do that?

My stomach flipped. Had they not wanted to be there with me? Oh, God.

I'd thought for the briefest second when I smelled them at The Agora that they were going to take me home right then. It would have been stupid and weak of me to forgive them so quickly, but I might have—instincts were hard to ignore.

Regardless, I'd have to manage it somehow if I was going to face my former friends and hold on to the shreds of dignity I had left.

Easier said than done.

I found a set of pajama pants and a T-shirt left for me. I held them up to my nose, breathing in the scent—hot and delicious. I frowned. My brain and my instincts didn't seem to be aligned. I opened the bathroom door and found the upstairs hall empty. I paused, unsure where to go. Was I supposed to go back to the nest? Or was I allowed to leave?

Voices drifted up from the main floor. "Call Lewinski. There's something wrong."

"I can't. You think the Institute will just ignore it if they know we have her here?"

"Fuck it, I don't care," Killian said.

"You should. Maybe there's nothing wrong. Maybe this is normal. How would we know?"

My stomach sank. They were talking about me. Typical.

The last thing I wanted was to go down there and face them—I wasn't sure what would be worse; if they tried to apologize, or if they wanted nothing to do with me.

Actually, that was a lie—I knew what would be worse. If they'd brought me here just to abandon me again, it would be far worse. I might as well rip that industrial strength band aid off now.

I crept down the hallway toward the voices and stepped into a dimly lit living room. Rafe, Killian and Nox all jumped up from their seats around a dark wood coffee table as I entered. My eyes narrowed slightly, noticing that once again, Ares wasn't with them. He was around here somewhere, though. I could smell him everywhere. Like an oncoming thunderstorm. His absence felt like further proof that they probably hadn't wanted to participate in my heat.

Not that I should care—did care. *I didn't care.*

"How are you feeling?" Rafe asked, quickly stepping forward into the forefront of the group.

"Um, better." I crossed my arms over my stomach. "I know where I am now...well, kind of."

His expression split into apparent relief as I trailed off, unsure how to finish my sentence. "You're at our house. We brought you here, because..." It was his turn to trail off.

"Yeah. I get the idea."

I bit my lip. This was painfully uncomfortable. My eyes darted to Nox and Killian, who both looked like they were in physical pain. Relatable.

"Do you need anything?" Killian asked, running both hands over his head. "Food, or are you cold, or..." He looked around, nervous.

"Water?" Nox offered.

"I'm fine."

Silence stretched.

Killian swung his arms in a wide arc, blowing out a breath. "Please let me just get you something. I feel like a fucking idiot just standing here."

I snorted a laugh despite myself. "I'll take some water."

Killian grinned and darted over to the kitchen.

Another small smile crossed my face. The interaction was sort of nostalgic. Some things had remained the same over the years.

A hopeful scent rose in the air and I gritted my teeth, a

shadow falling over the warm glow in my mind. Some things might have remained the same, but most things hadn't and the most important thing to remember was this wasn't my pack. These guys weren't even my friends anymore.

Nox adjusted his glasses. "Bliss, do you want to sit?"

Rafe crossed his arms. "We should talk."

Yes. We probably should.

God knew I didn't prefer alpha Nero, but they didn't know that when they'd barged into his house to stop my mating. They'd showed up at the Agora, after four years of complete silence, and what? Was it some biological bond instinct that made them follow me out of the Agora? They felt my fear and couldn't stop themselves? Maybe.

I'd spent enough time in classes about alphas and omegas over the years to know that was more than possible. God, I knew from experience that we'd felt each other's emotions from opposite ends of the country. I braced myself. Even putting aside the awkwardness of my heat, I deserved an explanation.

"Fine." I tried to channel Flora's bluntness, wishing she were here with me to bounce opinions off of. She'd have so much to say about this. "Let's hear it."

Maybe that's too blunt. Too blasé. What did you say to someone after four years of abandonment and a week of sex? *How've you been?*

I sat gingerly on the edge of the couch, facing them. Killian strode back over and pressed a full glass of water into my hand, his dark eyes meeting mine with an intensity that didn't match the benign action. I took the glass and averted my gaze, my neck heating.

"That didn't play out like we thought it would." Nox

shifted on his feet, where he stood behind the couch. "Are you okay? What we did. Are you okay with that? You know, helping you through your heat?"

I swallowed. "It's not like you had any choice. I'm sorry, I know you guys weren't expecting me to practically beg you for it after all this time, but I promise that was a one off. Not something you'll have to worry about happening again."

Three growls ripped through the air and I reeled back, nearly sloshing water over my lap in surprise.

"What the fuck are you talking about?" Rafe barked.

"Back off, you'll scare her," Killian snapped at Rafe, though he didn't seem to be much less angry himself. "Sorry."

"It's fine."

The growling didn't even phase me, which was something I didn't want to think too hard about right now. I should have been terrified. My eyes darted back and forth, confused by the intensity of their reaction. "I just meant that it was probably mostly the drugs, but I'll get out of your hair before my next heat anyway, so…"

Nox's eyes flashed black, his jaw tightening. "No."

"Where are you going?" Rafe bit out in a strained voice, clearly trying his best to stay calm.

"I'm not exactly sure," I said honestly.

The plan brewing in my mind was half-formed, and maybe twenty percent likely to work, but that was far better than no plan at all. The top of my list so far was to find Flora, and then regroup from there. Maybe I could sleep in the nest room for a night and start trying to find her tomorrow? The guys probably owed me that much—

"You can't leave. We just got you back," Killian blurted out.

My eyes widened, half in surprise, half in confusion. I glanced around the group of virtual strangers, and my pulse quickened. "What are you talking about?"

The scent of guilt and misery rose in the room, blocking out all other smells. I coughed, gagging as it invaded my mouth and nose, crushing me.

"Bliss, we're so sorry." Rafe said, dejected. "I should have led with that. I should always say that to you, every day. This wasn't the way we wanted to do things,"

Which part? I could think of several things they should apologize for, most of which I'd had quite a few years to dwell on.

I hadn't heard a word from them the entire time I was at the Institute. They'd abandoned me and given up any chance we had of being a normal pack. Then, in the heat, they hadn't wanted to mate.

"Why did you bring me here?" I asked, frustrated.

"What do you mean?" Killian asked, the sour scent of confusion mingling with his guilt.

"Why come find me? Is it just because you have to?"

Nox pushed his sleeves further up his muscled arms and crossed them over his chest. "What do you mean, we have to?"

I widened my eyes. I felt like we were speaking different languages—just on totally different planes of existence. "Why would you bring me back here after all this time? Is it because of the bond? Because I can live with a little pain."

A deluge of scent hit me all at once. I couldn't sort it. Couldn't figure out which emotions were coming from where, but as we all stood there, the tornado of misery surrounding us seemed to pick up steam.

"Bliss," Rafe said finally. "We've always regretted leaving you. Always. We wanted you back for years." He frowned, clearly frustrated. "Nothing went the way we all planned, but now Nero and the Institute will be after you. You need to lie low for a while so we can keep you safe while we figure it out, but there's no way we're letting you go again. We can't."

I licked my lips, tasting the emotions in the air as I took it all in.

Guilt, anger, protection, love, sadness, guilt again.

"Right," I sighed, resigned. "I understand."

I did understand.

It wasn't their fault, really. Well, being dicks who made selfish decisions was their fault, but there were some parts of this that were just biological. They literally could not let me leave.

They did regret leaving me and in some way they loved me—it was like a shard of glass to the heart. After four years of lessons in how these bonds worked, I couldn't even lie to myself and believe that they had any choice. They probably didn't even realize it was an instinct more than a real emotion.

"How about this?" I said, rubbing my tense eyebrows. "Can you guys help me get some blockers? I'll go back on them, and that will make it at least bearable for me to leave again. As long as I have them before my next heat, we'll probably be okay to separate."

"You want to go on blockers and leave?" Killian asked, slowly.

I raised my eyebrows. I'd admit it wasn't a perfect plan,

but it sounded to me like their issue was that they couldn't keep themselves from trying to protect me. The institute had been very clear about how that instinct worked. Still, four years ago as soon as I took blockers they seemed able to let me go, and maybe I still had some in my system over the last week, because they hadn't bit me. Ares hadn't even been in the room. That was supposed to be impossible.

"Yeah," I said quietly. "I think that would be better for everyone."

No one stopped me as I stood to leave the room, the scent of wilted dandelions following after me like a dark cloud.

I jogged up a set of concrete stairs at the end of the hall, not really paying attention to where I was going. I just needed to get some air. I wished I could talk to Flora. She would have something just on the edge of mean to say about all the guys that would undoubtedly make me feel better.

There was a time when the guys themselves were my only friends. When they would have been the only people I would have talked to about anything, but that was a long time ago. We weren't those kids anymore. The men in the living room were almost strangers, and the parts of them that were familiar were haunting and disorienting. Like switching out a favorite actor for a new cast member in the middle of a season without explanation.

I shoved at a heavy door at the top of the stairs marked "EXIT" and stepped out onto the roof.

I tipped my head back and stared at the sky. It was too

cloudy to see a single star. I sighed. Of course. Instead, I turned toward the skyline, and my heart squeezed.

I knew that skyline.

For some reason, I'd assumed we were still in New York. Brooklyn, or maybe Long Island, but we weren't. This was Stratford, New Jersey, where we'd grown up. And that meant that this warehouse was probably—

Movement to my left caught my eye. I stopped short.

A man's white-blonde head rose over the back of a beat up old couch ten yards away, his face turned from me. His arm was slung over the armrest, a bottle clutched in his hand.

Ares.

My heart pounded against my ribs as the fresh scent of night wafted toward me.

Every muscle in my body tensed.

Even if I didn't recognize his scent, the hair would have been a dead giveaway. I'd never seen anyone else so naturally devoid of color in real life.

I didn't speak, unsure if I should make my presence known or turn around and go back inside. I shifted on my feet, indecisive, my curiosity warring with my anxiety.

"Hello, Bliss." He put too much emphasis on the S at the end of my name, like "Blisssssss."

My breath caught. "How did you know it was me?"

I hadn't expected anyone to be up here, and I wasn't prepared for another confrontation with my past so soon. Or at all.

I should have said something more scathing. In a perfect world, I would rewind time and march back down the stairs. Or better, throw something at the back of his head before he said my name.

I was braver in my head.

Ares snorted and took a sip of the bottle. "I can smell you from here."

He didn't turn around, but I didn't have to see his face to know he was smirking. I frowned, affronted. I'd just showered and I was wearing someone else's clothes. "Yeah, well, you're not the only one and you smell awful."

Better. Sort of.

"Pft. Liar."

I narrowed my eyes, almost shaking with annoyance at being called out.

I was lying, and I'd forgotten for a moment he would know. I could have kicked myself—it had really been too long since I'd been around anyone not on blockers.

He smelled like rain and leather, but it was muted by burnt sugar and...something. This was stupid. I didn't know why I was still standing here.

I sniffed the air and frowned again. "Wait, are you drunk?"

Ares laughed bitterly. "Do you care?"

"I guess not..." I narrowed my eyes, annoyed for no one specific reason, but why wasn't he turning around? "Are you really not going to look at me?"

"No one is stopping you from coming over here."

My eye twitched. God, at least the others had made some kind of fumbling effort to apologize. This was–well, very Ares.

I moved without conscious thought. The couch was grouped around a beat up coffee table, with a few chairs scattered around it. None of the furniture matched, or had the same high-end appearance of the decor inside. In fact, from what I could see, this stuff looked second-hand at best.

I came to a halt directly in front of where Ares sat, feet up on the coffee table. He met my gaze, head on, expression unreadable. I faltered, hit suddenly with painful déjà vu. It was probably that I actually had seen him at some point during the transport out of Alpha Nero's mansion, I reasoned, or maybe just that Ares had always had very distinctive pale blue eyes.

He leaned forward, elbows on his knees, and looked me straight in the eye. A shiver traveled down my neck. "Hello, Bliss."

"You already said that."

"And you didn't respond."

I cocked an eyebrow, unsure what to make of this. With the metabolism of an adult alpha, getting legitimately drunk for any length of time would take enough alcohol to kill a horse. "Hello, Ares."

At the sound of my words, my chest seized with alien emotions. I could feel more than smell everything that ran through his head.

Pain, lust, resentment, protectiveness, loathing. Some feelings were the same as the rest of the guys, but most were sharper. Darker. It was impossible to tell how much of that was a conscious thought, and how much was a biological instinct.

I stepped back. "Sorry," I muttered, shaken by the intensity of his emotions. "I didn't know you were here."

"Well, I live here," he said lazily, but his posture was rigid. "Did you want me to leave?"

There was something loaded in that question, but I couldn't quite place it. "No. I'll go."

He blew air out his nose, resigned. "Don't."

"No—"

"Fuck, just sit down." He shoved the bottle he'd been drinking out of into my hand. "Here, drink this. You look like you need it."

I grimaced. That was probably true.

I turned around, trying to convince myself I had no choice. I didn't even believe my own lies. He hadn't barked at me—I didn't have to stay.

The liquid burnt the back of my mouth and traveled down my throat, warming me from the inside. I coughed, choking on the familiar sting. It had been years since I'd drank anything stronger than orange juice. "What is this?"

"Nothing good."

"Perfect." I took another sip and passed it back.

We sat in silence for a while, passing the bottle back and forth. I wondered if we had nothing to say to each other, or too much.

Both.

I leaned back on my elbows, looking up at the sky. The constellations were just a tiny bit fuzzy at the edges, the smallest stars hard to make out. I glanced over at him, but instead my eyes fixed on what he was sitting on. My heart stopped. "Oh my god."

"What?"

I gestured to the beat up burgundy sofa. "You kept our couch from our spot?"

"Oh." He glanced down as though expecting to see a different sofa. "Yeah."

When we were kids, we'd lived in a shitty foster home where we weren't allowed to hang out because of rules about fraternization between foster siblings of different genders. Outside of school, we spent most of our time at a clearing in the woods filled with a firepit and a bunch of stolen or dumpster dived furniture.

The couch was gross then, so it had to be a biohazard now. It had been through all sorts of weather, and it was far from new when we got it. Still, the fact that they kept it thawed my heart slightly. "Why would you guys keep this? It's got to be disgusting. "

I smelled his sudden nervousness and registered vaguely that it didn't correspond at all to his bored expression. "Don't know. We didn't have any shit when we moved in here and started working. It's nothing."

Lie.

His blatant lie tasted like acid and we both winced. God, if I'd had the ability to scent emotions as a teenager the way they did, things would have been so different.

Then again, maybe not. I still would have gotten carted off to the Institute. Not that it mattered right now.

"Why are you still here, anyway?" I swished the alcohol around in my mouth.

"I just told you, I live here," he said sardonically.

"No." I passed the bottle back again. "In this city. Why are you guys still hanging around?"

"We work here."

I wrinkled my nose. It wasn't a lie, but it wasn't the whole truth. His words smelled like Windex–I wasn't sure I cared enough to push it.

"Well, I'll try not to get in the way of your work while I'm staying here for however long it takes to get blockers," I said, as casually as possible. My voice came out a little higher pitched than I meant it. My head was nice and buzzy now.

"What?" He whipped his head over to look at me, eyes narrowing. Almost too alert. "What are you talking about?"

"I'm going to get blockers so I can leave. I just talked to the others about it."

He ground his teeth, the waves of anger in the air almost palpable as he stared at me for a full beat. "Fucking idiots." He pulled an iPhone out of his pocket, tapping something very fast onto the screen.

My gaze zeroed in on the phone. It was thinner, but larger than the kind that had been around before I'd entered the Institute. I assumed it still worked, more or less the same—maybe I could use it to find Flora. "What are you doing?"

"Texting Nox. Mother fucking…"

He trailed off and shoved the phone back into the pocket of his jacket and I watched it disappear. It was stupid. Before everything, I never would have hesitated to ask Ares for anything. I would have just taken that phone, but I had no idea where I stood anymore. I wasn't sure I should mention Flora—at least, not until I got some clarification on what they wanted from me.

"Why Nox?" I asked instead. I didn't want to deal with whatever he was upset about. Ares was always upset when we were kids. He probably just didn't want me here–he hadn't been in the nest. My brow furrowed.

He took another sip from the bottle he had clutched in his tattooed fingers. "Because someone needs to talk to you and it shouldn't be me."

Okay. That was good, I guess, but that wasn't what I meant. "No, I meant, why Nox? Why not Rafe?"

Rafe was Ares' best friend. We'd all been one group,

but whenever things split off, it was always Rafe and Ares and Killian and Nox. That was just how things were. The way Ares was looking at me right now, though, I was clearly missing something.

He snorted a derisive laugh. "You've been gone a long time, Love."

We both heard the term of endearment and froze. I coughed. "Well, whose fault is that?"

CHAPTER 12
Bliss

I stood in the center of my childhood bedroom at the foster home.

Sun shone through the thin blanket I'd tacked up as a curtain, warming my face. I turned in a circle, my eyes traveling over mine and Flora's beds up against the wall. Our nightstand stood in the center, my Institute textbooks piled on top.

No, that's not right.

My brain buzzed with distant confusion, but I let the thought wash away.

"Bliss."

Warmth pressed in on me from all sides, and hands fanned over my stomach, arms, and waist.

"Baby, come here."

I leaned my head back onto the nearest shoulder, and heat pooled in my core. I blinked as awareness filled me. "Where did you all come from?"

No one answered directly. I reached out, pulling them closer to me. Their skin was like fire, burning under my fingers.

I whimpered, arching my neck. Stretching, presenting my throat—

My eyes popped open.

My heart pounded with adrenaline as I blinked up at the off-white ceiling, the spots fading from my vision.

Just a dream.

I hadn't had a dream like that in a while. It was almost every night we'd first been separated, but after the first year or so at the Institute, it had dulled to every few months. This was probably due to my heat. *Or the smell.* I grimaced as I plucked at the T-shirt I wore, which definitely didn't smell like me.

I'd spent the night in the nesting room. It was obvious both from the smell and the decor that no one slept in here full-time, so I felt it was the safest place to hide.

I swung my legs over the side of the bed and stretched. In some ways, I was feeling more alive this morning than I had in years. I wasn't in pain. I'd actually slept alright, and the cloud of gloom that had covered my every thought since I was seventeen seemed to have cleared somewhat.

I didn't want to think about that too hard. It would make it all the harder to stay firm about what I needed to do and leave once I got the blockers. In the meantime, I would channel all my temporary energy into finding Flora.

I got out of bed and crossed to the closet. The guys had apparently planned this to some extent because there were some clothes in there. I flipped through the hangers, frowning.

I snorted, holding up a sundress I would have definitely worn four years ago but now barely covered my boobs. They seemed to think I would look exactly the same as I had at seventeen, pre-transition. I shrugged and tried it on anyway. It was a snug fit, and a little shorter than I'd like, but it was better than a T-shirt and no pants.

The kitchen of the warehouse was teeming with activity.

Rafe stood at the island, his black hair covering his eyes as he typed something out on his phone. He was actively ignoring Ares, who was talking to him—or, more accurately, *at* him—as he loaded bullets into the chamber of a handgun. I raised my eyes at the gun. That was new.

Nox crossed in front of me, carrying several large wooden crates stacked on top of each other, and passed them to Killian, who leaned against the doorway, looking relaxed in his unbuttoned blue-and-green flannel shirt, showing off his abs under his fitted white shirt.

When I appeared, all movement paused. All four of them stopped what they were doing to turn and look at me. Silence hung in the air as none of us knew what to say.

"Morning, B," Killian broke the tension. He dropped the crates, which looked heavy even for him. "Hungry?"

I shook my head, even as my stomach growled. I was famished, actually.

"Here, let me make you something before we go," Nox said quickly, crossing back over to the refrigerator. He wore a crisp white shirt, black vest, and pants, juxtaposed by his pierced ear and shaved head.

"Where are we going?"

Ares grabbed his gun off the counter and stalked out of the room without so much as a glance in my direction. After a long pause where the scent of guilt rose in the room, practically choking me, Rafe followed.

Killian ran a hand over the back of his head, watching the door where his two friends had left. "We've gotta work. You can stay here, of course. It's safe, and there's stuff to do." He glanced around. "Uh, here," He grabbed a remote control off the coffee table in the open-concept living room. "This works the TV and the sound system. You can use whatever. I think everything's logged in on the TV, but if you need a password, text me."

"Text you with what?" I raised an eyebrow.

"Oi!" Killian reached into his pocket and pressed a cell phone into my hand. "Use this if you need us."

My heart leapt as I took the sleek black iPhone and turned it over in my palm. Technology had definitely jumped a few generations, but I just needed to google Flora—that couldn't be that difficult.

Nox reappeared at my side, now holding a plate of toaster waffles I recognized as a childhood favorite of mine. "There's a ton of other stuff in the kitchen if you don't still like these," he said quickly. "And you can order whatever you want. There's money on the counter."

I blinked a couple of times, a little overwhelmed. "Where are you going?"

"Nowhere important." Nox backed up, scooping up the abandoned crates. "I'll see you—" He broke off, backing out of the room, and left his sentence hanging.

I laughed bitterly.

"What?" Killian asked, now the only guy left standing.

"I don't know, it's just funny. Even after all this time, you're still running with that stupid gang. Or, I don't know, maybe you guys have upped your game now." I glanced around at the expensive warehouse home, which must have cost a fortune. "And you guys are still lying to me about it. Like as though I didn't know."

It wasn't really funny, but it just felt so representative of all our issues. Back when we were teenagers, the guys were heavily involved in a local gang that dealt in alpha and omega party drugs. They always tried to keep me out of it and acted like I had no idea what was going on. Even then, their insistence on protecting me from everything was really keeping me at arm's length.

Killian tilted his head. "We're not lying, B. It's just not important. Taking over Alpha Lupi was how we found you in the first place, but the details are boring."

I could smell that he was telling the truth; I just didn't agree. Still, it wasn't really the time to get into it. The sooner they left, the sooner I could start trying to find Flora.

"Kill!"

Killian spun around in the direction of his name, then back to me. He took two steps forward, like he wasn't sure if he should give me a hug or something. He didn't. "Look, I know this is all messed up, but we're going to find a way to fix it. I promise."

"Right." I smiled awkwardly.

That was exactly what I was trying to do. Fix this. By finding Flora and getting out of here.

"Good." He smiled. "Please stay in the house."

I crossed the room and sat down on the stools near the large kitchen island to eat my waffles. "Um, have a good day?"

"You too, B. Don't do anything I wouldn't do."

The moment the door slammed, I powered on the phone and tapped the Safari icon. Thankfully, that hadn't changed since the last time I'd used one of these. I typed "Flora Cabot" into the search bar

Nothing came up.

This was pointless, she'd have a new last name. *Ummmm.*

"*Agora Ceremony. Mating announcements.*"

Several news articles appeared. Omega Blair from the Institute had been mated to a reality TV star. It was an upset—omegas never went to C-list celebrities. Politicians, tech moguls, and A-listers only.

I glanced around the warehouse. Good thing the media hadn't gotten wind of me yet.

I scrolled through several more articles speculating on the Agora Ceremony and stopped short at a picture of Flora. My heart pounded in my chest. In the photo, she was wearing her sparkling evening gown, her expression dazed. The man standing beside her was beaming in triumph. The caption of the photo read: *Former Congressmen, Judge Allen Raymond "Chip" Bishop IIII of Virginia, and his new mate, Omega Bishop.*

I ground my teeth. It didn't even mention Flora's name, but "Chip" got more names than a phonebook.

It did detail that Alpha Bishop lived in Brooks, Virginia, was a former congressman from the Sigma majority party, and was rumored to be on the short list for a Supreme Court seat in the next ten years.

Blood rushed in my ears when I came across a picture of Alpha Bishop shaking hands with Alpha Nero at some fundraiser. Nero's words came back to me, ringing in my head. "Speeding things up a bit... Some alphas do this, regardless."

I had to find her.

The only person I could think of who might know where Flora was and might be willing to help was her mother. Mrs. Cabot was an omega, and with any luck, she'd be something like Flora. When we were growing up, Flora had lived in one of the few nice houses in town. If I remembered right, it wasn't that far from the warehouse. I pulled up Google Maps on my phone, trying to remember what street she lived on.

I gave up, deciding that I would wing it.

When I reached the door to the warehouse, I paused. The guys told me not to go out—then again, they were saying that because they were afraid I'd be attacked. Years at the Institute taught me that I was currently about as safe as I was going to get without a mate.

The exterior of the warehouse looked nothing like I remembered. Years ago, this area was dirty, abandoned, and dilapidated—the kind of place five kids on the run could go unnoticed for a night because no one was around to see. Now, there were cars on the street, people on the sidewalks, and respectable storefronts surrounding the area. It was shocking how fast things had shifted. Practically impossible.

I set off down the street, drawing a few looks from passers-by. I wondered if they were staring because of my omega status or because of my too-short dress. Probably the latter. I hoped no one realized who or what I was, particularly since, as far as I could tell, the only people nearby were betas. The dress, though, was definitely eye-catching.

I turned a corner at the end of the street—noting the

newly painted crosswalks and installed stoplights—and passed a little strip mall that absolutely hadn't been there before. There was a dry cleaner, bank, and a CVS. I wished they had a Starbucks or something. It had been years since I'd had a coffee.

I stared up at the CVS sign. They sold Starbucks coffee in bottles in their refrigerator sections—at least they used to. I hesitated only briefly before ducking into the store. The guys had left me money for a reason, right?

The familiar and distinctive smell of the drugstore hit me like a long-lost memory—floor cleaner, stale gum, and Herbal Essences shampoo. I grabbed a red plastic basket from a small, haphazard stack by the door and strolled down the center aisle, making a beeline for the food.

There were too many types of coffee to choose from—lattes and frappes and coffee-flavored energy drinks. I selected a normal-ish caramel-colored bottle and dropped it into my basket.

"Is that all?" the woman at the checkout said.

I paused. "Um, actually, hang on."

I turned around, scanning the items placed by the register. They were all just there, begging me to take them. It had been years since I'd had anything for myself.

A package of stale marshmallow Easter candy landed on the counter, followed by a gossip magazine with a famous alpha movie star and his omega mate on the front, a box of purple hair dye, and a black eyeliner pencil as thick as my pinky finger. I held up two colorful plastic cases for my new phone. "Which do you like?"

The checkout woman gave me an odd look. "That one?" She pointed at the sparkly pink one on the right.

I frowned and handed her the black one with the stars instead, smiling. "Okay. I'm all set now."

———

I knocked lightly on the navy blue–painted door of Flora's parents' house and stepped back to wait. I shuffled my feet against the welcome mat, swinging my heavy CVS bag against my leg.

Flora's house was a white, two-story colonial with a huge, well-kept yard and a wraparound porch. There was blue wicker furniture on the porch that looked as though it had never been used.

Footsteps sounded on the other side of the door, and a boy appeared, staring at me with big brown eyes. I frowned, trying to decide how old he was. Alphas were weird like that—he was the size of the average fourteen-year-old beta, but he was probably only ten.

"Hi. Is your mom home?"

"Yeah. Who are you?"

"I'm friends with your sister."

It was the kid's turn to frown, seeming confused. "Flora doesn't live here."

"Charlie, who is it?"

Flora's mother appeared in the doorway behind her son, and her eyebrows rose ever so slightly as she took me in.

Flora's mother looked just like her—or rather, the other way around. She had long dark hair pulled back in a knot and wore minimal makeup. Her navy-blue sheath dress looked like it was chosen to match the house, and her heels clicked on the waxed wooden floor.

"Omega Nero." Her eyes traveled over my bare legs, tight dress, and visible cleavage. They lingered on my neck for half a second before she smiled. "To what do we owe the visit?"

I choked, both at the use of the name, and at the fact that Flora's mother knew who my mate was supposed to be. Maybe she read the Agora announcements? I crossed my arms over my ill-fitting sundress. "Omega Cabot. I was hoping to speak with you. It's about Flora."

Flora's mother smiled, her joy clearly genuine. "Come in. I'm so happy about Flora's mating. We're going to be attending the wedding at the end of the month. Of course, I'm beside myself."

My smile was brittle as I stepped into the bright white-painted foyer. That wasn't the reaction I'd been hoping for.

I didn't know Flora's mother, but I'd hoped that given how her daughter had turned out, they might have similar views on mating and bonding. I'd hoped maybe Omega Cabot was a secret ally. Then again, she still could be—her son was in the room.

As though thinking the same thing, Omega Cabot put her hand on her son's shoulder. "Charlie, go play upstairs."

"Fine." He went with very little argument, and I raised an eyebrow.

Omega Cabot laughed. "Wait till you have little ones of your own. They're fine at this age, but as soon as they learn to bark, it's duck and cover for us. That's when I let my mate step in."

I did the mental math, trying to remember the ages of Flora's siblings. "How many do you have?"

Flora's mother led me into her gleaming dining room and gestured for me to sit at the cherrywood table. "Only five, I'm afraid," she said a little sadly, as though five children was nothing. "Two omegas though." She perked up. "Well, we hope. Flora, of course, and then Lily is far too young to tell yet, but she has all the signs." She sat. "Did you want tea? Orange juice?"

"No, I'm fine." I wrung my hands. "What are the signs?" I asked, unable to hold in my curiosity.

The Institute had never talked much about how to tell if a kid was an omega. Had I shown the signs? If anyone who'd been around to notice had been paying attention, would I have been monitored?

"Oh, well." She looked surprised but not upset by the question. "She's fourteen, and she's already making nests in her room and collecting practice packmates at school. I'm just thrilled, obviously."

I nodded. It seemed like everything thrilled Omega Cabot.

"You said you wanted to talk about Flora?"

"Um, yes." Now that I was here, I was nervous. I didn't know how to bring this up. "We were roommates."

"Oh, that's nice. I'm still in touch with my nestmate."

I noted the soft correction of my terminology, and my heart sank. "I was wondering if you could tell me where she is exactly?"

Her eyes widened. "With her alpha, of course."

"Um, yes, right. I meant do you have an address?"

"Oh!" She looked relieved. "For a mating gift?"

I smiled. "Exactly. I'm so sorry, I should have led with that."

She laughed. "Not at all, dear. I'm thrilled you're still in touch. I'll get her address. Wait here."

She stood and left the room, and I let out a long breath. So, Omega Cabot wasn't going to help. At least not on purpose, but she would give me the address. That was something.

I drummed my fingers on the table as I waited for her to return. How Flora came from a mother like this was anyone's guess. In an odd way, I wondered if this was the promise the Institute gave in action. Flora's mom looked happy enough. Or maybe she was brainwashed? I did some quick math—she'd been with her assigned alpha for at least twenty years. Maybe she'd just acclimated.

Or she's drugged, a little voice in my head whispered.

I hoped when I saw Flora again, she would be the same person I left.

"Got it!" Omega Cabot returned. "I'm sorry to leave you waiting so long."

"No problem." I smiled.

She placed a piece of paper in front of me with an address scribbled on it. I grabbed it quickly and shoved it into my plastic CVS bag.

"Thank you."

"Of course." She sat back down, looking at me shrewdly. A shiver traveled up my neck. That wasn't the expression of someone drugged. "Darling, where's your alpha?" Her eyes darted to my neck, for what I now realized was not the first time.

My blood ran cold. *Damn.*

I warred with myself, unsure if I should move my hair to cover my unbitten neck or if that was more suspicious. Mated omegas always showed off their marks.

"Um, not with me. I—"

"What?" She sounded genuinely alarmed. "Then your security?"

I closed my eyes, horrified. What was I thinking?

I stood abruptly from the table, reaching for my CVS bag. "You know what, yes. I need to get back to my security. I'm sure they're wondering what's taking so long."

Flora's mom stood, her expression kind. "Darling, I reached out to Headmistress Omega DuPont. Something is clearly wrong, but we can help."

I took two large steps toward the door. "No!"

She looked scandalized. "Bliss."

"I really need to go." I was fully aware that if she thought I was strange before, now she had to know something was going on. "Thank you for everything."

I bolted out the door and down the front walk, ignoring Flora's mother's voice calling after me. "If there's something wrong, Headmistress Omega DuPont is the best person to help."

My vision blurred with frustrated tears as I ran down the sidewalk. I had to go back to the warehouse. Now. The guys were right; I should have stayed inside.

At the end of the road, I turned the corner, catching sight of a black limo driving straight toward me. My instincts screamed to turn around and go back the other way, but it was too late. The car came to a smooth stop against the curb next to where I stood.

The back window of the car rolled down to reveal the passenger. My knees shook, blood pounding in my ears.

"Hello, Bliss."

CHAPTER 13
Nox

A res burst out of the back door of the warehouse into the bright light of the parking lot. "This is fucking bullshit."

We followed him to the other end of the lot in silence. I couldn't say I disagreed with that sentiment.

We'd all been tense since last night when Bliss brought up blockers, but there had been no opportunity to talk without the risk of her overhearing.

Ares punched the side of one of the crates. "I'm not fucking doing this again."

I glanced at Rafe, surprised he hadn't commented on the splintered wood. He wasn't looking at any of us.

"What? You're suggesting we just hand her over blockers and let her go?" Killian choked on the words. His curly brown hair, still wet from his shower, dampened the collar of his plaid shirt.

Ares' pale blue eyes flashed up to him, his jaw muscle

ticking in his cheek. "Yeah, that's exactly what I'm saying. She told us flat out that she didn't want to stay."

"Did she though? Or have you decided that for her?" Killian pushed his fist into his pants pockets and rocked back on his heels. "She's freaked-out. She's barely out of her heat, and the last time she's seen any of us was four years ago."

Ares snorted a derisive laugh. "Yeah, when we fucking abandoned her."

"And we're not making that mistake again," I barked, putting more power into my words than I would usually bother exerting.

Killian stepped between us, hands raised at our chest. "Chill. We've got her now, and she's better with us than that rich asshole, right?"

Ares glared at me, evidently deciding if he felt like getting into it. I doubted he would. Sure enough, he collapsed onto the curb and dropped his head into his hands, his white-blond hair tumbling over his face. He looked wrecked. "Is she though? If we're just going to lie to her?" He snapped his gaze up to Rafe. "You're the leader now, right? So, fucking lead. What do you think?"

Rafe rubbed the back of his neck. "I don't know…"

A low rumble poured from my chest. *Of all the moments to fall behind the eight ball.* "What the hell is that supposed to mean? We're not letting her go."

Rafe's black eyes met mine before looking back at Ares. His voice was firm, almost a command. "I'm not saying we let her go. I'm saying we need to make her want to stay. Prove we love her and want her here."

"Well, leave me the hell out of it." Ares unfolded

himself from the sidewalk and stormed back toward the warehouse.

"Where the hell are you going?" I shouted, incredulous. This whole thing was lunacy.

Ares didn't bother glancing back, instead flipping me off.

I rubbed my hand over my hair. "Kill, can you?"

Killian ran backward after Ares. "Yup. I'll get him. Meet you there."

I let out a breath, turning to Rafe, who was staring up at the sky, still avoiding eye contact.

"Fuck," he barked at nothing in particular.

I tugged on my earring. "If you're about to lose it too, I need a warning."

Rafe didn't respond to that, but he did look at me, which I took as a positive sign. "We don't have time for this. Harrison is going to lose his shit."

"Since when did we care about Harrison? Bliss is the top priority, always."

"Since we don't need the Institute sniffing around when we don't supply their shipment." Rafe hit out a message on his phone, and within moments, our van pulled up to the curb. "This is about Bliss, I'm trying to protect her and that starts with doing our job like normal."

I nodded. He was right, but I didn't have to like it.

Wes rolled down his window and winked at us. "What happened? Your boyfriends leave you?"

Rafe narrowed his eyes as the beta pulled his coat closed to the gusts of wind pouring off the water into the abandoned fish market. Harrison had been our contact for the Institute for years now. He was alright, but that didn't make us friends.

"Aren't you guys fucking cold?"

Rafe raised a brow. He was only dressed in a thin henley shirt and jeans. I rolled up my sleeve that had slipped. We didn't get cold; our bodies naturally ran at a higher temperature. "You know better than that."

Harrison shifted from foot to foot, glancing away before speaking to Rafe. "You're late on the shipment."

Rafe sat down on one of the product-filled crates. A low growl of warning not to ask for clarification reverberated through his words. "We were preoccupied. Do you want the product or not?"

I ran my knuckles over the small, tattooed stars on my arm visible below my rolled shirtsleeve. It had been hours since we'd left Bliss. I tugged on the bond lightly, and a hint of apprehension traveled back. I could only make out the strongest of her emotions. What was she up to?

Memories of her smooth skin in my hands, sweet slick in my mouth, and pleading moans in my ears had me leaning my weight into the stall's post. Never in a million fucking fantasies did I foresee how earth-shattering it would be to finally be with her. The bond that connected us all hummed as we took her. The only thing stopping it from being completely satisfied was we didn't mark her. Fuck, I wanted to. I even let my teeth graze over her neck a few times. Not when she was lost to her heat like that.

I could barely look at her while we were leaving. She was going to stay until we found her blockers? *Life's a fucking joke.*

Harrison threw up his arms, looking entirely too

comfortable considering who he was speaking to. "Of course I fucking do, but I have to answer to why it's late."

Rafe crowded him, placing a hand on his shoulder. "You'd think the take you skim off the top would make that worth it."

Harrison's face drained of color, and he shook for an entirely new reason.

I rubbed my chest as the bond tugged, and I tried to make out the sensation. The feeling of her was stronger now. I wasn't sure if that was because of our proximity or the heat. All I knew was I wanted to get home to see what the little wolf was up to.

Rafe's fingers dug into the beta's arm, and he visibly flinched. "I wouldn't suggest underestimating our intelligence again."

"No, never. I just didn't think…I just…"

I gave him a break. "The shipment's here. Pay up and get the fuck out."

Harrison pulled out his phone and hit a few buttons. Mine beeped, showing the transfer complete.

I nodded toward Rafe. "It's all here."

Harrison made a nondescript sound, drawing our attention. He looked between us, his fingers wringing in front of him. He spent extra time on Rafe before taking a step further. "You asked about one of the omegas before."

I stiffened, and the air filled with the scent of ginger. The beta couldn't smell emotion, but his instincts had him taking another step at the shift in atmosphere.

I relaxed my shoulders and forced myself into a casual stance. "We asked about a lot of omegas."

"I know… This one…this one…you asked about more than once."

I clenched my teeth as fear trickled down my spine. I thought we'd hidden our interest in Bliss.

A growl rippled from Rafe as he stalked toward Harrison. His muscles strained in his back and up the tendons in his neck. He looked like he wanted to murder the guy.

I ran my tongue over my teeth. Actually, might not be a bad idea.

"We wanted to know how the product worked on *every* omega for research." Rafe's words held a sharp edge of warning.

The beta nodded emphatically. "Yeah, of course, I know that, but..." He shifted again, and his throat bobbed with his swallow. "Even if you aren't interested in her...specifically. I thought you'd be interested to know an omega was kidnapped from her mate."

"He's not her mate." I grabbed the guy by his jacket and debated the merits of throwing him in the frigid water.

Harrison's pleading eyes shot to Rafe. "Of course, yeah, of course not. What I meant was that she was taken from the guy that won her auction."

Rafe took his time studying the beta. It was a risk to let him go after seeing our reactions to news about Bliss. He took a deep breath. "Nox, let him go."

My grip loosened on the beta, who took several more steps away from us and held his hands up. "Let's say you knew who took her. The guy. Nero. He's on a warpath to get her back." His eyes danced between us, and he paused a moment. "Whoever...whoever is responsible is at serious risk...and so is the omega."

My chest tightened at the thought of putting Bliss in

danger, but leaving her there wasn't an option. "I'm sure whoever it was can handle it."

"Nero's not taking it lightly since he technically owns the omega." His face paled further as a growl pulled from my chest. I was normally the smart, rational one, but this guy was on thin fucking ice. Harrison's brows pinched in the middle, and his shoulders slumped. "I just don't want to see anything happen to her."

Rafe shook his head. "If someone wanted to hide her, she wouldn't be found."

"You'd be surprised what resources a guy like Nero has." Harrison pointed toward a city security camera that we'd had turned away from the market. "He's got eyes everywhere."

Wes was waiting for us, propped on the hood of the van. He had a black wool beanie pulled low over his ears, and his dirty-blond hair curled from below it. He was as close to the size of an alpha that any beta could hope to be. He tossed the keys in the air and caught them with a smile. "'Bout fucking time. I'm freezing my ass off."

"Fucking beta. Get in the car." I slipped into the back while Rafe took the front passenger seat. It was late afternoon, and I was buzzing with anticipation to get back to Bliss. Even if she only let me stare from a distance. The corner of my mouth rose. We were a long way from being back to normal, but we were a hell of a lot closer than we had been. When the fog of heat broke, she'd been curled against Killian's chest. He'd looked at her with soft eyes as he trailed his fingers over her arm and took a shuddering breath as he kissed her hair. I thought I'd stop breathing just to keep her there. It had been too fucking long since I'd seen him like that.

The idea that we would hand over some blockers and she'd disappear on us was laughable. Maybe it made me an asshole, but I'd have no issue destroying every last bit of our supply to keep it away from her. Was it forced confinement? Yes. Did I give a shit? Not in the slightest.

My stomach lurched as Bliss' fear pierced the bond gripping my thoughts. Rafe made an incoherent sound from the front seat as I whipped around, trying to get a grip of what I was feeling. My heart felt like I was running for my life.

Ice filled my veins as I clicked the pieces together. "Bliss."

Rafe spun in his seat, black gaze on mine. "Where is she?"

She was at home. We'd left her at the warehouse. She was safe. Bliss' rising panic mixed with mine, belittling that idea. I whipped out my phone and pulled up the tracker that I'd put on hers. My knuckles paled as I gripped the screen. "She's in that neighborhood over off of Park Street."

The tires screeched on pavement as Wes cut the wheel hard to take the off-ramp.

Endless ringing filled the air as Rafe tried to call her. "Come on. Pick up. Pick up. Pick up."

My hands shook as I watched the blinking dot of her location on my phone. She was moving down a residential street and then took a sharp turn into someone's yard.

What are you doing, Little Wolf?

Killian's and Ares' voices shouted through the van's

speakers as I looked at the intersections and the grayed-out boxes denoting buildings in the app. We were close. A few streets away.

The pain from the bond increased as we got closer. It was a live wire of panic on the other end.

We're coming. We're coming.

CHAPTER 14
Bliss

"Hello, Bliss."

Alpha Nero and I stared at each other through the window of his black limousine. His lip curled into a smile as his piercing deep blue eyes raked over my body, lingering on my neck.

"How did you find me?" My voice came out surprisingly steady, considering my heart hammered so hard it was like it was trying to escape my chest.

He cocked his head to the side, as though mildly amused. "Come get in the car. We'll talk about it."

His voice was smooth like silk—more pleasant and persuasive than I remembered. Maybe he was making some effort not to scare me. It didn't matter; I wasn't falling for it.

I took a large step back and to the left, feet scraping against the pavement as I fumbled to find my footing. The car inched forward, making it clear that wherever I went, it would follow.

Alpha Nero smiled pleasantly. "Bliss. Don't make this more difficult than it already is." He said it like he was speaking to a misbehaving toddler.

A cold calm fell over my entire body. He was going to take me. He was going to put me in that car, and I'd never see my guys, or Flora, or the light of day again.

Or, I could run.

I stumbled backward, tripping over my first step as I tore down the sidewalk. The car followed. I couldn't stay on the street if I wanted to have any chance of losing them.

I dove right, crashing through someone's front hedge and onto a well-manicured lawn. The bushes tore at the skin of my bare legs and the hem of my sundress, but the pain barely registered. There was no world where I was stopping because of a minor scratch.

My sandal caught around my foot and tugged, pitching me forward. "Damn!"

I panted, reaching down and throwing my shoes off as I dashed through the yard and down a driveway, coming out the opposite side on another suburban street. I had somewhat of an advantage having grown up in this town, but I wasn't so naïve to assume that Nero wouldn't have some kind of high-tech GPS. He was probably swinging around the block right now, about to catch up.

The houses on this street were shabbier than the ones where Flora lived but still bigger than the one I'd grown up in with the guys. I ducked under the fence of a triple-decker home on the corner and paused to catch my breath.

I doubled over, my lungs burning with the effort of running, fear licking up my skin. I put my twisted CVS bag on the ground and pressed my palms to my eyes, willing myself to calm down.

Without warning, a surge of rage that didn't belong to me shot through my system. My eyes shot open, and I straightened, letting the adrenaline course through my body.

They knew. They knew, and they were coming.

Bolstered by that idea, I allowed myself to borrow their adrenaline. My body was exhausted, traumatized, and not built for this, but alphas had endless stores of energy. Whether they realized it or not, four alphas were currently shoving massive amounts of life-saving adrenaline at me down our bond.

I stepped out from behind the fence again and turned, trying to find my bearings. I needed to get back to the warehouse.

I ran toward what I hoped was the main road, breathing in time to my own feet hitting the pavement. I could do this. I could get back.

A van pulled out in front of me, and I screamed, dropping my bag.

The van doors opened, and Nox leapt out. I nearly choked on my relief. Or it might have been tears.

"Bliss?" Our bond hummed, we were so close.

"He—" My voice cracked. "He tried…tried to take me."

I hadn't realized I'd fallen to the ground until Nox landed on the ground next to me and pulled me into his lap. "Shhh, shh, it's okay. We've got you."

I shivered, digging my fingers into Nox's black vest. I was so cold.

A growl ripped through the air, and I felt Nox speak to

someone out of my line of sight. "You're going to scare her, asshole."

He was wrong.

I looked up at Rafe as he sat down beside us, putting a phone to his ear. I opened my mouth to tell him I actually wasn't afraid of the growling—it was biologically impossible—but it got caught in my throat somewhere.

"You left us," Nox muttered against my hair.

"I know," I said, feeling only slightly guilty.

"Why?" Rafe asked. The phone was still against his ear, and I guessed it was Killian and Ares listening on the other end.

"There was something I had to do."

"Can you hurry the fuck up?" Ares barked at Wes as we rolled to a complete halt at a stop sign and sat there for a full three seconds before continuing on. In the distance, the warehouse loomed on the horizon.

"And risk getting in an accident with her in the back and you four breathing down my neck?" The beta shivered. "No fucking way, man. You can threaten me all you want. I like my throat attached to my neck."

Ares went back to grinding his teeth, obviously undecided where to direct his aggression.

It had barely been over an hour since the guys had picked me up, but the tension was still so high in the van it felt like five minutes. Torn between wanting to get me right home and wanting everyone there to protect me, Rafe had decided to make Wes pick up Killian and Ares. The van now felt tight.

"What's in the bag?" Killian asked me with a smirk, seeming to want to break the tension.

I glanced down at my bedraggled white-and-red plastic bag. "Oh. Nothing really."

I pulled out my forgotten coffee and unscrewed the cap. I sniffed it as we pulled back into the warehouse parking lot. The sugary beverage was almost too sweet—beyond anything I'd had in years. I wrinkled my nose in distaste and took one tentative sip. My stomach immediately woke up, growling loud enough for everyone to hear.

"Did you eat anything since breakfast?" Rafe asked a little too intensely for such a benign question.

I shook my head, suddenly realizing how hungry I was.

"Fuck that. Come inside," Nox barked. "We'll make you something."

Wes raised his eyebrows at me in the rearview mirror, and I shrugged sheepishly. I didn't know what to say—they couldn't help it. I wasn't sure they knew they were doing anything strange.

The scent inside of the warehouse hit me like an oncoming train as we traipsed back inside. Oh God.

I pressed my thighs together, willing my heart rate to slow down. The pull to mate shouldn't be coming back this quickly, and certainly not after I'd just used all my energy and then some. If it was going to be like this every time I left and came back, I needed to stay inside until I left for good. I wasn't sure I'd ever get used to stewing in the scent of all four guys in such a concentrated area, but the cognitive dissonance of wanting nothing to do with them while my body was happier than it had been in years was infuriating.

"Why did you guys keep this place?" I asked, mostly to distract myself.

Killian reached out to take my bag and drink from me. "Would you believe we just liked it?"

I let half a smile cross my face. "Probably not. I remember what it looked like before."

Killian opened his mouth to answer, and Nox cut him off. "What if we tell you after you tell us where you went today?"

"Can I eat before the third degree?"

They all glanced at each other, now caught between the two sides of the most important alpha trait—protectiveness. I sighed, knowing I'd just trapped them in what could be their own personal trolley problem.

"Food first, then we talk," Rafe declared for everyone.

I waved a resigned hand. "Fine."

Nox opened the refrigerator and pulled out a package of steaks. "Do you eat meat?"

I nodded. "I didn't really have a choice about what I ate."

He furrowed his brow. "What do you mean?"

"Uh." I wished I hadn't spoken. "Omega diets are very controlled."

"Is there a reason for that?" Rafe questioned, rubbing the back of his neck. Like he was afraid they were going to poison me with a steak. He probably was worried about that—literally.

"If you need something else, tell us." His voice was a command, not quite a bark.

I sighed. "No. Steak is fine, I promise."

Rafe didn't look convinced, but he wisely dropped it. He crossed the room and grabbed the steaks from Nox, lightly brushing my arm with his as he went. I ignored the jolt of electricity that traveled through me. It wasn't anything—just our bond and instincts trying to force us together and the stress of the day. Probably.

———

After dinner, they all sat in the living room, staring at their respective phones. No one spoke. Not even Killian, who bounced his knee with anxiety, looking like he was struggling to contain himself.

"Are you usually this quiet?" I asked finally.

Nox looked up at me. "No."

I nodded. I suspected as much.

"Quiet seething?" I asked, trying and failing to make a joke. It was like I'd forgotten how to be funny—or maybe this just wasn't funny to begin with.

"Where did you go today?" Killian glanced up from his phone. "That's all we're trying to know, B."

I froze, and my heart beat a little faster. He hadn't barked at me, but it was hard to ignore any alpha when questioned, and ignoring my own alphas was almost physically impossible.

"It's really not that important," I tried.

Rafe growled in frustration but made no command. "It's fucking killing me that you don't trust us."

"I didn't say I don't trust you."

Nox rolled his eyes and for a second looked a lot like the kid I remembered growing up with. "Like we can't smell it."

"Maybe you're smelling how you don't trust each other anymore?"

There was a long silence. That touched a nerve.

In all honesty, I wasn't trying to goad them. Whatever was going on here had piqued my interest. They'd trusted each other implicitly as children, but you'd have to be blind not to see the cracks in the foundation now.

Killian massaged his temples, clearly upset by this whole interaction. "All we wanted to do is protect you, B."

"I know. I know you want that."

"Then what's the problem?" He looked so sad for a minute I felt guilty.

"It's that we have to want that," Ares said bitterly. "Right?"

I opened my mouth to disagree and closed it. He'd sort of hit the nail on the head.

Them just wanting to protect me wasn't enough to repair our broken friendship, because of course they wanted that. That was like saying they wanted to keep breathing. Still, maybe I wasn't putting enough value in the bond.

I wasn't doing myself any favors trying to do everything alone. If today had proved anything, an unmated omega working independently wasn't going to get far. That was just the way of the world.

They had saved me twice now, and we did have a shared history, even if it had been overshadowed by their abandonment. Maybe I could give them an inch, if only because I wasn't going to be able to find Flora alone. If it didn't work out, I'd be no worse off than I was now.

I took a deep breath. "Do you remember Flora Cabot? From high school?"

All four guys looked up at me in surprise.

"Yeah. We saw her at the gala." Killian leaned over the chair, his curls flopping in his face. "Why?"

I swallowed thickly. So, they'd seen her.

If I'd brought this up sooner, would they have known where she was? Could we have found her already? "She's my best friend."

Nox gave me an incredulous look. "No."

"What?" I snapped indignantly. I clamped my mouth shut. "Sorry."

Killian's grin was mischievous. "Why are you sorry?"

I shook my head. "Nothing." They didn't need an explanation about how I wasn't allowed to raise my voice for the last four years.

Killian tilted his head to the side. "You hated Flora."

I grinned in spite of myself. It was so childish, I'd completely forgotten.

Flora was the only potential omega at our school growing up, which had felt very important to me, with four alpha best friends I was not-so-secretly in love with. If I'd realized at the time that she could never go near them anyway and that being an omega wasn't exactly winning the lottery, she wouldn't have bothered me so much.

Pain lanced through my chest at the thought of sitting in our room, laughing over the whole thing. We might never laugh like that again. The smile slid off my face. "Oh. Right, well, not anymore."

It was impossible that they didn't see my inconsistent reactions or at least smell them, but no one commented. Rafe crossed his arms over his broad chest. "What about her?"

"I went to see her mom today."

The collective feeling in the room shifted, becoming

more tense. "Why?" Killian asked, leaning forward in his chair as though to hear me better.

"I need to find her. I got her address and the name of her mate."

Nox ran a hand over the back of his neck. "Find her for what?"

I blinked incredulously. How were they not getting this? "Because she's my friend, and she's been forced to mate with some perverted old alpha. I need to help her."

They glanced at each other, and once again, silence stretched in the room.

"What do you mean 'forced'?" Killian asked.

I stared at him blankly. "All matings are forced...I feel like we're not on the same page, and I don't know why."

"Do the omegas not get some say in who they end up with?" Nox asked incredulously.

"What? No. Of course not. We're all drugged—when would we have a say?"

"What the fuck are you talking about?" Ares ground out.

"Weren't you guys all at the Agora? I assumed you knew."

My mind spun. This was too confusing—I didn't know how to go about explaining an entire subculture from scratch. What did they know? What were they missing?

"The Institute's designed to create perfect omegas. They controlled what we ate, said, did. All to make our alphas happy. The Institute teaches omegas exist to please their alphas. Not the other way around."

"Bliss," Rafe said slowly. "That's awful, and I'm so sorry, but if Flora's mated now, she might not want help."

My heart sank. Maybe. That was something that hadn't occurred to me, but they didn't know Flora like I did. They didn't know how against the system she was or how she hated the Institute. They didn't know how she'd refused her blockers for months and would have never allowed herself to be drugged before her heat. At least, not willingly.

"No," I said firmly. "I need to check. I just have to."

Rafe didn't react. He was the leader now, and Nox and Killian seemed to be waiting for his opinion. I didn't have the patience to wait.

Instead, my eyes found Ares' intense stare. He hovered several feet from everyone else toward the back of the room. To my surprise, he hadn't said much. Of the four of them, Ares had clearly become the wild card over the years. He raised an eyebrow at me. "I'm in."

"You're in for what?" Rafe barked, his posture going rigid.

Ares ran a thumb over his bottom lip, not taking his eyes off me. "Fuck it. Let's go get Flora."

My stomach leapt with excitement, and it must have shown on my face because Rafe growled at Ares.

"You can't do that. You can't suddenly decide you want to be a real part of this again. "

I narrowed my eyes, confused. I had no idea what he meant by "a real part of this," but the tension in the room was suffocating.

"And you're talking about her like she isn't here." Ares smirked at me. "You like when he does that, Love?"

"Alright, enough," Killian barked. "You two, cut the shit."

"Of course, you want to go after Flora," Nox muttered,

obviously not fully listening to the argument. "At least say what you mean, Ares."

Ares grinned at Nox, running his tongue over his teeth like this whole thing was a joke to him. "Yeah? What do I mean?"

"This is too dangerous, and you know it. You don't care about Bliss' friend. This is just another suicide mission."

"Or maybe I'm just not interested in pretending everything's fine like you three assholes." His statement sounded casual, but his posture and vibes were anything but.

Rafe stood, hands balled into fists. "Meaning what?"

Ares gave a derisive laugh and raised his arms and gestured around the room. "Is this how you pictured your happy family reunion? Get your head out of your ass." Sarcasm laced his words as he turned around, walking in the direction of what I now knew to be the roof. "I'm done with this. Come find me if we're going after Flora or something interesting happens. I won't hold my breath."

The door slammed, and I took a few labored breaths. I felt like I'd just run a mile when I hadn't moved an inch.

When we were kids, Ares was always the de facto leader. He was the oldest by a few months, and as children, that had meant something—especially when he could use his alpha bark before anyone else and spent most of his time compelling the others to stand on one leg or other stupid shit. The Ares I remembered would have insisted I stay safe. He would have taken charge of the situation. This was not the same man. "What happened to him?"

Rafe ran one hand through his coal-black hair. "You happened."

My eyes narrowed. "Excuse me?"

"He's never been normal again after what…" He seemed to struggle for words. "What we did. I'm not sure if it's possible to go back to before."

I sighed. Wasn't that the truth. There was no way to erase the last four years, for any of us.

———

I sat behind tempered glass.

The bright lights of the stage blinded me, the heat of them beating down on my face and scorching my skin. My hair clung to the back of my neck, sweat pooling at my nape and trickling down the back of my too-tight sequined dress.

I squinted out into the crowd, searching for a familiar face amongst the sea of strangers. The scent of all the alphas was overwhelming—musky and sharp inside my nose and on my tongue.

"And now," the announcer said, "lot number fourteen."

My breath came faster, and my gown pinched, holding me too tight. I couldn't breathe. I needed to get out of here.

"Omega Bliss is twenty-one years old from Stratford, New Jersey. She received top marks in all her etiquette and carnal lessons and enjoys gardening in her spare time. Her measurements are…"

I sucked in a deep breath and choked on the scent of testosterone as I tried to tune the announcer out. I couldn't listen to this. I couldn't be here.

I had to get out.

I looked down at the floor, and it swam, my head spinning. The glass walls of the box appeared seamless, like it was somehow one solid piece. There was no door. No exit. How was that possible? Someone had brought me in here. But when?

A familiar scent fought its way through the melee, finding me. Like home—coffee, peppers, lemon, and the fresh scent of the night sky. I whipped my head up, searching for it.

"Let's begin the bidding at one million dollars. Do I hear—"

"One million."

"Thank you, one million."

"One point five."

"I hear one point five, do I hear two—"

"Three million."

"Thank you, gentlemen. I hear three million, do I hear five?"

I ignored the voices, searching the room desperately for the smell. My body tipped forward, practically of its own accord, until my nose was almost pressed to the glass.

"Looks like someone is eager to meet her alpha! We've got a live one, gentlemen—you don't want to miss out on that heat. Do I hear twenty million?"

"Bliss! Wake up!"

I scanned the crowd, trying to focus on every face.

My heart pounded wildly when I saw them—they were there, all of them, dressed in tuxedos, laughing together.

"I'm here!" I waved. "Hey!"

They didn't look at me.

"Do I hear fifty million?"

"One hundred million," a voice spoke loudly from the table in the front.

My gaze snapped to Alpha Nero, now somehow clearly visible, while everyone else was still hard to see against the lights. He leaned over and spoke to a man next to him.

My foster father, Mr. Ward, shook hands with Alpha Nero and smiled up at me. "We're going to share her."

Someone shook my shoulder. "Bliss!"

I cracked open an eyelid and stared up into a familiar face.

Rafe leaned over me, hands on either side of my head. My face, sleepy and confused, was reflected back in his black, pupilless eyes. "You screamed."

"Huh?"

Tremors rocked my body, and I shook my head as if to clear it. The last fragments of the dream fell away. I had no idea what I was afraid of, but my heart wouldn't slow down. My breathing wouldn't slow.

"You still have nightmares," Rafe stated.

I shook my head again, then realized that was dumb given the circumstances. "Sometimes," I amended.

I'd had nightmares my entire childhood and well into my high school years. It was impossible to go a single night without waking up trapped in my own body or feeling stuck in some imagined hellscape.

Since we lived at the foster home, screaming all night wasn't exactly making me any friends. My roommates were rightly annoyed, and our foster parents had no time for "troublemakers." Eventually, the guys started sleeping in my room in shifts, and the nightmares went away.

After I moved to the Institute, they'd stopped for the most part. I'd privately wondered if it was because no matter how much I wished otherwise, I was never really alone. One small silver lining.

My brain quickly caught up with the situation. "I'm fine. It was nothing."

The scent of ammonia hit us both at once, and he wrinkled his nose.

"You always did that, you know," he muttered. "Lied about how it was nothing."

I snorted a laugh, and a tiny bit of the residual fear floated from my body. "Someone should have told me what it smelled like."

"And clue you in on our best superpower? No fucking way."

He smiled, and for half a second, everything was normal. This wasn't my alpha, and I wasn't an omega. It was just Rafe. We were seventeen again, and he was sneaking into my room because I'd had a nightmare. Perfect.

Heat coated my skin, and my stomach clenched. I squirmed. Despite the absurdity of the situation, my body was still very aware of the alpha—my alpha—on top of me. Maybe this was a dream too.

Rafe jerked and leaned back, clearly realizing he was still hovering over me, trapping me against the mattress with both arms. "What was it about?"

I felt my cheeks heat—this time from embarrassment rather than arousal. I was ninety-nine percent sure that he'd only realized the implication of his position after scenting my arousal. "I don't really remember."

"Okay..." He stood up, now looming over me next to the bed.

I tilted my head back to keep him in view. "Well, thanks, I guess. For waking me up."

"Yeah." He ran a hand over the back of his neck. "Is this about Flora? Your dream?"

"Oh. I don't know, maybe a bit."

In actuality, my nightmares rarely made much sense,

but I supposed it was possible I was thinking of Flora generally. The stress could be compounding.

He took a breath through his nose, as if steeling himself. "Okay. Fine."

I narrowed my eyes in confusion, squinting against the semi-darkness. "'Okay, fine,' what? What does that mean?"

He crossed the room, putting his hand on the doorknob. "We can go try to find her. I still think it's dangerous, and we have an order coming in the next few days we need to hang around town and finish first, but if you know where she is, we can at least go check it out."

My chest swelled, genuine gratitude filling me for the first time in living memory. I smiled. "Thank you."

A few days wasn't perfect, but it wasn't that long. Flora was strong—I had to believe she could hold on that long.

He coughed. "Sure. Well, good night."

My heart beat faster, my brain warring with my body. "Wait," I blurted out. "Please."

Rafe stopped short in the doorway and turned back to me. The light from the hall caught the edge of his sharp jaw and reflected off his hair, giving him the look of a bronze statue. "What's up?"

"Stay."

CHAPTER 15
Killian

I cracked my neck as I made my way down to the kitchen. Still exhausted, I didn't bother throwing anything on besides a pair of gym shorts. I swore I'd never been as tense as I was last night. I woke up in panic when Bliss' nightmare kicked in. Fuck. I would've killed to crawl up next to her like I used to, but God knew she'd hate that.

There were a few times in the last four years her fear had me bouncing from bed in the middle of the night, pacing at the fucking helplessness of not being able to be there for her. Knowing goddamn well how bad her dreams were. Which just made last night a million times worse because I *could* go to her, but I was terrified.

I'd just given up on all hope of controlling myself when her fear stopped. Relief flooded through me when I met calmness at the end of our bond. I should've been jealous that one of the guys must've grown the pair that I couldn't and gone to her, but all I could do was be grateful that someone did.

I couldn't stand another second of her feeling that way, and if the only way to stop it was for us to go lie with her like we did as kids, then so fucking be it. She'd just have to accept that.

I rubbed my hands over my face and tried not to walk into anything as the light from early morning barely lit the kitchen and living room areas. It was late for the others to still be asleep, but there was no way the others could've slept through her nightmares.

Even the idea of sleeping made me twitch. I put a pod into Nox's fancy-as-fuck coffee maker and hit the Start button. I grabbed a bowl bigger than my head and a spoon before sitting down on one of the island stalls to dig into my cereal.

I'd just finished tipping the bowl to get the last of the now cereal-flavored milk when Rafe walked in. His workout shorts hung low, and his black hair dripped in strands where he'd pushed it off his face. My gaze followed a drip down his shoulder, along his pec, and down his abs. The bowl clicked on the table when I absent-mindedly put it down too hard, but *damn*.

Rafe's gaze met mine, his black eyes shadowed by thick lashes. The intensity sucked the air from the room before he cleared his throat and turned his back to me, grabbing a sports drink from the fridge.

I took advantage of his distraction to adjust myself in my seat. I hadn't been so much as horny since we'd lost Bliss. There was something that always felt like I would betray her if I looked at anyone else. Clearly, that'd changed since her heat, because if Rafe had looked at me much longer, I'd have been on my knees convincing him of all the reasons acting like a real pack was a good fucking idea.

I choked on a cough as realization hit me: we were the only ones up. He…

Defined lines formed on Rafe's back as he tensed. He let out a breath, and his fist clenched at his sides as he turned to face me. "Just ask."

"So, you're the lucky bastard who went to Bliss last night?" I tilted my head to the side and took in his features. He looked rested, a pink tinge to his face that I doubted was from his workout. A million questions flew through my head. Did she touch him? Did they cuddle? Did she still do that thing where she nuzzled into your chest while gripping you so tight, you'd never be able to let go?

He brushed the strands of his black hair off his face. "Yes."

My mouth dried as I pictured them together, and then the tip of my lips tipped up. "Was she everything you remembered?"

He stared at the floor before his own sheepish grin tilted his mouth. "More."

"Wait, you didn't do anything, did you, right?"

"I'm choosing to ignore that." Rafe took another sip of his drink and wiped his mouth with the back of his hand. "She was scared."

An eagerness bubbled up my chest at the idea of it being my turn to comfort her. I wasn't ashamed to say I'd spent more than my share of nights trying damn hard to imagine her beside me. Sometimes, when I was just waking up, I would swear she was there. All that came of it was a bone-deep ache that she wasn't really there. I didn't give a shit what she needed me to do to earn her back her trust. I'd do anything.

Crawl through glass? Done.

Apologize every day for the rest of my life? No problem.

Buy her anything she wanted? A pleasure.

Spend every second reminding her how precious she was to me? A fucking honor.

Now I just had to do all that without scaring her off.

Rafe tossed his bottle in the recycling bin. "You'll be the first to stay home with Bliss. We're going to meet up with Harrison. See if he can get us any information on Flora."

I was up and out of my chair with such speed, my empty bowl tipped over. Spending the day *alone* with Bliss. Well, fuck. "The guys are going to be pissed."

"Don't rub it in their faces, and you'll be fine."

I huffed out a breath. "Wasn't worried."

"Out of all of us, you're the least…intimidating. We need her to settle in. We can't have a repeat of yesterday, and that requires her to trust us with finding her friend."

"Don't worry, I'll keep her happy." My tone didn't match my words as thoughts of yesterday crept in. I hadn't been there when the guys found Bliss, but I'd felt her through the bond. She'd been terrified. The only thing that stopped Ares and me from going after the asshole was the overriding instinct to take care of Bliss. She needed us with her, even if she didn't know it.

The absolute need in her voice when she asked us to get Flora had me dying to help. Even though I didn't understand. Mated omegas were happy omegas. There was something she wasn't telling us about the Institute.

Didn't matter—I didn't need to understand. She'd asked, so we'd do it.

She was stuck with me now, and I wasn't leaving her for any bullshit excuse.

―――

I pulled my hand from my pocket and hesitated before knocking on Bliss' bedroom door. I'd been in the hall the last five minutes but hadn't built up the courage to actually knock. I didn't know what I would do if she shut it in my face. It'd pissed me off when she'd told us about Flora, imagining the same thing happening to Bliss. We'd been damn close to that asshole, Nero, mating her.

I dropped my forehead to her door and took a deep breath.

Keep it together, Kill.

The guys had left more than an hour ago, and Bliss still hadn't woken up. The need to check her room for threats had been riding me all morning. Protectiveness was a part of being an alpha, but I didn't think Bliss would appreciate me going in there and doing a security check. Plus, the warehouse was on complete lockdown after her taking off yesterday. We'd installed systems that were hooked up to our phones. If one of her windows even cracked open, we'd know about it.

Which left her not wanting to come out.

My ribs tightened over my chest. In theory, I knew she was just getting used to the idea of being here, but I'd been picturing her here for the last four years. Everything finally felt like it was clicking into place. Sure, we had our issues, but I knew deep down she'd forgive us. She had to. Right?

Then why can't you knock on the damn door, Killian?

Shit. I sucked in a deep breath and was caught off guard by her sweet and spicy scent. Distracted, I nearly crashed forward when her door swung open.

"Hi." Bliss stood in front of me, brow raised over violet doe eyes. She didn't seem at all surprised to see me.

I froze. Her head tilted all the way back, exposing the soft column of her neck, and my teeth ached to graze over her mating glands. She looked perfect, fresh-faced, rosy like she'd just washed it, and she pulled her hair over her opposite shoulder.

I reached out and slid a strand of pastel purple through my fingers, careful not to touch her skin, and smirked at her gasp. I met her gaze, stunned. "You dyed it back?"

Her eyes darted around the space, anywhere but on me. "Yeah, I thought... I wanted to feel more like me."

My fingers itched at my sides, wanting nothing more than to slide my hand up her neck and bring her gaze back to mine. As if sensing me, she raised her face until she met my eyes, and I locked down the urge to growl when she exposed her neck more. "You look perfect. Fucking perfect, Bliss."

Her cheeks pinkened, and I followed the flush down her chest and over the swell of her pale breast. I swallowed hard at the curve of her hips and the softness of her stomach. Fuck.

Flashes from the heat had me gripping the doorframe to stay standing. The way her hips filled my large hands like she was fucking meant for me, or how they gripped the side of my head as I tasted—

A soft whine had my eyes darting back to hers, and a sheepish smile lifted my lips. The further away we got from her heat, the more her instincts were driving her to be with her mates. Her blush had taken over her face. She was practically crimson she was so red.

Her eyes narrowed, catching on my mouth. "What are you doing here?"

"It's just you and me, babe." The nickname slipped out of my mouth so easily it had me reaching to take it back, but fuck it. I'd been dying to call her that.

She shifted closer to me before pulling herself back, eyes flashing. "And where is everyone else?"

"Hunting for your friend, of course."

She sucked in a breath, eyes round, and I had to reach out a hand to steady her. The only thing distracting me from her touch was the shock on her face.

"We'll always do whatever will make you happy. We have a long time to make up for."

The air grew thick around us as we stared, trying to figure each other out. She wasn't the same Bliss we'd lost. There was something almost broken in her eyes that had me crowing to kill whoever put it there. The fact that it was us just made the need to fight all the stronger.

I stepped back into the hall, making space for her before I could do something stupid like get on the floor and beg her to forgive us. Although, I would if I thought for a second it would work.

"You hungry? Rafe made you pancakes before he left." Her stomach made a small rumble, and I smirked. "It'll be cold now, but I can warm it up for you. We even have that Quebec maple syrup we used to steal for you."

"You never told me you stole it."

I huffed out a laugh. "Well, we sure weren't buying it."

"I thought you were trading for it or something."

"It's like twenty bucks a bottle."

"Are you kidding me, Kill? I used to drench my pancakes." I felt a warm hum through the bond, and a sweet fruity scent tickled my nose. "We could've bought so many things with that. You guys are crazy."

My grin widened to a full smile, splitting my face. I didn't think she even noticed the use of my nickname. "We coulda, but I think I can speak for all of us when I say that the joy it brought you made it totally worth it. Plus, it always dripped down your lip and had my cock—"

The back of her hand smacked against my stomach, and I blew out a breath. "What? We were teenage boys."

"And I was practically your sister."

"No, you weren't, and you knew it."

"Whatever." She walked past me down the hall toward the kitchen. "Where is this pancakes you promised?"

Watching Bliss eat had my alpha instincts humming. I was naturally programmed to want to take care of my omega, but everything was more intense because it was her. I'd set her up on the island and leaned across from her, both hands planted on the counter. She didn't notice she preened under my full attention.

I laughed as Bliss shoved a fourth piece of pancake in her mouth in the last 2.5 seconds. She hummed around her food. "I freaking missed these."

She hadn't spoken about her time there, but whenever we brought it up, her scent soured. Right now, she was happily distracted by her maple syrup. She'd tied her long, now fully purple hair back and leaned over her plate, giving me a perfect view down her blue dress. It was made of a stretchy soft fabric that molded to each of her curves. The last time we'd seen her, she'd been rail thin, bones practically sticking out. The Bliss sitting in front of me looked like a siren, soft, supple. I wanted to mark every inch of her pretty pale skin.

I smelled a hint of jasmine, honey, and spice and looked over her flushed face. The three freckles to the left of her right eye, the natural pink tint to her lips, and the subtle violet color of her eyes had me sucked into the past. I pushed down a growl when her tongue cleaned syrup off her bottom lip. "You don't have to worry about that anymore. Rafe will make them for you every morning, noon, and night. All you have to do is ask."

She hummed as she took the last bite. "I'll be taking him up on that."

I knew he'd fucking love it.

She got up and reached for her dirty plate. I swiped it from her hands, tucking it into the dishwasher. The instinct to take care of her was still riding me hard.

Her eyes warmed as I handed her a freshly made coffee. "I left it black. You made a face when you drank the last one. I can make you a new one if you don't like it."

She took a sip, and I swore she purred as she took another. It took effort not to wrap her in my arms and taste the liquid on her lips. I cleared my throat. "So… I was thinking about giving you a tour of the warehouse, right?"

"It's about time."

I gestured to the door that led downstairs. "Well, you've seen the entire upstairs. Not much to go over up here."

Bliss passed me, and the bottom of her skirt skimmed my arm, and my skin broke out in goose bumps. I didn't want her to think I thought of her as an object, but damn did my body react to her, unable to resist touching her. She startled but didn't move away when I placed my hand on the small of her back, guiding her. Warmth flooded through me at her acceptance of my touch. I was going to wear down her walls one at a time. I wasn't great at patience, but I'd do whatever she needed. It helped that I was cocky enough now that we knew she wouldn't just take off, that she'd eventually forgive me for my part in letting her go to the Institute.

It helped that I had absolutely no shame in groveling and admitting how fucking wrong we were. Our instant regret, mixed with the inability to get her back, took a toll on all of us.

The warehouse was large, but there wasn't a whole lot to show. Her nose had scrunched up when I pointed out the boxing mats, and she didn't seem at all interested in the gym.

I brought her to the back of the building. The tall bay door was already open, letting in a soft breeze, and pointed to the small attached building. "Wes lives here. He can be a lot, but he means well."

A grin spread over her face. "*He* can be a lot to take in?"

"Hey now. I'm the epitome of calm and collected."

She laughed and spun around in the open space. "So, what's in the crates?"

My stomach dropped, and I looked away from her, not quite ready to fess up to what we'd done to get her back. "We aren't good people, Bliss."

"Don't keep secrets from me. I don't think I could take it."

I nodded, still looking at the ground. "What if I promise to tell you, just not yet?" I met her gaze, eyes pleading.

She took a deep breath, body relaxing, and tilted her head. "You aren't hiding bodies in there?"

I smirked back, grateful that she was willing to give me this reprieve. "I promise, we aren't hurting anyone."

"Okay, but you will need to tell me. I can't wait forever."

I swallowed and sucked in my bottom lip. "I know."

I flipped on an old movie, not that I paid any attention to it. She'd curled her legs under her, revealing a few more inches of her thighs. The girl would be the death of me.

Rafe, Nox, and Ares walked through the front door, and a small part of me ached knowing our time alone was ending. Only offset by the smile, she tried to hide from them.

She didn't know it yet, but she was already hooked.

Ares froze when his gaze locked on her, but he stumbled forward as if an invisible rope was pulling him. Bliss tugged on her hair, and I could feel her anxiety through the bond. I wanted to scream at Ares for making her doubt him. He needed to get over himself. We were all afraid we weren't good enough, but you didn't see the rest of us acting like assholes. If he didn't smarten the fuck up soon, I would make him.

My brows raised as he grabbed a bottle of water from the fridge and tucked himself into the corner, away from Rafe and Nox. Ares watched Bliss with soft eyes while she pummeled Rafe and Nox with questions about Flora.

A part of me wished she'd turn to Ares, that she could see the way he watched her like she was everything he needed. He wasn't as immune to the pull as he wanted us all to believe. Ares' gaze flashed to mine, and his jaw clenched. "I'm out of here."

The hurt I felt through the bond had me pushing down the urge to tackle him, but even I knew he had to come to terms with this on his own. I just hoped he wasn't too late when he did.

We only had one shot at winning her back, and he was royally fucking his up.

CHAPTER 16
Ares

I growled in frustration as I scrubbed the eraser over the page for the millionth time. I had locked myself in my room and was working on old drawings since I realized I didn't capture her right. There were countless drawings that needed work; the lines were too angular. They didn't have the soft feminine curves they needed. I sat at my small worktable, which was covered in an assortment of pencils and pens.

It had been over a week since we'd taken Bliss from her designated alpha, and it felt like I was going to go insane. When she asked us to get Flora back—a mated fucking omega—I realized just how wrong I'd been. The idea that a mated omega would choose to be away from her mate went against every instinct I had. Were there others out there confined by the alphas who fucking bet on them? Acid burned the back of my throat at the very idea of what that meant.

Now that we'd taken Bliss, were we any better than

them? She didn't choose this. She wasn't asking us to mate. No, she was adamant about getting her friend back, then planned to leave.

My breath came out on a shudder, and my hand twitched on the page, ruining the lines I'd just perfected. Bliss was an unmated omega; she'd be naturally drawn to any alpha in any situation. *But we're different. We're bonded.*

We had days, maybe hours before her instincts kicked in and she started craving us again, but it wouldn't be real. I'd betrayed her and didn't deserve to mate her in the first place, and I wouldn't do it now that she was being coerced by her own instincts. She told us flat out that it was best for Flora to be separated from her mate even if she wouldn't be able to understand that now that he'd bitten her.

Rafe, Nox, and Killian looked at Bliss with eagerness, like if they just waited her out, she'd come back to them. The truth was, she would come back, but it would be because of the bond and her instincts. Not because she accepted the reasons behind the bullshit we'd pulled when she transitioned.

I'd spent every second since the Institute drove her away wishing I'd listened to my gut and told the guys to screw off when they'd suggested it. Now it was too late, and the only thing I cared about was her happiness. Even if that meant helping her get away from us.

I fought down the growl that wanted to work its way out of my throat. It damn well may kill us to lose her again. Hell, the guys would definitely kill me for my part in it, but it wasn't up to us to make this decision for her.

It wasn't safe for an unmated omega to be on her own, especially accompanied by another omega, but we'd taken away her choice the last time. We'd decided what was best for her, and we'd been wrong. Unbelievably wrong.

We may have spent the time pining for her, but the glimpses she'd given us of the Institute made me want to vomit. Bliss had been a splash of joy in our lives growing up, completely oblivious to the fact that we were all madly in love with her. She was a free spirit none of us would ever try to control. At least that's what I had thought—turned out we'd been more than willing to control her. The Institute controlled every minute of her life, trying to snuff out all the things that made her *her*.

We'd done that to her.

I threw my pencil across the room, and it splintered against the wall.

I had to convince Rafe to get back into the ring before I broke something. Fighting was the only place I could get this roiling energy out of me.

Someone knocked on my door, and the knob shifted as they tried to open it. "Let us in, Ares." The force of Rafe's alpha bark bounced off me. He may be our pseudo leader, but he wasn't stronger than the rest of us.

"Fuck off, Rafe." I turned the music up, drowning them out, but the poor door didn't stand a chance.

Within seconds, Killian had the door off its hinges, placing it to the side of Nox. The three of them entered my room, eyes darting over my walls.

Rafe's fingers grazed over a drawing I'd done of Bliss last year. "Jesus, Ares. If you care for her this much, why the hell do you push her away?"

A growl pushed up my chest. "It's because of that, idiot."

I looked over my once best friends. There was a rift

between us so wide, we'd never be able to cross it. There were a few times over the years when Killian and Nox would worm their way back in, but I could never forget that they'd played their part in that night too. At least they'd regretted it just as much as me. Killian still held the weight of being the one to command her to leave.

Rafe though. I'd never forgive him for the part he'd played in convincing me to go along with it. I knew I made my own decisions and couldn't blame it all on him, but that didn't stop me from hating him. "What do you want?"

Rafe's eyes narrowed at my tone, but he straightened, his black gaze boring into mine, a command in his tone. "You'll be staying with Bliss today."

A jolt ran through me, and my hands fisted the table. "Who the fuck's idea was that?"

Rafe ignored my question. "The Institute has called us in for a meeting."

I raised a brow. "So? They want more supply?"

Nox stepped forward into my line of sight. His voice was low, and the air was coated with the smell of dead flowers. "A meeting about a missing omega."

"Fuck." I raked the loose strands of my hair from my face, looking between them. "That doesn't stop *you* from staying."

"They want to see all of us." Killian's smirk grew. "Well, except you. They see you as a wild card."

I rubbed my palms over my face and tried to calm my raging heart.

"You don't have to hang out with her. We just needed someone home. You know, in case someone breaks in or, more likely, she tries to take off again."

My chest vibrated with my suppressed growl. "She's smarter than that."

"Then you won't have any problems watching her."

My hands shook as I pictured someone breaking into the warehouse and Bliss calling out to us when we weren't here.

"Fine."

The three of them looked at me in surprise, clearly expecting a bigger fight. No matter what I projected, Bliss was the only thing that mattered. If that meant a day of being uncomfortable, so be it. I'd just have to hide out.

———

Sweat dripped into my eyes. I grabbed the white towel off the mat and ran it over my face. I'd been at this for hours. The ache in my arms and back helped mask the bond between us. I'd felt her curiosity as she explored the warehouse by herself. Over the last hour, there was a loneliness that traveled through it, damn near close to sadness. I had to tamp down my instincts that screamed at me to go to her. It wasn't me she wanted to see though. They'd be back soon enough; a few more hours and we'd go back to normal.

I slammed my unwrapped fist into the beat-up black punching bag. We had to replace them every other month —they weren't designed to take the abuse four alphas would put on it. I smirked as the sting of pain traveled up my fist into my forearm. Pain had been an addiction for me the past years. A way to distract me from everything else.

"What are you doing to yourself?" My head swirled, and I placed my hand on the bag to help steady myself as I breathed in the full force of Bliss' scent. It was coming in stronger the more time that passed since her heat. Her eyes were round, and she bit her bottom lip as her gaze traveled over me, catching on the blood covering my knuckles. She sucked in a breath, and her eyes turned glassy.

The bond screamed with her worry for me, and I tried to calm myself to send it to her. I wrapped the damp towel around my fist, hiding the evidence. "You shouldn't be here."

Hurt flashed through the bond, and it pained me not to take it back.

"I could feel your pain."

"I'm sorry. I'll stop."

Her head tilted to the side. "It was more than just physical pain. You're hurting."

A cynical smile curved my mouth. "Don't worry. I'll keep it to myself."

"No."

My eyes flashed to hers. She looked worried as she walked onto the mat and stood directly in front of me. "What's wrong?"

I huffed out a laugh and pinched the bridge of my nose between two fingers. "Nothing you can help with."

She visibly flinched, building that wall between us. That's a good girl. I didn't deserve a second of her pity. "Well, if I'm going to feel it, the least you could do is let me help."

I let out a breath, my shoulder slumping forward as I met her eyes. "You can't help with this, Bliss. It's not your problem to fix."

Anger flashed through the bond, and it mixed with the

scent of dead flowers as she struggled to sort me out. I didn't want her to figure it out. I had too many secrets.

That I wanted her more than the others, that it physically killed me to stay away from her. That I'd give her absolutely anything to make her happy. Which was exactly why I was staying the fuck away, because no matter how much I wanted to be the one for her, I could never make up for what we did. The trust we broke. She deserved the absolute best, and in the last four years, I'd just become worse. Bliss watched me, her face hardening. "I hope you aren't making decisions for me again. That didn't work out too well for us the last time."

The difference was this time, I knew her staying away from me was the best thing for her. I wasn't the alpha she'd known growing up. I'd turned myself into something I'd never ask her to love. Something damaged.

I picked up my water and took a long sip.

"I don't want you here." *Lie.*

Her nose scrunched up.

"You shouldn't be here." *Truth.*

She placed her hands on her hips, reminding me of the Bliss I used to know. "It's a good thing you don't control where I can and can't be."

Giving up, I softened my tone. "Have you eaten yet?"

"Yes. The alpha obsession with feeding me is getting old."

I clenched my jaw against arguing with her. There was no turning off our instincts to care for her. It was only made stronger by her near miss the other day. Even the thought of Nero getting to her had my blood boiling.

She crossed her arms in front of her. "I need to know how to defend myself if I'm caught."

"Didn't they teach you anything useful?"

"An omega's job is to be docile and listen to their alpha."

"Fuck that place."

Her violet eyes searched mine. "I need your help."

I tipped my head back, looking at the roof. An alpha couldn't just turn down a request from their omega, and even if I couldn't have her, she was still mine. "Ask one of the other guys."

She wrung her hands in front of her, staring at the floor before meeting my gaze head-on. "I'm asking you."

A growl rumbled through my chest, cutting off when she took a step back. Fuck. She had to know no matter what, I'd never hurt her.

She swallowed, highlighting her delicate neck. "Please."

Any willpower I had crumbled with that word. "You can't fight off an alpha. You just can't."

She bit her lip, nodding as she looked around the warehouse, disappointment trickling through the bond.

"I'll teach you how to break a hold. You can run, Bliss. Just get away and run."

Her posture straightened. "I can do that."

"I'm going to have to touch you." I didn't know which one of us I was warning more.

One side of her mouth quirked up with her smirk. "I know."

I placed my water bottle a few feet away and stepped up behind her. "If they're trying to take you, they'll most likely come from the back." Her chest rose and fell a mile a minute, and her anticipation colored the air. "Ready?"

"Yes." Her voice was barely above a whisper.

I placed my arm around her chest, pressing mine against her back. "You won't be able to overpower them, so your defense needs to take advantage of your opponent's weak spots. The key here is to get them to release you and run. Do not try to fight them. Okay?"

She nodded. "Okay."

"Every guy is going to protect their groin. So you're not going to go there. You're going to attack their eyes." She flinched in my arms. I never said it would be pretty. "I want you to reach back and act like you're going to dig your nails through my eyes. I'd prefer to keep mine, but if this was real, I want you to think about putting your nails through the back of their head with as much force as you can."

She shook in my hold but brought her hands back, grasping the sides of my head and placing her thumbs exactly where they needed to be.

"Good, now squeeze my head between your hands to give you leverage. He's going to let you go to stop you from taking out his eyes. When I go to break your hold, I want you to run. You understand me?"

She nodded.

I shot my hands up in an attempt to catch her off guard. The second they released her, she took off.

Her cheeks were flushed, a wide smile across her face. "Did I do it right?"

"You're perfect."

The sweet scent of jasmine, spice, and honey wrapped around me, and a groan traveled up my throat. Her eyes darkened, and she took a step forward.

Fuck. The way she looked at me, combined with her scent, had me aching to have her. Her gaze turned pleading, and my stomach clenched. Her body was demanding to be mated the only way it could—lust. Each passing day just made it harder for her to control, and it wouldn't stop until one of us claimed her.

I dropped my forehead to hers, unable to stop myself, and she grazed her lips against mine. Our scents were thick in the air, and my hands shook as they held her face.

"I can't. It can't be me."

She sucked in a breath, fingers digging into my shirt. "What if I want it to be you?"

Heat flooded me, and every muscle tightened with the force to hold myself back. "It's the bond talking. I won't be able to live with myself after."

She jerked away, eyes wide, and her scent turned sour. Hurt and embarrassment flooded the bond as she practically ran from me.

I desperately wanted to go to her and explain that I did want her, more than she could ever understand, but I stayed planted where I was. Her thinking I didn't was for the best. Even if her pain would kill me.

CHAPTER 17
Bliss

The ghost of Ares' fingers trailing down my face had me groaning into my pillow. A quick glance at the clock told me it was 2:00 a.m. I kicked at the blankets tangled between my legs, pushing them off me, and rolled over for the millionth time. It had been days since my heat finally broke, and my body didn't understand how my bonded were so close, but I still wasn't mated. Training with Ares was physical torture. Every touch felt like it ignited a fire from within. My cheeks and neck heated.

It can't be me.

Ares' words stung, but they were nothing compared to the embarrassment I felt after telling him I wanted it to be him and him replying he wouldn't be able to live with himself after. I felt like my chest was going to cave in, and the back of my eyes burned as I struggled not to cry in front of him. He'd accused me of being driven by the bond, and that wasn't completely wrong. If that were the case, I would have been happy he stopped me.

Against my better judgment, no matter what they did, a part of me still cared for them. I had learned years ago that time and anger didn't cancel out the feelings I had for them completely, even if it was what I wanted. Being back with them had only made everything that much more complicated, which was why Ares' rejection hurt so much more.

I flipped my pillow over to the cold side and squished it into the shape I liked. I was disappointed in myself for thinking maybe they felt the same. It sure felt like Killian wanted me back in their lives, that the only thing stopping us was me.

All the more motivation to find Flora and leave before I became more attached. It was going to hurt, though. It felt like they were tearing my heart out the first time we were separated, and I didn't think that would change with it being my choice.

Knowing they'd betrayed me didn't override everything else I was feeling, no matter how much I wanted it to.

A part of me buried deep down wanted *them* to claim me. Wanted them to take that decision from me. It would be so simple. Pain radiated up my chest. I couldn't forget what they'd done. They were my childhood loves, my bonded, and if it wasn't for their betrayal, they'd be mine. Anger burned through the pain, and I climbed out of bed, trying to escape my thoughts. I threw on a pair of pajama shorts and a large sweater one of the guys left me. I lifted the collar higher and breathed in the scent. It was freshly washed, but I could still smell Rafe's pepper-and-coffee scent. My body heated, and I rubbed my thighs together against the building ache. For how much I didn't want to take blockers, it was quickly becoming the only option to survive being an unmated omega.

Frustrated, I left my room and took the stairs two at a time to get to the roof. It had always been my safe space, where I could let everything go. I sighed as the cool night air lifted the ends of my hair off my heated neck, and I closed my eyes, taking a few calming breaths.

"Do you want me to leave, Little Wolf?" I startled as Nox's voice cut through the moment.

He was curled onto the couch, his normally crisp shirt mostly unbuttoned and a book in his hands. He'd brought a small lamp, surrounding him in a soft glow, and his cross earring flashed in the dark. I couldn't make out his expression, but his body was stiff, waiting for my reply.

Did he want me to tell him to leave or stay?

If he was Ares, I'd know the answer to that, but not Nox. He was different. A part of me desperately wanted to forget everything tonight. I could remember it tomorrow. My voice cracked around the word "Stay."

He let out a breath, and his posture softened as he dropped his legs to the floor to make space for me. I swallowed hard, taking the spot on the couch beside him, focusing on the familiar pattern. He shifted on his seat, and I felt a desperate need to end the awkwardness. We'd been friends once. Still not ready to meet his eyes, I gestured to his book with my chin. "What are you reading?"

I couldn't miss his soft smirk in my peripheral vision. "It's nothing." I looked at the title and sucked in a short breath. The entire time I'd known him, he'd been buried in textbooks. He tilted his head to the right, his smile growing, and held my gaze. "Wasn't what you were expecting? Schoolwork?"

I huffed out a laugh. "You could say that." His choice of books wasn't the only thing that had changed. I searched his face as he searched mine. He was more angular, harsher than I remembered, the youth I'd known washed away by time. What did he see when he looked at me?

My body had changed. Gone was the scrawny girl we'd all thought was a beta. I'd taken on all the soft curves and tempting femininity of an omega. His eyes darkened as they traveled over me, his teeth grazing over his bottom lip. "You're beautiful."

Warmth pooled in my stomach, falling dangerously lower, and I had to fight the urge to climb onto him. "It's the bond. You have to feel that way."

He choked on a laugh, his pale face turning bright red, and looked away from me. An ache passed through the bond as his lips tilted in a sad smile. I hated the uncertainty he exuded. Hated that I couldn't take it away without admitting that maybe, just maybe, I could forgive him. His gaze was warm when it met mine, and he reached over to a pile of books, shuffling through them until he found the one he was looking for. "Here." He held it out to me.

Our fingers grazed, and sparks flew up my arm. His hand opened and closed into a fist as if he felt the shock. The pull between us doubled like eternal magnets destined to be together. I focused on the book, desperate to ignore the feelings threatening to overwhelm me.

The description was a friends to enemies to lovers romance. I traced the edge of the book and read the first few pages until I couldn't ignore the weight of Nox's gaze on me. He watched me, green eyes shadowed black, with so much reverence I couldn't breathe. He used to look at me like this. I never knew what it meant, but I did now.

I took a shaky breath in and finally asked what I was dying to know. "Why did you do it?"

I felt his sadness before I could smell it. The feeling only grew stronger with each moment it took to answer. "It's the biggest mistake I've ever made. I regretted it the second it happened, but there is absolutely no reason I could give you that would make up for it. You trusted us, and we hurt you. *I* hurt you."

My breath caught in my chest as I forced myself not to cry. I wanted to trust them, but the four years that stood between us felt like a canyon to cross. His glasses hid his eyes as he turned through his pages too fast to be reading them, and something clicked in place. I may not trust them now, but I could give them a chance to earn it. We get Flora back and go from there. I lifted my legs onto the couch, pulling them up in front of me so I could rest my book on them. Nox stiffened but relaxed into his spot. After a few minutes, he settled into his book, and I let myself get lost in the words.

My fingers tightened on the book with each chapter. It had been hours, and the sky started to shift from black to blue. The pain the characters were feeling was a little too close to my own. Nox shifted, and his fingers grazed my bare calf, and goose bumps covered my skin.

"You're cold?" He pulled my legs over his lap, under his arms. The casualness of the action only made it more intense. There wasn't an inch of me that was cold. Being wrapped up in him had my blood humming, and my skin started to burn.

The bond wanted us to be mated and to solidify our pack. It didn't care about secrets or broken promises. Heat pooled between my legs, and my core grew slick. A barely there whine escaped my lips and was met by Nox's purr.

He ran his thumb over my calf, and a shiver ran down my spine as my legs opened a few inches. Ignoring the pull became physically painful.

"How long have you hurt?" Nox's voice was a low possessive growl.

Too long. I wasn't thinking of the neediness between my legs. He seemed to know that, and his fingers tightened on my ankle.

"Let me take care of this." His gaze was so hot it practically burned. He'd removed his glasses, leaving a clear view of his crisp green eyes, barely visible with the sunrise.

I hesitated. There was nothing I wanted more in this minute than to have him over me, touching me, *inside* of me. I wasn't ready for what that could mean.

His eyes went soft, reading my face. "It doesn't have to mean anything more than what it is." His words were undermined by the sadness through the bond.

He trailed his fingers higher up my calves until they were just over my knees, thumbs touching the sensitive skin on the inside. "Let me take care of you, Little Wolf."

Heat ignited under my skin, and I keened with the need to feel him. I could do this. I wanted to do this. It didn't have to mean I forgave him. I ignored the quiet voice deep within me, whispered that there was no going back, and nodded, biting my bottom lip.

Nox growled and tugged on my ankles until I was laid out on the couch and slid his hands up my legs, resting them on the sides of my apex. "We'll take it slow. This is all about you. Just tell me if it's too much. Okay?"

His green eyes were practically molten, but he didn't move, waiting for my response. Need poured through me, and I barely stopped myself from begging. "Yes."

My pulse pounded in my ears, and I whimpered when Nox crawled over me, resting his chest against mine. His purr vibrated through me until my scent enveloped us as my slick soaked through my shorts. Nox buried his face into the curve of my neck and snarled as I shifted, exposing it to him. He ran his nose along the column of my neck and licked over the mating glands, marking me as his. The sensation shot to my core, and I arched to press myself harder into him.

He grasped my jaw in one hand, holding my gaze while his other traveled down between us. "I've got you. Let go."

I cried out when his hot hand cupped my core, pressing his palm down on my clit and rotating it in small, torturing circles.

His grip tightened on my jaw as he slid his hand under my shorts and groaned. "You're so wet, so fucking perfect." His fingers circled my entrance before dragging over my clit and repeating the process until I was writhing under him. He held me down to the couch without letting my face go. He watched as I took gasping breaths, every other word an incoherent plea. I'd turned into a needy, writhing mess, completely at his mercy. His long fingers pushed inside my entrance, and a low growl formed in the back of his throat. His gaze darkened, the intensity almost too hard to watch, but he didn't let me turn my face, holding me in place as he pumped his fingers harder, circling my clit.

"I can't, I can't take it. Please."

His growl rocked through me, and he dragged his fingers over my inner wall, hitting a spot that had me combusting. Shards of pleasure spilt up my back through my limbs until I was panting with my release.

He dropped his forehead to mine, lips nearly millimeters away. "So fucking stunning."

My body turned to liquid, unable to move after the force of my orgasm. Nox moved me until I was tucked beside him on the couch, gently running his fingers from my temple through my hair, lulling me to sleep.

A car horn woke me up. It took me a moment to realize where I was, and then everything crashed into me. Nox's arm was still wrapped around me, gripping my waist.

Lust, fear, love, and pain all flashed through me, overwhelming my senses.

Careful not to wake him, I lifted his arm and slid out from underneath it. When I glanced down, my heart tightened. He looked peaceful, eyes closed, mouth slightly open. Would he miss me when he woke or be happy he didn't have to deal with the awkwardness of the morning?

I leaned over and grazed my lips over his temple, taking in his sandalwood scent. It hurt to be this close but not be able to stay. I sniffed and blinked away the burn behind my eyes. Four years was just too much hurt to let go of in one night. *What had I done?*

I shut the rooftop door silently behind me and made

my way to my room in the quiet hall. A door swung open, and Ares propped himself on the frame, watching me. I couldn't smell him from this far, but he was sending a mix of lust and longing that had me taking a breath.

I stepped toward him, but his eyes narrowed, and he slammed his bedroom door, cutting him off from me.

The rejection felt like a stab, but I straightened my shoulders. I couldn't let him have that kind of power over me. I thought he'd loved me once, and the embarrassment of my naivety stung.

CHAPTER 18
Bliss

The delicious smell of fresh coffee with a hint of hazelnut washed over me, warming me from the inside out. I rolled over and pressed my face into my pillow, refusing to open my eyes. I wasn't ready to wake up and face the day.

My brain had allowed me a brief vacation from crazy dreams, but that hardly mattered as last night may as well have been a dream.

I wasn't sure what was worse—how I was losing control of my body and hormones or how I wasn't fighting it hard enough.

When I was alone, my drive to complete our pack bond was still manageable, but it was growing worse the more time we all spent together. I wasn't due to go into heat again for another three months, but the way things were going, everything seemed accelerated. I had no way to know if that was normal.

Realistically, none of this was normal.

I dragged myself out of bed and stripped off one of the guys' shirts. I didn't dare think about why I kept wearing them. Careful not to get my hair wet, I stepped under the shower, sighing as the hot water beat at my muscles. My cheeks heated for all the reasons I was currently sore.

I opened a purple bottle of body wash, and a hint of lemon and vanilla coated the room and the corner of my lips tipped up at the familiar smell. Making quick work of washing, I turned off the shower and wrapped myself in a large white fluffy towel. Fully prepared to squeeze into another too-tight sundress, I gasped at the handful of new dresses hanging at the front of the closet. The first one was a deep green, and I ran my fingers along the delicate soft sleeve. A little thrill went through me. It was gorgeous.

Up close, I could make out a subtle monotone pattern of a small wolf print—each design couldn't have been much larger than a quarter. It was fun and flirty. Something I would have worn before.

Excitement skittered across my skin, and I pulled the dress over my head and instantly felt lighter. It was cut in a wrap pattern so that all the fabric pulled together at the side of my waist doing wonders to show off my omega figure. It fit perfectly over every inch of me. If I didn't know it was impossible, I'd have guessed it was custom made. I let out a little squeal and spun in a circle. It had felt like forever since I wore anything I really liked.

I followed the scent of the coffee and I fumbled with the ends of my hair, walking slower than was necessary. Who would be on babysitting duty today? It made no difference, really. I wanted them all equally—that was the problem.

I stopped short in the doorway to the kitchen, quirking an eyebrow. "Hey."

Wes looked up at me from where he sat at the kitchen counter. "Morning."

Relief and disappointment flooded me in equal measure, and I shook my head as if to clear it. I needed to get a grip, if only so the guys wouldn't feel my confusion down our bond and think it meant something.

"What's up?" Wes said jovially, spinning on his stool to face me.

"I feel like I should be asking you that."

No less than four guns were laid out in front of him, and two more were strapped to his legs. He looked like the hero of a low-budget action movie.

I crossed the room to the coffee maker and helped myself. "Everything okay?"

"Yeah, why?" he asked.

I raised a brow at the guns. "Planning a bank heist?"

Wes looked like the kind of beta guy I was supposed to like in high school. He was good-looking in a nonthreatening way. He was probably around six feet. Tall for a beta, but at least a head shorter than a small alpha. He had dirty-blond hair tied back in a messy bun and a square jaw, currently lifted in a grin. "Nope, but I'm glad you're feeling better than the last time I saw you. Things going better with the pack?"

"Oh my God." I rolled my eyes. "Don't change the subject. What's with the guns?"

"The guys had to run down to the dock really quick, and no one could stay back. They're still worried about that guy who's after you, obviously." He gestured to the guns. "They'll be home soon."

I took a sip of my coffee and savored it, thinking. "This is the job that they had to stick around in town to finish?"

"Uh, yeah, I guess so." He rubbed the back of his neck. "We do a lot of jobs, but this one was pretty big."

"What exactly are you guys doing?"

He held up both hands but kept his friendly smile. "Hey, don't get me in trouble, okay? I don't know what you're supposed to know. It's not my business."

"Fine." I sighed. "So, you're the watchdog today?"

"Something like that. Just for a couple hours."

I turned to the refrigerator and swung the door open "Want something to eat?"

He nodded happily. "Please."

I went through the motions of making breakfast, taking out the toaster waffles twice and putting them back in the freezer, as my mind was elsewhere. If whatever big job the guys had to do was done—or almost done—did that mean we could go find Flora?

Finally, I placed a plate and a ceramic coffee mug in front of Wes and backed out of the room down the hallway. "I'll be right back."

I'd left my phone in my room as I wasn't used to carrying it around with me anymore. I dashed back to my nest and scanned around for where I'd left the thing—ah, bedside table.

Powering on the iPhone, I checked Google—no new articles about Flora or her mate as of this morning—then opened the notes app to where I'd copied down her address.

Flora now lived one state over from us. Thank God, since she could have ended up anywhere. Her mate was a judge and former congressman who was known to have extremely polarizing views. According to Reddit, last year he'd made sizable donations to multiple pro-alpha extremist groups, but I couldn't find any paper trail to back it up.

I glanced at the calendar. Flora had now been with that nutjob for more than a week. I had a strong feeling that the longer we left her there, the harder it would be to get her back. The more likely it would become that she would acclimate to her new situation and become brainwashed like her mom, but that was just a hunch. I had no real way to test the theory and no one to ask.

"Do you know anything about Judge Chip Bishop?" I asked Wes as I walked back into the main part of the warehouse.

"Nope," Wes said with a smile. "Who's that?"

"Former congressman from Virginia. He's an alpha, maybe fortyish."

He laughed. "Darling, I don't follow politics."

"Fair. Worth a shot though."

"Who are you calling 'darling'?"

I glanced up as Rafe strode in, Killian right behind him. My skin immediately flushed, my pulse picking up. "Hey. I didn't hear you guys come in."

I took an involuntary step forward toward them and then halted. What was I doing?

Rafe faltered, his focus now stuck between me and Wes. I took that to mean it wasn't all that serious.

"Calm down." Wes hopped down off his stool and adjusted the guns at his hips. "I was just teasing your girl. She's fine."

"Well, don't," Rafe grumbled, tossing his jacket on the couch, revealing a deep blue henley shirt underneath.

"I make no promises. Where's Nox and the Antichrist?"

Killian barked a laugh. "On their way up."

"How did it go?" Wes asked.

Rafe tossed me a wary look before answering. "Good. Better than I expected."

I rolled my eyes. In addition to their normal scents, they were carrying salt air and the metallic tang of blood, but no one seemed hurt. "This was the big job you mentioned, right?"

Killian shot Rafe an alarmed look, and he stiffened. "Bliss…"

I barreled on. "Now that you're finished, we can go get Flora, right?"

Rafe rubbed the back of his neck. "Wait for Ares and Nox to get back, and we can talk about it, okay?"

I didn't have to wait long as the sound of the bay door opening announced Nox and Ares' arrival.

"The word of the day is 'paucity,'" Nox was saying as they walked in. "It means there's a scarcity of something."

Ares was actually smiling for once, and my heart squeezed—it had been so long since I'd seen that, it was almost eerie. "Take this how I mean it, which is offensively: I have a paucity of fucks to give about your words of the day."

They stopped short at the sight of us all standing in the kitchen, waiting for them. "What's up?" Nox asked, tugging on his cross earring.

He looked at me, a tentative smile crossing his face. A wave of lust and admiration hit me, for once without any of the usual accompanying guilt and pain. I blinked, surprised.

Ares made a noise in the back of his throat somewhere between a growl and a snort, and my eyes darted to him, my mood immediately souring as last night's rejection washed over me again. Had he and Nox talked to each other about what happened? What were they thinking?

No, I need to focus.

I turned to face the group. Wes hadn't moved from his spot sitting at the counter, while Killian was at the end of the island, helping himself to the rest of my forgotten breakfast. It was still early, and the sun shone through the large windows, giving everything a warm glow. I felt a little like a general directing troops. Which, I supposed, I was—kind of. "Alright, so you said we could go check on Flora when you were done with your job. When are we leaving?"

I expected immediate protest, but it didn't come. I tried to meet everyone's eyes, picking out individual emotions, but it was impossible when there were so many feelings in one room.

Killian threw me a smile, but there was an edge to it. Like he was trying to soften whatever he was about to say, but there wasn't room for argument. "We'll go check it out, but you're not going anywhere, B."

"Someone will have to stay with her," Nox said, more to the others than to me.

There was a general murmur of consent, and I frowned.

"Wait." I put my hands on my hips. "I'm going. I have to go."

"You can't." Nox set his jaw in a hard line. "You can't be seen in public."

There was a big part of me that loved the protectiveness, but it was also getting inconvenient. I groaned. "Then we'll be careful."

Ares kicked off his shoes by the door and strode over to the nearest armchair, throwing himself into it with a little too much force. "Fuck no. You know you can't be around other alphas."

He didn't say that as though he actually cared, more like just as a fact. It was the same condescending tone someone might say, "Santa Claus isn't real."

"Then we'll figure something out." I balled my hands into fists, my throat tightening. "Flora isn't just going to leave with you even if she wants to go. She doesn't know you."

"That's not the point. You smell unmated," Rafe said, stepping closer to me. He gestured vaguely at my neck, but I got the idea. It was confirmation of what I already knew—my scent was coming back too fast. "It's too dangerous. Remember what happened last time an alpha was around you like this?"

I blanched, a chill settling over me. "That was different."

"It wasn't," Killian said, more gently than I would have expected.

"What am I missing?" Wes asked, turning his head back and forth between the five of us like he was watching a very awkward Ping-Pong match. "I thought she was safe-ish to go out right now."

"They're not talking about the alpha from the other

day. They're talking about our foster dad," I muttered. "It's a long story."

"It's not a long story," Ares drawled. "He attacked her, so we killed him. That's it."

My stomach constricted painfully, and my breath caught as my skin burned hot. *Rage, love, possessiveness.*

I met Ares' bored, ice-blue eyes for half a second before looking away, shocked by the emotions that didn't belong to me now coursing through my body. "Yeah, I guess that's more or less how it was."

"Shit," Wes laughed. "And you were only seventeen."

I nodded. I'd only known I was an omega for twenty-four hours when our foster father tried to claim me. Killian and Nox had held me while Rafe and Ares beat him to death right in front of us. In retrospect, I should have been scared of them—teenagers shouldn't do things like that—but I wasn't. I still wasn't. Who knew what that said about me, or them, but I was glad he was dead.

"He had a fucking death wish, anyway," Ares continued. "You always smelled claimed, even then."

My eyebrows rose. "What does that mean?"

"Wait." Rafe stood up a little straighter, his eyes flashing. "That's a good point."

Killian coughed, choking on a bite of breakfast. "Sorry. I'm fine. What's a good point."

Rafe ignored Killian and scanned me, his gaze intense. "Right now. You don't smell mated." Rafe glanced at Nox. "But you don't smell available either."

My hand flew to my neck. "I don't understand."

Rafe took three steps closer to me, and I had to tilt my head back to keep him in view. The scent of coffee beans and sea salt wafted toward me, wrapping around my senses and muddling everything.

"I have an idea, and I just want to test something." His eyes darted to my neck, and his tongue darted out to wet his lower lip. "Can I?"

Is he saying what I think he's saying? I trembled slightly, my heart leaping into my throat. I nodded.

Rafe wrapped his fingers around my upper arms and pulled me in. He lowered his face to the crook of my neck, and his breath was hot on my skin for a moment before he ran his tongue up the smooth column of my neck, scenting himself over my glands.

Pleasure shot through me, and I melted, my entire body buzzing with need. A mewling sound erupted from the back of my throat. "Alpha."

I pressed closer, suddenly desperate to remove any space between us. Rafe wrenched his face away from my neck; his fingers collared my throat, and he held me back. "Fuck."

I stared up into completely black eyes, my brow furrowing in confusion. *Why did he stop?*

"Killian!" Rafe barked, his voice strained. "Come smell her."

"Maybe I should go," Wes muttered from somewhere to my left.

"Yeah, maybe," Killian said in a low voice as he made his way over to me.

He pressed his nose into my neck, inhaling deeply. I shivered as his fingers trailed absently up my back and his breath tickled my skin. *Mine, mine, mine,* my brain chanted.

Killian grunted, pulling back from me with what

seemed like great effort. He took a full step back. "Alright. I get what you're saying."

I shook my head, feeling a bit high. "What's going on?"

"If you smell like us, it might be enough of a deterrent to keep other alphas from noticing you, as long as we don't go anywhere really public," Rafe explained.

A jolt of excitement traveled through me, breaking through my haze of lust. "Great. Problem solved."

Nox shook his head. "No, it wears off too fast, Otherwise, we wouldn't have had the problem with that asshole Nero the other day."

A wicked smile pulled up Killian's lips. "I feel like the obvious answer is if it wears off too fast, we just need to do it better. Right?"

My pulse picked up, and I could practically feel my pupils dilate. If I could see myself in a mirror at that moment, I was sure my eyes had gone fully black. I pressed my thighs together in an attempt to remain casual, but it was pointless. Everyone—the beta excluded—could smell how much I liked that idea.

"Alright, now I'm definitely out," Wes said jovially. I spun around, surprised he was still here. He picked up his pile of guns off the counter, paused, and put one back down. "I think that one's yours. Give me a call when we're ready to go. I'm all for rescuing damsels in distress."

I pursed my lips, cocking my head to the side. "I'm not sure he has a good understanding of Flora if he thinks he's about to meet a damsel. She swears more than you guys, and she's pretty intense."

No one seemed wholly focused on my statement, and I didn't blame them. They were clearly still thinking about our travel plans.

"We'll leave tomorrow," Rafe said.

"And until then?" I hedged, trying not to sound too eager.

It was becoming almost impossible to ignore my growing instincts pushing me to complete my mating bond, and my nature loved the idea of being scented—whatever the reason. Keeping me safe and letting me travel was starting to feel like gravy.

"Killian's right. We'll just have to make sure it sticks."

CHAPTER 19
Rafe

Bliss' intoxicating scent swirled around me, filling my nose, mouth, lungs, until all I could think about was her. After tonight our scents would meld together until all she smelled like was ours. The thought had my cock hardening in my pants and my teeth aching to mate her.

Ares moved away from us but didn't leave the kitchen, eyes trained on Bliss. She trembled in Killian's arms as he gripped an arm around her waist from behind and licked up her neck, scenting himself all over her.

Mated omegas didn't smell all that interesting—like unsweetened oatmeal. Having our scent all over Bliss would be the closest possible thing to actually claiming her as our mate and hopefully confuse other alphas into not looking at her too long.

A groan rumbled at the back of my throat and my chest vibrated with a silent purr. I was close enough I could practically feel the heat rolling off them, their scent mixing together. Fuck, it was hot watching him possess her. My tongue wet my bottom lip, picturing it was Killian's. The overwhelming need to lay mine against his, claiming her together, had my dick pressing painfully hard against my zipper.

She was ours, and after tonight, no one would doubt it. Our little omega had no idea just how badly we wanted this, how many dreams she'd starred in.

I shifted, making room for Nox, and Bliss made soft, needy cries when Nox captured her mouth, pushing her harder into Killian. Kill's fingers traveled up her thighs, grazing the sensitive skin under the hem of her dress.

I stepped behind Killian, breathing against the shell of his ear. "Take it off."

He grunted and pushed his hips back into my cock. Nox broke from Bliss' lips as she arched between them, and Killian lifted her dress over her head. Her purple hair wound around one shoulder. We all groaned as her perky, pale breasts and rose-colored nipples were exposed. She was nearly bare between us. All soft curves, every inch of her skin flushed. My hot gaze trailed over her. She wore translucent pink panties, and my teeth clenched, knowing I would rip them off her.

I looked over Killian's shoulder, and Nox's gaze met mine, waiting for my command. "Touch her."

He growled, doing as he was told. I could just see over Killian's shoulder and was grateful for the few inches I had on him. Bliss' full breast pooled over Nox's hands as he gripped and massaged them, running his tongue over the peak of one while pressing his thumb on the other. He lifted her, pushing his legs between hers, and she rubbed herself over him, making sweet whimpering sounds.

Fuck. I unzipped my pants to relieve the pressure of my cock growing against my zipper and ground it against Killian's ass. I loved watching them take care of our girl.

Killian gripped Bliss' legs, and she wrapped them around Nox's hips like the good little omega she was.

"Such a good girl." I pushed my cock against Killian. Her scent threatened to throw us into a rut as her slick dripped down her legs. I backed us up until a wall supported us. "Eat that sweet pussy of hers."

She whimpered as her nipple popped out of Nox's mouth, and he sank down on his knees, lifting her legs over his shoulders.

I reached around Killian, yanking Nox's hair back. "Leave her panties on. They're mine."

His eyes turned black, biting his lip, and nodded. I let him go, and Bliss' skin pebbled under my hands as I ran them up her round stomach and lifted her heavy breast in my palms. I licked up Killian's neck and groaned when he exposed it for me. They were fucking mine.

Ares watched us from across the room, his eyes pitch-black as he pumped his cock slowly in his fist. The scent of his arousal mixed with ours, but his brows furrowed as he fought the need to join us. He was a fucking idiot.

Bliss jerked when Nox pulled her panties to the side and flattened his tongue over her clit. I sank my teeth into Killian's shoulder and rocked against his ass as he ground between Bliss and me, searching for his release. I gripped his hips hard, holding him still. "You're going to wait, Killian, and fill our girl up with your cum."

He growled, resting his head back on my shoulders, and his fingers gripped my thighs as he searched for control.

Bliss keened at the loss of friction, desperately moving against Nox's mouth. He groaned, his mouth making wet sucking sounds as he worked her over.

I gripped her breast, licking where I left teeth marks on Killian. "Finish her."

Bliss cried out as Nox thrust his fingers into her and slid them in and out until she stretched over three of them.

She made whimpering, needy sounds. "Please, Nox, please."

I rolled her nipples between my thumbs and nodded at Nox. "Since you asked so nicely."

Nox burried his face against her needy core, and I pinched her nipples hard. She cried out with her release, mewling, and her hips rocked between us. Killian's grip tightened where they held my thighs, fighting his own release.

Nox lowered her legs slowly from his shoulders and caught her before she could collapse.

Killian ran his tongue over her mating glands in repeated slow licks. "Baby girl, just wait until we knot you."

Nox lifted her, one hand under her back and the other under her legs. She clung to his shoulders and burrowed into his chest. He moved away from us, letting me and Killian move away from the wall.

The spot Ares had been was empty. Disappointment flooded through me, and Bliss' glazed eyes met mine.

I ran my fingers over her cheek. "It's not you."

She searched my face and went back to resting on Nox.

I circled Killian's neck in my hand and bit the bottom of his ear. "I'm going to make you come so hard, you'll never forget you're mine."

Killian growled, attempting to turn in my arms, but I walked around him, following Nox into the nest.

Nox lowered Bliss onto her knees on the nest cushions. She swayed, unable to hold herself up. I dropped behind her, pushing her panties down her legs. My chest vibrated with my groan as I licked up her neck, scenting myself over her while I tasted her sweet-as-fuck sweat. She trembled in my arms, and I slowly lowered her backward and laid her on the pillows, fully exposing her sweet pussy to us.

Nox held her hands against the cushions above her head, and I shifted down between her thighs. Her core was swollen, pink, and wet, already ready for us. I licked her slick off her thighs, cleaning her with my mouth, holding her hips steady as I slid my tongue through her slit. "Such a good omega, so fucking delicious."

She whined when I licked her again, and Killian captured the sound in his mouth. He dug his hands into her hair, tilting her head back and exposing her neck, and licked, sucked, and nipped until he left soft bruising, marking she was ours.

My dick twitched as he crushed his mouth against Nox's, sucking on his tongue like he would a cock. Nox's eyes rolled back, and he stripped, fisting his pierced cock. Steel bars ran up the length of him, and two round balls went through the tip. Bliss whimpered as I bit her thigh a little too hard, fucking my cock into the mattress.

Killian replaced Nox's hand and stroked him from base to tip, thumb grazing Nox's jewelry.

"Fuck." Nox groaned the word into Killian's mouth, thrusting his cock into his hand.

"Don't you dare come." I barked the words, and Nox

jerked back, gaze meeting mine where I watched over Bliss' sweet cunt. "Killian, come here. You're going to take this sweet pussy."

Bliss cried out, hips lifting against my mouth, and I sucked her clit hard before moving out of the way.

Killian removed his clothes and moved between her wide-open legs, lifting her so she could straighten them around him. She didn't waste time, digging her heels into his ass, pulling him closer. Killian's skin broke out in goose bumps. It hadn't been that long since her heat, but there was nothing like sliding into Bliss, and Kill knew it.

He thrust himself until he bottomed out and paused so she could adjust for him. She bit her lip, circling her hips. He didn't have to worry. She was made to fit us.

Nox moved to the side of Bliss and leaned over them, capturing Killian's mouth, sucking his lip between his teeth and biting hard. Killian's hips bucked faster as he lost himself in the rut.

I stripped naked and stroked my cock, gripping it in my fist. Fuck, his loss of control was hot.

Bliss captured the tip of Nox's cock in her mouth and ran her tongue over his piercing. He bucked hard, choking her with his cock. He went to pull back, but Bliss' cheeks hollowed as she sucked him harder.

Nox growled into Killian's mouth, thrusting his dick harder into Bliss, and a low, claiming growl started in Kill's chest. His hips rocked into her, pressing his knot further with each thrust. He shivered as I grazed my fingers down his back until I wrapped my fingers around his knot where he pumped into Bliss. Killian snarled and rocked harder. My hand dripping with Bliss' slick, I brought it up to Killian's ass, pushing two fingers over his entrance. He stilled momentarily but moved faster, pushing into her and back against my fingers with each thrust.

I pushed them slowly into Killian and groaned as he gripped around them. I couldn't fucking wait to feel it around my cock, but tonight was all about Bliss. I increased my pace, stroking the sensitive spot inside Killian, firmer each time.

Killian thrust hard, and Bliss cried out as she took his knot. Without moving my hand, I dropped myself closer to Bliss, where she was still devouring Nox's cock. "That's a good omega. You take them so well."

She moaned around Nox's cock, and he yanked himself out of her mouth with a growl. His hands fisted her head, preventing her from recapturing it. His dark gaze followed where my fingers, soaked with Bliss' slick, stroked inside Killian's ass, and he crashed his mouth against mine in a brutal, needy kiss. His voice came out on a groan. "I've wanted you to fuck me for so long."

My eyes rolled back, and my dick seeped precum, nearly losing control. He was going to pay for that. Nox's dark gaze met mine. He knew exactly what he was doing.

Bliss mewed, and Nox and I shifted to each lick up her neck, scent marking her thoroughly.

Killian's growl broke on a groan as his knot grew, locking him in place, and he moved in short demanding movements as he filled our girl with his cum. Her nails bit into my shoulder as her release broke over her.

I licked along her neck until I could catch my breath, then kissed her temple and headed to the bathroom. After quickly washing my hands, I grabbed a bottle of water from the minifridge we set up for her heats.

I found Killian still knotted in Bliss, but he'd rolled

onto his back, with Bliss laid out over him in a puddle. Nox helped her lift up on her arms as I brought the bottle of water to her lips, holding back a groan as it dripped down her chin. Nox licked it off her face, and she shifted on Killian's cock. He grunted and gripped her hips, holding her still.

After a few sips, Bliss looked between us. "Are we just going to hang out until he can let go?"

My lips tipped in a mischievous grin, and Nox bit down hard on his fist.

"Little Wolf, we're going to keep making you come until you've taken all of us."

Her breath came out on a whimper, her eyes wide, half-scared, half-delighted.

Killian ran his thumb along her jaw, drawing her attention. "We have you, baby girl."

This would be torture for him, his knot too sensitive to have her grind all over him, but he didn't try to stop us. I moved around the front of Bliss, holding her chin until she raised herself onto her hands, her mouth wrapped around the tip of my cock. The ripple of pleasure that sang through the bond as she tasted me on her tongue was nearly my undoing. I needed to hold off. The only place I was coming was her sweet pussy.

I waited for Nox to position himself behind her, running his hand from her core over her ass, making her nice and wet. He slid his cock between her crack but didn't push in. Her mouth opened on a gasp as he rocked against her.

I filled Bliss' mouth with my cock until it hit the back of her throat. Her violet eyes met mine as she swallowed me further, tears trailing down her face as she choked on me.

She sucked me harder, and I let her set the rhythm, Nox following her pace. "You're stunning with your mouth around my cock."

Killian grunted and groaned as her hips shifted, and he slid his hand between them to circle his fingers over her clit. She cried out, hips held in place by Killian's knot, unable to chase the friction she craved.

Nox, Killian, and I worked together until she was mewling around my cock. Killian reached up and pinched her nipple as she took me deeper, and her body trembled around us as she came apart.

Killian came free, his cock already hardening even as his knot deflated.

Nox's hands grazed up her front and gently pulled her onto her knees into his chest. He licked up her neck, whispering into her skin. "You're so perfect. You take us so well. You're everything we need."

She relaxed into him, her head falling back against his shoulder. Nox lifted her so Killian could get out of the way and collapsed on the mattress at their other side. Nox turned her and took Killian's place with Bliss over him. Her eyes widened as she stretched around his pierced cock, and her cry filled the room.

"That's it, Little Wolf." Nox guided her all the way down, gritting his teeth at the edge of his control. "You feel so good."

Bliss pressed her palms on his chest and rode him, increasing her tempo with each thrust. She trembled as I ran my tongue up her spine, over her shoulder, and grazed my teeth over her mating glands. "Lie forward."

She followed my command immediately, even without the alpha bark, laying her chest flat over Nox. She writhed over him, and he slowly guided her back and forth on his cock. He captured her mouth with his, sucking her tongue at the same pace as he entered her. Her slick puddled under them, running over his base and balls. I tilted over and took one into my mouth, tasting her all over him. He bucked into her, a grunt tumbling from his throat as I sucked in the second one until he was clean of her.

I ran my finger where her opening stretched around him, and his piercing appeared every time he pulled back. "You look so pretty stretched around him."

I trailed one finger with his cock, and she sucked in a breath as I pressed against her pussy until she stretched enough to fit me. She rocked against Nox's cock and my hand, and I added a second finger.

She was lost between us, body trembling, laid flush with Nox's chest. I met his gaze, silently communicating like we used to. He palmed her face. "Can you take both of us, beautiful?"

Her body stiffened when I lined my cock against them both, waiting for her answer. She dropped her cheek against his chest and nodded.

Fuck yes. I leaned over her back and pushed in slowly, and the feeling of her tight walls clamping me down against Nox's pierced cock had my eyes rolling back. She was too fucking tight. I kissed up her neck, licking her softly. "You have to relax, Bliss."

It took a few moments before she let out a breath and relaxed fully, letting me sink all the way in. "You're so fucking perfect."

When she squirmed around us, I took that as my cue to move. Nox's gaze met mine as my dick ran over his pierced cock. I could feel each bar as her pussy clamped us together. He sucked in a shaky breath after I pulled back, tilting my hips, and pressed forward. I was fucking him as much as I was fucking her.

Bliss' fingers dug into Nox's chest, leaving perfect crescents as she held herself perfectly still for us to take her.

Nox lifted his hips, angling her so we could go deeper, and they both cried out as he pressed his knot inside.

Bliss whimpered and took deep breaths. Nox and I stilled.

Killian lay beside her, sliding her wet hair off her face. "You're doing so well." He placed a soft kiss on her lips, and she keened painfully, sucking his tongue into her mouth. He smiled, licking her lips. "What do you want, baby? Do you want more?"

"Yes, Alpha."

Fuck. I shifted deeper, giving her my knot. I growled at the pressure, growing almost too intense as she stretched to fit both of our knots. "You're so perfect. I love the way you fit both of us."

Nox's knot swelled, locking mine in place, and it felt so good I damn near died. I thrust hard against him, only controlling the rut long enough to confirm with Killian that she was okay before losing myself to it. Fucking Bliss, fucking Nox, them fucking me. Bliss ground her clit against Nox until she came, moaning out our names. Nox followed, and hot liquid surrounded my cock as he filled her. I slammed in harder, overflowing her with my release.

I sank forward, careful to hold my weight off Bliss. My heart felt like it was going to break out of my chest as I sucked in calming breaths. Bliss' own breathing filled my ears, and I smiled as an overwhelming feeling of satisfaction came through the bond.

I kissed her back, and Nox and I delicately switched our positions so she lay on the bed between us. We'd be like this for at least another twenty minutes. I lifted Bliss' damp hair from her neck and nuzzled up her throat. Killian lay on the bed above us, fingers playing with her hair as his breathing evened out.

My heart clenched in my chest, and I held her sleeping form tight. She was stunning tonight, but the idea that this was all she would give us damn near ripped me apart. I kissed along her shoulder blade, wishing things had gone down differently. I said the things to her I couldn't say if she was awake.

"I'm so sorry we ruined this."

She snuggled into Nox's chest, voice barely above a whisper. "I forgive you."

Nox met my gaze, and it felt like my heart would explode. She wouldn't remember that in the morning, but it meant everything to us. I rested my head against hers and closed my eyes, taking deep breaths of her jasmine scent.

CHAPTER 20
Bliss

We sped west on the I-80, all six of us crammed tightly inside an inconspicuous silver Chevy Tahoe.

"We should have taken the van," Killian grumbled next to me, rolling his neck. His hand landed on my thigh as he shifted, trying to get more comfortable. I didn't correct him.

Since last night, my whole body hummed with energy. Like I was a battery that had been sputtering along at 1% without ever knowing it. I'd be lying to myself to say this wasn't making me question leaving them, if only a bit. If this was just a taste—a half charge—what would it be like to run on full power?

"I told you, the van is too obvious," Rafe snapped, glancing at Killian in the rearview mirror. "The Tahoe blends in with traffic."

"It won't matter if we blend in if we're driving to Virginia to start a shootout anyway."

I hoped we weren't driving to Flora's to start a shootout, but the guys had loaded enough guns into the back of the car—just in case—that it was definitely possible. "Well, I like it," I announced, lying back against my seat with a smile and closing my eyes. "The van smells like chemicals. This is way better."

"I wouldn't mind if Rafe ever let someone else drive." Killian kicked the back of Rafe's seat so hard the whole car shook and laughed. I laughed along with him.

"You're cheerful this morning," Wes observed with a Cheshire cat grin. I turned around in my seat just in time to see Nox punch him in the arm, hard enough that the beta visibly winced. "Ow. Chill, man."

"It's nothing." I shook my head, still smiling a bit. He was right—I was cheerful and trying to pretend we didn't all know why. "He just reminded me of when we used to drive to school like this."

Ares' head popped up from where he sat in the passenger seat, ignoring all of us. He had a pen cap in his mouth and one leg crossed over the other, with his pant leg rolled up to the knee.

"One of these days, someone is going to have to tell me about you all as kids." Wes raised his arms in the air, stretching, and hit his hands on the ceiling.

"There's not much to tell," I lied, ignoring the unpleasant taste on my tongue. "What happened to the old Impala, Ares?" I craned my neck to see he was sketching something on one of his few remaining un-tattooed patches of skin.

Ares spit his pen cap into his hand and put his leg down, hiding his drawing from me. "Crashed it." He shrugged, but the scent of pain lingered in the air and reverberated through my chest.

Well, alright then.

According to the GPS, Flora's house was about six hours away, giving us ample time to come up with a plan. I tried and failed not to roll my eyes as Rafe suggested I stay in the car while they checked on Flora—again.

"I told you," I said as patiently as possible, my teeth slightly bared. "She's not going to go anywhere with you. She doesn't know you."

Killian's hand squeezed my leg. "What if someone sees you? How are we going to explain why you're out in public without Nero?"

"Omegas don't always travel with their alphas," I insisted. "Sometimes they travel with security."

I thought back to the omega we'd seen briefly at the airport on the way to the Agora. Omega…what was her name? Donnelley. I pulled my phone out of my sundress pocket and quickly typed her name into Google.

"What are you looking at?" Nox asked, more curious than demanding.

"I've got an idea." I tapped on the first listing that came up without even reading the source and scanned the new article. "Here, look. Omega Donnelley. Her mate is a tech guy from Europe. Now lives in Silicon Valley and invests in start-ups…" I scanned further down the article, twisting my hair with my other hand. "She has four children. Three girls."

Nox tugged on his earring. "And?"

"I saw her at the airport on the way to the Agora, and she wasn't traveling with her alpha. She was just with her security.

"Who's her security? Betas?" Wes asked.

"Other alphas," I explained, still reading. "Since she's mated, it doesn't matter anymore."

"Wait, so instead of her alpha being with her, he's hiring other alphas to hang around her and keep her safe. And this is normal. Is that what you're saying?" Rafe said incredulously.

"Yes."

Rafe and Ares glanced at each other, both clearly thinking, *What the fuck,* and for half a second, it was like they were best friends again. Until they both looked away.

"That's fucking idiotic," Ares grumbled. "I'm not saying I give a shit, but this is the problem with the system. They've sanitized the mating process and created a dystopian hellscape where omegas are only with one alpha, so now they need a whole group of security to protect them. That's what a goddamn pack is. If I reached a point where I had to hire other alphas to do the job I was literally born to do, I'd pray to be put out of my misery right then and there. Fucking Institute ruining everything."

My eyebrows had crept so far up my forehead I probably looked like I'd been electrocuted. That was the longest statement I'd heard him make since being back. "Right. Well, in this case, it might work to our advantage."

Ares ducked his head and went back to drawing. Killian turned to me, a shit-eating smile on his face. "What's your plan?"

"So, what if we just go to her house and knock on the front door?" My voice rose with tentative excitement, and I sat up a little straighter. "Flora and I are friends, and her mating ceremony is this weekend. I'll say I got to town early and wanted to drop by and say hello but lost her phone number or something. You guys can be my security."

"Wait, slow down." Killian put his palm flat on my thigh again.

"What? Do you guys have a better idea?"

Killian grinned, probably getting blasted with the full force of my excitement. "No, but there are some issues. Didn't you say Nero knows this guy? Do you think he told him you disappeared?"

"That prick won't tell anyone." I could almost hear the wheels turning in Nox's head. "This looks bad for him. He'll be pretending you're just locked in his basement for the rest of his life."

I shuddered. That was probably true.

Rafe kept his eyes firmly on the road. "What about the fact that she has no claiming mark?"

"I'll wear a high-collared dress. Men don't really notice clothes."

Ares scoffed. "Clothes, no, but your neck? Yes, we do. An alpha will notice if you're hiding your mating glands."

"Okay, but would they ask me about it directly? Probably not."

There was a general murmur of agreement, and my stomach jumped, my excitement building again.

"You still don't smell mated though," Rafe pointed out. "You're fine to walk down the street or roll down the window, but we'd be pushing it to have a long conversation with another alpha."

I tugged on a loose bit of my hair, thinking. "Her mate is a judge, right? So, he probably goes to work. We'll try to time it for when he's gone and only talk to her. Worst-case scenario, we run into security."

"There's no way for us to know for sure if the mate is home," Nox pointed out. "We should go to the house first and make sure."

"Alright," Rafe said, as though everything was settled. "We'll go. Bliss will stay in the car while we check it out, and if the mate isn't home, we can do this security plan thing, but if anything goes wrong—" He turned around to look at me directly. "—you leave right away, no questions."

"Fine. I can live with that."

Fifteen minutes from the state line, we stopped at a dingy strip mall so I could find something to wear that looked more like Flora's mom and less like teenage me wearing the wrong size. My options were pretty limited, but I finally found a cream turtleneck sweater and a navy-blue flared skirt, neither of which clashed too badly with my hair. Then we swung into a relatively nice rest stop so I could change.

"May as well just stick around here while you guys go see if the mate is home." Wes shrugged. "I'll hang out with Bliss. We can get pretzels." He gestured to one of the rest stop food stands with a smile.

The pack looked at each other, and dead flowers scented in the air.

"Not the worst idea." Nox ran a hand over his shaved head. "But maybe one of us should stay."

I sighed, grabbing my shopping bag out of the back

seat. "You guys decide who's staying, and I'll see the rest of you in an hour. I'm going to change."

I kept my head down as I crossed the parking lot, trying not to draw any attention to myself. I'd had a lot of practice with walking while keeping my eyes on the floor rather than on where I was going, but it was harder when I wasn't following the black patent leather shoes of the girl in front of me.

My heart beat with misplaced anxiety, and I took deep breaths through my nose. The last time we'd visited a rest stop, I'd come out to find the Institute waiting for me. Not that I thought something was going to happen again, but my body felt like it was in fight-or-flight mode.

A group of three men stood outside the rest stop, chain-smoking. The hair on the back of my neck stood up as I passed them, and their scent wafted toward me over the strong odor of Marlboro Reds. At least one was an alpha.

"Alright, honey?" one yelled, and his friends laughed.

I muttered something noncommittal and gave half a wave before ducking inside and making a beeline for the restrooms.

The rest stop smelled of fast food, gasoline, and the lingering imprint of hundreds of travelers. I walked quickly past the racks of brochures and Pepsi-brand vending machines and a closed Auntie Annie's pretzel stand—looked like Wes was out of luck on the snack front. The whole building was surprisingly empty, given that it was a main road and barely midafternoon, but I almost preferred it that way.

I changed and used the bathroom as fast as possible, then examined myself in the long mirror as I washed my hands. While the fabric of the sweater and skirt was cheap, the tags on the inside nothing that would impress anyone, from the outside, I still looked the part of a traditional omega—mostly. The sweater clung to my curves in all the right places and, aside from the turtleneck, resembled something that I'd seen headmistress Omega DuPont wear to dinner on Sundays. Except for my hair, which had faded to a lighter lavender after only a few washes.

I dried my hands and gathered up my rumpled sundress, turning toward the door just as it swung open. The scent of an unfamiliar alpha wafted inside the small four-stall women's bathroom, along with a plume of cigarette smoke. The hair on the back of my neck stood on end.

Three men stepped inside. They each wore some variation of beat-up jeans and a graphic T-shirt emblazoned with the logo for a sports team I neither recognized nor cared about. A jolt of panic shot through me as I recognized them from outside the rest stop.

Of the two in the back, one was a short but muscular beta. The other was tall and broad enough that he was probably an alpha, though his smell wasn't very dominant. The one in the front was the real problem.

The alpha in the front stepped closer to me, smiling. "Hi, honey. What are you doing here by yourself?"

He was probably late twenties or early thirties, with black hair and mean eyes. Clearly dominant enough that he was used to getting his way and probably had these other two to back him up one hundred percent of the time.

"I would have thought that was obvious," I laughed, trying and failing for bravado.

The cranberry scent of my fear permeated the room,

and the mean-looking alpha took a long breath through his nose, his smile growing broader. "Are you in town long?"

"No," I stammered. "Actually, I need to go."

"Why?" They laughed, nudging each other as though this was all some big joke.

My heartbeat pounded against my ribs as I realized they were moving further into the bathroom. I took an involuntary step back. There was nowhere to go. Just a tile wall behind me and three men between me and the door.

"I have people waiting for me." I fought to keep my voice steady. "My alphas will—"

The alpha in the front jerked his head up, his eyes widening. "Say again? Who's waiting for you, honey?"

A cold chill fell over my body as my eyes darted between them, taking in their similar looks of confused delight. The alpha in the back laughed incredulously. "No shit, an omega? I knew you smelled good, baby. I've never seen one'a you in real life."

"Fuck off," the dominant alpha spat at his friend. "She's mine."

"Come on, Scott. We can share. I heard omegas are freaks. She'll love it."

My heartbeat reached dangerous levels as I caught fingers out of the corner of my eye reaching for my arm. I'd never be able to fight off an alpha—it was impossible. God, it was pretty unlikely I'd be able to fight off most betas if they wanted to hurt me. That just wasn't how omegas were built. I might be able to break his hold, though, and run back into the rest stop. Where the hell were—

"Bliss!"

The door banged open again, and hot relief flooded my body.

Ares strode inside, his expression murderous as he whipped his head from me to the three men cornering me against the wall. "Back away from her," Ares barked. "Now."

The force of his bark reverberated off the tile and had the two men in the back immediately dropping their eyes and stepping away toward the door.

The tall, loud one in the front faltered, surprised, but gritted his teeth, fighting to ignore the command. He watched the door slam as his buddies took off and set his jaw in stubborn resolve. "Nah, fuck off. I found her, she's mine."

I gasped in mingled surprise and fear. The alpha was more dominant than he looked. He reached out again and ran one finger down my right cheek. Ares snarled.

Judging by his smug grin, the other alpha thought he had this one in the bag. He was older and dominant enough that he probably wasn't used to losing. But he couldn't feel Ares pounding adrenaline down our bond and hadn't seen Ares kill our foster dad with his bare hands when he was only seventeen.

The alpha, while large and naturally strong, gave the impression he was used to fighting outside bars and at sporting events. The kind of fights where no one really knew what they were doing, everyone was most of the way to blackout anyway, and the guy who stayed upright the longest was declared the winner. Ares was not that kind of fighter.

"You should walk away before you get hurt," I blurted out.

The alpha laughed. "Aw, that's sweet. She don't want you to ruin your pretty-boy face, kid. Listen to the girl and walk away."

I narrowed my eyes. "I wasn't talking to him. You need to leave before he kills you."

The alpha gaped at me for a second, then guffawed. He reached out and pinched my nipple through my sweater, still grinning. "Mouthy bitch. I'll enjoy breaking you in."

I yanked backward out of the alpha's grip, and Ares growled in rage. "Bliss, get the fuck out of here."

The tug of the command pulled at my middle, but now Ares blocked the door as he advanced on the grinning alpha, and my survival instinct warred with my desire to obey. I shrunk back into the stall at the end of the row and closed the door halfway, trying to satisfy both urges at once.

The alpha tried to throw a punch, and Ares sidestepped him easily, turned, and drove his elbow into the man's neck. The alpha made a noise somewhere between a scream and a wheeze.

Miraculously, the alpha stumbled back to standing, going for a tackle this time. Ares grabbed him by the hair, slamming his face into the edge of the long row of sinks. I winced, closing my eyes as bones crunched, and I heard a wet thunk as the alpha's head hit the sink again.

The metallic scent of blood filled the air, washing over everything

"Hey," I called through the crack in the stall door. I eased the door open. "You can stop now."

Ares dropped the bleeding alpha on the previously white tile floor and turned to look at me. My heart pounded in time to my erratic breathing as he held me transfixed by his completely black gaze. It was almost as eerie as it was beautiful, only because it was so opposite to his normal eye color.

"Did they touch you?" he growled, his voice shaking with barely contained anger.

I trembled, but I was half-ashamed with myself that it wasn't from fear. Ares had already made it perfectly clear several times over that he wasn't interested in me, but still, this level of dominance had my omega side practically begging to be claimed. "No. They didn't touch me. They tried, but—" I gestured toward the floor, trailing off.

I gasped as each wave crested, crashing right into me. *Rage, possession, fear.*

My gut instinct was to fix it. *Your alpha is angry with you. Make it better.*

"I'm not hurt." I grabbed his hands and held them tightly in mine, bringing them up to my face. "See?"

He held my face gently between his palms. "I should have come in here sooner."

"Why did you stay?" I asked.

He shook his head, eyes still black and wild, not seeming to understand the question. "Why wouldn't I stay?"

Because you rejected me. Because you didn't want to scent me last night, even for my protection. Because you don't want to be a part of the pack. "Because I thought you would think it was more important to go check out Flora's house."

"Nothing is more important than you."

I whimpered as a wave of lust and something more, stronger, ineffable, crested over me. His palms shook against my burning cheeks. He took half a step closer, inhaling deeply through his nose. "You should back up, Love."

"W-what? Why?" My voice came out breathy and foreign as I tried to remember what I was doing here in the first place. My head spun, drunk on a cocktail of overpotent pheromones and adrenaline.

His hands fell from my cheeks to my hips, and he tugged me to him, growling low in the back of his throat. "You need to give me some space, because I want you so bad, I can't think straight. I'm going to fuck you up against that wall and make you come all over my knot so no one ever questions that you're mine again."

Every nerve ending in my body hummed with need. The sharpness of his words and the strong scent of our combined arousal made me desperate to close the remaining distance between us. "Please."

Ares growled, the remainder of his self-control snapping as he backed me into the sinks behind us. He pushed aside the fabric of my skirt to cup me between my legs. I whimpered as his fingers brushed me over my panties, and the honey scent of my slick hit both of us. "Fuck, Love."

I shifted, wanting more. I wanted him to touch me. Own me.

There was a tiny part of me that wondered if it was me or the bond pushing me to complete the pack. As long as Ares rejected me, and by extension, the pack, the bond would never feel right.

As he stroked up and down my entrance over my panties and finally pushed them aside to sink two fingers into me, I keened, surrendering to the sensation. Maybe it didn't matter why I wanted it. Maybe all that mattered was that I did.

He withdrew his fingers and brought them to his mouth, sucking them clean. "Perfect. I can't wait to taste you again."

My eyes widened. *Again? When*—

He wrapped both hands around my thighs, lifting me onto the sink, distracting me from my thoughts as he slammed his lips down on mine, punishing me with his kiss. He thrust his tongue past my lips forcefully, demanding my submission.

I wrapped my legs around his waist and held on, grinding myself down on his cock through his jeans as I grew drunk on greedy kisses.

His hands dug into my ass, pressing me, if possible, closer. I whined, writhing against Ares' hard body. I wanted more—to be full. I needed more.

"Mine." He pulled his mouth from mine to look me in the eye. "You're mine, Love."

I moaned. "Yes, Alpha."

He pressed his face into my neck, speaking against my skin. "That's my good girl."

"I want…" I couldn't find the words as he rocked into me, and his mouth moved to the sensitive skin of my neck. "I want…"

Ares scraped his teeth up the column of my neck, and I cried out in unexpected pleasure as one of his sharp incisors nicked my skin. Everything narrowed to a point, and my heart beat a crescendo in my ears, roaring its approval.

I craned my neck further, pressing against his mouth as

though I could somehow impale myself on his teeth. "Do it," I gasped. "Please."

Ares didn't move.

For a full beat, I waited, the only sound now my own ragged breathing. I pulled my head back to look at him. His eyes were shifting back to blue right in front of me. I frowned—I'd never seen that. It was quick, like a cat walking from a dark room into sunlight.

His gaze darted from my face to my neck, a look of sheer horror on his face. A chill settled over me, my heartbeat in my ears becoming a roar as embarrassment and rejection sunk in.

"Bliss, I'm so fucking sorry," he blurted out. "Fuck. I can't do this."

CHAPTER 21
Bliss

The bathroom door slammed, and I stared dumbstruck at the empty space where Ares had just been. My chest heaved as I fought to catch my breath, a cold chill washing over me.

"Wait!" I slid off the counter, nearly tripping over the beaten and bloody alpha still lying on the floor.

I tore across the slippery tile floor, trying to straighten my skirt as I went, and threw open the door. Expecting to find the lobby of the rest stop deserted again, I skidded to a halt, shocked, when Ares was standing right in front of me.

Aside from the blood in his white hair and covering his T-shirt, you wouldn't know anything had just happened. His expression had returned to completely neutral. "Let's go."

My brain spluttered, short-circuiting. "Is this a joke? Are you serious right now?"

"The guys will be back any second, and we don't want to hang around near that." He jerked his head toward the bathroom door. "We'll wait outside."

He set off across the lobby toward the front doors, and I had to jog to keep up. Hurt, confusion, and indignation bubbled in my stomach, quickly morphing into anger. "Are you really going to pretend nothing just happened?"

He turned back to me, one hand on the door to the parking lot. "Don't worry. I don't think that will do anything." His eyes darted to my neck. "It's more of a scratch. I didn't really bite you. We're not any more connected now than—"

"Than we already are," I finished for him acidly. "Except, according to you, there's nothing between us anyway."

"I never said that."

We stepped outside and turned to face each other on the sidewalk in front of the rest stop. I crossed my arms over my chest, as though somehow that would shield me. "You didn't have to. You're making it very clear you want nothing to do with me, or the rest of the pack for that matter."

He made a noise in the back of his throat that might have been a growl, or maybe a scoff, it was hard to tell. "There is no pack, Bliss. And don't tell me now you want to stay and make one."

I looked down, suddenly unsure. "I don't know. Maybe I would if I had that option, but it's not like you guys are offering me that. No one is asking to mate with me."

"Because we know you only think you want that because of the bond," he said bitterly. "You're not thinking clearly."

I laughed, but there was no humor in it. "Don't tell me how I feel. I loved you all before any of this. I would have stayed with you no matter what and just hoped being a beta was enough. It was you guys who changed and abandoned me, and you're the ones who still won't be with me now."

His eyes widened, staring at me in obvious shock. "Love…"

The SUV pulled up outside the rest stop and skidded to a halt, brakes screeching. Ares and I turned in unison to look as the doors flew open and everyone leapt out.

"Are you okay, baby?" Killian rushed to me, his hands trailing over my hair.

"Fine," I breathed—struggling for a moment to remember what they were talking about.

"What happened?" Rafe demanded, more to Ares than me.

My eyes landed on Ares' bloodied knuckles. A hot flush rushed up my neck. Had they felt *everything* through the bond? From the way Nox was now eying my neck, a curious look on his face, the answer was a resounding "yes." Perfect.

I took a large step toward the car, willing myself to get it together. What was I doing? I was supposed to be focused on my best friend—nothing else should matter right now. "Everything is fine now. Was Flora's mate home?"

"No, wait, tell us what happened. Is she hurt?" Rafe snapped his fingers at Ares, who was still staring at me, an unreadable expression on his face.

Ares seemed to wake up. "Later." He glanced up at the

security cameras mounted above the door. "We should get the fuck out of here, anyway."

My stomach did a nervous flip. The law protected alphas defending their omegas—it was understood that they couldn't help it, and therefore, even if Ares had killed that man, nothing would happen. Except that, technically, I didn't belong to the guys. I belonged to Nero. I nearly gagged thinking about it.

"Let's leave," I said urgently. "Please."

We piled back into the car, my shaking hands and the scent of blood the only indication that anything unusual had gone on in the last hour.

"Looks like her mate is at work," Wes said from his seat in the back row. "They have a security gate around the whole house, and the guard keeps a log of arrivals and departures."

I nodded. I wasn't sure I wanted to know how they got their hands on the arrivals and departures log in the span of forty minutes. Some things were better left to the imagination.

Alpha Bishop lived in a six-bedroom, eight-bathroom mini-mansion with an Olympic-sized pool and a nine-hole golf course. We knew this because the house was renovated last year and was featured in an issue of *Better Homes and Gardens* alongside the homes of several other political figures. In the photos, the house was decked out in flags and bunting, as though it were the bicentennial. When we arrived, it looked far less festive.

It was painted a pale gray, with wide stone columns in the front. It reminded me a little of a prison with its high walls and stone arches—more austere than impressive. We pulled up to the iron front gate, finding it already open. I supposed that confirmed my suspicions about the fate of the security guard.

I reached up, twirling a strand of my hair. That brought our body count for the day up to two, and we weren't even inside the house yet. That couldn't be a good omen.

The gravel of the long driveway crunched under our tires, kicking tiny pebbling up against the windshield. I sat up a little straighter, trying to channel a good omega. The kind of omega that would travel with security. "Remember." I smoothed my hair as the car came to a halt near the front door. "I am nothing to you."

Growls tore through the car, and Wes winced. "Cut that shit out. It's unnerving as fuck."

I ignored him. "Seriously. You can't talk for me or do anything unless I'm seriously threatened. Security wouldn't do that because you wouldn't have the urge to. You're just there because you're getting paid."

"I don't like this." Killian reached over and squeezed my thigh.

I shivered at the casual touch. Had we moved on to that? Was he just nervous? Never knowing where things stood was, as Wes put it, unnerving as fuck. I nudged Killian away, climbing out of the car. "I can't think of anything else, and we're already here, so let's just get it over with."

The guys stood slightly behind me as I knocked on Flora's front door. My heart beat a violent rhythm against my breastbone, seeming to count out the seconds while we waited for someone to answer.

Would Flora answer the door, or did she have staff? I

imagined in a house this large, there would be a butler or something, but I was also basing my opinion off movies.

"Maybe no one's home." Killian shifted behind me.

I knocked again, louder. They didn't seem to have a doorbell—maybe there was a side entrance? Footsteps sounded on the other side of the door, and my stomach jumped with nervous anticipation. The door creaked open.

A brunette beta woman in her mid-twenties poked her head around the door and stared at me. "Hello?"

My skin went clammy as panic washed over me. I didn't know if I was supposed to look at her directly. I'd had a thousand etiquette classes on interacting with alphas and other omegas, but no one had ever told me how to talk to betas in this sort of social situation. I settled on staring at her right shoulder. "Um, hi. I'm Omega Nero. Is Omega Bishop taking visitors this afternoon?"

I internally cringed. That sounded painful. If I were this woman, I would immediately assume something was going on from the awkwardness of that statement alone.

The beta woman shuffled her feet, a salty scent rising around her. "She's not here, ma'am."

I wrinkled my nose, swallowing against the sour taste of the lie. I looked up, staring into the woman's warm brown eyes—etiquette be damned. "Really?"

"Yes. She left with Judge Bishop."

Lie.

Behind me, the guys shifted, obviously also bothered by the lies. I frowned, confused. This woman worked in an alpha's household—why wouldn't she realize she couldn't lie without us knowing?

"Your boss never told you that alphas and omegas can smell lies, did he?" Nox said flatly from behind me. "Probably helps keep his staff in line."

The maid gasped. "I'm sorry, ma'am. Miss Flora is very ill."

Lie.

I raised my eyebrows. "Are you sure?"

Her eyes widened. "I mean, she's too tired from the planning for the mating ceremony."

Lie.

I rubbed my temples—the smell was starting to make my head spin. "Please stop lying."

She slapped her hand over her mouth, clearly struggling with this new realization. She shifted, now trying to shut the door. "I think you should leave."

That, at least, was true.

"Look, I get it," I said, trying to give the woman a reassuring smile, even as sweat beaded on the back of my neck. "I'm sure you were told not to say anything, but I really need to see my friend. Please let us in. This doesn't need to have anything to do with you."

The maid ducked her head, staring at my shoes. The scent of cranberries and salt overwhelmed my senses, lingering on my tongue. "If he can tell I'm lying like you said, he'll know I let you in."

I closed my eyes against the deluge of emotions hitting me from all sides. If she was so afraid of her boss, I couldn't imagine what state Flora was in. I didn't want us to turn into the kind of people who bulldozed over innocent bystanders, but at what point did we have to escalate this? We were wasting time, and I didn't see any other security. It was just one maid standing between me and finding Flora. "Look—"

The maid looked over my shoulder, an idea sparking behind her eyes. "You can do that thing, right? Just tell me to let you in, then it's not my fault."

"Let us in," Nox barked immediately, the strength of his voice raising goose bumps on my arms.

The maid stepped aside immediately, and I let out a sigh of relief, following her inside the house. The foyer was almost exactly what I would have guessed from looking at the outside—white, clean, and devoid of personality. "Can you show us where Flora is?" I asked quickly.

The maid gave a pointed look at the guys, waiting for the command.

"I don't like the idea of a staff being familiar with getting barked at," Killian said under his breath once we were being led down a long, wide hallway and up a flight of stairs dotted with crystal sconces along the walls.

"Me neither," I whispered back. I kept my back rigid, expecting to come across other staff or security, but no one appeared. "Is there anyone else here?"

"Miss Flora, me, the cook, and the gardener," the maid said, her tone robotic.

"No alphas?"

"No."

I glanced back at the guys as we climbed a second flight of stairs to the third floor, wondering if they found that as odd as I did. Flora should have security.

The maid came to a halt outside a heavy oak-paneled door and wiped her sweating palms on the skirt of her black uniform. "This is Miss Flora's room,"

I glanced at the knob, immediately zeroing in on a

large, old-fashioned brass key sticking out of the lock. "Is she locked in?"

The maid nodded, stepping back to let me take a closer look. A shiver traveled down my spine as a combined feeling of dread and anger settled over me. I reached for the knob, then paused, glancing back at the guys. "Maybe you should all step back."

Rafe growled, reaching for my hand to stop me. "No. We don't know what's in there."

"Exactly." I jutted my lip out. "We don't know what state she's in. We're not all going to rush in there together and scare her."

In almost all situations, I was happy to defer to the guys. It was my nature to let them protect me, but not this time. My instincts screamed not to let them in that room, and my instincts hadn't been wrong yet.

"There's no one else on this level, ma'am," the maid said. "Just us and Miss Flora."

"Fine," Rafe muttered, stepping back. "We'll wait here while you go in."

I faced the door again and took a deep breath, shaking out my shoulders. Raising my knuckles, I knocked softly. "Flora? It's Bliss. I'm coming in."

My heart beat so loudly it drowned out all other sound as I turned the key and hesitantly eased the door open on a darkened bedroom. The scent of sweat, sex, and rotting food came at me in a rush, and I choked as I tried to identify the source of everything—to pick apart the emotions from the physical scents. I blinked and stumbled back as something moved abruptly in the darkness, and a bedside light flicked on. My hand flew to my mouth, stifling a cry.

Flora sat up in the center of the bed, a tangled sheet

wrapped around her naked and bruised body. Her hair fell in crumpled and battered curls, and she had glitter smeared across her face, like she hadn't bathed since the Agora Ceremony. She squinted at me, leaning forward into the light, and I nearly gagged at the dried blood stuck to her neck near half-healed bite marks. "Bliss? Is that you?"

CHAPTER 22
Wes

Bliss unlocked the door and stepped inside, and Rafe stiffened next to me. "What the fuck is going on in there?" he growled at the maid.

The rest of the guys shifted behind me, and the maid backed up, looking half-scared, half-guilty. I frowned. "Leave her alone. We can't even see inside."

The guys didn't understand what it was like to have someone barking at you and not be able to control your own body. Fucking weird was what it was, and that maid was a tiny woman. I shuddered. I couldn't imagine.

Somehow, I'd ended up near the front of the group, and I peered into the room. It was dark in there, and unless they had some kind of Superman X-ray vision I didn't know about, they couldn't see shit either.

"You can't smell it," Killian muttered, his voice relatively even. He wasn't trying to be an asshole, just stating a fact. "It's a shitshow."

I grimaced. He was right; I couldn't smell what was

going on, but I'd have to be a fucking moron not to notice the way the guys had stiffened behind me like they were about to attack the moment the door opened and Bliss stepped into the room. I wasn't totally useless at reading people—alphas in particular. I'd been hanging around Alpha Lupi since I was fourteen and was tight with the pack for the better part of three years. I loved the guys, but they weren't what I'd call subtle.

A light flicked on in the room, and I leaned forward further, trying to get a glimpse of the so-called shitshow. My stomach rolled.

Bliss knelt on a king-sized bed, her back to the door. Her shoulders shook slightly, like she was crying as she spoke to her friend. I warred with myself, half-transfixed by the woman on the bed, half-horrified by what I was seeing.

"How long has she been like this?" Rafe bit out, echoing my thoughts.

"I—I—" The maid was struggling, wringing her hands. "A little over a week? Since Miss Flora arrived, sirs."

Flora. Pretty name. I hadn't paid much attention until now, but suddenly, I couldn't focus on anything else.

"And you didn't do shit about it?" Ares jostled my arm as he tried to sidestep me to get to the door.

I kept my feet firmly planted on the floor, more out of spite than anything else. Sure, he could knock me out of the way if he wanted to, and we both knew it, but I sure as hell wasn't going to just bow out of the way and make it easier for him.

"I can't." The maid set her jaw, her face reddening with anger. "I'm ordered not to."

I balled my hands into fists, hot rage pounding

through me for the sake of both women. That was fucked. "When does her…" I trailed off, unsure if I should say husband or mate. "When does your boss get back?"

"Tonight," the maid replied. "Unless Miss Flora is seriously hurt, then he'll come back right away."

I swallowed thickly, not liking the implication of why the maid knew that.

Bliss stood, walking back toward the open door on wobbling legs. Her face was set in as serious an expression as I'd ever seen her wear, her mouth a thin line. "Can someone help me carry her?"

"Where, baby?" Killian's voice was soft.

Bliss looked lost. "The car, I guess? I don't know what to do, but she's not staying here. All I can think of right now is to go to her parents."

"What happened?" I asked, already sure I knew the answer.

A flash of unbridled rage crossed Bliss' face. "I explained how the Institute works and the point of the Agora. This shouldn't come as a surprise."

Nox leaned around my shoulder to get a better look into the room, and I stepped to the side to let him see. This was fucking ridiculous with so many of us crammed up here. Fuck, the hallway was as tightly packed as a strip club on half-price wings night. "We can't take her out of here and have her abandon her mate while in that condition."

Bliss shook her head, dejected. "I know, but we can't leave her here."

They'd lost me. I gritted my teeth in frustration at not understanding what was going on, my skin crawling with nervous energy. "Can someone explain to me what the hell you all are talking about?"

Rafe growled, his voice barely under control. "Flora is mated and clearly in bad shape. Separating mates is incredibly painful. We don't know if she'd survive it."

Bliss pulled at the ends of her lavender hair. "That's why I'm thinking we should go to her parents. Like a visit? I don't really know how this kind of thing works, but that's all I've got right now."

It nagged at the back of my mind that we were talking about this woman without her input, making even more decisions for her. Bliss was clearly doing her best, but what the hell did Flora want to do?

"I'll carry her downstairs," Killian offered before I could voice that opinion.

Something hot and protective rose in my chest, and I straightened, intending to say no, I could help instead.

I blinked, leaning back against the wall as I swallowed the insane urge back down.

What the fuck am I thinking.

Killian followed Bliss into the room, and I suddenly remembered they'd all gone to high school together. They at least all knew each other; this had absolutely nothing to do with me. Inserting my opinion was not only unnecessary, but it would probably make things harder for everyone.

My spine straightened as a high-pitched scream shattered my eardrums. "No! Don't touch me."

"Flora. It's Killian," Bliss panicked. "You remember Killian, right?"

Flora screamed again, her terror evident. "Fucking alphas. Stay away from me."

Killian darted back out of the bedroom, his eyes wide, expression somewhere between sad and horrified. I almost felt bad for the big guy. Of all of them, he was by far the least naturally violent. I could see being scared of Ares or Rafe, who both gave off kind of an "I kill people and like it" energy. Maybe even Nox with all the piercings and shaved head, but Killian? Nah.

"Wes," Bliss called from out of sight. She sounded like she was on the verge of crying again. "Can you come here?"

My stomach seized with something like anxiety, but I pushed off the wall, not making eye contact with anyone as I stepped into the bedroom.

My eyes landed on Flora, and I regretted it instantly. If the situation had looked bad from my position in the hall, it was nothing to how she looked up close. She was probably around Bliss' age, so several years younger than my twenty-five, but the look in her eyes made her seem far older. She had bruises all along her face and neck, like someone had grabbed her or smacked her around, dried blood stuck to her collarbones. I squinted at her neck, my stomach rolling. It looked almost like an animal attack. I knew that alphas and omegas bit each other, but I'd never seen anything like that.

Flora didn't look at me. Her hollow eyes were fixed on Bliss, who stood on the opposite side of the bed now, holding up a sparkly evening gown. "Do you have any other clothes?"

Her voice came out soft, compared to the scream I'd just heard. Like a different person. "No."

Without thinking, I shrugged off my sweatshirt and held it out to Flora. She didn't take it. Instead, Bliss darted around the bed and grabbed it and helped to push the neck of the rumpled garment over her friend's head. She was so small, the material practically drowned her. Flora didn't seem to care.

"Can you please just take her out of here?" Bliss implored, her voice shaking.

"Sure. Of course." My breath caught in the back of my throat as I bent to lift the woman off the bed. She was too frail. Too delicate—like a wounded bird. I paused. "Hey there, Buttercup. My name is Wes," I told her, not sure if she was paying attention to me. "I promise not to hurt you. We're going to take you somewhere safe."

Where that somewhere was, I had no fucking idea, but I'd be damned if we were going to leave her here. I couldn't live with myself.

Flora shifted her gaze and stared up at me with surprising clarity. "My name is Flora, not Buttercup."

"Alright then. Do you mind if I pick you up?"

She nodded, and I lifted her carefully, and an unfamiliar feeling of protectiveness washed over me as I looked down at the shaking woman in my arms. She was beautiful, despite the bruising along her face and under her eyes. Rage boiled in my veins. What kind of sick, twisted asshole would do this to a woman like this? Any woman. I couldn't wrap my mind around it.

"I'll be right behind you," Bliss said quickly.

I nodded, turning toward the door. Flora shifted in my arms, raising her head enough to press her face into the crook of my neck. She took a deep breath, and her ragged breathing slowed. I froze, unsure what to do. Was this normal omega behavior?

I felt the eyes of the pack and the maid on us as they

parted to let me pass, pressing themselves as flat as possible to the walls of the tight hallway. Flora kept her face hidden against my arm. How the fuck could a system be so broken that this was the outcome? Weren't omegas supposed to be meant for alphas? But now, here was evidence that the system didn't always work.

I paused at the top of the first flight of stairs, adjusting my arm under Flora's knees. I internally cursed whoever the fuck her mate was. He was already going to hell, and I hoped to help him get there, but putting her room on the third floor was an extra fuck-you I didn't need right now. I looked down at her apologetically. "I promise not to drop you. Let me know if I'm jostling you around too much and I'll stop."

She stiffened in my arms, clearly not listening. Her huge brown eyes widened in fear. "He's coming."

I frowned. "Who's coming?"

I should've known what she meant. This was part of their thing, right? Alphas and omegas had freaky telepathy almost, so they knew when their mates were in danger. It didn't seem like an issue when the pack did it with Bliss, but a whole new hellish world suddenly opened up for me. Did they have control over it? Could they hide certain emotions, or did they have to broadcast everything? That sounded like my worst fucking nightmare.

"Guys!" I bellowed over my shoulder.

I didn't really need to yell, since they were still assembled outside the room waiting for Bliss. Ares turned at the back of the group to face me, brow furrowed in confusion. "What?"

Flora whimpered, struggling to get down from my hold. Her whole body quivered, though it was impossible to tell if it was from her fear of alphas or her fear of her mate coming home. Both, probably. Fuck.

"Please, just go!" she insisted.

I jerked my head for the guys to hurry up and jogged down the stairs, hoping they got the message. "Do you know how long until—"

I didn't get a chance to finish my sentence.

The front door banged open. The hollow sound rocketed through the house, making my hair stand on end and Flora stiffen in my arms. She let out a strangled noise of panic that shot straight to my heart. My eyes darted left, then right, but we were standing in the middle of the narrow staircase with nowhere to go but up or down. This was so fucked.

"Where do I go?" I hissed over the roar of my own racing pulse.

"Fuck if I know!" she whispered back. "All I've seen of this house is that bedroom."

A flash of anger shined behind her eyes and I drew back a fraction. Even through her panic, that wasn't what I would've expected her—or any omega—to say. I liked it.

Making a split decision, I dashed down the three remaining steps onto the second-floor landing and turned right into another long, white-painted hallway. There was no decor—no rugs, no giant vases to hide behind like in a movie. I tried the nearest door—locked.

Footsteps thundered up the stairs below us, as I could only guess her mate ran up to the third-floor.

"I'm going to put you down," I whispered.

Flora grabbed onto my shirt, eyes wide. "No!"

My chest squeezed. "Just for a minute. Stand flat up against the wall and don't move."

Her expression was a mask of fear, but she let me lower her to the floor, even as the footsteps drew nearer. "Wait here."

I hoped the bastard would be too single-minded to look where he was going and just run right past us and straight into the pack. Still, if he didn't, I wanted to be between him and Flora. I reached down and pulled the gun out of my waistband and ran my finger over the trigger. I couldn't fight an alpha physically, but a shot to the head would stop anyone.

I stepped carefully back down the hall, aiming the gun at the landing. Labored breathing joined the pounding footsteps, and then a bluish blur darted past the illuminated doorway on its way up to the third-floor. My breath caught, my heartbeat jumping as I waited to see if Flora's mate would turn back around, realizing he'd blown past us.

He didn't.

"He's going to realize I'm not up there and go berserk," Flora called, her voice losing its fire again. "Wait, is Bliss still up there?"

My gaze flew from her beautiful tear-stained face to the mouth of the hallway where the footsteps were only getting louder. She was probably right, her mate would lose his shit, but the pack could hold their own. Somehow, I didn't think Flora needed to hear that.

"Bliss is fine. Don't move," I hissed over my shoulder at Flora, already sprinting back down the hall toward the stairs.

I burst back out of the hallway, skidding to a halt. I raised my gun again, my blood pumping with adrenaline. Above, footsteps, shouts, and muffled voices rang through the house—the mate must have found the pack. I started back up the stairs again, just as the group came into view on the landing above.

Flora's mate was huge—nearly seven feet tall. He had brownish hair and was dressed like a weekend anchor on a cable news show. Maybe it was just because I'd seen her bruises, but he looked like a fucking asshole to me.

The asshole pushed forward, as though he intended to go through the pack blocking his way. Literally.

Rafe snapped his teeth, seeming more feral then I'd seen him before, and shoved the man back away from Flora's room. He said something, but I couldn't make it out.

I hovered my finger over the trigger of my gun, sighting my shot, but they kept fucking moving. Flora's mate growled, darting backwards out of the way as Killian swiped at him. His foot landed on the edge of the stairs.

Time seemed to slow as the gigantic alpha teetered on the top step, arms windmilling. My stomach leapt, like I'd missed a stair myself, as I watched him tip backwards. Over his shoulder, Bliss's violet eyes had turned to saucers. Killian was in front of her, hand still hanging in the air like he'd forgotten they were there.

The large alpha tumbled backward, and collided with the steps. Crash after sickening crash reverberated down the stairs, like a gigantic bass drum.

"Move!" Nox screamed from somewhere too far away.

Fuck.

I dove out of the way, back into the mouth of the second-floor hallway. My heart pounded with mingled shock and adrenaline, and I whipped my head up to see Flora's reaction.

No.

I was running again before my brain had connected cause to action. I fell to my knees Next to Flora's limp body on the floor at the end of the hallway, and scanned her face for signs of what was happening. She was fine a minute ago. She'd been fine.

Flora was limp in my arms, her eyes rolling back in her head and in that moment the room seemed to tilt. Nausea swept through my body and my arms went numb, my throat suddenly tight and swollen. I heard myself yell something, but the words didn't make sense.

Footsteps thundered down the stairs and more shouts joined the cacophony of noise. I couldn't focus. That didn't matter.

"Let me see her." Bliss suddenly appeared next to me. Where the hell had she come from?

"No," I said harshly, pulling Flora's frail body away from Bliss. Then, my brain caught up with my mouth, and I had no idea why I'd refused. "What's wrong with her?"

"Her mate is dead. Wes, let me see."

"Dead? What the fuck just—"

"Let me see!"

I held Flora out to Bliss, refusing to let go completely. Bliss gave me an odd look, but didn't say anything. Her purple hair stuck to her face as she bent over her friend, pressing her fingers to Flora's pulse.

"I think she's fine. We need water, and to get her in the car."

"What the hell does that mean?" I said angrily.

She glared at me, clearly unwilling to give an inch when it came to her friend's safety. "Exactly what I said."

Killian appeared behind Bliss, putting a hand on her

back as she got in my face. I raised an eyebrow. Incidentally, this level of intensity was more how I'd pictured Bliss, after three years of hearing stories about her from the guys day in and day out. Interesting.

Fortunately, if it was about Flora's safety, Bliss and I were in total agreement. I adjusted Flora in my arms and turned back toward the door. Her chest rose and fell, but she was still too limp, her eyes closed and lifeless.

She stirred as I laid her across the back seat of the Tahoe and my heart leapt with relief. Thank fucking God. "Be right back, Buttercup. I'm going to grab you some water."

I stepped back into the front hall of the house and into the center of the group, now staring at the crumpled body on the first-floor landing I nearly gagged. With his neck twisted 'round like the goddamn exorcist, the asshole didn't look that intimidating,

"Oh my God," the maid muttered. "Shit."

"You can just leave," Bliss told her. "What's your name?"

"Clary."

"Okay, Clary. If you want, one of them can make it so you have to lie if anyone asks you about this. Otherwise you can just go."

I raised my eyebrows, more impressed than anything else. I supposed that's what you got for treating your staff like shit. I should be a cautionary tale, except that it would probably be best for the maid if no one ever heard about it.

Clary danced back and forth between her feet, clearly unsure what to do. I didn't blame her.

"No, wait."

I whipped my head up, my heart suddenly beating double time.

Flora stood in the doorway again. My sweatshirt covered the worst of her bruising but only emphasized the cuts and bruises on her bare legs and feet. Her hair was a mess, and she swayed slightly where she stood, but her expression was hard. Alert.

"Flora!" Bliss exclaimed. "Go back to the car. We—"

"No. You're making a plan, right? I want to help."

Bliss wrung her hands, obviously torn. "But you're hurt and…"

"I'm fine."

She clearly wasn't fine, but no one seemed to want to argue with that.

"Okay," Rafe said, clearly struggling to keep his voice even. Bliss reached out and grabbed his hand, seemingly without conscious thought. "So her mate is dead."

"No shit," Killian kicked the body with the toe of his boot, his voice half-awed, half-disgusted.

"I mean, we can't just take her to her parents now. There will be questions. This asshole was important, no matter what other twisted shit he got up to."

"We hide the body," Flora said flatly. She met Bliss' eyes across the group. "That's what I want. I want to hide the body and leave. I don't want to tell my parents."

Bliss bit her lip. "Okay. That's what we're doing, then. I hope no one has any moral objections 'cause you can leave."

I noticed her eyes lingering on me for half a second, and it didn't take a genius to know why. For every man in this house, the sun rose and set because of Bliss. Everyone but me. The pack wouldn't give two fucks what she wanted them to do or what they had to do to help her friend. They had no morals; their code of ethics was Bliss' happiness.

Except all of a sudden, I'd come up with my own code of ethics, and she was standing in the doorway, wearing a shitty, beat-up sweatshirt.

"I'll help," Clary said finally in a quiet voice from the furthest corner of the foyer. "Tell me I have to go to the police and lie. Or whatever you want to say." She looked up at Flora, and tears rose in her eyes. "I'll say whatever you want."

I didn't have to be able to smell anyone's emotions to know the mood in the room was heavy.

"There's only one thing," Nox said quietly, speaking only to Bliss. "If they both disappear, the Institute will come looking for them."

"What if it looks like I'm dead?" Flora asked, her voice rising in strength.

"Sure," Nox said. "But how?"

"Can I borrow that?" Flora stepped toward me, nodding at the pocketknife clipped on my belt.

I swallowed, nodding mutely, and handed her the knife handle-first.

Again, time seemed to slow. My blood ran cold the moment the cool metal left my hand and I spotted the conviction in her eyes.

"Wait!" Bliss yelled, darting forward.

Flora flipped the blade open, pushed up the sleeve of my sweatshirt, and ran it hard and fast over the skin of her forearm. Shouts and growls erupted as blood sprayed across the white tile floor, smattering the walls. She raised the knife again, and I reached her this time, grabbing her hand before it connected with anything major. "Stop."

"No." She met my eyes, jutting her lip out. "It has to look real."

"What are you trying to do?"

"Let go of my fucking arm and find out."

Behind us, Bliss choked on a sob, and I could hear the muffled sounds of someone trying to comfort her, but my focus was totally on the woman in front of me. I let go of her arm. "As you wish."

Flora grabbed a chunk of her long dark hair and hacked it off, tossing it across the floor. "For the scent," she said as though that explained everything. "Let's go."

CHAPTER 23
Bliss

The scent of Flora's emotions soured the air. She'd grown frail in the few weeks since the ceremony and looked tiny in Wes' arms. Her tan skin had turned a grayish white, made worse by the deep hollows under her eyes.

My heart clenched as she twitched in his arms and her hands tightened into fists. Wes whispered calming sounds too low for me to hear. He hadn't taken his eyes away from her from the second she'd let him pick her up.

She'd been restless for the first hour of the drive. She shrank away from my guys, eyes round. The only person who seemed to calm her was Wes. He tucked her into his chest and stroked a large hand up and down her back until her breathing evened out with sleep.

Nox ran his hand over his reddish-brown shaved hair. The earrings that lined his right ear caught the light from the lamppost, and their reflection danced around the car. His eyes searched mine. "Are you alright, Little Wolf?"

Am I? I glanced at Flora, who'd wrapped her hand with Wes' shirt as if she was holding on to a lifeline. I knew it would be bad, but this was somehow worse.

The guys had been on edge the entire ride. Flora's pain overwhelmed the smell of their emotions, but I could make them out through the bond.

Shock.

Fear.

Anguish.

Relief.

Possession.

Each one of them took the time to check in on me every few minutes, as if the need to confirm I was here was driving them insane.

"I think so," I murmured. Not quite a lie and not quite the truth.

Staring at my best friend, there was nothing alright about this situation. The only comfort was in knowing we got her out of there. That we'd protect her.

The thought pulled on my mind. *We.*

The doubt that gripped me over the last four years loosened, leaving behind the inkling of everything that *we* could mean.

At least, most of us.

My chest tightened as I glanced at Ares in the passenger seat. His brows furrowed as he drew an intricate design over his calf. His face snapped up, and I studied my fingers before he could catch me staring. I held my breath as his gaze heated my skin like a brand. A chill passed through me as he looked away.

Killian slid his hand over my thigh and gently squeezed. "Ignore him."

If only it was that easy.

I could barely keep my eyes open as the heavy weight of tonight's events took over. As I drifted off, images of Alpha Bishop tumbling down the stairs and the way his neck landed at such a disturbing angle had my stomach turning. Nox's warm hands pulled me over his lap to rest between him and Killian.

"We've got you. Go to sleep." Nox's soft lips touched my forehead, and I burrowed deeper into his chest while Killian ran his hands soothingly over my legs.

It was early dawn, the sky still too dark to see as we pulled up to the warehouse. We'd driven through the night, unwilling to risk stopping. The more distance we put between us and that house, the better.

Rafe jumped out of the driver's seat, slamming his door, and Flora startled awake. I glared at him, and he lifted his shoulders and hands in a "sorry" motion, backing up slowly. Flora turned out of Wes' arms, and his jaw clenched as he gently led her out of the car before releasing her completely.

Everyone jumped out of the Tahoe. Nox, Killian, Rafe, and Ares moved toward the warehouse, but Wes still hovered around Flora. I gestured my head toward where the guys stood twenty feet away. "Can I have a minute with Flora?"

Wes' eyes darted to me, then to Flora, where she stared at the ground. He paused for a moment before folding his arms over his chest, making it clear he wasn't leaving.

I was about to become way less polite to get him to

leave, but Flora took a small step in his direction, her shoulders dropping slightly.

Whatever was happening, she was more comfortable with the beta than my alphas.

"Hey, girl, you're okay now." I lifted a hand to push back a long piece of her ebony hair but dropped it away when she flinched. I swallowed hard and took a step back.

Flora was slightly crouched in on herself, arms crossed tight over her middle as she looked around. "Where are we?"

My eyes burned at the break in her voice. "We..." I let my breath out in a huff. I didn't know how exactly to answer that. I settled for the bare minimum. "We're with the guys I told you about."

Flora's gaze snapped to mine, a hint of the sparkle they used to hold. "*The* guys?"

I could feel my cheeks grow hot, and the glow of amusement trickled through the bond. "The same."

Killian walked up to us, placing a hand on my shoulder, and all traces of improvement dropped from Flora's face. Her chin touched her chest, and the distinct scent of cranberries coated my nose. Killian stiffened behind me, then immediately put distance between himself and Flora.

Wes uncrossed his arms, allowing Flora to step back without him touching her. He kept his hands at his sides but didn't increase the bare inch that was between them.

She didn't seem to mind his proximity.

Wes' brows pulled together, his gaze focused on Flora, all traces of his playful expression wiped off his face. I glanced between him and the guys. They weren't throwing off a hint of their emotions, like they were doing everything possible to tone down their scents. Meanwhile, Wes was a powder keg of worry mixed with anger.

I rubbed my hands over my face. This was going to be harder than I thought. I walked up to where Ares, Rafe, Killian, and Nox stood, all equally exhausted. "She's not going to go anywhere near you."

"Fuck." Rafe put his hands on the back of his head and looked at the quickly lightening sky. "Okay. Get her in your room, then we'll come in once she's settled."

Flora was still staring at her bare feet, completely shut in on herself. Her hair tumbled over her shoulder, covering her mating marks, and Wes' hoodie practically swallowed her up.

I bit my thumb, unsure if this was a good idea or not. "What if she doesn't…"

All four guys watched me, no doubt feeling my anxiousness through the bond. Nox closed the distance between us and gently lowered my hand from my mouth. "What if what?"

"Maybe we should bring her to her parents?"

"No."

All heads turned to Wes, including the small omega inches away from him.

"Well, if she won't come upstairs, where would you like her to go?"

"She can stay with me." Wes blurted the words before stiffening, slowly meeting Flora's eyes. "I mean, you can stay with me if that's what you want."

Flora let her gaze roam over Wes, his hands, his chest, his neck. He may not be an alpha, but he was still more than capable of overpowering her. I was just about to say forget about it when she spoke. "I'd like that."

Wes seemed to try to shrink his size so as not to overwhelm her as he gestured toward his small home. He wasn't trying to loom over her like some protective alpha. He was using his betaness to help her feel comfortable.

I smiled widely at Wes. He won some brownie points for that one.

Growls rumbled from behind me, and I sent back a quick glare. The growling stopped as all four of them were suddenly interested in their shoes.

I hooked my arm into Flora's and spoke low enough that only she could hear me. "You okay with this?"

She leaned her exhausted body against me and looked between Wes and the guys. "I can't go in there with them." She squeezed my hand.

"Okay, you heard her. Show us your home."

A hint of a smirk tipped up Wes' mouth, the first sign of the man I'd grown to know since he first laid eyes on Flora. "It's not much, but I have the perfect spot for you."

Wes' keys jingled in his hand as he worked at getting the large steel door unlocked. It was a small industrial building, probably an old office of some sort converted into his living space. He swung the door wide and held it open for Flora and me.

Wes looked between us, bottom lip tucked under his teeth as he waited for Flora's reaction. She came around me, wide brown eyes scanning the open space. We'd stepped into a small kitchen with old slatted wood cabinets and vinyl flooring. Unlike the warehouse, Wes' place was closed off into individual rooms instead of an open concept. The coziness eased some of my anxiety. Flora moved through the space, toward the hallway, and turned toward Wes.

Her eyes didn't lift from the ground, and her hands twisted in Wes' sweater. "Can I look around?"

Wes looked green, and the scent of sour milk wafted off him as he stared at her dejected form. "You can do whatever you want, Buttercup." The corner of his mouth kicked up when she met his gaze. "My place is yours."

Flora huffed out a breath, nearly a laugh, before entering the room across the hall. It was a living area with a couch and two matching love seats that looked like they were from the 1970s. A lemon scent lingered, leaving the room smelling clean and well cared for. There was wall-to-wall wood paneling, driving home the warm cocoon-like tones. Flora dragged her hand over the back of a long mahogany table covered in cards and poker chips. A few mostly empty glasses at each chair. She raised a brow at Wes, and he cleared his throat.

"Don't worry. No one will be in here if you're here."

She nodded, looking at her toes, then me. "It's nice."

"'Nice' as in you want to stay here?"

She sucked her bottom lip between her teeth, then took a deep breath. "Yeah, I think it's a good idea."

I wasn't sure if I agreed this was the best idea. She was an omega who'd just lost her mate, and no matter how much of an asshole he was, that wouldn't stop the devastating physiological response she was having. I strangled the part of me that wanted to insist she'd be better off with me. She'd had enough people telling her what to do for a lifetime. What she needed was a shower, a snack, and a nice long nap.

I locked our arms together and let her rest her head on my shoulder. "Okay. Wes, where's your guest room?"

Wes' brows raised, and his eyes went round, giving

him an almost boyish look. "I don't have one. She'll stay in my room."

My mouth dropped open and closed a few times before I recovered from my shock. "Absolutely not."

"Don't look at me like that. I'll stay on the pullout couch."

Flora's hand squeezed mine. "It's fine. We can figure something else out tomorrow."

I let out a sweeping breath. "Tomorrow, then." I raised a brow in Wes' direction. "How about a shower?"

Wes made short work of showing us the bathroom that was next door to the only bedroom in this dwelling. It was a simple design: small wood vanity, toilet, and shower, only large enough to fit one person. Steam drifted from around the curtain, filling the small space.

Flora winced as she tried to take her sweater off, the sleeve catching on her makeshift bandage. I tamped down the cold shudder threatening to overcome me after last night.

"Here." I held my hand out to her. "Let me help."

She stiffened, eyes lost for a moment before coming back to mine, and held out her arm. I carefully shifted the fabric over her cut and guided the sweater above her head. My breath caught when her hair lifted with the garment, revealing a row of partially healed bites along her neck, still rimmed with dried blood. Finger-sized bruises covered her from being held too hard.

"Flora…" The words caught on my tongue. "I'm sorry this happened to you."

Flora turned her back to me and shielded herself from my gaze with the shower curtain. The room quickly filled with the scent of male bodywash. The smell was something you'd expect from the college football team. It kept getting stronger, but she didn't make a sound except for the occasional pained hisses.

I slowly pushed the curtain back, leaving plenty of time for her to stop me. "Let me smell."

Flora's eyes rounded on me with a flare of fear, but she leaned her neck toward me. "You don't smell like him anymore. The bond is broken. He's dead. Now you smell like a teenage boy trying to get laid."

She choked on her laugh, eyes welling with tears, and nodded. "I smell better than you. My nose is burning with your alphas' claiming scents." She wrapped the towel I handed her around her body, taking extra care with her arm.

"They aren't really my alphas. They scent marked me so I could leave the house without everyone freaking out about meeting an unmated omega."

Her head tilted to the side, scanning over my face. "Keep telling yourself that."

Wes had dropped off a change of clothes, a hairbrush, and a fresh bandage for her cut. By the time she was ready, Wes was waiting outside the bathroom door. He took one look at Flora, lifted her from her feet, and carried her to her bed, taking extra care to pull the covers over her.

Wes closed the door behind him, and my nose singed with the scent of iron.

"He's fucking lucky he's already dead."

CHAPTER 24
Nox

"Can you stop?" Ares barked at Killian, who'd been pacing the length of the roof for the last hour. "Fuck! Sit down."

Killian gestured to where Ares had covered every last inch of available skin with a black Sharpie. "Like you're any better."

Ares sat on the rooftop chair to the right of the sofa, his foot crossed over his ankle, giving him ample access to his calf. His pale blond hair was pushed off his face, and his brows were pulled tight as he drew intricate lines.

The cascade of emotions Bliss was sending down the bond was driving us all insane. The steady stream of deep-seated sadness for her friend had my heart tearing in two. The spikes of her guilt had me practically doubled over on the couch. I'd do anything to take this away from her.

I pulled my glasses off, letting them drop to my lap, and rubbed both hands over my head. "Maybe we should check on her?"

Rafe handed me a beer from the cooler from across the couch. He leaned into the shadows, and his dark hair and eyes made it hard to read his expression. "We're staying here. We can't stress Flora any more than we already have."

Flora. The once lively, if annoying, girl we'd known in high school was a shadow of what she once was. My blood boiled, thinking of the bruises along her face and jaw. Her hair, which looked like it hadn't been washed in weeks, and the leftover blood from her mating marks.

That girl had gone through hell.

Killian pulled off his black-and-red flannel button-up, leaving him in a fitted gray T-shirt. "I don't fucking get it. Alphas are programmed to protect their mate. To love and care for them. How did he let her get like that?"

My stomach roiled at the notion of hurting Bliss. "Clearly, there's more to it than we thought." I sucked on my teeth, racking my brain for any possible conclusion. "The bond isn't a sentient thing. It doesn't give a shit about love or caring; it's about possessing the omega." The words felt like acid on my tongue. "He locked her in a fucking room."

Rafe took a long sip of his beer. "That doesn't make sense. That would mean hundreds, if not thousands, of omegas would be in the same situation."

I stared at him, my eyes narrowed. "And what makes you think that isn't the case?"

Ares laughed, harsh and cold. "I'd believe it. Fuck the Institute."

"Hang on," I cut him off, "that's not what I said."

"It should've been. What makes you think the Institute doesn't know? They get paid. Why give a shit about the omegas afterward?" Ares' laugh ran a chill down my spine. "They fucking orchestrated this. Making the Agora Ceremony seem like a good thing, not letting the omegas mate on their own, only being sold to the highest bidder."

I clamped my mouth shut. He was right. It sounded like a damn conspiracy theory, but it made sense, and after everything Bliss said, I'd be lying if I said I didn't believe it.

Killian held his hands up. "But why?"

"You can't be that naïve. It's fucking money. It's always about fucking money and power," Ares hissed. "We aided and abetted them with fucking blockers this whole time."

My stomach plummeted to the floor, thinking of the role we played in this disgusting industry. "Fuck that. I don't give a shit if we lose everything. We're done." I narrowed my gaze, and a soft rumble formed in my chest, daring them to disagree, but they all nodded like it was a given we'd give up our livelihood after this. Maybe there was hope for us after all.

Ares lifted his head, gaze darting around us, and capped his Sharpie. "There's something else we need to talk about."

Killian threw his hands up. "Well, don't try and hold us in suspense."

"Bliss thinks we don't want to mate with her."

My breath left me like he'd punched me in the stomach. Out of everything, I thought he'd say that wasn't even on the radar. How could she be so wrong? "How do you know?"

"She told me," he said acidly.

Rafe leaned forward, resting his elbows on his knees, eyeing Ares. "Why the hell would she think that?"

Growls blocked out every other sound as Ares' words sank in.

His pale eyes met mine. He clenched his jaw, his expression tormented. "She said she loved us. She still believes all that bullshit Rafe spouted four years ago. That we didn't want her with us because she'd get us killed." He huffed out a laugh. "Meanwhile, we spent all that time killing and nearly dying to fucking get her back."

Killian collapsed into the chair to the left of the sofa. "What the hell do we do now?"

A calmness settled over Rafe. "We convince her we want to be a pack."

I watched him with dark eyes. "You think it's that simple?"

"Yeah, it's that simple. And we start right fucking now."

I hopped up from my spot on the sofa and headed for the exit door, running my hands over my head as I went. I didn't need our bond to know our girl was hurting, and I wasn't going to sit around and wait anymore.

"Where are you going, Nox?"

"Where the hell do you think I'm going? I'm going to find her."

Ares' gaze bored into mine. "When she's done at Wes', bring her here. We'll comfort her as a pack."

The muddle of emotions filled the air with scent. To be a pack, and for Ares of all of us to suggest it. A slow, warm feeling filled my limbs and sank into my chest. *A pack.*

"So that's it, then?" Rafe crossed his arms over his chest. "You're just all in—you're going to act like you haven't been a fucking nightmare for four straight years?

"Yeah." Ares gave him a hard look. "That's exactly

what I'm saying. Do you think I was doing this for my fucking health? You think I like being miserable?"

"I don't get it," Rafe snapped.

"Yeah, you never fucking got it. You were always happy to move forward. I wasn't."

"Okay, let's all try and calm down." Killian grinned nervously. "Take a breath, man."

"No," Rafe barked. "What did I do to offend you other than hold everything together?"

"I didn't ask you to do that. It's not my problem that you decided to play daddy and then resented it. We're all adults."

Rafe growled, his face turning red, as Ares' eyes flashed dark. I rubbed my hand over my head. This was some toxic shit that no one needed, and worst of all, it was going to keep us from Bliss. "Alright, stop. No one wants to listen to you two fight it out."

"Then don't listen," Rafe barked.

I ignored him. "Ares, if you're really all in, why? What happened?"

He met my eyes, and I shivered at the intensity. "Because that's what Bliss said she wants, and this has always been about her."

I waited for half a second to see if there would be any hint of deception in that statement, or even confusion, but there wasn't. Killian and I glanced at each other across the circle. He shrugged as if to say, "Good enough for me."

The waves of frustration rolling off Rafe were still enough to make his opinion perfectly clear, but I doubted he'd be able to stay that way for long. It was the same reason that, despite everything, we'd never been able to separate.

Bliss had bonded us all together. Not just to her, but to each other as well, and I had a feeling that the moment all five of us got on the same page, there would be no turning back.

Bliss was opening her bedroom door by the time I caught up to her. She looked exhausted, and a part of me wanted to just let her rest and figure it out in the morning, but that was overshadowed by a raging, swirling need to show her how fucking wrong she was. How much we cared, craved, loved her.

Red rimmed her violet eyes, and she crossed her arms over her middle as she radiated desolation down the bond. I stepped closer, sliding a strand of her hair behind her shoulder. I dropped my forehead to hers. "Come sit with us."

I held my breath. This felt like a test. It made more sense for her to tell me it was late, but love didn't care about making sense. My body hummed with the want to care for her. To lift some of her sadness and carry it for her.

She paused for a minute before nodding. "Okay, but only for a bit."

A small smirk formed on my lips. She'd soon learn it would be forever.

I guided her up the stairs to the roof and tugged her along with me to sit between Rafe and me on the couch. He made quick work of handing her a beer. "How is she?"

Bliss took a deep sip from the bottle. Her scent of burnt sugar and dead flowers had my heart aching in my chest.

Bliss sucked in her breath, and her voice cracked around her words. "I don't know. The things she's lived through…. She's so scared."

I stroked a hand over her chin, encouraging her to face me. "We'll take care of her, Little Wolf. She'll have a safe place here with us."

Bliss' lips wobbled as she looked between all of us, eyes landing on Ares. "As in stay?"

Ares was completely still, all of his attention pinpointed on Bliss. His voice was devoid of its usual snark. "We want you to stay."

Bliss sucked in a breath and pulled her feet up on the couch. Her emotions swirled in a mix of confusion, desperation, and guilt.

I wrapped my arms under hers and pulled her sideways over my lap, placing delicate kisses along her temple and jaw as Rafe pulled her legs over his thighs. She leaned into my touch, and her distress lifted a fraction.

"You don't have to agree now." I kissed along her jaw, and her sweet jasmine, honey, and chillies scent met my tongue. "Let us take care of you. We can make you forget, and we can deal with it *together* tomorrow."

She stiffened, teeth biting into her lower lip. She was fighting against this, guilt still coming through the bond.

Ares' took two steps across the circle, closing the space between us, and kneeled in front of the couch. The top of Ares head just reached Bliss' middle, with her sitting on my lap. His chest purred low as he slipped her hair behind her ear. "This is what we're here for, Love. You want your alphas to comfort you, don't you?"

She licked her lips and nodded. "Yes."

CHAPTER 25
Bliss

My mind swirled, tipping to the side, and I felt like I would topple over. Ares knelt on the ground beside me, trailing biting kisses up my neck. "That's my good girl."

Ares.

Ares watched me like I hung the moon— like everything had somehow changed. His ice-blue eyes begged me not to question it. Every emotion threatened to overtake me as he trailed up my skin.

Rafe ran a hand up my calf, his fingers grazing the sensitive skin behind my knees.

Nox's growl rumbled against my side. "I want you to let yourself go, Little Wolf. We'll catch you." I squirmed on his lap when his tongue stroked over my mating gland, and my legs tried to squeeze together. "Can you trust us, Bliss? Even for just tonight?"

After everything that happened and the years that

stood between us, the answer was still simple: I'd always trusted them entirely too much, and I still did. "Yes."

Ares leaned in closer, and his fingers grazed the hem of my sweater, brushing the bare skin above the waistband of my skirt. He pulled my sweater over my head, revealing my black bra. "You're so good, Love."

I didn't know what had happened to change his mind, and right now, I didn't care. I'd think about it later. Tomorrow. Right now, I was done pretending I didn't need him.

"Fuck, babe," Killian said hoarsely from his seat across the circle.

A thrill ran through me as I looked up, meeting his darkening gaze. Growls erupted as I reached back and undid the clasp, letting it slip off my arms and onto the couch.

The pupils of Ares' eyes expanded until they were almost completely black, with only the barest hint of blueish silver showing, like a lunar eclipse. He leaned even closer, his hands sliding further up my thighs until they were so close to where I needed them I was practically shaking. He bit down on his lip. "Fuck, I've dreamed of this."

Heat burned down my stomach into my core. Nox against my side, Rafe holding my legs across his lap, and Killian's hungry gaze made me bold. I tilted my chin up in a very un-omega gesture and forced my voice not to shake. "Yeah? What did we do in your dreams?"

Ares' gaze danced up to Nox, curling his lip. Nox shifted under me and ran his hands up the sides of my bare waist and cupped my breasts. His voice practically dripped with lust. "You sure you want to know?"

My body hummed with anticipation as I looked around

at all four of them. All of my boys were here, and I wanted to play. I'd never been more sure of anything before. "Show me."

Ares growled and lifted me off Nox's lap. As soon as my feet hit the ground, he made quick work of my skirt and underwear, leaving me bare in front of them. Standing there naked, I should've felt exposed, but I felt empowered.

They were watching me like I was the only thing that mattered.

Ares smiled and pulled his shirt over his head. Nox and Rafe quickly followed suit. They removed the rest of their clothes, standing proudly while my heated gaze traveled over every naked inch of them.

Nox placed his hands on my hips, guiding me onto his lap, my back pressed against his chest. I gasped as his hard cock slid through my folds but didn't enter. His piercing rolled over me, sending a shiver down my legs.

Rafe kneeled on the couch to my right. Strands of his near-black hair covered his dark gaze. The deep olive tan of his skin made each hill and valley of muscle stand out in sharp contrast. I was losing my mind following the deep v-cut abs down—

"We're going to play a game." Ares' words stole my attention, and he stared at me with heat in his gaze.

"What game?" My voice wavered.

Killian stood from his chair and crossed to stand in front of me, shedding his clothes as he went. His honey-brown curls wrapped around his ears, and my eyes traveled down his chest. His cock bobbed when my gaze caught on it.

He leaned down, capturing my mouth in a long, slow

kiss. He smirked against my lips. "Keep looking at my cock like that and I won't last long."

"Don't distract her," Ares barked, more playful than angry.

Killian grinned and sank onto the couch on my left, mirroring Rafe's position on my right side. "I think I'm going to like this game."

Ares gripped my knees and pulled them to the outside of Nox's, leaving me completely exposed. A low growl rumbled from his throat as he stared at my exposed core, now perfectly aligned with his face. I tried to close my legs, but Nox just held me open wider.

Ares ran his nose along my thigh, inches away from my apex. "We're going to see if we can make you come without touching this sweet pussy of yours."

I whined, and Killian and Rafe simultaneously sucked on my mating glands on my neck, bruising the skin there. The intensity had my eyes rolling back as heat flooded me, washing away every thought with it until they reduced me to a writhing mess.

Ares searched my face, and a wicked smile lifted his lips. Without looking away, he ran his tongue along my inner thigh, and a jolt went through me as he grazed his teeth over the mating gland there. "You want us to bite you, don't you, Love?"

My hips bucked up, and Nox's held on to my knees, spreading them wider. "Yes."

Ares bit my skin millimeters from the gland, and I cried out at the torture of it. My body rioted, knowing it was so close to being mated.

Ares bit again, his teeth bruising the skin all around my

gland. I gasped, my chest rising, only to have Killian and Rafe sink their teeth into my breasts.

The mix of pain and anticipation had me rocking against Nox. His cock slid easily between my crack, soaked with my slick. I pushed back against him, and he groaned, mouth brushing my neck. "Hold still, Little Wolf."

I froze, every molecule pinpointed on where his teeth grazed over me. He let his tongue trace my mating gland before sinking his teeth in the curve of my neck an inch below it. I bucked up, pressure building with each touch. They were so close to what my body craved.

I grasped Ares' hair and tried to force him against my clit, but Killian and Rafe caught my hands and placed them around Nox's neck behind me.

My fingers dug into his soft, shaved hair as my breaths came out in harsh pants. I craved their teeth to sink into the gland. To crack it open and complete our bond.

This was too much.

Killian nipped the bottom of my breast, then licked over the spot to soothe it. My thoughts had turned to flames as each of their bites stoked the fire until I thought I would combust.

The sweetest ache formed in my core, throbbing as the intensity of their touches grew. They alternated between licking and sucking, and my core throbbed with their tempo.

"Please, Alpha." I didn't know who I was calling to, but I didn't care. I needed them. Needed them to take care of me. Needed my alphas to push me over the edge.

Nox's hands gripped my hips and moved me until he was fucking against my ass, leaving my core empty.

"Please."

Four sets of teeth broke my skin simultaneously just outside of my mating glands. The constant buildup of pleasure detonated around me as I came. I shook in their arms and continued to spasm as more orgasms passed through me.

Rafe placed a soft kiss on my temple. "Fucking perfect."

I took a deep breath, and my lungs burned as I took in their scents. Lemon vanilla, smooth sandalwood, coffee beans, and the fresh scent of a new night. Heat swirled in my chest, down my stomach, until it pulsed in my core.

I needed, wanted, craved to touch them. I lifted until Nox's cock slipped over my core. His jewelry hit my clit perfectly, and I rocked myself against it, purring when his breath hitched.

I reached for Killian's and Rafe's cocks and stroked them from bottom to top. Their precum coated my fingers, letting me slide over their smooth, hard skin with ease. Killian groaned, his teeth catching my nipple, and I rolled my hips with the tempo, chasing my second release. They gasped when I squeezed over their tips, so I did it harder, faster, the next time, until they were both pumping into my hands.

Killian pulled out of my hand and lifted until his cock was positioned beside Nox's mouth. I shifted to the side and leaned back so I could see the exact moment Killian's head breached Nox's lips. They both groaned low, and the vibration traveled directly between my thighs. Killian started to pump harder, holding the back of Nox's head as he made him force it down. Nox's cock jerked against me, moving faster with each of Killian's thrusts.

I stroked Rafe's cock, and he licked up the side of my

neck. "You're perfect. See how they watch you as they fuck each other? They've been denying themselves this for *years.*" Rafe ran his thumb over my bottom lip and pushed between my teeth. "I want to take this sweet mouth of yours."

I hummed and tugged on him until he lifted his hips to my mouth. I licked his tip, purring at his salty taste, and I sucked his cock down my throat.

Ares groaned from between my legs, finally sucking on my clit. I lost control and started to suck Rafe harder, pumping him with my fist at the same time. Rafe's hips stuttered as he filled my mouth with his release, and I worked to swallow it all. He sat back and licked the cum that dripped from the corner of my mouth. "Fucking perfect."

Nox groaned, and his hot cum dripped down my thighs as Killian burst in his mouth.

Ares growled, and his tongue ran over his bottom lip as he looked at the mess Nox made of me. Ares' nearly black eyes burned into mine as he licked Nox's cum, cleaning me.

My chest heaved as my body chased its own orgasm. I needed to feel it rip through me so I could pour myself out.

Ares moved until his chest met mine, and his fingers dug into my jaw as his gaze bored into mine. He ran his tongue over my lips, and I opened for him, the taste of Nox filling my mouth. "Fuck," Ares growled. "We'll torture you later."

He slammed his cock hilt-deep into my needy core, and my orgasm burst like a million stars, shattering my world around me.

Ares lifted me from Nox and rolled us to the ground so his back was to the rooftop and I straddled him. Killian and Rafe watched from the couch, their chests rising and falling with their panting breaths.

Ares groaned as I took him all the way in, and his fingers dug into my hips as he guided me up and down in slow, languid motions. "That's it, Love. You take me so well."

My lungs burned as I sucked in a breath, and fire singed through my damp skin.

Nox knelt at our heads and cupped my jaw in his hand, tilting my head back, and read my mind. "Do you need more, Little Wolf?"

"Yes," I keened.

Ares' rhythm increased as he pushed more of himself into me with each thrust until his knot pressed against my entrance. I shifted, trying to take it in, but his hands stilled me. "Patience, Love."

I growled, and he smiled. The air sucked out of my lungs at how much he looked like the Ares I remembered.

My eyes burned. "I missed you."

He choked on his breath. "Fuck, Bliss. We missed you too." He slammed into me, driving his point home. I arched back, and Nox caught my moan with his mouth.

Rafe dropped from the couch and caught my ear between his teeth. "You're meant for us. Our mate."

"What?" I asked, my voice barely above a whisper. Everyone stilled. Warmth flooded my chest that had nothing to do with sex. *Our mate.*

I met Rafe's gaze. "Say it again."

"Our mate."

I shook my head. "But you didn't want me."

"I fucking lied." He pushed a strand of damp hair behind my shoulder. "We've always loved you. You're our mate, and it has nothing to with the fucking scent bond."

"That's if you'll have us." Killian's voice broke around the words.

Happiness bubbled in my stomach as I met each of their eager eyes. "A pack?"

Nox kissed me, smiling against my mouth. "Yes, Little Wolf. A pack."

Rafe let his teeth graze where my gland throbbed. "A few more months until your next heat, then we'll claim you as ours."

My body shook under his touch, and the air smelled sweet and fruity as their pleasure tumbled through the bond. I shifted, and Ares' cock moved deeper inside me, drawing a groan from the back of his throat. Honey filled my nose as lust coated my skin, taking over the moment. They were my pack, and I wanted all of them.

I gasped as fingers trailed up my back, and goose bumps erupted in their wake. Killian's growl rumbled through me as he kissed up my spine. "You ready for me, B?"

His hand trailed down my ass and wrapped around where Ares was pumping into my core. I clenched around him, anticipating taking them both.

Killian chuckled, his hand sliding back, stroking over my second hole. His fingers swirled around it, coating it in my slick. "I want to take you here. You'd like that, wouldn't you?"

I nodded, and shivers broke out over my skin. *Yes, please.*

He kissed along my shoulder blades, and I gasped

when he pushed a finger into my ass. He swirled it before pulling it back and pushing in a second one.

Ares groaned. "Fuck. She's clamped down on me. Killian, do it again."

Killian's hand pulled away from me, and Ares growled.

I kissed Ares, sucking in his bottom lip. "Who's impatient now?"

He purred and nipped at me, and I laughed.

Killian lined himself up, and I stilled completely. He started working himself into my ass. I sucked in a breath. It was too much.

"Look at me, Little Wolf." My gaze obeyed, and Nox's face was so close he ran his nose along mine, our lips brushing. "Breathe. You're made for them. Just breathe."

I followed his breathing pattern and relaxed into their touch. Killian pushed deeper, drawing a moan from both me and Ares.

My head tipped back as Killian sank to his hilt, pulling out before slamming back in, and I cried out between them. "Alpha."

"My turn." Rafe kissed up my neck, swirling his tongue over my mating gland.

I hummed, having no idea where I'd take him but more than willing to try.

I had to contort my body to see him move behind Killian. Rafe raked his fingers into Killian's hair, pulling it back to expose his neck, and licked up the column of muscle. "Do you want me to bite you here?"

Killian shivered against my back. "Yes."

Rafe leaned over, his hand turning me back toward Ares. "Bliss, I need you to take his knot so I can take Killian's ass. You want that, don't you?"

"Yes, please."

Ares growled, and his hips slammed into mine until I adjusted to fit all of him. His chest rumbled as his knot grew, locking me in place. I whined and ground against him as he rutted his hips up.

Rafe growled, and Killian moaned as Rafe sank into his ass. Killian's cock slammed into me with each of Rafe's thrusts, causing me to squirm, but Ares' knot still locked me firmly in place.

Nox's usually green gaze was pitch-black as he watched his friends take me. "That's it, Little Wolf. You're so fucking stunning."

Ares' hand slipped between us, and his thumb circled my clit with the perfect amount of pressure.

I closed my eyes, mouth falling open, and a smooth head touched my lips, coating them in salt. My gaze snapped to Nox's as he slowly pushed his cock into my mouth.

His eyes rolled back as my tongue slid over each piercing, and I hummed around him.

"That's it, Love," Ares encouraged me as they all slammed into me until it felt like I was going to lose my mind. His thumb circled my clit with steady motions until I came apart around him, my muscles clenching with my release. He grunted, his hips shuddering as he filled me with cum.

Killian leaned over and bit my shoulder as he rutted against my ass, grunting with his orgasm.

Rafe came while telling Killian how good he felt. I hollowed out my cheeks and sucked hard on Nox, determined to drive him just as far over the edge as I was. He choked back a groan, and bitter salt painted the back of my throat as he lost himself to the sensation.

Killian rolled off my back, and we collapsed around each other, doing our best to suck in air. I lay motionless over Ares as his heart pounded against my ear. There was no world where I could lift myself from this position.

"You're such a perfect omega." Rafe's hands ran up and down my back in a soothing pattern until my breaths evened out and my eyes grew heavy.

They must have let me sleep because Ares was no longer knotted inside me. We descended the stairs, and panic started to set in as we moved down the hall. The bond ached at the idea of being apart from any of them. "I don't want to go to sleep. I need all of you."

Ares ran his fingers along my jaw and opened a door. "Shh, Love. We're just going to the nest. No one's going anywhere."

I snuggled into Killian, breathing in his scent, basking in the feeling of satisfaction.

They were finally *mine*.

CHAPTER 26
Bliss

My nightmares stayed just on the edge of my consciousness all night, never breaking through the warm cocoon of familiar scents I'd wrapped myself in. Citrus, coffee, warm spices, and midnight sky.

I snuggled deeper into the warmth of the arms circling my waist and pressed my face against someone's hard bicep. I never wanted to leave this place—between dream and reality.

Still, that wasn't realistic.

Sighing, I cracked an eye open and rolled over. I looked over at the bodies surrounding me on all sides, and a small smile crossed my face. My body ached in all the right places, reminding me in the most perfect way of last night. For the first time, we felt like a pack. I'd let them comfort me and put aside all our past trauma. Maybe, for once, I could let myself have this. I could believe that I was home.

Yet, with the morning sunlight streaming across the bed, the doubt started to creep back in.

I sat up and gingerly slithered out of the tangle of limbs, trying not to wake anyone. I grabbed a shirt off the floor, not bothering to check who it belonged to, and tossed it over my head. *Thank God they're all the size of a house.*

The air of the hallway was cold compared with that of the nest. It was like our combined body heat and breath had warmed the room—that was probably literally what it was, since there were no windows and barely any ventilation. When I'd been at the Institute, I'd never understood what they meant about omegas liking small and dark places. Now, I realized that I actually did. I just hadn't liked the Institute. There was a difference.

My nest at the warehouse was—I almost hated myself for using the Institute's favorite word—soothing.

It was things like how the guys had made me a nest. They'd bought me clothes—even if they weren't quite right. They'd fought for Flora, and last night, they said they loved me. Things like that made it seem like maybe I should stay.

And that wasn't even taking into account all the emotions I was getting blasted with on a daily basis.

Maybe I wasn't putting enough stock into that. I'd dismissed a lot of their feelings of lust and affection as part of the bond. Something they couldn't help. Was that hypocritical when I'd just yelled at Ares for ignoring my feelings from before the bond came into effect?

I sighed as I padded down the hallway to the living room and sank onto the nearest armchair. I could argue both sides of this dilemma. Rationalize my way into leaving or staying, based on love or pride, and I had no idea what to do. There was no rule book for this kind of thing. No one way to forgive a betrayal or move on from trauma. Just like there was no rule book to love.

"Hey."

I glanced up at the sound of footsteps in time to see Rafe wander into the room. He wore only wrinkled sweatpants and no shirt and was rubbing sleep from his face. My eyes immediately darted to the V of his abs, and heat rose up the back of my neck.

"Did I wake you?" I asked, pushing my hair behind my ears.

I wasn't sure if it was his expression or our bond letting me know he was anxious. Maybe both. Maybe it was that I'd known him for so long, I could read him without having to dig into his feelings or hope he was projecting them. When I first arrived, it had seemed to me like all the guys were completely different, but they weren't. Not really. Only in the same way that I was. Lost but not forgotten.

"Yes, but I'm glad you did." Rafe sat down on the edge of the couch facing me. "What are you doing out here?"

"Just getting coffee, I guess." He gave me a look to tell me without words he knew I was lying. "Fine. I just wanted a second to think about everything. I thought I might go see how Flora is doing. Maybe go for a walk."

"Do you want someone to come with you?"

I frowned, skeptical. "Do you want to come with me?"

"Always."

My heart panged at that. I twirled my hair around my fingers, trying to find the right words for what I meant. "I think we all need to talk."

He snorted a laugh, and my eyes narrowed slightly. He stopped immediately, seeing my face. "No, don't take that the wrong way. You're right—we definitely need to talk. It's just, this is such a fucking mess."

I pulled my hair over my shoulders like a security blanket, smiling to myself now. "You think? I don't know what the hell is going on anymore."

I heard myself swear, and I almost apologized, then forced myself not to. No one was going to tell me what I could and couldn't say anymore. There was no headmistress Omega DuPont hanging over my shoulder. No Alpha Nero. Rafe didn't give two fucks. I grinned.

"What now?" he asked, matching my smile.

My stomach jolted at his smile, and it was odd. We kept having sex. We were already bonded, but a rare smile had the potential to give me butterflies. "You wouldn't understand."

"Try me."

"You guys say 'fuck' all the time, but you have no idea. The Institute didn't even let us talk about being angry. We had to say 'upsetting our balance.'" I grimaced. "I'm just getting used to no one policing what I can say anymore."

His eyes widened. "Bliss. Holy fuck. I don't..."

"Don't say anything," I said quickly, shrugging. "That's not what I want to talk about. That's just what I was thinking."

He ran his hands through his hair, tilting his head up to the ceiling. "Bliss, we meant everything last night. I know we fucked up. Years ago, but also basically every moment since you got here. Every time you mention something else about what you've gone through, it kills me."

"Wait," I blurted out.

"No." He leaned toward me, black eyes wide and earnest. "I am so sorry. We handled this all wrong, and that's a lot on me. I should have controlled the situation better."

I opened my mouth to reply, but my words were drowned by a knock on the door. Rafe turned toward the door and then back to me, smiling awkwardly. "Think Flora is sick of Wes already?"

I frowned. I hoped not because I didn't know what else to do if she was.

Rafe rose from the couch and crossed the room, swinging open the front door with more enthusiasm than I'd seen him show in a while. Then, he froze.

"Hello. Are you Rafe Farral?"

"Yes," Rafe said. "Why?"

I leaned forward on the couch at the sound of the unfamiliar female voice and caught the scent of leather, metal, and polyester.

"I'm Officer Sanderson."

"Yeah? Who are they?"

The woman outside laughed without humor. "Don't worry about them. Just some extra security. Does the rest of your pack also live here?"

I leaned forward further, trying to see what Rafe was talking about and how many people were on our doorstep.

"Why?" Rafe asked, putting far too much power in his voice.

A sickly sweet smell filled the room, wafting toward me as the wind shifted outside. "You don't want to bark at me, kid. That's not going to look good for you in court."

I jumped up, half-confused, half-scared as Ares and

Nox came skidding into the living room, Killian two steps behind them.

"No," I whispered, "Go back." They didn't seem to hear me.

"Who the hell is here?" Ares barked.

Down the bond, I could feel more than smell Rafe's mingled exasperation and, to my surprise, fear. Why fear?

Instinctively, I backed up toward the kitchen, out of view of the front door. Nox and I made eye contact across the room, and he nodded slightly at me, telling me, yes, I was doing the right thing.

"Roof," he mouthed.

My eyes darted toward the staircase. I could get there, but I'd have to pass in front of the windows, where my reflection would be completely visible from the doorway. Would anyone notice?

"What is this regarding?" Nox said loudly, stepping up beside Rafe.

"Could we come inside?" the officer asked. "We'd love to discuss it."

"Only if you tell us what this is regarding," Nox snapped.

I edged toward the stairs to the roof, half-doubled-over as I tried to make myself as small as possible.

"Is there any chance you boys have been harboring an unclaimed omega?"

Silence stretched in the room.

Rafe shuffled to the side, further blocking any view of the warehouse. "Excuse me?"

"What about any recent trips out of state?" the officer asked. "Do any of you know a Mr. Scott Carver?"

The room filled with the mingled scent of vinegar and lemons.

"Sorry," the officer said cheerfully. "I'll rephrase. Did anyone here kidnap an omega, bring her to a rest stop near the Virginia border, and slaughter an innocent alpha who just happened to get too close?"

In a rush of memory, the scent of Marlboro Reds, the wet crack of Ares slamming that alpha's face into the sink, and the crimson trail of blood across a slippery bathroom floor came back to me in a rush, garbled and from a distance, as though through the crack in a door.

Ares and I stared at each other across the room, and my blood ran cold as I caught the determination down our bond.

"I did it," Ares said, his jaw tense.

"No!" Rafe barked at the same time as I took an unconscious step forward

Rafe tried to put himself between Ares and the officer, but Ares shoved him out of the way, hard enough that he lost his balance and hit the opposite wall. "I did it. I killed that asshole. The rest of these guys weren't even there."

"Alright," the officer said, and it was clear from her tone that she was skeptical. "And what about the missing omega? Bliss Nero."

"She's gone," Ares said.

The layered scents of bitter citrus annoyance and sour confusion mingled with the ammonia of the lie. The officer didn't believe him.

If I had to guess, the officer had seen the security footage, and they already knew that Ares was the only one in the bathroom with me. They suspected the entire pack, but they couldn't prove it.

I pulled on the ends of my hair, my anxiety rising. Next, they'd search the warehouse and then probably the outbuildings. They'd find Flora and Wes and realize Flora wasn't dead. They'd arrest everyone anyway. *No, I can't let that happen.*

I tripped over my own feet, stumbling into view. "Wait!"

I stared at the wall of the drab, gray holding station, tapping my nails in time to the incessant ticking of the clock on the wall. My thighs stuck to the beige plastic chair I'd been confined to for the last several hours, and the metal of the table dug into my arms. Still, I couldn't be bothered to get up and stretch my legs. Pacing felt too cliché.

It seemed to me that the clock was slow, but maybe that was only because I'd had no updates on where they'd taken Ares or if they had arrested the other three guys. I wasn't under arrest, as the officers had reminded me several times upon arrival, but I was being held until they figured out "next steps." When those next steps were going to happen, I had no idea.

Every so often, a flash of anger or anxiety would reach me down the bond, but it was impossible to tell whose emotion it was. My own anxiety rose to the surface, and I was sure I was projecting it back. I closed my eyes, trying to think happy thoughts, more for their sake than my own.

A knock sounded on the door for the first time in

hours, and my eyes flew open, and I whipped my head around so fast I cricked my neck. Ow.

"Omega Nero."

"My last name is Davis," I said automatically.

The same officer who arrived at the warehouse gave me a patronizing smile. She was in her mid-forties, with red hair and lines around her eyes. She didn't look like she was a bad person, but the sour fruit scent in the air made me wonder if she just didn't like omegas. I sighed. *One problem at a time, Bliss.*

"Your mate is here to pick you up."

"Which one?" My heartbeat kicked up a notch. "I can go home?"

She gave me an odd look and stepped aside to let another figure step into the room. My heart sank, and fear washed over me, cooling my blood. Of course. I should have realized.

Nero smiled down at me, his gaze taking in everything from my pajama top and disheveled appearance to my now shaking hands. His gaze lingered for half a second on my neck before I pushed my hair over it. His lip curled. "Having fun, are we, Pet?"

"Don't call me that," I muttered.

"Leave us," Nero barked at the officer.

She stepped out of the room, closing the door, and I narrowed my eyes. She didn't seem to mind when he barked at her, only my guys.

"You have caused me such a fucking headache," Nero hissed at me, his smile never wavering. "Consider yourself lucky I can't punish you the way you deserve right here and now."

I shuddered, unnerved by the unmoving grin, then

followed his gaze up to the camera in the corner. So, we weren't completely alone.

"I'm not sorry," I whispered.

"You will be." He reached out and pushed the hair off my neck. "Looks like after all this, they didn't even mate you. I hear that's nearly impossible. They must have wanted to protect their own asses more than they wanted you."

If he'd said that to me even a day ago, it would have cut me, but I knew better now. I angled my chair, making sure my back was to the camera. I let a benign smile fall over my face, refusing to react. "Bullshit."

Nero's face twisted, his smile slipping. He raised a hand and brought it down across my cheek. "You've forgotten your place, Omega. I own you. You do not speak to me like an equal."

Pain burst across my cheek as my head jerked to the side with the force of the blow, and I clenched my teeth together, forcing myself not to cry out. "You've never owned me. My place is with them."

Sounds of footsteps sounded outside the door, and there were voices in the hall. Nero forced his smile back into place, probably realizing at the same time someone saw what happened on the cameras. He leaned close to me to hide what he was saying from view, his voice growing low.

"You stupid bitch. You're trying to embarrass me over a group of fucking barely adult criminals who won't mate you and have been lying to you since the moment they took you from my bed."

I narrowed my eyes, confused. "You don't know them—"

"Of course I do. The whole industry knows them. Where do you think the blockers come from?" Alpha looked down at me, his expression almost pitying.

I wrinkled my brow in confusion. "I don't know what you're talking about."

"Your boyfriends have been responsible for drugging you for years. Everyone is saying that the most recent batch circulating through the Institute is making the omegas practically comatose. It's so strong. You wouldn't know how that happened, would you?"

I waited for the ammonia scent of his lie to tear through the room. Nothing happened.

My heart pounded out of control.

The pain of betrayal, like a physical wound, burned through the center of my chest, and I gasped, staggering at the weight of it. I pressed my fingers to my chest, willing it to stop, but it was as though I was being torn in half.

Not again.

Pack Bliss

To the readers that think one knot is never enough.

PACK BLISS

A BLISSFUL OMEGAVERSE NOVEL

INTERNATIONAL BESTSELLING AUTHORS

KATE KING   JESSA WILDER

CHAPTER 1

Ares

"I will fucking kill you if you've hurt her." My bark rang around the small windowless room, useless against the beta wearing military-grade ear protection.

Officer Asshole bent over and banged his fists on the steel table between us. His eye twitched, and a muscle ticked in his jaw. "Why did you kill Alpha Carver?"

I smirked at him. "You keep asking that like you're going to get a different answer."

"You're cocky for someone in a holding cell," he said, straightening to his full height. He'd started out clean-cut, but in the hours I'd been in here, he'd disintegrated. His face had grown a ruddy red, and his once-styled hair drooped to the side and revealed his thinning hairline.

I leaned back in the hard chair as far as I could go with my hands cuffed to the table in front of me. I was going for a bored look, and by the way a red flush crept up Officer Asshole's face, I'd say it was working. "You don't have enough to keep me here." My voice came out on a low growl that had the hairs on his arms standing up. "Tell me where she is."

I leaned forward and stared him down. He might not scent my pheromones, but he sure as shit could see the danger.

He glanced between my hands and my face and took a small step back. His fear burned my nose, like salt and cranberries. "Why? So you can kidnap her again?"

"You would think that. Fucking brainwashed, idiot."

"You're telling me you didn't break into Alpha Nero's place? Grab the omega and take off with her?"

"Bliss."

"What?"

White lines formed on my knuckles as my fingers curled into fists. "Her name is Bliss."

The officer rocked back on his heels and rubbed his palm over his face, pushing his hair back. He let out a breathy sigh. "Whatever. We've told Alpha Nero we found her. He's had the entire precinct looking for his omega."

A growl ripped through me. She was *our* omega. Visions of Nero's body limp, on the floor coated in blood, had my own blood humming. "Let me see her."

"Kid, you murdered a guy in a bathroom." He sounded almost incredulous. "You're never going to see the omega again. Hell, you aren't ever getting out of here."

I jumped out of my chair, hands colliding with the table. "That *guy* tried to fucking attack her."

I sucked in a breath and reined myself back, sitting down. Our lawyer would kill me if I said anything to incriminate myself. My metal chair grated on the floor as I shifted and kicked my feet on the table. My pose was relaxed, but my voice was edged. "Whoever killed him did the world a favor."

Officer Asshole shook his head and knocked on the door, and a beta opened it from the outside. The officer turned back to look at me. "You're going to jail, and the pretty omega is going back to her mate. Whatever finders keepers right you think you have to her, you're wrong." He stepped through the door and snipped at the younger officer. "Get him to the cell."

Anger rippled through me. The only alphas Bliss was going back to was us.

Where the fuck are they?

I cracked my knuckles as I paced around the small, cagelike room. After the pointless interrogation, the Institute threw me in what was effectively a drunk tank while they worked on the paperwork to charge me.

Good luck with that.

You didn't get where we were without the right connections.

I leaned against the wall, resting my head back on the salmon-colored cinder blocks, and tried to even out my breathing. I'd been stuck in here for hours, and I was about to kill someone if I didn't find out what the hell was happening to Bliss.

The fucking Institute was integrated into every level of government, manipulating and controlling the alphas and omegas.

And we fucking helped them.

I hit my head back against the wall hard enough to

make my teeth chatter.

Fuck. Energy crawled under my skin as my fight instincts threatened to take over the longer I was stuck in here. I tugged on my hair and walked around the small room.

One of the three low-strength alphas huddled on the steel bench lining the wall attempted to stand and slurred his words. "Stop fucking pacing. You're creeping me out."

A spark flashed through me, and the bitter stench of cranberries burned my nose when I turned my attention to him. The alpha pheromones I threw off were enough to have him stumbling back into his friends.

My lips tipped up in the corner. Thought so.

There was a darkness rolling off me in waves ever since Bliss' panic pierced through the bond a few hours after we got here. Since then, there had been a constant dull pit in my stomach that I wasn't sure was hers or mine.

I rubbed my hands over my face, digging my palms into my eyes. Why the fuck would she give herself up? Could she really still have doubts? After everything that happened last night, the way she fit perfectly between us as we each took her, she had to have known things were different. That we would've protected her.

Fuck, there wasn't one of us that wouldn't die for her. We were finally figuring things out.

Then I had to fuck it up again by killing that alpha in the gas station. The only saving grace was they clearly didn't know about the rich fucker we'd killed directly after that.

I wouldn't regret it though. Anyone who came close to Bliss was a dead man.

We had years to atone for, and we'd been doing a shit

job of it. No one had fucked up more than me. I raked my fingers through my hair and tugged on the ends until my scalp ached. Anything to take my mind away from what was happening to Bliss.

I knew she was in the police station. So close. Too close.

I cracked my neck and did another lap, my boots sticking to the piss-stained holding cell floor. She shouldn't be here at all. I trembled as another wave of her fear rocked through me, and a low, menacing growl rumbled my chest. My alpha instincts drove me to go to her to comfort our omega.

I clenched my teeth and slammed my fist into the cell door. I couldn't just sit here. The guys were taking longer than they should've to bail us out, and it took all my willpower not to fuck this up even more by ripping the door off its hinges.

I sucked in a breath as a low rumble formed in my chest. I was going to get her home and chain her to her goddamn bed if she did anything like this again. The need to protect her rivaled with the ultimate desire to sink my teeth deep into her neck and finally claim her as ours.

I was such a fucking idiot. I'd spent the last four years angry that we let her go. Then, the second I got her within reach, I pushed her away. I was fooling myself by pretending to be selfless. I was fucking scared.

Scared I'd ruined everything.

Scared she'd never forgive us.

Terrified she'd never look at us the same way.

I was the leader back then. It was my responsibility to keep us all in line, and I fucked up, and we all paid for it.

Then I kept fucking up every day since then.

The guys—my pack—had been putting up with my

bullshit for years.

They'd all lost themselves to climbing up the ranks in the Alpha Lupi, but I let myself go. Couldn't stand the idea of being happy if she wasn't with us. Instead, I shut down, turned cold. I did everything necessary to get her back, but I never thought it would happen. It was a dream I was chasing. Never in a million fucking years was she supposed to take us back.

Not our Bliss. Not after she'd looked at me with huge pleading eyes, begging me to tell her it wasn't true. That we didn't call the Institute to take her. That we weren't sending her away like we promised we wouldn't.

But we were.

The desperate, destroyed look she gave us as she fought against Killian's bark had imprinted in my mind. It haunted my nightmares. Always her walking away, begging me to not let her go. Biggest fucking mistake of my life.

Everything was going to change now. By some sheer miracle, we had another chance, and I wasn't fucking this one up. The second we all got home, I'd lay this all out. I was fucking wrong. About all of it. Last night was only the beginning. I knew we had a long way to go until we were back to where we were. First thing was no more secrets. Keeping things from Bliss inevitably blew up in our faces. We wanted to keep her out of it, but now that we'd learned more about the Institute and the shit she went through...

Just another fuckup in a string of fuckups.

I didn't give a shit what the guys said now. We'd tell her about working with the Institute. Being the blocker supplier. We couldn't continue to keep things from her.

She'd be pissed, but if it came from us, if we explained

why, we could work it out. We just needed to get her home.

Shouts came from the other side of the door, Rafe's unmistakable bark so dominant it had the alphas beside me cowering.

Fucking finally.

The second the doorknob turned, I yanked it open. The beta officer stood there scowling like he'd eaten something sour. "This is total bullshit, but you're free to go."

I grabbed him by his collar, and his breath came out in a rush as I slammed him into the wall. The blue plugs in his ears stopped him from being commanded, but his body still vibrated with my alpha bark. "Where is she?"

The room filled with the smell of sour cranberries, and the officer stared at me with wide eyes. Fucking useless.

I dropped him, not bothering to slow his descent, and took off down the hallway. The walls were lined with doors, and my shout reverberated in the corridor.

"Bliss?"

She didn't answer, and panic rose inside me at the thought of not finding her.

"Bliss!"

I caught the faint hint of jasmine growing stronger as my feet ate up space.

A snarl vibrated my chest as I stopped in front of a black steel door. The nameplate said "Interrogation room."

I would fucking kill them.

"Open the fucking door." I slammed my fist against the metal surface.

Nothing came from the other side. No attempt to open the door, no whispers, not even the sound of shifting.

I pressed my face closer to the doorjamb and breathed

in through my nose. Bliss's honey, jasmine, and pepper scent whipped around my head, and I slammed my shoulder into the door.

"Bliss. Answer me."

Bliss' sweet scent grew acidic, only to be overpowered by the scent of cigars and whiskey. *Nero.*

My heart pummeled my rib cage as I struggled to take my next breath. "Bliss, Love. Answer me."

The guy's pounding feet took up the hall, but all I could do was take in the smell of Bliss' panic. It was so quiet. Too fucking quiet.

Rafe came up to my side. "What's happening?"

I ignored the bark rolling off his voice. At this point, I didn't think he could help it. Not after years of me fucking around and forcing him into the role of pack leader. I could've helped him if I wasn't so far up my own ass.

I moved away from the door so Rafe could get closer. "She's not fucking here."

Rafe sucked in an audible breath and stiffened. A muscle ticked in his jaw, and his fists opened and closed, barely containing his reaction. There was no mistaking the smell of the asshole that tried to buy her.

"Hey!" An officer came running after Rafe. "Hey! You can't be in here."

Killian and Nox came running up behind the beta. They both looked worse for wear. Nox wasn't wearing his coat or vest. His signature white shirt was wrinkled and unbuttoned halfway. Killian wasn't much better. He looked like he was still wearing the clothes he threw on this morning.

"Where the fuck is she?" Rafe's growl had the officer stumbling back. A police station should really hire only alphas. Even if they wore special bark-proof ear protection, it clearly wasn't fully effective. Or it just wasn't effective against high-powered alphas like Rafe.

"She's gone."

My ribs compressed around my lungs as I struggled to take my next breath. Fuck no.

I grabbed the officer and pulled him forward. "Open the fucking door."

The officer stumbled through the motions. His keys rattled around, and I did my best not to bark at him again. I didn't want to break him, but he needed to hurry the fuck up. Right the fuck now.

The door swung wide, and I pushed the beta out of the way. The room couldn't have been over ten by ten. Light gray walls and a steel table in the center. A mirror image of the room I'd been shoved into hours earlier. The only thing left of Bliss was her panic.

Cranberries burned my nose as Killian lifted the officer by his neck. Beating up the police was a lot even for us, but we'd deal with those consequences later. Nothing a few good bribes couldn't take care of.

"What the fuck did you do to her?" Killian's fingers tightened around the beta's neck, the scent of iron rolling off him in waves.

Nox pulled back on Kill's shoulder. "Back off. Give him room to tell us."

Killian's grip loosened, and he took an enormous step. The sharp smell of piss hit me hard as the beta shook. "Her alpha came and got her."

Our growls blocked out his next words, and Nox's fist collided with the officer's face. "He's not her fucking alpha."

The beta slumped to the floor, out cold. A smirk twisted my lips. "What happened to 'back off'?"

Nox glanced back at me as we stepped over the officer and made our way toward the reception desk. His lip curled. "I didn't like his answer." Nox gave the administrator at the front desk a card for our lawyer and followed us into the parking lot, never once looking up from his phone. "Nero's mansion's the closest. If he took her anywhere, I'm betting there."

They illegally parked the van in front of the building, two of its tires sitting on the curb, half over the sidewalk. "Where's Wes?"

Rafe gave me a knowing look. "He stayed back with Flora."

I shook my head. Wes had no idea what he was getting himself into. He was already falling all over himself for her. He was going to get his heart shattered when she fell for some alpha. I was intimately familiar with having my heart ripped out.

I didn't get three steps around the van before Rafe was gripping my arm. His gaze bored into mine. It had been years since we'd really looked at each other. Not without me trying to pick a fight.

He looked older. Tired. Like I'd dropped the weight of the world on him. I braced for the punch I expected for getting us into this mess.

Instead, Rafe tossed keys at me and smiled as I fumbled catching them. "You're faster. We get her back. Then figure out whatever the fuck has been going on with you. Deal?"

I ran my tongue over my teeth and closed my fist over the keys. "Nero's a fucking dead man."

CHAPTER 2
Bliss

I pressed my nose to the tinted window of Alpha Nero's huge black limousine, staring out at the miles of identical highway whipping by. My teeth rattled against each other as the car drifted into the grooved pavement on the shoulder of the road, letting us know we were too close to veering into the grassy ditch along the side, before the limo driver quickly righted us again.

"Pay attention!" Alpha Nero barked for the second time in the last hour.

That was all he'd said since forcing me out of the police station and into the limo. He didn't even look up. He kept his head down, eyes glued to his phone as his thumbs flew across the screen.

"Yes, sir," the driver said warily.

I grimaced, turning my head slightly to peek at the driver. His scent was exhausted—like damp leaves.

The day I'd begun my transition into an omega four years ago, I realized all emotions had a scent. Not in the obvious way that all people know of—how you can smell dinner cooking from down the hall or can't help but take a deep breath every time you get into a new car. No, pheromones smelled and tasted different from anything I'd ever encountered during my seventeen years of normal beta existence. Every time anyone felt a powerful emotion, their pheromones would shift just slightly, and that smell hit me like a freight train.

Most emotions were simple scents. Disgust always smelled like sour milk. Fear was bitter, like unsweetened cranberry juice. Happiness was sweet with a hint of fruit, like ripe berries. Some emotions smelled more complicated—a blend, or were different for different people. The grapefruit scent of suspicion was the combination of bitter fear and sour confusion. It was like emotional math.

The most obvious scent of all was the strong ammonia odor of a lie. It was unmistakable—it burned at the inside of my nose and throat, impossible to miss.

Yet, somehow, people kept lying to me, and I was the idiot who kept letting it happen.

I shook myself, turning to press my nose back into the window, and swallowed down the lump rising in my throat. Alpha Nero could smell my emotions just as well as I could scent him, and all I needed was to give him more ammunition. Not that he seemed to be paying attention.

"Your boyfriends have been responsible for drugging you for years. Everyone is saying that the most recent batch circulating through the Institute is making the omegas practically comatose, it's so strong," Nero said, leaning toward me across the police interrogation table. *"You wouldn't know how that happened, would you?"*

I stared at him for a full beat, unable to form the words to answer. That couldn't be right.

It was right. I took a deep breath. *Focus.*

Nero's intentions for telling me were no doubt nefarious, but he hadn't lied. When we were growing up in Stratford, the local gang, Alpha Lupi, dealt alpha pheromone drugs for betas. The guys tried to keep me away from their business, but I would have had to live under a mountain-sized boulder not to know. Switching from party drugs to blockers didn't feel like a stretch. None of the guys ever lied to my face—they couldn't—but they may as well have. Almost as soon as I'd arrived at the warehouse, I'd suggested going on blockers myself so I could leave. No one pointed out they had a stash on hand. What was worse, when I'd explained how the Institute kept all the omegas drugged and docile through the use of constant overdose, no one spoke up.

"I hope you're not over there planning anything stupid," Nero drawled.

I refused to look at him. "Hmm."

I couldn't answer because he would smell the lie. I wasn't just planning—I was plotting my revenge.

I should have been terrified of Nero—part of me was. I was when we'd sat across from each other in the police station. But a low simmer had mostly replaced that fear. Not quite anger and not quite sadness—a chaotic energy, with no outlet.

I'd only been willing to come this far because I figured it would be easier to escape one person than a whole police station of armed officers. It was the "play dead" approach. Pretend he'd worn me down long enough to be left alone and then run like hell.

I shifted a little in my seat—in case he made any sudden movements—but to my surprise, Nero didn't push for a reply. Maybe he'd just stopped caring at this point. I would have. This wasn't going that well for him.

"What are you going to do with me, anyway?" I asked, still keeping my eyes on the window.

"Excuse me?" His tone was tight.

"What are you doing with me?" I repeated.

At least he'd answered. That was more than I'd expected. I chanced a glance at Nero. He was leaning away from me, his face still buried in his phone. I narrowed my eyes. His breathing was shallow. Strange.

"Shut up," he snapped. Again, his tone was tight. He was definitely trying not to breathe.

I grinned. I probably smelled like other alphas and sex. Not that I wanted to smell like the guys—not anymore—but I didn't want to be attractive to Nero either. Equal-opportunity disgusting would be perfect. "Why do you want me when you can't even stand to scent me?"

"Do not test me," he said through his teeth, leaning forward as if to reach for me. "You can still be useful to me somehow. Just wait. You don't need to leave the house to have children."

My heartbeat kicked up, and I reeled back. Even in my defiance, I couldn't completely ignore the instinct to flee. Nero was a lion, and I was a furious rabbit. I took a deep breath. I needed to be smart about this.

I bit the inside of my cheek and turned back to the window. Alpha Nero was picturing keeping me around for events and mandatory baby making, just to make it appear that he still had an omega like all the other most powerful men in society. That sounded about right. It sounded like I was about to end up like Flora.

Or I would if I didn't plan to get out of here at the very first opportunity.

The limo driver pulled down Nero's long driveway, and I immediately recognized the house. A shiver traveled up my spine as I remembered the last time I'd been here. What if Nero planned to drug me again the moment we walked inside? That was something I hadn't immediately considered and should have.

He didn't bother to speak to me or open my door as he got out of the car. I bit my lip. I might be too optimistic, but he didn't seem in the mood for a week of sex. At the very least, he'd probably make me shower first—maybe the bathroom would have a window?

I jumped out of the car and followed two steps behind him up the walk—less out of manners and more out of a desire to keep my distance. The house was dark, except for the lamps lining the porch and the path to the door. As with the last time we were here, it struck me how there were no houses surrounding us. No lights from neighbors in the distance. Weird.

"Where are we?" I asked as Nero unlocked the front door.

He snorted a derisive laugh, the scent of iron rising between us. "Going to call your criminal boyfriends to pick you up? They already know the address."

"No," I said and was glad that I could tell the truth. I had no intention of calling for help from the guys ever again. "I don't want to see them. I just wanted to know where we are." *Because I'm going to run away by myself.*

Nero turned to face me in the foyer. The wide stairwell

rose behind him, intimidating in its grandeur. "Go." He nodded for me to walk ahead of him.

I deflated a little, realizing he had no intention of answering my question. "Where are we going?"

He didn't bother to explain. Clearly finished chatting, Nero's fingers shot out, and fire raced over my scalp as he grasped a handful of my hair and pulled. A scream escaped me, and my feet lifted off the ground for a moment before I was scrambling to run along after him.

"Stop!" Pain shot up my neck, and I tried to push his hands away from my hair as he dragged me down a wide hallway.

Nero tightened his fingers. "I don't want to hear another word out of you unless it's 'Yes, Alpha. Fuck me, Alpha.'"

I stumbled, my knees hitting the hardwood floor, and whimpered in pain when Nero didn't stop moving, merely dragging me along with him as though I weighed nothing. I twisted, only succeeding in pulling my own hair out and scraping my knees. Hot tears of mingled pain and anger sprang to my eyes and poured down my face.

We stopped moving, and Nero dropped my hair. I landed on the floor in a heap, panting, my head both burning and numb at the same time.

A door opened above me. "Get in."

I gasped for breath and pushed myself up on my palms. My heartbeat pounded in my ears, so loud I wouldn't be surprised if Nero could hear it.

"Did you not hear me?" Nero barked. "Get in!"

My body snapped to attention, moving without my consent. I couldn't ignore a full bark—not when it was given with that much force. Stumbling to my feet, I stepped into the room, bracing myself.

It was a bedroom—smaller than the one I remembered Alpha Nero bringing me to the first time I'd been here but just as fancy and sparsely decorated.

The bedroom had a huge, four-poster cherrywood bed with a carved head and footboard that took up most of the floor space. There was a bedside table with a lamp, a matching dresser, and not much else. The walls were bare but for the blue-and-white patterned wallpaper, which matched the thin white quilt on the bed. It wasn't a hideous room, but it looked like a prison to me.

My blood ran cold. I spun to him in a panic. What could we be doing in a bedroom except... "I—"

"Stay here." He slammed the door, the metallic scent of his rage lingering after him.

The lock clicked, and the sound reverberated through me, resonating a thousand times over until I knew I'd never forget it. It would replay over and over in nightmares for the rest of my life.

I stepped back, shaking, and leaned against the foot of the enormous bed. My breath caught in my throat, and I choked. My adrenaline left me in a whoosh.

In the last several hours, my life had come crashing down. I woke up this morning with the guys. I hadn't even showered. My scalp and knees throbbed. I wanted to lie down on this bed, curl into a ball, and cry, but I couldn't. I had to get out of here while I still could.

I pressed my palms into my eyes as though I could push the tears back inside. "Get it together," I whispered to the empty room. "Escape now, cry later."

The room had two windows on either side of the bed. I

stood and ran over and checked the distance to the ground, ignoring the pain in my knees. We were on the second floor. Of course, the first floor would be too much to hope for.

One window overlooked the driveway, so that wasn't an ideal landing spot. The other would put me into the grass on the side of the house. Neither seemed to have any handholds or trees or anything, but I'd rather jump onto grass than pavement.

I ran my fingers over the top of the windowsill until I reached the latch. I let out a shaking breath of pained relief when it flipped over with no resistance.

Unless it's a trap.

I stepped back from the window, my heart pounding and my eyes narrowing with suspicion. I glanced back at the locked door, listening hard. No sound came from the hall. Maybe Nero just didn't think I could ever escape from this height? It could be that omegas weren't known for our self-sufficiency or athletic ability or just that he had a low opinion of me personally. Maybe both. Either way, I was in no hurry to correct him.

I hauled the window open. It was heavy, giving more resistance than I would've hoped. Clearly, no one had aired out this room in a while.

My heart pounded too loud as I scanned the edges of the wire screen. It wasn't the kind that easily popped out for cleaning. Damn. If I was too loud, someone would come running, whether or not they were waiting outside. Then, no doubt, Nero would lock me in a closet next or put bars on the window.

I scanned the room for something to help me pry the screen out. There wasn't much in here—a lamp on the bedside table, a dresser with nothing on it. I crossed the room and opened the door just in case I was missing something—I wasn't.

Gripping the edge of the window with both hands, I lined my foot up. The angle was awkward, and I closed my eyes and held my breath as I kicked.

My heart immediately stuttered at the hollow thunk of my shoe hitting against the wire of the screen. The screen didn't pop out, and I was making noise. Damn.

"Come on," I told myself. "You can do this."

I needed to commit and do it well, once, not half-ass several times, until someone came to investigate.

I switched my grip, holding on to the bedpost instead and lining my foot up more evenly with the middle of the screen, keeping my eyes firmly open. *I can do this. It's just a screen, not cement.*

I slammed my heel into the middle of the screen and lost my balance as my foot hit thin air. Catching myself on the bedpost, my heart pounding out of control, I quickly scrambled to look.

The screen had fallen with a quiet thud into the yard below. I paused, holding my breath. Had anyone heard that?

Outside, the yard was dark and still. The trees swayed in a light breeze, still visible in the light from the house. The only sound was the wind, the crickets, and the buzz of cicadas—no footsteps, no voices. I released my breath.

I stuck my head all the way out of the window and again judged the distance to the ground with slightly better accuracy. A couple of yards to the right, there was a drainpipe. In a movie, I would use it to shimmy down, but in reality, I was pretty sure it couldn't hold my weight even if I could get to it. I would just end up pulling the thing off the house and making more noise than if I just jumped. But would I survive a jump? Yes, but maybe not with both ankles intact.

I pulled my head back inside and searched the room again for something to aid my escape. I zeroed in on the bed.

One time when we were about fifteen, the guys made a rope out of bedsheets so all of us could sneak out of our foster home. Of course, the sheets ripped because they were already six and a half feet tall each, but I might fare better.

Pulling the sheets off the bed, I tied them end to end and quickly lowered them out the window, tying the opposite end to the bedpost. I frowned at my makeshift rope—it wasn't nearly as long or as sturdy as I'd pictured, but I couldn't be choosy.

I stopped at the edge of the window, both hands on the sill. I checked the distance to the ground again, and my mouth went dry.

Okay. Well, here we go.

I threw a leg over the edge, and my whole body shook. I really wasn't built for heights. Or athletics. I suddenly remembered with more clarity that when the guys had made the rope to sneak out when we were younger, I'd refused to go with them, and we all ended up staying home in the end. My heart clenched at the thought—I had no idea what happened to us, but the guys who would have stayed home with me didn't exist anymore.

"Focus," I muttered under my breath.

I flipped over, trying to lower my feet out first. I squeezed my eyes shut, and my stomach leapt into my chest as I slid down my rope. The sheets ended several feet before the ground, and I landed on my back on the grass with an oomph and braced myself as the vibration of the impact rattled through my body.

A phantom stab of anxiety shot through my chest, and I jumped. I'd probably sent some wild emotions down the bond in the last hour. Oh well. I lay flat for a moment, taking stock of myself. *Not broken. Not dead. Okay.*

My makeshift rope swung overhead, like a white flag waving surrender. Freezing, I waited again to see if anyone would come around the corner or appear at the window. It seemed impossible that Nero wasn't having me watched. There had to be guards or cameras around here somewhere.

I needed to get off this property and figure out where the hell I was. Find a phone. Go…

I stopped dead in my tracks, realizing with a jolt I didn't have anywhere to go.

The guys were my only friends before the Institute. I had no family. No connections. My only friend in the world, Flora, was still at the warehouse.

I gasped. Dammit. Flora was still at the warehouse, which meant that, at the very least, I had to go back to get her.

Good. It's time I confront the guys and get some actual answers. It's been a long time coming.

I glanced back up at Nero's house, still half waiting for someone to follow me. He'd realize what happened soon enough and would be on my tail again. That was another reason not to go back to the warehouse—where he'd know right where to look for me.

But I couldn't leave Flora—especially not after how I'd found her only yesterday.

I sucked on my teeth. It was probably too much to hope that there was a gas station or something around here that would let me borrow their phone. Hell, there wasn't even another house. Still, I had to try.

I said a silent prayer to no one in particular that whoever I ran into first would be a beta and took a step in the driveway's direction. Something rustled in the distance, and I froze again.

My ears pricked up, straining for another hint of sound. Someone shouted in the front of the house, their words indistinguishable.

Dammit. Even knowing there was no way I'd get out of here without running into someone, it hadn't stopped the faint hope that maybe Nero just assumed I was so useless I didn't need guards.

I glanced back up at the window, my heart pounding. Was it possible to go back up? Was that stupid? Should I run? My thoughts raced, caught somewhere between fight, flight, and freeze. It was naive to think no one would be out here at all, but did they know I was here too?

"Calm down. Think!" I hissed at myself.

I grabbed for the end of my sheet rope, which would be the first thing to give me away, and tugged. It didn't give—obviously, since it had held my weight. Groaning in frustration, I abandoned the rope and ducked behind a large bush. The scent of damp earth and the floral plants filled my nose as I crouched on the ground, peeking through the leaves.

The long shadow of a person was just visible around the edge of the house. It hadn't moved, like there was someone standing on the corner just out of sight. I swore silently. Maybe Nero stationed top guys on all the corners? Or maybe there was a door over there?

I turned to my right, away from the shadow and the driveway. That would be going toward the back of the house and away from the only known road, but there weren't any people over there as far as I knew… It wasn't a great gamble either way.

"Hey!" a man's voice shouted.

I stopped breathing.

"Yeah?" another man replied—closer. The man on the corner, maybe?

"Can you swap places with me for a minute? I gotta run inside and take a piss."

"Sure."

I let out a breath in a whoosh. They weren't talking to me.

The shadow moved away from the edge of the house. My heart pounded double time. I might not get another chance to run, but what if they saw me? Then again, what if they didn't?

The longer I sat in this bush, the more likely it was that Nero would go into my room to check on me, or someone else would walk around the house from the opposite side. There just weren't a lot of good options.

Making a split-second decision, I angled myself toward the backyard. There had to be another road somewhere. A house. *Something*. At the very least, it was better than walking straight down the driveway.

I got to my feet and forced myself to step out into the open. When no one yelled or tackled me immediately, I put another foot in front of the other, darting toward the darkness of the shadowed lawn.

With every step away from the house, the panic ebbed out of me, only to be replaced by a simmering rage. It rattled through my entire body, ominous, like the distant war chant of an oncoming siege.

I wasn't helpless, and I shouldn't be underestimated. Not anymore.

CHAPTER 3
Bliss

The taxi driver pulled up outside the warehouse over an hour later. "This what you wanted?"

I sighed, leaning over to look out the window at the tall brick building. "Yeah."

He glanced at the meter and whistled. I winced—less at the price and more because I'd need to go inside. "Can you wait a second? I need to go get someone to pay you."

"Wait, hang on—"

"I swear I'll be right back." I was already halfway out of the car. In some ways, it was too bad betas couldn't smell the truth.

I strode purposefully toward Wes's little outbuilding apartment. The taxi horn honked behind me, and I gritted my teeth. I was ninety percent sure the guys weren't home —I'd know—nevertheless, I wanted to make everything as quick as possible. I raised my hand to knock, but the door swung open.

"Oh my God!" Flora shrieked, throwing her arms

around me as she launched herself out the door. "I saw you on the security cameras. What's going on?"

My best friend wore a pair of baggy gray men's sweatpants rolled at the bottom and an oversized black sweater. It mostly covered the bruising on her body but didn't quite disguise the marks on her neck. Her waist-length chestnut hair was clean and bouncy again but had an asymmetrical section in the front where she'd hacked off a chunk with a knife only yesterday. I grimaced.

"Where's Wes?" I asked quickly, looking behind her into the small apartment. "I need him to pay—"

The taxi driver honked again. "Hang on, please!" I called. "I'll be right back."

"Bliss?" Wes appeared behind Flora, pulling his longish brown hair into a bun at the top of his head. "What happened?"

It had taken me about forty minutes of walking from Alpha Nero's mansion to hit a main road and a gas station, but thankfully, the beta working the desk was happy to let me use the phone to call a cab. My feet ached from the entire ordeal, and my body would no doubt give out shortly, but right now, I was still in go mode. I closed my eyes. "Too much. Are you the only ones here?"

"Yeah, I think so," Flora said. "What—"

Wes spotted the screaming cab driver and stepped around us to go outside and pay him. I waited a beat until he was out of earshot.

"We need to leave." My chest squeezed, pushing the air from my lungs. "Now."

Flora's large brown eyes grew wide. "Why? What happened?"

"It was them all along. They were the ones doing it…"

Her hands gripped mine, her brows pulled together, and her voice was soft. "Who? Doing what? I need you to fill in the Mad Libs here, Bliss, come on."

I cracked a smile. That sounded like something Flora would have said before we'd left the Institute. I took a deep breath and gave her the CliffsNotes in a fast whisper, glancing over my shoulder to make sure Wes wasn't coming back.

As I explained everything—the guys and their involvement with the Institute, the lies, Nero, Ares being arrested—the back of my eyes burned. I fought against my overwhelming emotions coming in like a tidal wave and pushed down the undertow of betrayal, hurt, disbelief, and loss before it could drown me.

To Flora's credit, she didn't panic or ask too many questions. "Where do you want to go?"

I sighed. I wasn't aware I'd been afraid of her reaction until she affirmed her willingness to come with me. "I'm working on that part. Hotel?"

The second the words left my lips, frustration banded around me, and I wanted to punch something. We couldn't leave.

Flora's grimace told me she was thinking the same thing. "I'll come with you if you want to get out of here, you know that, but we can't just go to a hotel."

The helplessness of the situation had my nails digging into my forearms. There was nowhere to go, not for two unmated, penniless omegas. The unfairness of reality slammed into me. I'd been trapped since the second I presented as an omega. "We could get blockers?"

Flora stared at the ground, her fingers twisting together, before meeting my gaze with wet eyes and shaking her head. "I can't go back on them. They affect me more than they ever did you."

She was right. Blockers made most omegas—really, everyone except me—practically zombies. Anger boiled under my skin. How could the alphas I'd considered family be the ones responsible for providing the drugs the Institute used to control us?

"Staying here is not an option." I groaned in frustration, and it came out as almost a growl.

I knew deep in my core that staying in that apartment with them would break me. Not after all the lies and all the harm they caused. Flora had just gone through hell herself, and was I really about to tell her we needed to run again? The idea was practically suicide.

Flora's gaze darted over my shoulder. "What about him?"

"Wes?"

"Yeah."

My stomach squeezed with guilt. It was so apparent that the guy's beta had already become more than attached to my friend. I glanced over my shoulder. "You can stay with him if you want. I didn't mean to assume—"

"No, it's not that," she blurted out. "What if we both stay with him? At least until we sort something out?" She gave me a playful smirk that didn't quite reach her eyes. "You can share my bed."

I blinked at her, stunned silent as I ran through the idea. We'd still be under the pack's protection. "He works for them. He makes blockers too."

Flora bit her lip. "I'll keep trying to think of something, but that's all I've got right now."

I crossed my arms. I didn't like it, but she was right. It

was probably the best we were going to come up with, with no time to plan. "Just until we think of something else."

She looked over my shoulder again. "He's a beta. I doubt he understands what's going on the same way your guys do."

"They're not mine."

She ignored that statement, which I appreciated. I didn't think I could say it again. Once was hard enough. "Do you need me to come with you to pack?"

I bit my lip. "No. I only have like five dresses. I'll be right back."

I darted back toward the main warehouse, still running on adrenaline. The buzzing in my whole body was incessant, like I was just short of catching fire.

The scent in the warehouse nearly knocked me over when I opened the door. They weren't even home and my body begged me to go to them. To pretend I'd heard nothing, Nero said, and go back to the happy ignorance of last night. But even last night, I'd known something was off. It was too fast. Too perfect. There was too much between us to just pretend nothing had happened.

I rushed to the nest that had become my bedroom and threw open the closet, pulling the dresses they'd bought me off the hangers and tossing them on the unmade bed. I scowled at the dresses, annoyed that I didn't really have any other clothes.

It was things like this—the dresses, the food, the nest—that had made me think I could live with things the way they were. Like those gestures were enough, but they weren't. It was painfully obvious now that we'd never aired out what was really wrong with us.

We'd been friends first and a pack second, and from the moment they burst into Nero's house, they'd treated me like an omega and not myself. It was like in the last four years, we'd all forgotten what had made us friends and what we actually liked about each other. That couldn't be blamed on instinct—that was just miscommunication.

I wasn't going to hang around for a third chance to be lied to or abandoned while being treated like less than myself. I was worth more than that.

I pulled the last dress off the hanger and reached to gather them all up off the bed, then froze. My skin prickled with sudden awareness.

The front door banged open. Damn.

"Bliss?" Rafe's voice echoed through the house, and four sets of footsteps pounded down the hall.

My spine went rigid, and I turned slowly to face the door, setting my jaw. I held the dresses out in front of me, as though keeping the barrier between us could protect me.

Killian appeared in the doorway first, and his face split into a smile at the sight of me. He bounded two steps closer, his curly hair swinging. The scent of his relief hit me full force.

"Don't," I said firmly before he could lift me off the ground.

Killian skidded to a halt at the foot of the bed, his arms outstretched inches from me. He let them hang there in the air, comically empty. "Baby, what's wrong?"

Without waiting for my reply—typical—Rafe stepped up next to him, dark brows furrowed. "We went to find you, and you were gone."

Distantly, I wondered what he meant—they'd gone

looking for me where? Had they broken into Nero's again? Did that matter? No. I couldn't let myself get distracted.

"I was here," I replied vaguely.

Not a lie, not quite the whole truth. A confused citrus scent replaced the happy relief.

Nox ran his hand over his head. He still stood in the doorway, just behind Ares, as though he was wary of coming all the way inside. "Are you hurt?"

My annoyance spiked. "Not permanently."

I *was* hurt, and it had nothing to do with the throbbing pain still shooting through my knees or the stinging in my palms from sliding down the sheets. Those weren't serious injuries and would fade quickly. It would take far longer to get over the pain of yet another betrayal.

Ares' pale eyes widened as he seemed to catch on. "Love…we should explain."

A mix of frustration and hurt had my heart banging against my ribs. I clutched my dresses tighter, wishing with everything in me I had moved faster to avoid this conversation altogether. "What is there to explain? I already heard all about your connection to the Institute."

The acidic scent of vinegar filled the room, but it was tinged with something else. A resolve. Something tugged at my chest, but I ignored it, shutting down that link between us by sheer force of will. I didn't want to know what they were feeling. It wasn't mind-reading anyway—clearly, or I wouldn't be in this situation. Feelings weren't thoughts, and they sure as hell weren't actions.

"Heard from Nero?" Rafe asked sharply. "You can't listen to anything he says. He's only trying—"

"Shut the fuck up," Ares snapped, reaching out to pull Rafe back. "We're not trying to defend this."

I was slightly surprised that Rafe snapped his mouth shut. An awkward silence fell on the group, with no one seeming to know what to say. Finally, Killian moved to step into me again. "B, there's no excuse, but it wasn't..." He broke off, his voice one step away from begging. "Just hear us out, okay?"

My chest ached with the need for answers, wanting desperately for them to have a reason that would make this all go away. That they somehow had the magic words to make everything alright. "Fine. Explain."

Rafe took a deep breath, clearly struggling to remain calm. The tension in his neck spoke volumes, even if I couldn't smell his stress. "We are so sorry. There's no excuse. There were things we had to do—"

"*Things?*" My heartbeat rang in my ears, and I threw up one arm. "Don't you dare water this down. For once, be specific. Tell me the truth."

All four of them gaped at me, stunned, only fueling the fire building under my skin. It was like they'd forgotten that I'd ever had a backbone. Maybe we all needed a reminder.

"How far back do you want to go?" Nox said quickly, nudging Ares out of the way lightly so he could move to the front of the group. "Right after you left? Before we found you again?"

I gritted my teeth, already getting frustrated. "What's relevant?"

"Sorry." He tugged on his earring nervously. "Fuck. Okay. After we sent you to the Institute, we couldn't just go back to foster care after everything with Mr. Ward, but we hadn't aged out of the system either."

I blanched, shocked that he was going this far back. My

stomach churned with old hurt, mixing with my new anger. If I'd thought for a minute I was over their abandonment four years ago, I'd been wrong. "Why? Why did you do any of it? Why did you send me away?"

Nox put his hands up. "We fucked up, over and over again. We should never have sent you away."

I dropped my dresses back on the bed, throwing my hands up in frustration. "You think? It's a bit too late for that apology though. You had some twisted idea of protecting me, right?"

"Yeah," Killian jumped in, relieving Nox, who looked completely lost. "Mr. Ward had just attacked you, and that was only day one. We had no money and no way to protect you, so we panicked."

"Right. The only thing there is you didn't ask me what I wanted. But I'm the one that paid the consequences."

"We were fucking idiots for letting you go." Nox's voice cracked, and he coughed. "We thought we were doing the right thing. We thought you'd be safer." He ran a hand over his shaved head. "But we fucking knew the second you were gone, it was a mistake. Everything we've done has been to get you back—"

"Don't you make this about me. I would have told you a million times over that it wasn't what I wanted. Four years ago, you were the only thing that mattered to me. I was madly in love with you. I thought…I thought you felt the same. That you could love me back. But you didn't because I'd have never let you go. I would have fought for you."

Killian's soft voice rubbed against my skin. His eyes were wide and pleading. "We did fight for you."

Tears stung my eyes, but I met each of their gazes.

"How did you fight for me? By hurting hundreds of omegas? By helping to take away their choice?"

"We didn't know." Rafe's voice was thick around the words.

I let out a sarcastic laugh. "How did you not know? How could that possibly happen?"

Killian responded quickly, speaking practically at double time. "Everything was so fucked-up after what we did, so we split up at first, but pretty quickly, we realized we couldn't be apart from each other any more than we could be away from you."

"We learned fast that the way to get you back was the Agora," Ares said quietly. His expression was dark, like he didn't like the memory. "The Agora meant we needed money, and the only way to get money—"

"Was the gang," I finished for him.

"Yeah."

I looked between them. Their sad but hopeful expressions, like this, might be the end of it. They seemed to be completely missing the point. It wasn't about the gang or even them abandoning me—though that still hurt. It wasn't even about only us anymore. This problem stretched beyond us.

"Do you understand what you've done though?" I asked, my voice quaking a little as my anger built. "I don't understand how you heard me talk about the Institute and still worked with them. How you met Flora and didn't tell me. Do you even know the harm you caused?" I was screaming now. "I'm the one who spent four years being forced to be the perfect omega." I pointed toward where Wes' place was located. "I'm the one who saw my friends be drugged by *you*!"

They flinched back from me, eyes downcast.

"Bliss—" Rafe tried to speak, but it was clear he had no idea what to say.

My chest heaved as I continued. "So, go on. I'd love to hear why you thought it was okay to make the choice to send me to that hellhole or help the damn Institute of all things."

"This wasn't what we wanted to happen." Nox's eyes were rimmed with red, making his beautiful green eyes stand out in contrast. "Any of us."

Tears welled over my cheeks. "Having good intentions doesn't erase the harm you caused." I made a pained sound, and they stumbled toward me but stopped when I held my hand up. "Had you taken the time to look, instead of just making decisions, you'd have seen what the Institute was doing."

Ares ran his hand through his hair and pleaded. "We are so sorry. We can fix this—"

Anger rushed through me, washing away the overwhelming sadness. "Sorry's not enough. 'Sorry' doesn't erase the harm you caused. 'Sorry' doesn't give me back the four years we could have had together."

Rafe's eyes narrowed in on the dresses tucked under my arm. "Where do you think you're going?"

"Away from you!" I went to rush out of the room, but Killian's arms wrapped around my middle, and his lemon vanilla scent filled my nose. I choked on a sob and fought against the urge to turn into him. To just forget all of this and have them back. But they ruined that. "Please let me go."

Killian's arms dropped, and the overwhelming scent of ash replaced his. "I know you want to, but we can't just let you go. There isn't a world where we could let you put yourself in danger like that. Every alpha within a mile of where you end up will be a predator."

"Don't you think I know that? What kind of fool do you take me for?" I huffed out a sardonic laugh at the unfairness of it all. "I'm going to stay at Wes' with Flora until we figure something else out."

Rafe sat on the arm of a chair and pressed his palms into his eyes. "You'd rather stay in a place with only one room than with us."

"Yes." I prayed it wasn't a lie.

Nox was the next to speak. "Okay, Little Wolf. We're done making your decisions for you. If leaving is what you want, then we'll help you do it."

The other three turned on him, the look of betrayal in their eyes, but Nox continued as if he didn't notice them. "You might not be able to roam around, but you aren't completely out of options. We have a house."

"I'm not moving into a house with you."

Nox nodded. "I know. Yourself, Flora, and maybe even Wes can move in. We'll stay here. The Institute isn't going to stop looking for you just because you left Nero."

I flipped his words over in my mind, looking for a catch. "You're really just going to let me live in your house?"

A sad smile crossed Killian's mouth. "Yes. We'll do anything you need. Just tell us."

"I want you to leave me alone." Their noses scrunched with the sharp ammonia smell of my lie.

Ares growled. "Except that."

They followed me down the stairs and through the parking lot, and I sighed and looked at Wes' door as though I could see through the metal to where Flora was undoubtedly waiting for me. She'd come with me wherever—she was that kind of friend—but should she have to? I didn't have a plan. I didn't know where we were going or how we would make ends meet once we got there. All I knew was that being near them hurt. I sucked in a breath as my ribs squeezed around my chest. It hurt so freaking much. I twisted my finger through my hair, running the debate through my mind. In the end, Flora's safety and mental health were more important than my broken heart. "Fine, but just until I figure it out."

Four collective sighs of relief set my teeth on edge. This wasn't a surrender, and they shouldn't be happy about it.

"Thank you," Nox said in one breath.

"Don't thank me. I'm going to go get Flora, then Wes can take us to the new house. Just give me space."

Killian reached out and grabbed my arm. "We can give you space, but we aren't going anywhere. Never again, Bliss. Do you understand? Never. Fucking. Again. I'm so sorry for not telling you. So fucking sorry. We are going to fix this." His grip tightened to punctuate his words, and his warm brown eyes pleaded with me. "I love you."

I choked back a sob and pressed my palm to my chest as his words tried to rip me open. "It's too late."

"Not for us, it isn't. And we will spend every fucking day proving to you that you will always belong with us."

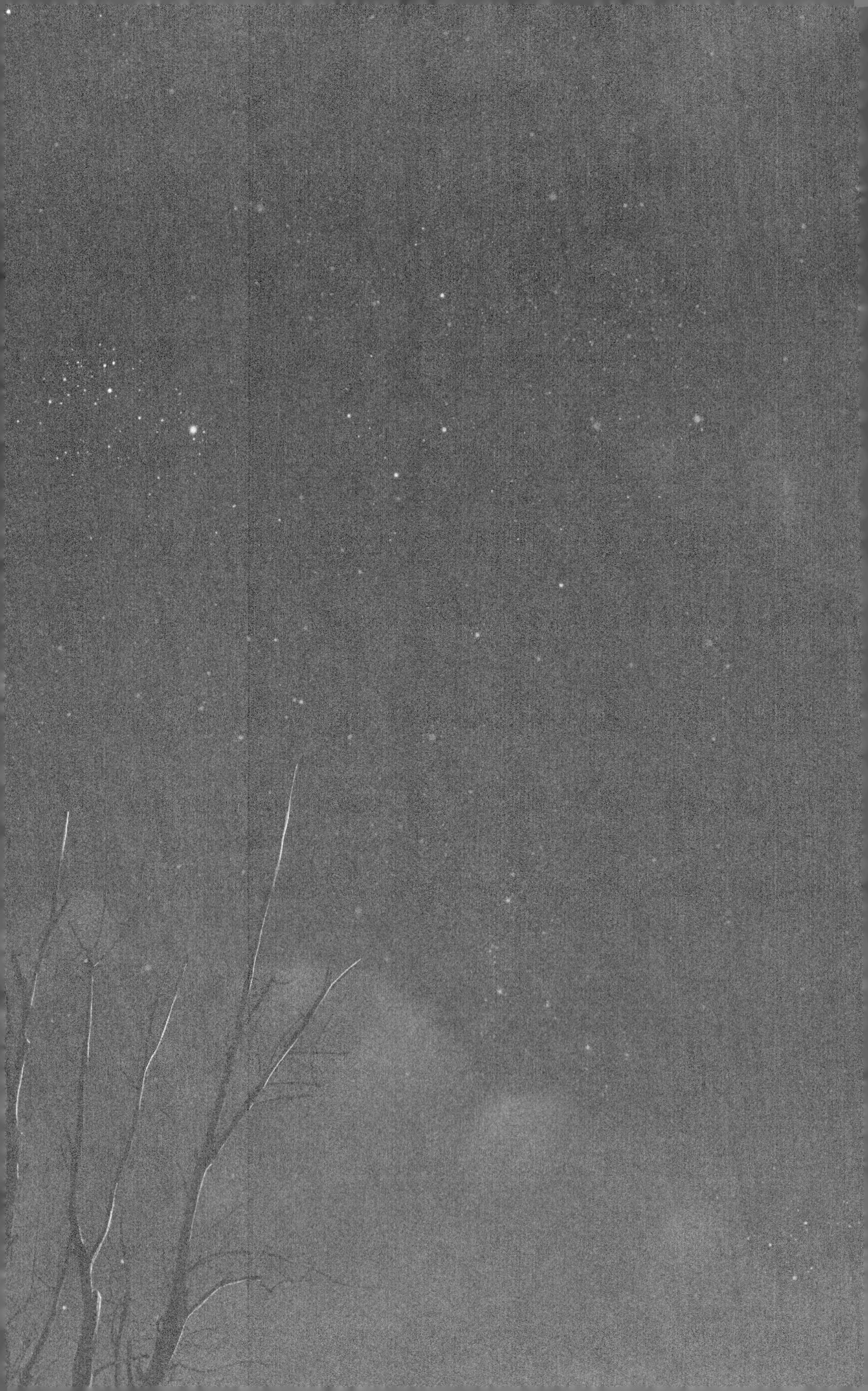

CHAPTER 4
Rafe

The wind from Ares' flying fist brushed against my cheek. I danced back, barely missing his follow-up jab. "You can't retreat forever."

We'd been in the ring for hours, burning off our collective pain and energy. For once, I could see what Ares liked about fighting. Every time his fist connected with my face, I reminded myself I deserved this and worse.

Stay the hell away from me. The last thing she said before slamming Wes' front door shut behind her still rang in my head, a constant refrain. The words bit through my chest, and I lunged for Ares.

He danced away, and a sneer curved his lips, the heavy cranberry scent of bitterness mingling with our sweat. "That your best shot?"

It wasn't, but I wasn't trying that hard. This wasn't working. Both of us were trying harder to get hit than to attack each other. "Just talk to me."

His eyes narrowed and darted to the side, like he was

looking for the right words. Four years ago, we never had problems talking—but that was before the bastard had practically abandoned us after we called the Institute on Bliss.

I met his eyes, waiting for him to open up. I needed my friend back. I'd needed him before, fucking wished he'd just talk to me, but I needed him more now.

His voice was barely over a whisper, growing louder with each word. "It was my fucking fault that she was sent to that fucking place. I should've done something."

I grimaced, breathing in the rotten scent of his misery and frustration that no doubt mirrored my own. It really wasn't his fault. It was true that for a couple of years, Ares could order the rest of us around just because he was the oldest, but by the time Bliss presented as an omega, that wasn't really an issue anymore.

"Well, it's my fault that we fucked up the blockers, so I guess we're even," I said sarcastically.

"That's not only your fault. We'd all seen the peaceful omegas..." Ares' voice cracked at the end, the smell of burnt marshmallows and damp leaves surrounding us.

"Yeah, and we all sent Bliss away," I countered. I circled him, looking for his weak spot. "You need to snap out of your four-year-long pity party. We're all fucking morons, so now what?"

Ares rocked back on his heels, leaving the opportunity I was waiting for. I ducked in and landed a solid uppercut to his jaw. He collapsed back, landing on his ass and bouncing with the impact on the red gym mat.

White, sweat-damp hair raked back from his face, a small frown pulling down the corner of his mouth, now split open. He scanned my face for several moments, and his shoulders relaxed. Hopefully, he finally realized we were on the same side.

I reached my hand down to where Ares was laid out on the mat and hauled him up. "You left yourself wide open."

He narrowed his eyes, looking like he wanted nothing more than to take out his anger on me. "Oh yeah? Let's try again. See how it goes for you."

Ares was a legitimate threat in the ring. He'd always been a wild card. Even when we were kids, he'd always had an edge to him. I leaned over and grabbed two cloths from the edge of the mat, tossing one toward him. He caught it easily, wiping off his face and neck.

I sucked back my water and took my shot at getting him to work with us. "What the hell are we going to do about Bliss?"

Ares' eyes bored into mine, and his body went rigid. "Whatever it takes."

For once in the last four years, we agreed on something, and it was like threads wove back through the rip between us, knitting our pack bond back together as we focused on the only thing that ever mattered.

I sighed. "I just wish I knew where to start."

"Yesterday, I was down to just forget about everything and move forward like nothing happened. That's obviously not the play though."

"No, for sure, not that." I wiped the sweat off my forehead. "Does 'whatever it takes' include shutting down the business?" I asked, already knowing what I would do.

"What the fuck do you think? That's the easy part of this whole thing." Ares pulled a white T-shirt over his tattoo-covered chest. He was leaner than the rest of us. His muscles carved into his pale skin like marble, offset by the dark ink that covered nearly every inch of him. "We've got enough in savings to get us by. The hard part is dismantling it so no one can do what we did."

I ran my hands through my black hair, pushing it off my face. "We'll have to make it worth the doctor's while to disappear. He's the only one that knows how we did it."

"Just saying, I'd be down with killing him and blowing the lab up." Ares' mouth tipped up in a smirk. "I'm not fucking around when I say I'd do anything."

I reached through the bond to Bliss and was met with a deep sadness. I flinched. Never mind—she wasn't ready for any eavesdroppers on her feelings yet. "It's going to take more than words. She needs us. I know she does, but why the hell would she trust us after all the shit we pulled? We're the bad guys in her narrative, and we fucking earned that title."

Ares headed toward the stairs to our loft. "Which means we're absolutely fucked."

I followed him, nodding even though he couldn't see me. Whining wouldn't do a damn thing to help get her back. I wanted to get started on actually fucking doing something—I wasn't good at sitting still.

I stepped through the door to the upstairs apartment and stopped dead in my tracks. *The air smelled of salt, anxiety, and determination. What the fuck?*

Books covered every surface. I moved further into the room, eyes roaming over the covers. Some were handbook-type things, like *The Ultimate Guide to Caring for Omegas*, and *Omega 101: Ten Surprising Things Omegas Need (and One They Don't!)*. Others were huge textbooks like *The Core Principals of Omega Anatomy and Physiology*.

Nox lay slumped over the arm of the couch and didn't look up as I approached. "Dude…"

He didn't react. I wasn't sure he even heard me. His head was buried in a book as his fingers typed rapidly over his keyboard. His red hair had grown out, he was overdue for a shave, and he was dressed in what looked like pajama pants and a white T-shirt. While we'd been busy beating the crap out of each other, he'd obviously gotten to work. I tapped him on the shoulder. "What *is* all this?"

Ares came into the room, echoing my surprise. "Nox. What the hell are you doing?"

Nox finally looked up, his brows pinched together. "What we should have done already. Do you want to get Bliss back? Do you want to make her happy?" He held up a book and read from the text. "Omegas require quiet, dim spaces."

Ares huffed. "We fucking know that. The architect designed the apartment around that."

Nox shook his head. "Did you know they like to be covered in their alpha's scents? That it can cause anxiety if they're away too long?"

I placed my hands on the back of a lounge chair and shook my head. "But we aren't her mates." *God, I fucking wish we were.*

"But we are scent bound. You must have noticed it's grown stronger since her heat?"

I thought back to every time I'd sensed her emotions through the bond. For years, it had only been a faint tug, but I could now feel her emotions from miles away.

Ares sat on the sofa beside Nox and placed his elbows on his knees. "So what now? We study?"

Nox laughed. "You haven't properly studied a day in your life."

No lie there.

Nox stared me down, his chin lifted. "I will study, and for once, you're going to do as I say."

I raised my hands as relief that at least one of us had some inkling of a plan. "You won't get a complaint out of me. If it helps Bliss, just tell me what to do."

Ares rubbed his palms over his face. "Same."

I went to the kitchen and grabbed a bottle of water from the fridge. "Where the hell is Killian?"

"He's way ahead of you. He's sitting his watch with Bliss."

I had to hold back my bark to demand what that meant. I had no business bossing these guys around anymore. I did an absolute shit job of getting back in her good graces. Well, I did until last night when we'd finally come clean with how we felt. My heart clenched. That just made it all the more brutal that we'd lost her again.

"What the fuck does that mean?" Ares leaned back on the couch, taking the words from my mouth, his arm slung over the back where Nox sat.

"We'll take turns watching out for her. Unless you think she's safe just because she's with Wes?" Nox's right brow rose, clearly knowing the answer.

"She's not going to let us hang out with her. She was pretty damn clear that she wants nothing to do with us."

"I didn't say anything about hanging out with her. I said keep an eye. Killian is currently stationed in front of the house, but I made him swear to stay outside."

It was my turn to rub my hands over my face. "You really think Killian, of all people, can manage that?"

Nox grinned. "No, but I also think he's the one Bliss is most likely to forgive first."

"You really think that's a good idea? What if she doesn't want that?"

Ares's low growl rumbled in his chest. "We're fucking done deciding what Bliss can and can't handle. If Killian's bothering her, she'll tell him." He smirked at us. "There's no resisting him once he goes golden retriever mode. We fucked up by holding him back."

He was right about the fucking-up part. "Just tell me what to do."

Nox pointed at the stacks of books. "The main thing is being open about how we feel and start showing her in ways she'll understand."

"How are we going to do that?" I asked.

"Well, that is what we are going to find out. For now, we pay attention to what she needs and figure out how to get it for her."

Show her how we feel. Every instinct in me wanted to crash in her place and just flat out beg to get her back, but I could do this. I could do whatever it took. "I'm taking a shower, then I'm relieving Killian." Even if it wasn't as close as I wanted, I needed to be near her.

Ares stood from the couch, a flash of his old self coming through. "The fuck you are."

Nox just waved us off. "Give it up. Fighting is just going to make it worse." He picked up his phone, hitting a few buttons, and a schedule came through mine.

I smirked at Ares. "Looks like I'm next in line, after all."

My smile melted from my face at why Bliss needed

protection. My growl filled the room. "What are we going to do about Nero?"

Nox took his off glasses and shrugged. "Kill him."

Ares nodded, and my chest eased. Good. That was decided, then.

I left them and headed directly for the shower. Hot water poured down my back, and a part of me wished I hadn't gotten in here. I still smelled like her, and the idea of washing her away made me want to throw up. Not now that I knew there was a good chance I wouldn't smell like her again. Unfortunately, I also smelled like sweat from my ring match with Ares. I lathered a cloth and scrubbed over myself before rinsing off. I made quick work of shampooing my hair and rushed out of the shower. It was my fucking turn to be near Bliss, and I wasn't going to miss a second of it.

It took no time to get dressed and head out to the other house. Killian sat on a porch swing, his feet stretched out in front of him. The streetlights were the only thing lighting the space. The night air held a chill, but I barely registered it.

The house was an old Victorian style with a wraparound deck. It loomed above me, painted a deep green with white trim.

Killian crossed his arms and leaned back in his chair. "I'm not done."

"Yeah, you are." My voice slipped back into the commanding tone easily.

He placed his hands behind his head and smirked. "You can join me, but I'm staying."

"Fuck, fine." I didn't bother sitting beside him, instead propping my back up directly against the front door, and kicked my feet out in front of me. We sat in silence for several minutes until Killian started to whistle.

"Why are you so happy? We're literally stuck outside her door."

Killian's smile grew, his obvious smug excitement like the scent of cardamom in the back of my throat. "Not for long though."

"How the hell do you know that?"

Kills' eyes darkened as he looked at me. "Because it's not a fucking option. I don't give a single shit what needs to happen to earn her trust back. I will do it."

"You can't be sure she'll take us back," I said.

Killian turned back to the house. "Who the hell said anything about *us*? You guys are on your own."

I took a deep breath, the faint smell of Bliss filling my nose, and my chest squeezed. I wish I was as certain as Killian was.

CHAPTER 5
Bliss

I shut the door of my new room and leaned against the wood, breathing heavily. It was as though I'd run a mile, though I hadn't done more than climb the stairs.

I reached out, fingers stretching to catch the light switch on the wall, and flicked it on. I blinked against the sudden brightness as the bedroom came into sharper focus. The room I'd chosen was directly at the top of the stairs and cozy, though simply furnished. The rug under my toes was braided wool, and the blanket on the double bed a blue flannel—cute, but not the same kind of designer decorating happening at the warehouse. I took a deep breath. It smelled like…what I expected a grandparents' house to smell like. Cotton laundry and maybe something floral.

Wes was in the room across the hall from me in the main bedroom, and Flora was in the smallest room at the end of the hall next to the bathroom. Wes had put up a fight about taking the largest bedroom, which just showed how little he understood about omegas, despite clearly trying. The man had a lot to learn—assuming he wanted to take the time to learn it. Judging from the way he kept looking at my friend, I'd guess he would.

I pushed off the door and dropped my small bundle of clothes and other belongings on the bed. The faint smell of lemon and vanilla filled my nose, and I turned, expecting to see Killian. A tiny part of me was disappointed when he wasn't there. The fact that I was imagining their scent was just proof of how bad I had it.

I removed the elastic from my wrist and twisted my hair into a high bun. I turned to open the window to let in a breeze and gasped, stumbling back.

Killian knocked gently on the glass from where he perched outside of my window.

At least I wasn't hallucinating his scent.

I shook my head and waved my hands in front of me. "No. No, no, no. Absolutely not."

He gave me the saddest puppy dog eyes I'd ever seen, impossible to ignore. I opened the window, prepared to tell him he had to go, when he jumped in, crowding me deeper into the room.

"What are you—"

Killian covered my mouth with his hand, and I jerked back, but he held me firm. "I'm going to let you go. Just hear me out."

He slowly lifted his hand from my mouth, and I pushed him back. "Out, now—"

My mouth fell open, and I sucked in a breath when all two hundred plus pounds of alpha dropped down on his knees in front of me.

"Please. Listen to me. I promise to leave right after."

Stunned, all I could do was nod.

"I am so fucking sorry, B." He lowered his head in a fully submissive display that had me frozen in place. "I'm going to prove to you how sorry I am. From now on, I'm on Team Bliss, and everyone else can fuck off. I'll never keep secrets again. Whatever you say goes. Just please, please give me a shot."

I wanted to. Every single molecule in me wanted to drop down in front of him, wrap my arms around him, and tell him I forgave him. That everything would go back to normal. But that wasn't the truth. I wasn't the same naive Bliss anymore. "It's not that easy."

I wasn't expecting a smirk to tip the side of his mouth. "Good. Don't make it easy on me. I don't care what I have to do. I'm not going anywhere, Bliss. Never again. You're the only one for me, and if that means the only part of you I get is watching you from the sidelines, then that's enough. Because any part of you is worth a million of anyone else."

I swallowed hard as his words warmed me and steeled myself for what had to happen next. "Killian, you have to go."

He stood immediately and stripped off his shirt, tossing it on my bed, and backed up to the window. "I'm looking forward to proving it to you, Bliss."

My body heated at the promise in his eyes, right before he swooped out of my room like it wasn't a two-story fall.

I lifted his shirt to my nose and pressed my palm to where my heart was going wild in my chest. If I wasn't careful, I'd fall right back into him.

CHAPTER 6
Bliss

I opened my eyes to the faded paint of an unfamiliar ceiling.

It took me a full thirty seconds to remember where I was as the sleep cleared from my brain and reality sunk in. I was in the guys' safe house. Ironic. I didn't feel all that safe right now.

I lay awake last night in my new bed for longer than I should have, given my level of exhaustion. I expected the moment I shut my eyes, I'd wake up again, terrified by the slamming of Nero's door, falling out a window where there was no rope, or some twisted version of my fight with the guys. And that would be just the nightmares that made sense—I shuddered to think what my brain could come up with. Thankfully, though, I'd slept through the night without incident. *Lucky me.*

I frowned. I didn't believe in luck anymore.

I threw off my pale blue flannel covers, swung my legs over the side of the bed, and stretched. My eyes darted to the window across from the bed, still open a crack, and I frowned.

In the light of day, that entire conversation seemed so surreal. Everything about last night was surreal. Part of me wondered if I'd done the right thing in refusing to just let Killian back in. I needed someone to talk to, but Flora was going through her own mess, and it was hard to justify unloading on her.

I grabbed one of my sundresses—the one with the small wolf print—and ducked into the bathroom in the hall. My pale reflection stared back at me in the mirror over the sink. The circles under my eyes betrayed my exhaustion, despite having just woken up. I splashed water on my face and pulled my lavender hair into a messy crown on the top of my head. I'd never been into heavy makeup, but God, I would kill for some concealer right now.

Making my way downstairs, I avoided stepping on any of the creaky hardwood steps. It was like being back in the foster home, except now I was doing it so I wouldn't wake up my friends, not to hide from my foster parents.

The safe house was actually near where the guys and I grew up. We were only a few streets over from our old school and the woods where we spent summers at the fire pit. It probably wasn't there anymore. Not that four years was a long time, but for an outdoor space on the East Coast? The winters had probably killed it without upkeep.

I wished I could go check. Hell, I wished I could go anywhere.

I'd never considered myself an ornery person. I'd been happy to spend most of my life going with the flow, following along with whatever the guys wanted to do. In retrospect, maybe that was an omega trait. Maybe it was just because I'd never been out in the world or done anything alone.

Now, suddenly, being told that I couldn't go anywhere alone—that no omegas could go anywhere alone—was making me want it more. The injustice of that was intolerable. We needed to find a way for omegas to take blockers without losing all ability to think, and they needed to become accessible to everyone. Omegas should be able to live freely without being mated or hunted just for existing.

I reached the bottom of the stairs and glanced around. I hadn't spent much, if any, time exploring the house since we'd arrived. Short of glancing in all the bedrooms and locating the bathroom, I'd basically gone straight to bed last night without so much as a walk-through. Now, I did a quick scan of the downstairs.

The layout was simple enough—the staircase was in the center of the house like many older East Coast homes. When you walked in, the living room was on your immediate right, and the kitchen was down the narrow hall toward the back of the house. There was a back door off the kitchen leading out to a small concrete patio covered in crabgrass and leaves. There was nothing wrong with the house—it was cute, even—but today, it felt like a prison.

I crossed to the living room window and pushed aside the thick, white curtain.

The gray morning light shone dully on the street outside. Everything was overcast and hazy, like the sky was trying to decide if it felt like raining. I peered out at the lone, pale-haired figure in the leather jacket hovering on the edge of the yard. My chest squeezed.

"It's like a scene out of an emo music video." Flora's

voice sounded behind me. "Cue the rain and the flock of doves."

I turned around to see her coming down the stairs wearing the same clothes she'd worn yesterday. "This is serious."

"I'm being totally serious. Film that shit."

I took a small step to the side, giving her space to stand next to me. We both watched as Rafe pulled up in an SUV next to Ares. They spoke for a moment through the window, and then Rafe got out, and they swapped. Ares took the car and left as Rafe sat down at the bottom of the tree at the edge of the yard.

"Looks like they're taking shifts," Flora said unnecessarily.

"Yup." That should have made me feel safer, but all it was doing at the moment was serving as a constant reminder that we were never really safe. "I can't watch this."

"Making you want to go out there and let him in?" Flora asked, her tone light but eyes serious.

"No!" I said indignantly.

Flora wrinkled her nose and swallowed a few times, as though trying not to gag on the taste of my lie. "Whatever you say."

I glanced at her as I let the curtain fall back into place. "How did you know he was out there?"

"My window overlooks the street, and I've been up for a bit." She pushed her hair behind her ears.

I pursed my lips. I was pretty sure "I've been up for a bit" meant "I didn't sleep at all." Her tone was flippant, but her scent was total chaos. I'd need to keep an eye on that.

Over the next few days, my hunch turned out to be correct.

A few days later, I hovered in the hallway outside Flora's room, dancing between my feet. "Hey!" I knocked lightly. "Are you up?"

She didn't reply. Today, we seemed to have swung in the opposite direction—instead of not sleeping at all, Flora was being a little *too* quiet. Under normal circumstances, I wouldn't wake her up, but this wasn't normal circumstances...

I turned the knob and poked my head inside. I let out a breath of relief I hadn't realized I'd been holding as soon as my eyes adjusted to the darkness of the room.

The curtains were drawn, and Flora was curled in the middle of her bed, her chest rising and falling as she slept. Wes' musky scent hung lightly in the air, though he wasn't here. I raised an eyebrow. *Interesting.*

Her expression was perfectly peaceful, and her hands lay folded serenely under her head. If I hadn't lived with her for four years, I would think she was faking it, but I knew better. Flora looked like a Disney princess—a foul-mouthed, sharp-tongued, feral Disney princess. I slept with my mouth open and all my limbs spread out like a starfish. Life wasn't fair.

I closed the door quietly again and trotted down the stairs for breakfast.

The hair on the back of my neck stood up as a copper scent hit my nose and pooled at the back of my throat. I came to an abrupt halt. "What the hell are you doing here?"

Ares sat at the kitchen table, facing away from me. His white-blond head was bent low, so all I could see were the tops of his shoulders and leather jacket over the back of his chair, but that was all I needed to see. The smell alone was recognizable enough.

At my words, he spun around and dropped the Sharpie he was holding. "Hi."

I watched the Sharpie roll across the floor, making a thin black line across the wood. I scowled, crossing my arms. "Don't do that."

His stare was too intense for any time of day, but especially for 7:00 a.m. pre-caffeine. "Do what?"

"*Hi.*" I mimicked his deep voice. "You're not supposed to be in here."

He *wasn't* supposed to be here. He definitely wasn't supposed to act like it was no big deal.

I crossed the room to the counter and checked the coffeepot. Empty. Clearly, Wes wasn't up yet. I wasn't sure if Flora had had any coffee since getting out of the Institute, but she was about to get some. I smiled slightly at that idea.

"I'm not here," Ares said, pushing to his feet to retrieve his Sharpie from where it had landed near the dishwasher. "Not really."

My frown deepened. "What the hell does that mean?"

He smirked at me. "Are we leaning into 'hell'? Fuck, I'm into it."

"Don't do that!" It was all I could do not to stamp my foot, but that felt incredibly childish. If ever there was a time though...

"Sorry." He put his hands up in surrender. "It's my turn to guard. It's cold out today. I came inside."

I narrowed my eyes. That was...a specifically phrased

statement. *"It's cold out today. *Pause* I came inside."* Not *"It's cold out, so I came inside."*

"You don't get cold," I said. "Didn't you tell me once your base temperature is like 101?"

The scent of his amusement was suffocating. "True."

I rolled my eyes and made my way to the refrigerator, sighing. "This is dumb, and it's too early. I don't want to talk to you."

"That's fine." He picked his pen back up. "Pretend I'm not here."

"Fine."

The sound of Sharpie scratching against skin filled my ears as I turned back to the coffee maker. It was a marvel he had any free skin left to draw on—I resisted the urge to turn around and look.

Refocusing, I paused, realizing I had no idea where anything was in this new kitchen. Crap. I turned in a half circle, scanning the cabinets above the counter for one that looked like it held pantry items.

The pen stopped scratching. "Over the stove."

I frowned, gritting my teeth. "Thanks."

I stood on my toes to reach for the cabinet over the stove and pulled out an unopened bag of breakfast blend. The bottom of my dress lifted as I stretched to graze the backs of my thighs, and the scent of sweet honey filled my mouth. I shivered.

I tugged on the bottom of my dress as I landed back on flat feet. "Stop that." I forced myself not to respond to the scent in the room through sheer willpower.

Ares made a noise that might have been a laugh. "Sorry, Love, won't happen again."

I wrinkled my nose at the ammonia scent of the blatant

lie. *Asshole.*

I jammed my finger onto the Start button of the coffee maker with more force than needed and whirled to face him. "This isn't going to work."

Ares was watching me again, Sharpie held limp in his hand, expression unreadable. "It's only been three minutes, Love. I thought you'd last at least five."

"Don't be cute."

"I was serious about that one."

I narrowed my eyes. "I can't pretend you're not there."

"Then come talk to me."

"No," I snapped. "I meant you should leave."

He gave me another serious look. "I can't do that. One of us has to be here at all times."

"I know. I meant you don't have to be in the kitchen watching me."

"True," he conceded the point. "I want to be in here, but I'll go if it really bothers you. Does it?"

I opened my mouth and then shut it again. What if I said I wanted him to go and I didn't really mean it? Suddenly, I wasn't sure what I meant. Instead, I asked, "Why do you want to be here?"

"Making up for lost time. You're angry now, and I get that, but you're still mine. You wanted me to be there before, and I wasn't, so I'm just going to be here now whenever you're ready to talk."

I mentally slapped myself. *Stop it.* "What if I never want to talk?"

He raised an eyebrow. "Honestly, I'd be lying if I said I thought that would happen, but I guess if it does, then I'll just be hanging around forever, waiting quietly...patiently. It's your call."

I had no words for that.

I turned around and opened a few cabinets until I found the mugs and pulled the half-full coffeepot off the burner to pour myself some. The drip landed on the hot burner and sizzled loudly before I put the pot back on. I took a sip and pulled a face. Disgusting.

Ares got to his feet and held out his hand. "Give me that."

I recoiled. "No."

He rolled his eyes, pulled the creamer out of the fridge, and handed it to me. "Use that. There's sugar in the cabinet."

"Thanks, I guess."

"You're welcome."

I gave him a suspicious look. He was being unusually nice—no sarcasm, no backhanded banter. It was freaking me out. "I guess if you insist on lurking, you could make yourself useful."

"With what?"

He was a little too eager, his expression more like Killian than like himself. Again, it was freaking me out. I sort of preferred him rude. Not that I should have any preference—he wasn't supposed to be here at all. "I'd rather not stay in the house all day. I'm going crazy here."

His expression flattened. *Better.* "I can't. You know that."

"If you came with me though?"

Even as I spoke, I realized the problem. It was a bad idea, born of desperation and boredom. The last time I'd been out in public, Ares had killed someone, and that was not the kind of attention we needed right now.

That whole situation was made all the more frustrating

now by the knowledge that I could have been taking blockers. They didn't affect me the same way as everyone else, and the guys had access to them the whole time, so presumably, the whole reason they never gave them to me was so I wouldn't leave. Infuriating.

"Wait, do you still have blockers? Can I have some?"

"Love..." His anxiety was poignant, like rock salt. "What do you want to do?"

I thought for a second, biting my lip. Anything would be better than staying inside. "What time is it, anyway?"

Ares glanced at his phone. "Ten-ish."

I frowned. "And Wes and Flora aren't up? Flora I get, but..."

"Wes isn't here," Ares replied. "He left with Killian hours ago when I got here."

I frowned. Then we couldn't leave, because Flora couldn't be left alone. She probably shouldn't be left alone with just Wes anyway, but that was kind of another issue altogether. "Never mind," I sighed.

Ares grimaced, looking genuinely apologetic. "Another day?"

"Yeah." I sighed again. "I would have wanted to go see the fire pit or something simple like that."

"I don't think it's there anymore." He rubbed the back of his neck.

"Yeah, I figured, but still."

My gloom hung heavy in the air between us. Looked like we'd be spending the day in the house. *Kill me.*

I could at least go outside. I crossed to the back door and tugged it open with more force than I should have needed—clearly, no one had been here in a while.

Ares stood from his seat at the kitchen table and

followed me out the back door, a dubious expression on his face. "Love…"

"I'm just going to the yard. Come if you must." I glanced up at him as we stepped outside. "It's not cold."

"Yeah, you're right, but it was."

I gave him a sideways look. That was a total missed opportunity for a snarky comment. "Whatever."

A breeze kicked up, pinwheeling the leaves across the patio, and my breath caught as the scent in the air shifted and cleared. The back of my neck heated, and my stomach did a little flip, somewhere between nerves and rising tension.

God, I hadn't even realized Ares' scent was affecting me.

Before everything had changed, my hormones had already been all out of whack. If I'd had to guess, it seemed like my heat was coming on quicker than it should have been—probably all the proximity to alphas while still being unmated. My body had no way of knowing what was good for me emotionally. All my stupid hormones cared about was getting bitten and pregnant.

Ooph. That was a terrifying thought.

I needed to see a doctor about some birth control ASAP. Blockers. Birth control. Emotional independence. Not difficult or anything.

I scanned the backyard, my eyes catching on a swing hanging from a tall oak tree. Like the kind that was probably put up for a kid at some point. "Why do you guys have this place, anyway?"

"Backup plan," he said immediately. "We weren't sure if you would like the warehouse."

I cocked my head to the side, trying to see this place

from that point of view. It was kind of cute—like a nicer version of the house we grew up in. Not that I had perfect memories of our foster home by any means, but there were some great times there. I mean, we'd all met there.

My chest squeezed, and I swallowed hard. This wasn't going to work. This was why I needed better separation—we had too much history, and it was too easy to forget for a second why I was angry. *They lied to you. They abandoned you. They worked with the Institute for years—get it together.*

"Do you want to go on the swing?" Ares asked. His tone made it clear he could smell my turbulent emotions—probably feel some of them too through our bond.

"No, I'm fine." *I should have brought a book or something.*

Ares turned to me, intense gaze seeming to do an X-ray. "Okay. I get it, you're bored."

"I'm not bored. I'm pissed off."

"Pissed off and bored," he amended.

I gave his shoulder a shove. "I'm going to punch you if you keep doing that. I don't care if it breaks my hand."

His eyes sparked. "Okay."

I furrowed my brow. "Okay, what?"

"Hit me."

I took a step back, feeling my face heat, the sweet scent of honey and a tinge of embarrassment rising around me. "Is this a kink thing? I..."

His smile turned feral. "No, but I'm going to remember that you went there. You wanted to learn self-defense, right?"

I took a breath, my entire body flushing. God, what were my hormones doing to me? "There was no chance I was going to be able to fight off anyone. Even a beta."

He gave me an appraising once-over. "Eh... I don't

know."

I raised my eyebrows. "You told me yourself I couldn't fight off anyone."

"No, I said you couldn't fight an alpha. You can't."

I deflated. "I don't understand."

"A full-grown beta male couldn't fight off an alpha if it really came down to it. That's why they always carry guns and wear earpieces." He looked contemplative. "Maybe we should just get you a gun."

"I don't want a gun, God. I'd probably shoot myself before I'd hit anyone else."

"I doubt that, Love, but fine." He gave me half a smile, and my stomach did an annoying flip against my will. "You said there was no chance you could fight off anyone, and I don't think that's right. I think we could teach you to hurt a beta and at least escape an alpha better."

"Most people coming after me are alphas," I pointed out.

"Most, but not all. It's a start."

I took a step back, appraising him. "Last time I asked for your help, you weren't nearly this enthusiastic about it."

"Last time, I hadn't seen you attacked twice in forty-eight hours. I'd prefer that you're never alone, but I'd feel better knowing that you can also throw a punch."

I frowned. There was no reason at all for me not to take this offer—except maybe that we'd have to touch each other, and I was already a little more affected by his proximity than I wanted to be. Still, I agreed with him. I'd also feel better if I could throw a punch. "Okay, fine. What do you want me to do?"

Ares took a couple of steps away from me, leaving the

patio and standing in the middle of the grassy lawn. The yard wasn't perfectly flat, but it wasn't a hill either. Just slightly slanted and more than fine for sparring. He pulled off his leather jacket, revealing the white T-shirt underneath, and tossed it on the ground. I swallowed hard, my throat suddenly dry.

"Come here," Ares said, voice suddenly all business.

I went without question, suddenly unsure if that was a subtle, unintentional command or if I just responded well to directness. I stood stock-still, skin tingling. "What now?"

"Do you have any other clothes?"

I glanced down at my dress. "No."

"If you're going to work out, we need to get you something else to wear immediately."

"I mean, I guess, but in a real self-defense situation, I wouldn't be dressed to run, so this is probably better." I gave a little mock kick to illustrate my point, and my skirt flapped around my legs. I could have kicked myself instead. *Why? What the hell was that?*

He looked pained, and I tried to ignore the scent of honey that would have given away the direction of both our thoughts even without the bond. "You're killing me, Love."

Him and me both. "Alright, are we doing this or not?"

He cleared his throat. "Yeah. Okay, so I don't think we should do any boxing until we get you some real gear and are in the ring back at the warehouse..." He seemed to be speaking more to himself than to me, thinking out loud. "You'll hurt your hands. Let's try escaping if someone grabs you."

All I could think of was being dragged by my hair

down a blurred hallway. "I can't."

"You can. What's your advantage here?"

"I don't know. You outweigh me by a hundred pounds."

"Yeah. You ever hear that expression 'the bigger they are, the harder they fall'?"

Without warning, he grabbed me from behind, his arms wrapping tight around my middle and pinning my hands to my sides. I screamed instinctively, twisting to get free.

"Try not to scream or thrash around," he said hoarsely. "It wastes energy."

"Oh, I'm sorry," I said sarcastically, still trying to pull out of his arms. "Next time, I'll temper my reaction to being manhandled. Let me go."

"Make me." His words were hot against the shell of my ear.

A shiver traveled up my neck, and my skin heated. That wasn't supposed to be the reaction to being held like this, but with my heart beating so fast and the close proximity, my body was betraying me. I needed to get free for more reasons than one. "What do I do?"

"If someone grabs you like this, step to the side." He nudged my foot out with the inside of his boot. "And duck under my arm."

I raised my eyebrows. That sounded easy. I stepped out and backward, ducking under his arm. I frowned. "Except that you're huge. You'll lift me off my feet. I can't step out."

"Right. So, it's way harder to carry dead weight." He rolled his neck and held out his arms again. "I'm going to pick you up."

"Now you're giving warnings?"

"Fuck, just get over here and let me help you."

I bit the inside of my cheek, hiding a smile. "That was only thirty minutes. I thought you'd last at least an hour," I said, paraphrasing his early statement.

"At what?" His aggravation was clearing the smell in the air—thank God.

"Whatever sad, polite thing you're going for. You don't do contrite all that well."

His eyes flashed. "Fuck, you're right. Do you care?"

"I care about authenticity."

"I authentically want you to get your ass over here so I can pick you up and teach you something."

I rolled my eyes. "Fine."

Ares wrapped his arms around me again, this time lifting me into the air. I ignored the swooping in my stomach, chalking it up to the motion of my feet leaving the ground and not the scent enveloping me from all sides.

"I'm expecting you to struggle and pull forward," he said, businesslike again. "Instead, go limp."

"What?"

"Limp. It's hard to hold dead weight, especially if you're not expecting it. It's pretty likely you can slip out of their grasp, or the person will outright drop you."

I tried to relax, but it was totally counterintuitive. Even though I knew the point was to escape, I was somehow afraid he would drop me. "How far off the ground am I?"

He shifted so we were lower. "Six inches. Go limp."

I tried again, envisioning my whole body relaxing muscle by muscle. Ares loosened his arms slightly, and my feet slid to the ground. "Good. That was perfect."

I smiled, glowing a bit under the praise. "Let's go again."

CHAPTER 7
Nox

As I paced around the parking lot, I kicked a piece of broken concrete. I spent hours last night studying omega facts. I now knew the three best thread counts for an omega's nest bedding, but nothing meaningful. Nothing that would show Bliss how much she meant to us. I rubbed a palm over my head and huffed out a breath.

I'd kill for a book like *The Fundamentals of Apology* or *Groveling 101: An Essential Guide*.

The look on her face as she'd put everything together would stay with me forever. She was strong and fierce, laying out the consequences of our actions. Even while shredding my heart, she was fucking beautiful. I'd held myself back when the tears fell from her eyes. My alpha instincts raged to life, screaming at me to kill whoever did this to her, but it was us. We hurt her. We broke her trust.

She'd never asked for any of this. Her words about

loving us four years ago had sucked the air from my lungs. What I would give to go back to that day. Hit the rewind button on my life and do it all differently.

Our bond pulsed with heartache while she delivered the killing blow. *"'Sorry' doesn't erase the harm you caused."* I wasn't sure anything ever could.

She was actively planning a way to get away from us. I knew she would. We didn't deserve her. Never did. But the idea of her out on her own while every fucked-up alpha tried to chase her down had my vision going red. I had spun through her options at warp speed, desperately trying to keep her safe without forcing her to live with us. I never wanted to take away her choice again. I also knew we'd wind up locking Bliss in the basement if it was the only way to protect her.

Thank God we had the house. She wouldn't be with us, but she'd still be under the protection of the pack umbrella. She was one hundred percent right to cut us loose. That didn't stop my overwhelming need to wrap her in my arms and drag her back to my room as she left.

"Let's go." Rafe's bark traveled over my neck and shivered down my spine, pulling me back to the present.

I jogged up beside him, his scent of dead flowers clogging my nose that had nothing to do with where we were going. "Took you long enough."

Shutting down the blocker business was the only thing that felt right in all of this. Killian was all for it. The only thing he asked was to take care of disposing of the poison blockers himself. Something told me it would involve some form of explosion. He'd locked the crazy side of himself away since we got Bliss back, and it would be good for him to let some of it out.

Rafe grimaced. "Just get in the van."

He wore a set of guns in his holster, a matching set to the ones I wore. His black hair was a disaster, and the skin under his eyes was bruised. None of us got much sleep last night.

I jumped in the passenger seat, and we took off. It was a short, silent drive to the fish market where we conducted all our business, neither of us wanting to talk about how thoroughly we fucked up with Bliss. Rafe parked the van in the near-empty parking area next to a long shabby white van with a faded New York plate—probably stolen. A flock of chattering seagulls sat on top of the van and took flight as we approached, landing instead at the end of the long gray dock.

Rafe cleared his throat. "In and out. I don't want to fuck around here."

"In and out," I parroted, checking my gun and flipping off the safety.

I hopped out of the van and wound my way through the maze of abandoned stalls and broken lobster traps until I reached the end of the dock. I wasn't overly worried about Harrison. We'd been working with the beta for years, and although I didn't like him, he'd never caused trouble. Which was the only reason he was still around.

Harrison leaned against a worn and splintered post, his brows pulled together under a black knit cap. His jeans were dirty and his arms crossed against the cold, salty air coming off the water. He looked up as we approached, watery eyes struggling to focus.

"Hey. You're late." He gestured to the large empty space between us. "Where the fuck is the product?"

My sneer slid into place. "What product?"

The beta's face turned red. He pushed off the post and took a step toward me, and the scent of his mingled anger and confusion overpowered the cranberry smell of his fear. "What are you playing at?"

I raised an eyebrow. What was he playing at was a better question. There was no world where picking a fight as a beta was a good idea, no matter what the stakes were.

Rafe walked through the opening between the market stalls. "Back the fuck off."

Harrison stumbled back with the force of Rafe's bark, and the air filled with the scent of sour cranberries. He glanced at me, then to Rafe, and his voice shook as he seemed to remember he was outmatched. "Okay, sorry. Do you need an extension? It'll be tough, but I can make it happen."

A smirk tipped my lips, and I pushed my glasses up my nose with my thumb. "That won't be necessary."

Harrison visibly relaxed, his shoulders drooping. He pushed his hat up off his forehead and turned in a circle, looking around like an idiot for the missing crates of blockers. "So where is it?"

Rafe stood to his full height, and intimidation wafted off him, daring the beta to comment. "We don't have it. We're getting out of the business."

Harrison's brows hit his hairline, and his voice came out a squeak. "What? Why?"

I slid my hands into my pockets and rocked back on my heels. "That's none of your business, don't you think?"

The beta blinked a few times, as though waiting for someone to say this was all a joke. Then, his face flashed with rage as reality set him. His nice cushy job working as a go-between for Alpha Lupi and the Institute was going up in smoke. "You can't…"

"We can," I said lightly. This conversation was already boring.

"Is this about the omega slut—"

Rafe had Harrison pinned to the post, his feet dangling as his hand circled the beta's neck. A low menacing growl vibrated Rafe's words. "The only reason you're still alive after that comment is because we need you to tell the Institute to fuck off."

Harrison made a choking sound that might have been an apology, but it was hard to tell when his windpipe was being crushed. Rafe let go of his grip, and Harrison collapsed to the ground, gasping for breath.

I toed him with my boot. "I suggest you hurry. Your boss is going to want to hear the news."

Harrison stood and practically spit his words at us as he backed away. "The Institute is going to be pissed. You're fucked in the head if you think they will let you just drop the business. They'll come for you."

My lips curved. "Counting on it."

———

I took off my glasses and rubbed my thumb in a small circle between my brows. A dull ache had formed as I watched Bliss leave, and it had grown stronger ever since. It had been hours since our meeting with Harrison, and I was impatient to get to Bliss.

I grabbed my bag from the passenger seat of the van

and made my way up Bliss's driveway. While technically still our house, it was hers for all intents and purposes. I took a deep breath, nervous about how tonight would go. It had only been a day since she left, and already it felt like the distance was eating away at me.

Bliss was the best thing that happened to us growing up, and we'd formed a pack around her like she was the center of our universe. She was bright, lively, and carefree when nothing felt right. The sunshine to our grumpy. Alphas were a handful, but multiple teenage alphas living in the same house? Fucking disaster.

Bliss balanced us without even trying, like she was specially made for each of us. Ares had always held a darkness to him that would disappear whenever he was near her. When Killian arrived at the group home, he was so lost, but from the moment she smiled at him, she became the only thing that mattered. Rafe needed to feel needed, and Bliss' innocence had him bending over backward. For me, Bliss was my source of peace. She was the only one that understood when the world became too much. It was why I escaped for hours in books or lay on the roof, looking at the stars. Not that I hated my life. I was surrounded by my best friends and the girl I knew was made for us. She understood that. Bliss was my mirror. She craved those quiet moments as much as I did. Even long before the scent bond, it felt like she was a small piece of my soul walking around free.

I sucked a breath through my nose, and a hint of a smile curved my lips as the sweet smell of jasmine laced with honey and spice hit me. Fuck, I missed her.

I knocked on the door, listening to the click of the lock. Ares swung it open and stood in front of me, pushing his white-blond hair from his eyes. "I told you I didn't need to be relieved."

I held up my phone, showing his unanswered text. "I got it, and yet here I am." He'd been with Bliss all day. He was delusional if he thought I was giving up my turn. My gaze scanned the room, but I didn't catch sight of her. "Where's Bliss?"

Ares lifted his chin toward the stairs before grabbing his wallet, phone, and keys off the counter. "She's taking a shower. Don't come on too strong."

I flipped my backpack onto the living room sofa. "So it didn't go well, I take it?"

"It went fine."

He wasn't lying exactly, but there was something off there. "You're in the house, at least…"

"Barely." He stepped in close until his boots touched the tips of mine. "I'm serious, Nox. Don't fuck this up."

He didn't have to worry about that. "I promise, I won't. I need her as much as you do."

He fell silent for a moment, unable to meet my eyes. Like the question he wanted to ask was eating him alive. "Yeah, but…what if she doesn't need us? What then?"

I just shrugged. "I'll do whatever it takes to make her life happy, even if that doesn't include me." The words tasted like bile in my mouth, but they were true. "What about you?"

His pale blue eyes met mine, a seriousness holding them steady. "She may hold us to that."

I swallowed hard, knowing it would be torture to let her go. "Good. She deserves to be happy. No matter what happens to the rest of us."

I opened up my laptop and flipped on the TV, hitting a few buttons until they synced together. She'd loved this movie as a kid. We must have watched it fifty times, just her and I.

A door creaked open upstairs, and Bliss came down the stairs on silent feet. She watched me hesitantly as I removed textbooks from my bag and placed them on one of the sofas.

She twirled a strand of her lavender hair between her fingers, and her gaze didn't meet mine. "Hi."

My muscles strained against the want to tip her chin up until her violet eyes stared into mine. She was perfect, in a green wrap dress that hit just above her knees. I pulled the fourth book from my bag and tried to get my breathing under control. "Hi, Little Wolf."

She sucked in a breath at the sound of her nickname and searched my face. Her eyes moved, darting around the room. "Where's Ares?"

"He had to go. It's my turn to be near you."

She frowned. "Fine, but I'm not hanging out with you."

A hint of a smile tugged at my lip. "I'm not asking you to."

Her nose crinkled at my lie, and she rolled her eyes, turning halfway toward the stairs. "Alright. I'm leaving now."

This was my chance. I couldn't just stay silent. My body screamed at me to say something. *Provide, tend, care.* "I will always want you with me," I called after her. "But not...not if it's going to hurt you. It's all for you, Bliss."

Her cheeks pinkened, traveling to the tips of her ears, and she looked away, eyes landing on the TV. "How did you find this?"

"Luck."

She hovered in the doorway, dancing from foot to foot, eyes darting from the movie to the stairs to me.

"You could stay and watch it, you know… I promise I won't bother you. I'm just going to read," I said, holding up my open book with both hands. "You don't have to talk to me."

She made a happy sound and curled up on the couch across from me, where there was already a throw blanket and pillow. She sat tucked into the corner, the blanket over her knees. My fingers clenched at the million memories of us doing this, but in all of those, she was curled against me.

I cleared my throat, doing my best to pretend I was reading. How could I sit quietly and read when her presence made my every nerve spark like a live wire? It had been hard enough to hide it when I was a teenager, but now? Now that I'd lost her and found her, only to lose her again, it was damn near impossible not to openly stare.

Some of the sadness on the bond lifted when she laughed at the movie. Her smile fell when she noticed me watching her. "Thank you," she murmured and gestured vaguely at the TV. "For finding this."

I lifted my book in front of my face. "Of course."

She was at the halfway mark of the movie, but she'd wiggled and twitched herself into every position. She'd been feeding a mix of frustration, anxiousness, worry, and helplessness down the bond nonstop. My nose twitched with every change in her mood, and I tried not to react to the scent in the air.

My phone buzzed in my pocket, and I groaned, not at all surprised.

Ares: What the fuck are you doing to her?

Me: Nothing. She's watching a movie.

Killian: Sounds like I should start my shift early.

Rafe: Enough. Nox figure out what's going on. If she hasn't calmed down in 30 we're coming over there.

Bliss chewed on her thumbnail, her lavender hair drifting over her eyes. Her distress was killing me. "I know we aren't great right now, but you know you can talk to me, right?"

"I don't think that's a good idea."

"Why's that?"

Her jaw set, and her chin raised. "I don't think this is a subject you'll be happy about."

Unease settled in my stomach, but there was nothing I didn't want to help her with. "Try me."

"Flora and I have been trying to sort out how we can leave, but no matter what, it always comes down to the fact that it's unsafe for us to be alone." Her gaze narrowed on mine, waiting for my reaction.

My lungs collapsed with the force of her words. Of course, I knew she was planning to leave, but hearing her say it? This was what it must feel like to get shot in the chest. I had to force myself to take a breath.

She shifted uncomfortably, no doubt sensing my distress. "I told you talking to you was a bad idea."

Fuck. I swallowed and pushed down my emotions as far as I could and ground out, "It's fine."

Bliss tilted her head, her tongue darting over her lower lip. "Survey says that was a lie."

I didn't feel fine. "Trust me, I can take this."

"Mmm-hmm." Bliss pulled her knees to her chest, pausing while she studied me. She let out a sigh. "It's just not fair, you know? Omegas are helpless, and for how much I hate the Institute and how much shit they…you…did, I can't come up with another option." A wave of frustration pounded off her, and my phone buzzed in my pocket.

Ignoring it, I stood and reached out a hand. I had to help her the only way I knew how. "Let's go outside."

She looked at my hand, then back into my eyes. *Please, Bliss.* I knew exactly what she needed; I just needed her to trust me enough to do it.

She slid her delicate fingers over mine and visibly shivered. A low purring sound formed in my chest. She went to pull away, but I closed my fingers gently around hers. "It's fine. I promise."

Without letting her hand go, I scooped up the blanket from the couch and led her out the back doors. There was a large wood patio set up for entertainment we never used. I led her to the large daybed. I'd spent more than my share of drunk nights stretched out on this bed, staring at the sky.

I kicked off my shoes and got onto the seat and pulled her with me, letting go of her fingers the second she lay flat. I didn't want to. Hell, I wanted to pull her hard into my chest and bury my face in her neck. I wanted to beg and scream, but that's not what she needed. She needed me to be her friend. It was going to hurt like hell, but I wanted her happy more.

Shifting to put my forearm below my head caused my other hand to drift against hers. Bliss made a small whine sound as our skin brushed. I had to work to ignore it. Her scent had become richer over the course of the last few days, her heat coming up sooner rather than later. I focused on the sky, not wanting her to see the need in my gaze until I got myself under control. I spotted Orion looking down on us, and my chest tugged.

I pushed my emotions aside, wanting to be whatever Bliss needed, and right now, that was a solid friend. "You and Flora want to leave, or do you want every omega to leave?"

She was silent for several minutes, but the gentle hum coming through the bond told me she was awake. "I want every omega to do what they want to do. Right now, even if we could convince the Institute not to give blockers to the omegas, there still wouldn't be a safe place for omegas to go after. They'd still be sold off to some strange alpha. Just like I was."

A growl broke through my chest. "It should never have happened."

"A lot of things shouldn't have happened."

Fuck, did I know it. I twisted my head until my neck cracked, trying to sort through it all. "So the problem and solution are blockers." The words tasted bad on my tongue as I pushed them out. "If we can figure out how to get blockers not to turn omegas into walking zombies, you'd have a shot to leave."

Bliss' laugh was harsh. "Unless you've been sitting on some side-effect-free recipe I don't know about, I'm not sure how that's possible."

I shifted, uncomfortable with what I had to say next.

"We were only concentrating on potency."

The scent of anger surrounded us, mixed with the hurt coming through the bond. My phone buzzed again. I turned to look at her, where she stared directly at the sky, a silver line running from the corner of her eye into her hairline. "I'm so sorry, Bliss. I'm so fucking sorry."

She turned her head, violet eyes meeting mine. "You all keep saying that, but it's not going to fix anything."

"What if we could help fix it? We have access to a lab and a doctor. What if it's possible?"

"You're telling me you'd help me find the only chance I have to get away from you?" Her right eyebrow lifted high.

"I'm telling you, there is nothing I wouldn't do to make you happy. Even if that includes letting you go."

She sucked in a breath, and I'd never been so happy she had the ability to smell a lie because every word I said was true.

We ran ideas back and forth on potential solutions for the blockers. The later it got, the twitchier she became, but from the heat she was throwing off through the bond, I knew it had nothing to do with the conversation. All the reading I'd done told me the closer she got to her next heat, the more her instincts would drive her to mate. Her desire for us was strengthened by our scent bond and us helping her through her first heat. I took a chance and entwined our fingers, running my thumb over her wrist in a soothing motion. Her gaze met mine, eyes wide, before she settled into her spot. The anxiousness that had been pouring off her lessened to a trickle.

As sleep took her under, I drew circles with my thumb on her wrist. I lifted her in my arms, breathing in her scent, and brought her to her room, tucking her covers to her chin. I closed her door quietly behind me when a door down the hall opened.

Flora stood backlit from her room. "Don't hurt her again."

"Never."

CHAPTER 8
Bliss

I stood under the warm spray of the shower and dug my fingers into my scalp. I scrubbed harder than necessary as a million ideas for how to fix the blocker problem ran through my brain.

What if every omega gets her own contracted security? It's not like there are that many omegas, maybe...no.

I shut off the water and let out a little growl of frustration—the obvious problem with that idea was similar to everything else I'd come up with. Every omega would end up scent bound to their bodyguard.

Dammit.

I wrapped myself in a towel and stepped into the steam-filled bathroom. I had woken up before the sun, my skin flushed red from my dreams and Nox's lingering scent. I may have been set on keeping my distance from the guys during the day, but dream me was all over them. Unfortunately, dream sex wasn't very satisfying.

I must have fallen asleep because the last thing I

remembered was talking about blockers. Nox's willingness to even have that conversation shocked me. According to them, they'd spent years trying to get me back, and now he was willing to help me find a way to leave?

My chest warmed as I dropped my towel in the hamper and got dressed for the day. I couldn't forget the consequences of their lies, or I'd easily find myself back where I started. Still, even with the hurt that radiated off Nox as he offered his support, there wasn't any hint of ammonia in the air. He'd been telling the truth even though it clearly cost him, and I couldn't ignore that.

Maybe if we'd actually come up with a solution, things would be more clear. Unfortunately, we didn't, which only left me feeling more helpless.

I darted back down the hall to my room and halted at the sight of a small, perfectly wrapped purple gift box with a giant black bow. My eyes narrowed.

There was no chance it was from anyone else but one of the guys. I stared at it like it had personally offended me. *I should dump that right in the trash.* I glanced back at the door as though someone were going to come in and see me. *I guess I could pick it up. For just a second...*

I held it close to my ear, shaking gently, like one of those kids in an old Christmas movie. The soft, muted scent of peppers and coffee beans met my nose, and I hummed at the back of my throat. I glanced back at the door again, then shook my head. I was being stupid, feeling guilty over nothing. I'd just put it away and think about it later.

I pulled open the bottom drawer of my nearly empty dresser and pushed the gift all the way to the back so I wouldn't have to see it. *There. Like it never happened.*

The rich scent of coffee lured me downstairs.

I stepped into the kitchen and nearly choked. Killian turned to look at me, grinning. "Morning, B."

He was shirtless, for Christ's sake, and the way his mouth was tipping up in one corner told me he knew exactly what he was doing. That didn't stop me from taking in every inch of his tanned, chiseled chest, over the V-shaped muscles and the shadow of hair leading into his low-hanging jeans. *Holy shit, that man is sin incarnate.*

I swallowed hard as my body heated. I cleared my throat and met his sparkling honey-brown eyes. "Morning. I didn't know you were here."

He smirked at me, nodding to the coffeepot as if in explanation. "Strong smell, yeah?" He winked. "Sleep well?"

My ears heated, and I swallowed hard, wondering just how much of my dreams I pushed down the bond while asleep. "It was hot."

He let out a growl that had heat pooling between my legs. *There's the answer to that question, I guess. I must be sending them all lots of mixed messages overnight.*

This was a very dangerous game. For all his boyish charm, there was an edge to him, present even when we were kids, but he'd never shown me that side. Instead, we'd spent our childhood laughing and goofing around. Basically, being the bane of Ares' and Rafe's existence. I wouldn't have traded it for the world. A deep-seated sadness sank in my stomach at all the time lost and what we were going to miss out on. Killian stepped toward me, his boots millimeters from the tip of my bare toes. His eyes searched mine before his fingers grazed my cheek, sliding a loose strand behind my ear. "You're beautiful this morning, B."

A shiver ran down my spine, and my cheeks heated as I fought against leaning into him. What I would give to wrap my body into his and let the stress from the last few days be wiped away. I was exhausted from fighting against my traitorous body's constant ache to go to them. His strong arms banded around me, tightening until my cheek pressed flush against his very naked chest.

"Let go of me, Killian." I tried to keep my words harsh, but they came out breathy as I breathed him in.

He ran his hand through the ends of my hair in a soothing motion. "I can feel how stressed you are. Just please let me do this for you."

"It doesn't change anything."

He stiffened for a moment, and I swore he wasn't breathing before he said with a strained voice, "I know."

I snuggled my nose against him, feeling my resolve snap. "Just for a little bit."

His low purring vibrated my chest, and I found myself relaxing further into him. "Whatever you say, baby."

I groaned as I stepped back. "Don't call me that."

He bit his bottom lip, but his dimples gave away his smile. He looked delicious, and every thought washed from my brain as he dropped his head to mine. "Are you telling me you don't like it?"

I kept my mouth firmly shut, knowing he'd be able to smell the lie.

His smile lit his face. "That's what I thought."

I didn't realize I was still holding on to him until he pulled away, letting my hands drop to my sides and graze over my hips. I bit back the moan threatening to crawl up my mouth. My rational brain knew all the reasons curling up against Killian was a bad idea, but my body didn't care.

Killian took a deep breath through his nose, and his gaze turned black as he scented my arousal. It would've been embarrassing if he didn't look like he was one second from devouring me. He tugged at his hair. "You can't look at me like that."

This time, I didn't stop the sound escaping my mouth. I took a step backward, heat pooling in my lower stomach.

His eyes flashed bright, and his voice came out low and dangerous. "I wouldn't suggest you run from me, Babe."

I didn't know why, but I was dying to know what would happen if I did.

A snore pulled my attention. I turned to look at a sleeping Nox buried under a pile of textbooks, the sharpness of his features softened by his relaxed state. "Was he like this when you got here?"

"Yes," Killian's reply was more growl than anything. "The bastard fell asleep on his shift."

"It was fine. Nothing happened. Plus, he was still right here." I gestured to Nox's passed-out form. His sleeping through our conversation wasn't helping my point. I stepped around Killian, barely escaping his grasp, and walked around the kitchen island searching for coffee when I found a cup already made for me. I took a sip and hummed. "Perfect."

Killian smiled, some of the tension leaving him. "Good. I've been paying attention. I'm starting to learn exactly how you like it."

His words on their own were innocent but, mixed with

the way he said it, had my knees going weak. I put down my cup a little too hard, and the clanking sound had Nox sitting up.

He looked bleary-eyed as he rubbed a hand over his shaved head and looked around, as if trying to figure out where he was. His gaze landed on mine, and his eyes widened as he jumped to his feet. "Oh, shit."

The normally chipper Killian turned an icy look at his friend. "You fell asleep."

Nox looked genuinely put out by the idea. "I'll give you a free shot."

"Deal."

"What? No."

Killian just wrapped his arms around me from behind, pulling me into his chest and resting his chin on my head. I would pull away in a minute—instead, I leaned further into his warmth.

Nox came into the kitchen, a flare of jealousy coming down the bond, but he didn't mention it. I didn't like them being jealous of each other, and I half wanted to pull him against my front, but something told me that would be an even worse idea. Nox grabbed a coffee and leaned against the counter, watching us.

Seeing him reminded me of our fruitless conversation last night, which had my frustration growing. I unraveled Killian's arms and ignored his short growl. I had to concentrate, and I couldn't do that with a shirtless giant wrapped around me. And that wasn't including the fact that he shouldn't have been touching me to begin with. Although, I think I accepted it at this point.

I closed my eyes and rolled my neck, trying to work through a solution. A small idea started to form. I opened my eyes and faced them. "What makes your blockers so special that the Institute would buy from you?"

Killian smirked. "That's a trade secret that a lot of people would literally kill to know."

My brows furrowed as I fought the urge to scream. "And? Are you going to clue me in, or is this just another secret?"

Nox stepped up to me and brushed my hair behind my ear. "No more secrets, Little Wolf. We use our blood."

I jerked up in surprise. "Blood? I've been eating your blood?"

Killian purred, seemingly happy with that idea. I wasn't sure if I liked that or not.

Nox laughed, and I narrowed my eyes at him. "Not quite. We use our Alpha blood in the formula. It's what makes it stronger than the rest. Unfortunately, it's probably also why they had such a strong impact on the omegas."

I scrunched my nose, trying to stay impersonal through this conversation. There were important things to figure out outside of our pack dynamics. "Could you make it less strong? Water it down somehow?"

Nox tilted his head and took a few minutes to respond. "We could try weaker alphas." A thrill went through me, but his eyes dimmed. "But it wouldn't eliminate it completely."

I huffed out a breath, the thick scent of hopelessness pushing away the mingled scents of two alphas. If the secret to their product was in their blood, there had to be a way to manipulate it into working for me. I played with the end of my hair when my brain caught on a thought. "What about omega blood?"

"What?" Nox's eyes locked with mine, but he looked

lost in his thoughts. The way he used to when he was trying to pass a particularly hard math quiz. "It could work."

I jumped with excitement, and Killian dropped his mouth to the curve of my neck, whispering in my ear. Goose bumps exploded down my arms. "We've got a lab to test everything."

A thrill went through me but shorted as I watched Nox pick up his stuff and head toward the door. I looked up at Killian. "I'm coming with you to the lab. You aren't leaving me behind."

"I wouldn't dream of it."

I watched through the passenger-side window as we went further into the city. The stores had changed from regular shopping to dentist and doctors' offices. Killian pulled the van into a small parking lot. A small, practically windowless building with the name Medilife glowed in big letters on the sign overhead. I let out a long breath. This was the first time I'd gotten anywhere near their business. The fact that they'd brought me here, where they actually made the product, was a bit of a surprise. I thought they'd fight me tooth and nail, but both Nox and Killian just ushered me to the van.

Nox gestured for me to go in first, and I was surprised to see it looked like a regular reception area. I'm not sure what I expected for a top secret lab, but this wasn't it.

"You look disappointed, Little Wolf."

"No. It just looks so...normal."

"That's kinda the point." Killian took my hand and

guided me around to the back of the office. My mouth dropped open as I took it all in. It was definitely a research lab, but there were four beds hooked up with tall hospital poles beside each of them. Killian tugged me deeper into the room, and my gaze roamed over everything. It was clinical and way more professional than I expected. Not sure why I pictured some kind of sketchy hole-in-the-wall.

"You must be Bliss." A man in his late fifties with skin a little too orange to be a natural tan and kind eyes came out of a back room.

I stumbled back into Killian's chest, taking comfort in the arm he banded around my middle. "Um...yeah. That's me." Freaking awkward, but I had no idea what to say to this guy.

Nox jumped up on one of the cots and leaned back on his elbows. "Bliss has an idea for a side-effect-free blocker."

The doctor's eyes widened with interest. I thought he would for sure dismiss me; instead, he pulled out a tablet and looked ready to take notes. "Alright, Bliss. What do you have for me?"

I stalled for a few seconds, but each breath of Killian's vanilla lemon scent had me a bit braver. "If alpha blood is what makes the current blockers so strong, what would happen if you used omega blood?"

The doctor's eyebrows rose, and a smile crossed his face. "Honestly, I never thought to try. Omegas aren't easy to come by."

I chose to ignore how his words made it sound like omegas were a commodity. It was how the world saw us. "Well, here I am, Doc. Care to give it a try?"

The doctor grabbed some things from his desk and

gestured with his chin to one of the free cots. "Lie down there, and I'll take some of your blood."

I felt the color drain from my face, and Killian wrapped me in his arms. "It's nothing. Promise."

I didn't mention the fact that the last time I got close to a needle, I'd been put into an induced heat. I knew this wasn't the same, but that didn't stop me from leaning harder into Killian.

There was paper on the hospital bed that scratched at my skin when I hopped on. The doctor stepped up to my left side. "Now, relax your arm for me. It'll only take a moment."

My heart rate picked up as he tied a rubber band around my upper arm and told me to make a fist a few times. I shifted in my seat, and the doctor gently held my wrist. "You need to stay still for this next part."

I took a deep breath and let it out when warm fingers twined with my right hand. Killian sat on the edge of my bed and ran his finger along my jaw, drawing every molecule of my attention. I felt a small pinch in my arm. "That's it, B. Look at me. He's almost done." Killian didn't have to worry about me looking away; he was so close, his nose nearly brushed against mine. I leaned in further, feeling his breath over my lips. I tilted my head back, my mouth nearly grazing his.

"Okay, Bliss. All done." The doctor undid the band on my arm, and blood rushed back to my fingers. "We should have the sample in a few days."

My heart rate pounded for an entirely new reason, and I'd never been so happy that nearly all doctors were betas.

CHAPTER 9
Bliss

"I never noticed how unrealistic these movies are," Flora said, popping a chip into her mouth. "I don't know what annoys me more—that all the omegas are madly in love with their alphas at first sight or that even though I know that's bullshit, I keep watching them."

I sighed. "I think it's how all the alphas and omegas are played by betas, but honestly, I don't think the Hallmark channel is going for realism."

Nox glanced up from where he sat on the end of the couch reading a book called *History of Omegas*. "This says there used to be more designations. Do you want to hear about the deltas and the gammas?"

I opened my mouth to reply—I didn't really care about the textbook, but I liked listening to his voice. Was that entirely rational? No. My brain was playing weird tricks on me lately.

"Are they in this movie?" Flora asked before I could say anything.

"No." Nox tapped his fingers along my shin—the closest part of me he could reach from where he was sitting.

"Then hold that thought," Flora said. "We're like an hour in. The couple is about to mate."

I rolled my eyes, trying not to notice Nox's fingers on my leg. "All these movies have the same formula. You know they'll mate and then break up in thirty minutes."

"I know." She ate another chip. "I fucking love it. Let's do a holiday one next."

I smiled. It was nice to see her at least halfway back to her usual self.

Flora's bruises had faded, and the bites on her neck were mostly healed. She'd have scars from the worst of them, but she didn't want to talk about it, so I didn't bring it up. Slowly, she was getting back to her normal, sassy personality—at least during the day.

At night, sometimes I could hear her crying or downstairs pacing the kitchen. I glanced over at Wes, who sat in the chair across from Nox. Every so often, he looked up from his phone to watch Flora. He looked up as I assessed him, and we shared brief, meaningful eye contact.

"How's she doing?" I asked with my eyes.

"No idea. Better maybe?" he seemed to say back.

I gave a little jerk of my head, asking, *"Your shift or mine tonight?"*

He gave an imperceptible nod. *"Mine."*

Wes and I never really spoke out loud, but we'd come to a weird sort of agreement since moving into the safe house. An alliance of sorts centered around taking care of my best friend.

Wes stood from his chair. "Anyone want anything from the kitchen?"

I shook my head, but Flora held out her bowl. "More chips, please."

He took the bowl and left. Nox stood as well, following him without comment. He let his palm trail along the back of my neck almost unconsciously as he left, and I shivered, pressing my knees together.

Flora wrenched her gaze away from the movie. "Oh my God."

"What?" I said self-consciously, already knowing what.

"Girl, he's barely touching you, and the smell is enough to set *me* off."

I shoved her lightly with my foot. "That's your movie."

She scoffed. "No, it's really not. You're going back into heat soon."

I shrugged, but there was really no denying it. What had started as a need to get a little closer to the guys, maybe some overreaction to scent, was morphing into something far worse. "I shouldn't be though. I should have months."

She reached for the remote and turned up the volume so loud it made my ears ring, shooting a look at the hallway to the kitchen. "Maybe? But I'm not sure since you're not claimed and you spend so much time with the pack. You're tempting fate at this point. You have a giant blinking neon sign pointed at your vagina saying 'alphas eat free.'"

"Oh, shut up."

I wrapped my arms around myself and sank deeper

into Rafe's oversized hoodie, which I was wearing like a blanket. Flora raised an eyebrow but didn't comment.

It wasn't even that I was in denial—I wasn't—I just couldn't go into heat right now. Last week, all I'd wanted in the world was to be claimed, but if it happened now, it would feel all wrong, tainted by everything else that was happening. I couldn't imagine that the guys could go through another heat cycle—especially now that all four of them seemed to be clearly on the same page—and not bite me, so I needed to stop my body in its tracks. My best and only chance for that was the new blockers.

We both jumped as the front door swung open and Rafe stepped into the front hall. My entire body went stiff, the new scent washing over me and waking up all my nerve endings. I looked up, and my eyes widened.

His pitch-black hair hung in his eyes, and his navy Henley shirtsleeves were pushed back over his elbows, exposing his muscular forearms.

Flora glanced at me. "You're screwed," she mouthed.

"Why is the TV so loud?" Rafe asked, squinting like the sound was hurting him.

"Sorry." I reached for the remote and turned down the volume.

He grinned at me. "I have something to tell you." He glanced around. "Wait, where's Nox?"

"Here," Nox called from out of sight. "Kitchen."

I could feel Rafe's relief down our bond and nearly laughed. As though any of them would actually leave. "What did you want to tell me?"

He crossed the room and sat in Wes's vacated chair across from Flora and me on the couch. "I just got back from meeting with one of the small local suppliers."

I narrowed my eyes. "I'm going to be honest, not a great opener."

He put his hands up. "No, wait. We've been working on dismantling the business. We had to shut down all the contracts and supply lines, but that was the last one."

"So what does that mean? In layman's terms," I said slowly, just wanting to make sure I understood.

"It means we're not working with the Institute anymore. No more blockers."

I jumped up off the couch. "Seriously? Wait, what are you going to do for money?"

"Right now, we have money," Nox's voice came from behind me. "But in the long term, there are other options. We'll figure it out."

"That's less important than shutting this down," Rafe said firmly.

My smile was so broad my cheeks hurt. "Wait, did you shut down the lab though? We still need the lab."

"No," Rafe said quickly. "Oh, wait, I have something for you." He stood up to reach into his jeans pocket and pulled out a plastic bag. "This is from Lewinsky."

I took the bag and stared at it. Inside was a handful of white pills, nearly identical to the blockers they gave us at the Institute. "Are these the new ones?"

"Yeah. New formula made with your blood instead of ours."

Flora held out her hand. "Ooh, let me see."

I passed her the bag. "Good morning, ladies, time for vitamins," I said sarcastically, mimicking the nurse who would pass out our blockers at the Institute in the mornings.

Flora laughed and tipped back her head as she popped

the pills into her mouth. I grabbed my half-empty water glass off the coffee table and handed it to her.

Flora gulped, sticking her tongue out at me. "How long do you think it will take?"

I looked to Rafe for confirmation as I answered. "Ten minutes?"

"Probably." He nodded.

I grinned. "Thank you."

Without thinking about it, I launched myself at him, wrapping my arms around his neck in a hug. It was half about the blockers, half about disabling the business. I knew it was the entire pack who had decided on the business, and I hoped Nox behind me realized I was grateful to him too—they were clearly trying.

Rafe stiffened briefly in surprise. Then his arms came up to wrap around my back, pulling me closer. I let out a contented sigh, pressing my nose into the center of his chest.

My skin flushed, every nerve in my body tingling, and immediately, I realized my mistake.

"Um—" I stammered.

Warmth pooled between my legs. My eyes shot open, and I could all but feel my pupils dilate. The scent of honey filled the room, warm and inviting. *Oh, no.*

I wrenched myself away. "I'll be right back."

"Bliss—"

I ignored his call after me and darted backward out of the room and into the hall bathroom. I slammed the door shut, leaning back against the wood with a heavy sigh.

Flora's muffled voice made its way through the door, her smugness obvious even without seeing her face. "Damn. We better hope these blockers work."

I sighed. This wasn't going to work. I was grateful that the guys were trying to make amends. It was nice to get to know each other again. I wasn't ready to jump back into bed with all of them just because my body couldn't get its shit together.

Maybe it's just me who can't get my shit together.

Sometimes I wondered how much of my attraction could really be blamed on biology and how much was just me. Me, lying to myself and behaving at odds with my own desires.

Leaning over the basin of the sink, I splashed water on my heated face and held a cool hand to my flaming neck. My reflection stared back at me from the spotted mirror, wide-eyed and flushed, my dilated pupils nearly eclipsing the violet of my eyes. I groaned in exasperation.

Ten minutes later, I left the bathroom as though nothing had happened.

Barely anyone had moved since I'd left. Nox now sat on the arm of the couch, a spiral-bound notebook and pen in hand, scribbling rapid notes. Flora was now watching her movie on mute with subtitles, Wes beside her on the couch, and Rafe hadn't moved a muscle from where he'd been standing when I left, like he'd turned to stone. I didn't dare make eye contact.

"How are you feeling?" I asked Flora in a voice of forced calm. "Blocked? Do you know what your name is?"

"Yes," she replied, rolling her eyes. "I don't feel any different, but I don't think I'm supposed to. How do we know if it works?"

Nox glanced up at me. "It's not working. If anything, it's worse."

"You can smell her." I narrowed my eyes. For some

reason, that bothered me, even though it shouldn't have. Obviously, if there was another omega in the house, everyone could smell her—actually, why had I never thought about that? "Wait, does she not affect you guys?"

Rafe and Nox glanced at each other. "No," they said emphatically.

"I can tell it's not working, but in an objective way." Nox shrugged. "No offense, Flora."

"Absolutely none taken." Flora made a mock salute. "Keep your gross alpha hands away from me. Thanks."

I sank onto the couch. "So now what? If this isn't working, then what do we do?"

"Drugs have trials," Flora pointed out. "Like I'm sure there's a way the doctor can tweak the formula or something else we can test. Or we could use another omega's blood or…" She trailed off, clearly out of ideas.

I bit my lip, twisting one long tendril of hair around my fingers. I'd put all my eggs in one basket, which I knew was stupid, but I had no other plan. Rafe tentatively reached out to pat my shoulder.

"Don't," I said quickly, flinching away. I couldn't have another attack right now.

His eyes widened, and I felt his pang of horror in the center of my chest. I closed my eyes. "Sorry."

Dammit. "No, it's not…"

"I know." He looked at me and my wet hair. "Are you hot?"

I flushed, from embarrassment this time rather than my stupid hormones, and nodded. "No, this is a new look I'm trying out for fun."

Flora snorted but kept her eyes fixed on the TV, pretending she wasn't paying attention.

"Go take a shower. I'm going to the store. I'll be back."

"You just got here." I glanced at Nox. "Don't you guys have to switch?"

"I have nowhere I'd rather be," Nox said, picking his book back up and settling back on the couch.

I pursed my lips, looking back at Rafe. "What are you getting?"

His black eyes danced. "It's a surprise. I'll be right back. Now, come on, go shower."

My temperature was going through the roof. My heat was coming on way too fast. "Wait a freaking second. You said it was stronger?"

Rafe and Nox looked at each other worriedly before nodding.

"Yeah," Rafe said, one hand on the door.

"We're idiots." I shook my head. "We can't use pre-heat omega blood."

Everyone stared at me, not understanding the epiphany I'd just had. I widened my eyes at Flora, willing her to grasp my point.

She sat up a little straighter, face splitting into a grin. "Oh! Damn, I get it. We can't use an omega who's giving off pheromones, so we need someone who just came out of heat."

I smiled. There was a few-day rest period after every heat where an omega stopped giving off scent. It was about the only time she would be naturally safe, and if my idea was right, we might be able to take advantage of that protection. "Exactly. Now we just need to find someone to help before I, um…" I glanced around and flushed, trailing off.

"Or you could be our test subject." Flora raised her

eyebrows at me meaningfully. "Just saying."

"Let's hope it doesn't come to that."

I had to admit the shower helped. My temperature was still a little off but much better than it was. I climbed into my bed in nothing but a T-shirt and panties and lay on top of the covers. God, what I needed was to spend an hour in an industrial freezer. Like a reverse sauna.

I needed to write that down—million-dollar idea, right there. Reverse saunas for uncomfortable omegas.

In the back of my mind, I knew that what I really needed was to stabilize my bond—pack—whatever. As long as we stayed so out of sync, my body would continue to try and force us back together. It was simple biology.

This was yet another argument for why we needed the blockers more than anything. If the only time omegas were safe was right after their heats, that left them vulnerable ninety percent of the time and still required an alpha to step in at some point.

Someone knocked on my door. "Bliss?"

"Yeah?"

"I brought you stuff," Rafe replied, his voice a little muffled, like he'd taken a step back.

I debated with myself. To put on more clothes and deal with the feel of the hot fabric or have the potential temptation of less clothes? I compromised and threw the end of my blanket over my lap, sitting up. "Come in."

The doorknob turned, and Rafe stepped into the room. He held a grocery bag in one hand and a large cardboard shipping box in the other. He halted as soon as he entered, his dark eyes raking over me. Hungry. I swallowed. I wasn't sure who was giving off the heavy scent of lust—him or me—but it wasn't making it any easier to keep a clear head.

"Hey." I tried to sound casual, but it came out sounding like a whine.

"Hi. This is stuff I ordered a few days ago that just got delivered." He held up the box. "Not really related to right now, but it's clothes and things. Ares mentioned you needed workout clothes, and there's other stuff in there if you want to look for what you like."

I raised my eyebrows. "Oh. Wow, okay, thank you." My gaze darted to the bag. "What's that?"

He grinned and reached inside, pulling out Chocolate Peanut Butter Split. "They still make this stuff. I can't believe it since you're the only one to ever eat it, but here you go."

I squealed in excitement and then immediately snapped my lips shut, trying to temper my reaction. "Thanks."

He laughed. "Just 'thanks'?"

"Yeah, it's okay, I guess," I lied, and we both smelled it.

"If you don't want it, I can take it back." He took a step backward.

"No, wait." I lunged for him, reaching for the bag.

Rafe threw an arm out to steady me, catching me around the waist, then quickly let go. A pained expression crossed his face. "Unless you want a repeat of downstairs, I should go."

I bit my lip, my face flaming, and his gaze immediately went to my mouth. My breath caught in my throat. "Right. And I definitely don't want that."

His nose wrinkled, the scent of another lie wafting across the room. Time seemed to slow in the beat before his dark eyes flashed and he realized the meaning of what I'd said. My heart pounded double time, and my chest ached, an odd combination of desire and fear that didn't belong to me settling there.

He held the bag with the ice cream back out to me, and I took it, our fingers brushing. Rafe growled low in the back of his throat. "Bliss..."

I dropped the bag as he took a step toward me, closing the remaining space between us. My stomach leapt in excitement, and I gasped, my mind giving over to instinct.

Alpha, alpha, alpha, the back of my mind chanted, but it wasn't overpowering.

Rafe reached up, his fingers dancing along my jawline, and met my eyes for a moment before he pulled my mouth to his. I whimpered against his mouth, immediately coming alive as he ran his hands up my sides under my T-shirt, fingers twisting in the fabric.

I arched my back, and he growled, nipping my bottom lip, and another wave of heat washed over me. I threaded my fingers through his hair to try and urge him closer.

The fruity, candy scent of my own happiness mingled with the honey of lust in the air. I stepped back further, my knees bumping the edge of my mattress, and Rafe froze. He pulled back, looking down at me for a moment, still breathing heavily.

I blinked up at him, and I could see myself reflected in his dilated eyes. "Hey."

He groaned, and the scent in the air shifted to a note of dandelions. "God, I fucking hate myself for this, but I should go."

My eyes narrowed, and I deflated, rejection washing over me. "What?"

"No, not like that."

His eyes widened, and he winced like he'd been physically struck, and I was momentarily distracted. How much of my emotional turmoil was I sending down our bond? Maybe he was just good at reading my face.

He tilted his head back to look up at the ceiling. "Fuck, I feel like I'm goddamn seventeen again." He pinched the skin between his eyes. "This will set off your heat, and I don't want to be the one who does that again."

I groaned in exasperation. "Isn't Ares also trying to blame himself for setting off my heat? I'm not mad about that—let's focus on things I am mad about."

Rafe snorted a humorless laugh. "Okay, but I'm being serious. You just made it pretty clear downstairs you don't want to go into heat right now, and I want you to have everything you want in life. I want to be the person to give you everything, but if that's not what you want, that's okay too."

I opened my mouth to reply, and nothing came out. Maybe I'd been wrong downstairs, because right now all I wanted was for him to stay, but was that a bad idea? Would I regret that tomorrow? I couldn't say I always wanted the best things for me—case in point, I wanted more than anything to go back in time and never find out that the guys were working with the Institute.

My heart pounded as I warred with myself, and my indecision must have shown on my face.

Rafe took a huge step back and bent to retrieve the dropped shopping bag from the floor. He pressed it into my hands. "Enjoy your ice cream, Peanut."

CHAPTER 10
Killian

"Here, give it to me." I held out my hand to grab the C4 from Ares. He'd been helping me pack up my gear in one of the warehouse crates for the last half an hour and looked at me sideways. He hadn't been worried about me going off the deep end in so long, it looked strange on him. I grinned in his direction. I'd destroyed the remaining blockers in a fireball from hell. Fuck, it felt good to see it go up in flames.

Every snap, crackle, and pop a step toward making things right with Bliss.

"You smell like a medical bonfire." Ares' nose scrunched as he handed me the last piece. I closed the crate lid and cocked my head to the side, taking a long look at him. He'd chucked his leather jacket, leaving him in a plain, crisp white T-shirt and jeans. "You smelling me now, Ares?"

His gaze darkened, the pupils overwhelming the silver rims, and for a split second, I thought he might come on to me. Not that long ago, we'd all been fucking each other in a giant Bliss-filled orgy.

Ares looked away. "Don't be too full of yourself. You're not my type."

"Right. Sure I'm not." The sweet smell of honey had me groaning, and my dick twitched in my pants. *Fuck.* I had to get a grip on myself.

Bliss' hormones were growing stronger with each day, and it was damn near driving me insane to ignore them pounding down the bond. It was a fucking miracle our pack hadn't killed each other with how thick the tension was. We weren't exactly keeping it from Bliss, but no one wanted to be the one to push her further than she wanted to go. No one wanted her to look at them with regret once her instincts got what they craved. And right now, that was some alpha knot, preferably with a side of deep mating bites.

No, when I mated her, I needed her to be sure of what she was asking because once I got her, there was no letting go. Instead, I wanted her to smile every time she ran her fingers over the mark, thinking of me. I wanted to be so fucking ingrained in her she couldn't find where her soul ended and mine began. That's what it felt like for me. That's the way it had always felt.

Until then, I'd fight against the instincts driving me closer to a rut. We had time before Bliss' next heat, and we weren't fucking it up by getting greedy. I wiped the sweat from my face, deciding on an ice-cold shower. Fucking frigid.

I didn't make it three steps before someone pounded on the warehouse door.

"Who the fuck is that?" Ares gave me a look, a coldness

taking over him. We weren't expecting any company.

I shrugged, my lips tipping in a sneer. "Whoever it is picked the wrong day."

Ares opened the door, and my eyebrows hit my hairline as Headmistress Omega DuPont stepped into the warehouse. "Good evening," she said stiffly, notably leaving off any courtesy title.

Ares stepped in front of her, blocking access to the warehouse. "Why the fuck are you here?"

"Dear, I have reason to believe you are harboring a recently misplaced omega. You wouldn't know anything about that, would you?"

A growl escaped from my chest. *Misplaced.* Like Bliss was something instead of someone. My chest squeezed, knowing she'd been treated like this for years because of us.

"I suggest you fuck right off." Ares went to slam the door in the headmistress' face, but a giant of an alpha came from behind her and held it open. He didn't feel more powerful than us, but he was fucking huge. We weren't going to move him easily.

I cracked my knuckles, looking forward to the challenge. I had a lot of excess energy to burn off lately.

The headmistress took a proud step into the warehouse, forcing Ares back. She was an omega, but she moved like she was royalty. *Pompous bitch.*

"When I heard our local blocker supplier was going out of business, I thought something had happened. Imagine my surprise when I found out that not only were they choosing to close their doors to us, but that every other known supplier was suddenly out of product." She tsked, and the sound made my skin crawl. "We've had to purchase blockers from a small shop in LA. Unfortunately, the side effects are quite nasty."

I flinched. I hated we were a part of that, and I hated that to get ourselves out of it, more harm would come to omegas. Anger rose in my chest until it felt like it was going to bubble over. This bitch didn't have to keep the omegas on blockers. They were in a fucking school, for Christ's sake. It couldn't be that hard to keep alphas out. No, they didn't do that because they wanted them to be sedated. Compliant so they wouldn't question their future. So they wouldn't question how the Institute made the government so rich.

In the number of years since the creation of the Institute, the government body in charge of everything omega, there had been a large annual surplus on the budget, not that any of that trickled down. Instead, it lined the pockets of greedy politicians willing to look away for the right price. Or worse, assholes like Flora's governor alpha.

"Leave." Ares' bark echoed through the open warehouse, and the condescending look on the headmistress' face disappeared as it forced her to walk backward.

"I wouldn't do that. I'm just the messenger." What the hell was this old bitch talking about?

"Stop." Ares stared her down as she stopped one foot out the door. "Tell us your message, then leave."

The headmistress straightened to her full height, barely to my shoulders, and tilted her chin high. "You will return to your duties and continue to supply blockers to the Institute."

I choked on a laugh. "Yeah? And why would we do that?"

Her stony gaze cut to mine. "There will be repercussions if you don't."

Relaxing, I said, "We'll take our chances. Now, fuck off before you outstay your welcome. Wouldn't want you to destroy your perfect illusion of decorum."

"You might not be afraid of what the Institute can do, but there are other ways I can make problems for you, and I'm not alone. Alpha Nero has many ways of causing you trouble and an invested reason to help."

Ares' growl matched mine. "Leave her out of it."

"I don't know who you mean, dear. Alpha Nero and I are simply concerned government employees with an obligation to make sure that the best interest of alphas and omegas everywhere is upheld. It is in the best interest of the community for the Institute to succeed and for prominent couples to be seen as happy. Nero has been devastated since his poor omega went missing. Tragedy, really." The words dripped off her tongue with sweet poison.

I wanted to smack the self-satisfied look off her face. She knew she had us by dangling Bliss. What she didn't know was that it only drove us to go against them more.

"This is the last time I'm telling you. Fucking leave." Ares' bark rang out, and even the headmistress' security alphas stepped back.

I smirked and waved as Ares slammed the door. He looked at me. "Fuck, I want to kill her."

"Same, man. Fucking same."

I shifted uncomfortably against the hard wood of Bliss' front door. A quick glance at my phone told me it was after one in the morning. I'd started my shift over an hour ago but hadn't gone inside yet. I was too on edge from the headmistress' little visit today, and I didn't want to interrupt her sleep with all of my bullshit. Instead, I'd planted myself on the ground and wondered what the hell Bliss and Nox were looking at when they stared at the sky, because the city lights nearly blurred out the stars.

Air caught in my throat as I collapsed back, the door swinging out from behind me, and I lost my balance. I landed a foot away from a timid-looking Flora. She'd been sorta okay with us being near her, which was an enormous improvement from when we'd first brought her back, but I didn't think that applied to me practically landing on her. I got up slowly, my hands raised, and took a small step back.

She looked frantic, chest heaving and her eyes wide. I thought she was afraid of me before she said, "You need to go to Bliss. Now."

"Wait, what?" My brows pulled together as I tried to catch up to what was happening.

"You idiots don't understand anything about omegas, do you?"

I know she was talking to me, but all my focus was on one thing. "What's wrong with Bliss?"

"She needs help."

A low growl reverberated in my throat. "You're just telling me this now?" I stepped into the house and felt an intense need through the bond. *Oh shit.*

Flora grabbed my arms, then pulled back as if burned when I looked at her. I did my best to soften my features, but every instinct was screaming at me to get to Bliss now.

Flora straightened, dropping her arm. "She's been having heat spikes. Killian, if you bite her, I'll—"

A growl rumbled in my chest, and I immediately regretted it when she took a step back. I softened my voice. "I'm never hurting her again."

A small smile curved Bliss' best friend's mouth. "Don't fuck this up." I was happy Bliss had someone on her side when she was at the Institute. I'd have to make a point to thank her.

"Never." I took off up the stairs and opened Bliss' door. She looked tiny on the bed, her lavender hair splayed out behind where she was lying on her side. Her top leg was pulled close to her stomach, and the hem of my shirt raised a bare inch above her delicious fucking pussy. I groaned, biting my fists, and got my shit together.

She made a pained keening sound, and my stomach bottomed out. I sat on the bed and pushed her damp hair from her face. She shifted into my palm, and her eyes slowly opened. "Killian?"

I dropped my forehead to hers. "Fuck, babe. Why didn't you tell us it was this bad?"

"I'm fine. I have it under control."

My chest rumbled, and I lifted off her. "You are a lot of things, but you are not fucking fine right now, B." She was burning from within, and there was a sheer sheen of sweat coating her skin. She was spiking hard and needed to break out of it, or she'd crash directly into her next heat. For how much that tempted me, I wanted her in our pack before that happened. I could help her through this though. I could make this better.

"Bliss, babe."

"Hmmm." She snuggled closer to me but pulled away. Her nose scrunched up, and hurt flashed through her eyes. "Why do you smell like the Institute?"

Fuck, I didn't want to tell her. She'd already been worried about so much.

Her hand grazed my cheek, and her gaze fixed on mine. "No more secrets?"

I leaned in and pressed my forehead against her, breathing out. "No more secrets. I promise. Don't for a second think we're working for them. That bitch of a headmistress showed up at the warehouse threatening to sic Nero and the fucking government or some shit on us if we didn't go back to supplying them blockers."

"What?" Bliss jerked back. "Nero's coming after you?"

I smirked, and I was sure it looked more sinister than happy. "I'd like to see him try. It'll make killing him easier."

Heat flushed my girl's cheeks and rippled down the bond. She liked that.

"So, how did this happen?" I growled, looking down at her flushed body.

She mumbled something incoherent, then cleared her throat and tried again. "Don't blame Rafe. He tried to warn me."

My eyes widened in surprise. What the hell? Rafe and I had switched shifts several hours ago. I'd have to worry about it later.

"Tell me, B. Have you touched yourself before?" My voice was low and rough as I bit back a groan, imagining it.

Her bright eyes met mine, pupils blown wide, making them appear near black. "I tried…" Pain trickled through the bond, and my grip tightened on her. "It doesn't work. It doesn't help. Not like when you…"

"Shit. Okay. I'm going to take care of you. Okay?"

Her eyes softened, and she licked her bottom lip. "Please."

I groaned and captured her mouth in mine. She tasted sweet and seductive, and I could've gotten lost in that kiss. I wanted to be lost to her forever, but I pulled back and fought against her whine. She needed me to help her, not fuck her.

I went through her clothes and found a deep blue silk robe, grabbing the sash from it. I'd seen what Rafe bought for her and dug through the partially open boxes until I found a small velvet bag. I guess our girl hadn't gotten to this part yet.

I crowded her on the bed. "I've got you. Move to the middle."

She shifted over half a foot until she was laid out in front of me. Her hands wrapped around my neck, trying to pull me against her. "Please, Killian."

I knew if I touched her, I wouldn't be able to hold back, and no matter how much her eyes were begging me now, I couldn't take advantage of her.

"Trust me, I'll take care of you." I wrapped my hands around her wrists and pulled them from my neck, pinning them above her with one hand. I grabbed the silk sash and gently wound it around her delicate wrists, and secured them to the headboard. She keened and shifted in her spot, eyes wide on me.

I dropped my mouth to hers, just out of her reach, and moved down to her ear. She full-body shivered when I whispered in her ear. "I'm going to make you come so fucking hard, without touching a single part of you. Do you want that? Do you want to come, baby?"

Her gaze was hooded, and she wiggled to get closer to

me. "Now, please."

I breathed over her neck, enjoying the goose bumps that spread in its wake. "I love the way you beg, pretty girl."

Her hips bucked up, and I had to shift to not touch her. I lifted her T-shirt, exposing the silky smooth skin of her breast. I was damn close to grinding into her; the game be damned, but I loved the challenge of making her lose her goddamn mind.

"Be a good girl, stay still for me, and I'll give you what you need."

She stilled, her body vibrating with anticipation. The room was thick with her spicy, honey jasmine scent as I moved lower and barely brushed my bottom lip over her nipple, so feather soft she might not have felt it.

She moaned and pulled against her restraints, her legs lifting to wrap around mine. "Do you need me to tie your legs, B? Is that what you want?"

She pushed out a breath, holding herself still. "No."

"Good girl."

I grabbed the velvet bag, and her eyes went wide at the sight of the vibrator. "Where did you get that?"

"It was a present from Rafe." I smirked. "He's going to be so fucking pissed when he finds out I used it first."

I turned it on, the low vibration making a buzz in the air, and trailed it down her stomach, painfully slowly, until we were both struggling for air.

Her hips writhed, and her back arched as I barely touched it against her clit. She growled low in frustration when I lifted it off. "Killian, if you don't stop torturing me—"

I cut off her words, sliding the length of the wand deep

inside her, causing her hips to roll, and her head pressed into the pillow. The silk wound around her wrists pulled taut as she moved herself over the wand, chasing the right speed to put her over. I kneeled between her legs, biting my lower lip. "Fuck, you look so good. I can't wait until your pussy is wrapped around my cock like that, burying my knot so deep inside you, you won't remember your own name."

I moved the wand at the speed I desperately wanted to take her, listening to her cries until I found the perfect angle. I hit the spot over and over, chasing her release until her whole body shuddered as her orgasm took over.

I lowered my head and placed a gentle kiss on her stomach. I was panting, barely in control of myself. Every muscle strained against the need to take her. I took a deep breath before lifting up and untying her wrists. She watched me with hooded sex-dazed eyes as I rubbed her pink wrist between my fingers and pulled her T-shirt down to cover her.

Her gaze traveled down to my very hard cock, tenting my pants, her gaze already warming. "What about you?"

I dropped my forehead to her, breathing in her sweet scent, and leaned in for a gentle kiss. "Ask me tomorrow and I'm yours."

She reached out and grabbed my shirt when I pulled back to leave. "Stay."

Fuck. I didn't think she understood the state she had me in, but I couldn't deny her if I wanted to. I slid in beside her, and she laughed when I placed a pillow between us.

I ran my finger over her cheek, purring calmly until her eyes closed and she was lost to sleep.

CHAPTER 11
Bliss

"Spread your legs wider, Love."

I shifted my feet. "Like this?"

Ares put his hands on my hips, guiding my legs further apart. "Little more. Yeah. Good, Girl."

Goose bumps sprung down the length of my neck as his breath fanned against my skin. I settled into the new stance, bouncing a bit in my new sneakers, and gave an experimental kick with my right leg. "That's better."

He walked around me in a circle, assessing from all sides. "Almost perfect. You need to stop locking your back knee. You're going to fall over."

"She looks perfect to me," Killian called from the back patio, where he was watching me and Ares spar. He'd taken off his plaid button-up, leaving him in a tight black T-shirt. My gaze traveled over him, but I shook myself out of it before Ares caught me drooling. He'd probably make me run laps or something sadistic like that.

"Kiss-ass." Ares' tone was more joking than angry. "You have no fucking idea what you're talking about."

"True," Killian conceded. "I've never needed technique to make my point."

Ares turned back to me, ignoring Killian. The sun had turned his already white hair brighter, and he looked a little like he was glowing.

"Hands back up. Let's go again."

Since last night, my temperature had returned to normal—mostly. I still felt a bit on edge but not so wound up I couldn't let anyone touch me. Thank God, because sparring would have been impossible. As it was, their scent was getting to me, and that was with the wind muffling most of it.

Mostly, I was just a little annoyed. Not about what had happened—no, that had been almost too good—but that Rafe was completely right. I was still a slave to my hormones.

I wasn't blind to what was going on or totally in denial —the guys had been making a huge effort to change and prove to me they were different. I just wished I could take my biological drive to mate out of the equation. Ideally, I'd be on blockers if and when I told them I wanted to be together for real so I'd know for sure that was how I felt.

That was also why I didn't want to be the omega to go into heat and donate blood to the blocker project. I'd do it if there was no other choice, but I'd much rather find someone else if we could.

Ares stepped back and circled me again. I raised my hands in front of my face, preparing for the next attack. Behind us, the back door swung open.

Flora stood on the threshold, the door partially

shielding her, and she bit her bottom lip. "I think I know an omega who was recently out of heat."

A little thrill skittered through me, and I broke out of Ares' arms, heading straight for her, a smile stretching my mouth wide. "How on earth do you know that?"

Her nose wrinkled, and for the first time since I'd met her, she blushed crimson red.

I crossed my arms over my chest. "Okay, out with it."

"My mom. She'd have just come out of her heat."

The guys made grossed-out sounds, and I couldn't suppress my own. The excitement slowly building within me vanished, and my shoulders slumped, my disgust only to be outdone by my disappointment.

Killian's voice dripped with distaste. "How in the hell do you even know that?"

Flora turned sharp eyes on him. "Some of us understand how omega biology works."

Ares and Killian flinched at the dig, and a smirk formed on Flora's lips.

I stepped in before their argument could escalate any further, not wanting Flora to eat them alive no matter how entertaining that would be. I lowered my voice so only she could hear. "Okay. So really. How do you know?"

She looked a little green. "You don't just forget when you were sent to Grandma's house for a week for the entirety of your childhood. The fact that it's a consistent schedule helped too, I guess."

"That's gross." I laughed, but the moment was broken by what I knew. "Flora, there's something you need to know about your mom."

The smell of dead flowers wrapped around her, and her eyes widened. "Is she okay?"

"She's fine. She's home."

Flora took a hesitant breath. "Then why do you look like you have some kind of terrible news?"

Shit. I didn't know how to tell her. My skin felt too tight, my heart rate ramping up until warm hands landed on my shoulders, giving them a gentle squeeze. Killian's lemon vanilla scent wrapped around me, and I fought against the urge to rest against him. The weight of his hands and the closeness helped calm me, giving me the courage I needed. "Flora, I went to see your mom after the auction."

"What?" Her eyes widened, and she stepped fully through the door.

I swallowed hard. "I was trying to find help to get you back."

"You mean trying to get yourself killed?" Ares murmured from where he sat on a patio chair, and I ignored him.

"I'm sorry, but she wouldn't help me." Tears welled in my eyes that matched my best friend's. She had enough hanging over her without me layering on mommy issues.

Flora shook her head. "No, that's not possible—"

"She called the Institute while I was there. Nero almost got me."

The guys growled, and I cut them off with a quick glare. Flora had barely gotten used to being near them. She didn't need to put up with the alpha bullshit.

She walked onto the patio, dropping heavily onto a plastic chair, and lowered her head into her hands. She stayed silent for several moments before her gaze met mine. "She didn't know."

"Flora." My heart broke for her, but she needed to realize what was happening.

Her voice was firm. "You don't understand. My dad treats her like she hung the moon." Flora's gaze drifted from Ares and Killian to me. "She didn't know."

Ares' warm gaze drifted over me. "Okay, let's say she didn't know. How do we confirm that without putting you both in danger? People think you're dead, remember?"

Flora rolled her eyes. "My mom isn't going to call them on me. Not after I explain."

I wasn't as sure as she was, and from the swirl of emotions coming off the guys, neither were they.

She looked at me. "Please, trust me."

Flora was strong, feisty, and smart, and right now, she was begging me to believe her. "Alright, what's next, then? We just show up?"

"You've got to be kidding me." Wes was in the doorframe, brows pulled over his eyes as he stared at Flora. The air between them crackled, and she stood her ground, staring back.

"No, *Wesley*, I'm not kidding."

"You're not going."

"You don't have a say."

My head snapped back and forth between them like a ping-pong ball, and Killian's chest rumbled with his quiet laugh as he pressed against my back. His breath tickled my ear as he breathed. "Did you know this was going on between them?"

Flora's gaze snapped to us, color high in her cheeks. "Nothing is going on."

Wes growled and stepped toward her. "Like hell there's not."

She huffed and pushed him out of the way and muttered about arrogant, overprotective, possessive betas. I followed close behind her as she took the stairs two at a time, practically running to get away from him. She opened her bedroom door for me, slamming it shut behind us, and the bang reverberated around the room.

"Wanna talk about it?" I sat on her bed, unable to hide my smirk.

She glared at me before collapsing beside me. "No."

Whatever she thought wasn't happening between them was definitely happening. Whether she liked it or not.

"So, what are we going to do about your mom?"

"She'll be at home. She never liked going out while Dad's at work." Flora's fingers wrapped delicately around my wrist, and her voice dipped low. "She won't turn me in. Not after I explain. She didn't know. Couldn't have."

"Okay, okay. I believe you. The guys won't be happy about it."

She smiled at me. "For some reason, I think if you ask, they'll do whatever you want."

It was my turn to blush. She wasn't wrong.

Wes parked in front of Flora's childhood home and shot us a look where Flora and I sat in the back seat. "Stay in the van."

Rafe's eyebrow rose in a warning look, telling me the same, before he exited the van himself.

Nox, Killian, and Ares looked pissed when I told them they were staying behind, but there was no way we were rolling up with four alphas and a beta. One look at Wes had told me there was no point in suggesting he didn't come. The guys played rock paper scissors, and fair was square.

Flora jumped out of the van before anyone could stop her, and she rushed past them. "There's no way she's opening the door to you guys."

She'd already hit the doorbell when the guys caught up and was in the middle of arguing with them when the door swung open. Flora sucked in a breath, taking in the woman dressed head to toe in black, with hunched-over shoulders, sallow cheeks, and dark circles under her eyes. There was nothing visible of her mother's feminine vibrancy she always exuded. "Mom?"

Omega Cabot cried out, wrapping her arms around Flora before pulling back, searching her face, then pulling her back into a tight hug. "They told me you died." Her voice broke on a sob, and my heart broke for her. She may have tried to send me back to the Institute, but she obviously loved her daughter.

Flora stepped back and gestured to the door with her chin. "Can we come in? I can explain."

Flora's mom's eyes widened as she looked at us, then back to her daughter. "What did you get involved with, Flora?" Her voice was stern, like a mother reprimanding her child. Her reaction wasn't giving me the warm and fuzzies about how this was going to go.

"I'll explain. We just need to get inside." She pushed past her mom, not giving her a chance to disagree. I gave her an apologetic look as I walked into her house, completely ignoring her protest. My heart squeezed, knowing Flora was going to see her mom differently after this.

I shifted back, blocking her mom from following her, and held out my hand. "Give me your phone."

"Excuse me?" Omega Cabot's shoulders rolled back, and she looked down her nose at me.

My voice came out with a small growl I was proud of. "I said, give me your phone."

Rafe's gaze met mine quickly, but he didn't intervene in letting me do this on my own. Flora's mom huffed out a breath, but she handed over her phone.

Wes, Rafe, and I stood to the left of the couch, where Omega Cabot sat beside Flora, her gaze roaming every inch of her daughter. It didn't feel right to sit with them, but there was no chance we were leaving Flora alone. Which left us standing awkwardly while her mom lifted her hand to touch Flora's sheared hair. Flora grabbed her mom's wrist. "Mom, we need to talk about something. We need your help."

Her mom's gaze shifted around the room wearily, then fell back on her daughter's. "We'll call the Institute, and they'll get you out of whatever mess you've gotten yourself into." She squeezed Flora's hands. "Everything will be alright. They'll figure it out."

Flora yanked her hands back, shaking her head. "We're not going to do that, Mom. The last thing the Institute wants to do is help."

"Honey, I know you've been through a traumatic experience losing your mate." Omega Cabot's eyes were rimmed red as tears formed at the corners. "They'll know what to do. They'll know how to help you."

Frustration rolled over me as I watched my best friend see her mom in a new light. Rafe's strong arms banded around my middle, pulling me back against his chest, and for once, I didn't care about all the things between us. I just wanted him close.

"Mom, they did this. The Institute are not the good guys."

Her mom's eyes narrowed as she glared at Wes, Rafe, and me, then turned back to her daughter. "Did they tell you that? The Institute is there to protect you."

"Mom, the Institute sold me."

Her mom's eyes softened. "I know that part is scary, but it was only a short moment before you got your mate." Her eyes soften. "I'm so sorry you lost your mate, Flora. I can't imagine."

Flora huffed out a laugh, jumping back from her mom on the couch. "I'm happy he's dead."

Omega Cabot's head snapped up, her mouth falling open. "What—"

"I said I'm happy he's dead."

Flora's mom leaned back, staring at her like she barely recognized her daughter. "That's the mating bond tearing. The Institute will help with that."

Flora let out a frustrated breath. "No, Mom. I hated him. I hated them, and if you don't snap out of this fairy-tale haze and realize the truth, we won't have a relationship going forward. I will hate you."

Omega Cabot reached out, pulling her daughter's hands into hers, her voice low like she was coaxing a wounded animal. "It's okay. It'll be okay. I'll just call the headmistress, and she'll fix everything."

My heart plummeted as Flora's gaze dropped, the deep scent of burnt marshmallows and sour milk surrounding her. Flora's voice came out soft but hard. "They sold me against my will. Sent me to live with a stranger who—"

"Not a stranger, honey. Your mate."

Flora jumped up from the couch, her body stiff and her scent shifting to hot ginger. "My mate? My mate, Mom? Seriously? Let me tell you what my mate did."

Flora's mom stood, eyes wide on her daughter, and went to say something but stopped when Flora held up her hand.

"My mate drugged me. Then…" Her voice caught, and Wes caught her as she started to sink, holding her and whispering in her ear until she was strong enough to stand on her own and face her mom. "He forced himself on me for an entire week. Then he locked me in a room. I wasn't mated. I was kidnapped."

Her mom's eyes widened, and she shook her head. "No. That's not how it works. Alphas love their mates."

Flora hissed. "That's not how it worked for *you*. For once, look outside of your perfect little bubble. Where are your omega friends from 'school'?" Flora crossed her arms, some of her spark coming back. "Have you talked to them? Have you even seen them?"

"They're busy with their mates and kids." Flora's mom's voice was defensive, but it broke at the end. "Omegas don't really stay friends."

"No, Mom. That's what they told you." Flora looked at her, her voice pleading. "Are you going to believe me or them?"

Omega Cabot stood, hands wringing in front of her. "There must have been a mistake. The Institute cares about their omegas."

"Do they? Mom, think. Tell me about other omegas you know."

"There aren't that many. We're spread out. Just because

we don't speak doesn't mean you're right in your assessment."

"You've never heard of anything bad happening from the omegas you were with at the Institute, Mom?"

Omega Cabot looked at her daughter, her hand flying to her chest. "Omega Lynn, we were friends, but she never contacted me after we left the Institute. I tried to find her, but…there weren't even any photos of her."

Flora stepped closer to her mom, ignoring Wes' growl. "Is it possible she was mated to an asshole? Is it so hard to believe that some of these alphas are in it for the social standing an omega provides and the power trip he can have over her?"

"I sent you there." Omega Cabot's voice was frail, as if she was barely holding on as her delusions crashed down around her. "They take care of omegas. I sent you there so you could have a beautiful life like I did. They were supposed to take care of you."

Flora gripped her mom's shoulders. "Look at me, Mom."

Omega Cabot watched her daughter, flinching with each word Flora said.

"They drugged me. They sold me."

Flora's voice shook, and Wes' arms were back around her, holding her up like her mother should've been doing. "He raped me."

Omega Cabot wrapped herself around her daughter with a sob. "He forced you?"

Flora broke away from Wes and squeezed her mom, giving her comfort that Flora needed. I wanted to snap at her, scream that she was part of the reason this happened.

Omega Cabot pulled her head back, tears still running

down her cheeks, and her voice dripped venom. "I'm happy he's dead, and I hope you killed him."

Shock rushed through me, and a smile tipped my lips at the sight of her mom shifting into momma bear status. "Will you help us?"

She looked between me and Flora. "Whatever you need."

CHAPTER 12
Bliss

Over the next few days, nothing really changed—at least, not as far as our routine. My mood swings were a different story.

We were still waiting for the doctor to finish making the blockers, and my anxiety was getting worse every day. Flora had been spending some of her time out of the house visiting her parents, and I was happy for her, but that meant that there was one less buffer between me and the guys. I needed that buffer more than life itself, because my heat seemed like it was only days away.

Everyone was doing their best to ignore the scent I knew I was giving off at all times, but it had to be impossible. Hell, it was giving me a headache. Even Rafe's gift wasn't doing the trick, no matter how many extra-long showers I took. What I needed was one of my alphas, but for all I knew, that would make it worse, and I couldn't afford to speed up the timeline.

I wandered outside to the backyard. I leaned against

the side of the house for a moment, letting the light breeze soothe my warm face.

This was all coming back far too fast. The other night had given me some reprieve, but evidently not enough. If I kept going like this, I'd fall over the cliff into full-blown heat by the end of the week.

"What are you doing, Love?" Ares appeared at the door behind me.

I flinched out of the way to avoid touching him directly. It would only make things worse. "Wishing we had a pool."

He raised an eyebrow. "I don't know about that, but I have a proposal for you."

It was my turn to raise my eyebrows. "Excuse me?"

"Offer," he corrected. "Do you want to get out of here for a bit?"

My stomach leapt in excitement before plummeting back down. "Why? Since when can I leave?"

"Since we're going straight into the car and then to another spot where no one else will be. Trust me, I thought this through."

My heartbeat sped up. I didn't know why I was hesitating, except maybe that I knew Ares—a little too well. "Don't take this the wrong way, but does anyone else know about this?"

He smirked, but his shoulders tensed. A pang of sadness rocketed through my chest. "Afraid I'm kidnapping you? Do you think I'd put you in danger?"

"No, not at all," I said firmly. He stiffened, like he was waiting for the scent of my lie, then relaxed when it didn't come. "I know you wouldn't put me in danger. It's more like I'm worried you're doing something self-destructive."

He rolled his eyes, but I could smell his relief.

"Don't worry, Little Wolf," Nox called from the living room. His voice got louder, and he appeared in the doorway as he spoke. "I'm coming too."

I let out a breath. "Okay."

"Oh, so you trust him to make rational decisions but not me?" Ares said with mock offense.

I thought about that for a second. "Yeah, pretty much. Let's go."

―――

Ares pulled our SUV into the small parking lot at the edge of the familiar woods, and I sat up a little straighter. My face split into a grin. "No way. I thought you said this wasn't here anymore."

We were in the woods near the old park where we'd spent the last summer before I'd gone to the Institute. Back then, we'd had a fire pit area with old broken furniture, the beat-up couch that now lived on the roof of the warehouse, and a bunch of fallen logs. It was gross and hideous, and I loved it.

"It wasn't," Ares replied cagily.

At the very least, they'd taken the couch, and most of the other furniture hadn't been much of anything. Old, broken lawn chairs and scrap wood. Still, I was dying to check it out. I practically bounced out of the car—half in excitement, half because I couldn't roll down the windows and the heat and scent in there were getting to me.

The path to the fire pit had overgrown somewhat, but clearly, someone had been here recently. Footsteps were fresh in the mud and twigs broken along the side of the bushes. I strained my eyes, leaning forward as something came into view up ahead. "Oh my God."

"Don't get too excited," Nox joked. "It's not done."

I picked up my pace, jogging ahead of them toward the clearing. My eyes widened. Where the pit used to be, there was a permanent stone circle with an iron grate. New gravel lay along the ground, and a couple of comfortable-looking loungers, large enough to fit several people, were up along the side.

"Did you guys just do this? But isn't it public land?"

Ares ran his hand over the back of his neck. "Not anymore. You'd be surprised what you can buy if you just ask."

"Bribe." Nox rolled his eyes. "We need more landscaping, another couch…"

My throat seized. "I love it." I walked in a circle around the pit. "Can we stay for a bit?"

Ares smiled. "Yeah. Hang on, I'll be right back."

He jogged back down the path toward the car, and I watched him go, my chest fuller than it had been in a while.

I sunk down on the soft cushions of one of the new loungers. "Damn," I laughed. "If we'd had this back when we hung out here, I never would have left."

Nox lay on his back next to me, arms under his head, staring up at the sky. "You barely did anyway."

"True."

This had been such an incredibly thoughtful gesture—something completely out of the blue that I would never have thought to ask for. The best part was it was something that I would have loved before the Institute, and not just because I was an omega. I rolled onto my side, propping my head on my hand to watch Nox. I'd be lying if I didn't admit that everything they were doing to change was wearing me down.

His jaw was sharp in profile, his lip curling into a satisfied smile. He turned his face toward me, bright green eyes squinting against the setting sun. "What are you thinking about?"

"Nothing," I said automatically.

Lie. I wasn't even sure what the truth would have been in that moment, but no one was ever thinking about nothing.

Nox gave me a shrewd look. "Truth or dare," he said, laughter in his voice.

I rolled my eyes and nudged his shoulder with the back of my hand. "Stop it."

I immediately regretted the contact as fire raced up my skin. *You have got to be kidding me.*

"I wasn't joking."

I pushed my hair off my neck, subtly trying to get air to my now heated skin before I started sweating. "If I remember right, that game never worked out that well for us."

"I don't know," Nox said thoughtfully. "Rafe might disagree with you on that."

I flushed slightly, which I knew was stupid. We were talking about kisses between teenagers, and God knew we'd done far more than that, more times than I could count. That memory shouldn't even register, but of course, it did. "You're the worst."

I shifted back a little on the blanket and raised a hand to my neck, just above my collarbone. My skin was hot, my blush refusing to fade. My stomach did a little nervous flip.

Nox's nostrils flared, and he sat up a little. "Are you okay?"

I shot him a sideways glance. Was it even worth trying to lie? He watched me with too-intense eyes. Judging from his expression, no, absolutely not.

I fanned myself with one hand. "What do you think?"

I stretched out tentative fingers toward his face, then changed my mind at the last second and moved them to his arm instead. It didn't matter. With the briefest contact, my skin flared, my temperature rising another ten degrees.

Nox caught my hand as it trailed up his arm, almost independent of my conscious thought, and pulled me closer until I was lying almost completely on top of him. "I think you need to tell me what you want, Little Wolf."

"I..." What did I want? I tried to detangle my thoughts from my hormones. My gaze drifted to the new fire pit—something they'd done just because they thought I would like it—and a warmth that had nothing to do with sex spread through my center. "I want you to take care of me."

His eyes flashed hot just as my insides spasmed, and a whimper escaped my lips. Fire licked up my stomach, burning me from the inside out. It was like the worst stomach cramps of my life, made worse by an oncoming fever.

Nox's eyes widened, and he pressed his lips to mine, swallowing my next moan of pain. One hand trailed up the bare skin of my back between the straps of my sundress to caress the back of my neck and pull me closer.

All my nerve endings came alive, and I let out a breathy sound into his mouth.

Footsteps barely registered behind me. There was a thunk as something dropped onto the lounger, and then Ares' twilight smell invaded my senses, his warmth pressing against my back. He nipped at my shoulder blade, and I pulled back to look at him. His eyes were wild, panicked, and he leaned down to inspect me for injuries. "What happened?"

Nox pulled back, and I chased his lips with my own, my entire body crying at the lack of contact. Seeing my distress, he pressed his face into my neck instead, speaking low against my skin. "She's too close to heat. It's hurting her."

The scent of Ares' panic mingled with my arousal—an odd mix of sweet and bitter. "Let's get the fuck out of here," he barked.

"No," I said quickly, clinging to Nox's shoulders. There wasn't a chance in the world I wouldn't throw up if we got in the car right now. "I need the fresh air."

Ares threw an arm over my waist, pulling me back toward him. "Love, you can't go into heat out here."

I twisted halfway away from Nox to look at him. "I won't," I whined and winced at the needy sound of my voice. "It's just a spike."

I wasn't even sure I believed that, but maybe just by saying it out loud, it would magically become true.

Ares held my face with both hands. Maybe it was my fever, but his ever-intense gaze seemed somehow brighter. "You're sure about this?" He clearly wasn't asking if I was sure if it was a spike. "This might make it worse, not better."

I held Ares' gaze as Nox moved his mouth up the column of my neck. I whined. "I need you. Please."

I understood what the risk was, but with my stomach burning from the inside out, that didn't seem that important right now—vaguely, I registered that if I could even have a thought that coherent, I probably wasn't in full heat yet, but damn, it felt like it.

I twisted back, pulling Nox's mouth to mine. He kissed me hard, parting my lips easily as I whimpered against his mouth.

Ares nudged the underside of my jaw with his nose, and I turned my face slightly, meeting his lips instead. Sandwiched between them, so much of me touching them, my skin heated even as my breathing seemed to even out. Like this was where I was supposed to be.

Nox pulled my attention for a moment and met my eyes as though asking my permission before he tugged down the front of my sundress and pushed the straps off my shoulders. The cool air hit my burning skin and pebbled my exposed nipples, and I arched my back into Ares' chest, giving Nox better access to my breasts.

I ran my fingers over the back of Nox's scalp, and he purred low in the back of his throat. He pulled one nipple into his mouth, sucking lightly. A thrill of pleasure shot through me, settling in my core, and I let out a needy whimper.

Ares moved his mouth to the back of my shoulder, running his hand up the length of my bare arm and back down again before sucking on my ear. I craned my neck to the side, letting out a shuddering breath as he grazed his teeth over my mating gland. "What do you need, Love?"

I bit my lip, heart pounding so hard against my chest I was sure they could hear it. "More."

Nox ran his free hand up my leg, pushing the fabric of my dress up to pool around my waist. He growled low in his throat and pulled back to look at me. His eyes had gone fully black, the green no longer visible. "More what?" he pressed, pushing more command into his tone. "What do you want?"

I whimpered, rubbing my thighs together, desperate to relieve the ache. "Please, fuck me. I need…" I couldn't even finish my thought.

Behind me, Ares sat up, fumbling to pull off his T-shirt and undo the button of his low-slung jeans. He flipped up the rest of my dress in the back, bunching the fabric over my ass, and ran two fingers over me, rubbing lightly over my soaked panties. "Fuck, you're perfect."

I moaned, my entire body erupting in tingles at just that lightest touch. "Alpha, please."

"Hold her," Ares said, giving Nox a hungry look.

Nox wrapped his long fingers around my chin and pulled my face to his in a fierce kiss as Ares tore off my soaked panties, sliding into me in one swift motion. I gasped, holding tighter to Nox's shoulders for balance as Ares pulled me back against his chest and thrust into me from behind. I cried out, shocked at the feeling of fullness.

Ares rolled me upright and turned us so I was sitting on his lap, facing outwards. "You okay, Love?"

My only reply was to move, desperately needing the friction. I bounced up and down, always coming just short of taking his knot fully inside.

Nox disentangled himself from us and moved down to the base of the lounger. He paused for a moment to strip his shirt off in one fluid motion before looking up at me with mischief in his eyes. He pressed his mouth to the spot where Ares and I were joined. He ran his tongue up my center to my clit and along the edge of Ares' knot.

Behind me, Ares jerked against the sudden contact. "Fuck."

I whimpered, shifting to give Nox better access. He pressed a kiss to my throbbing clit, licking and sucking harder with every sound I made. I reached down, digging my nails into his short hair, urging him on.

The warmth built in my core, and my breathing sped up. Ares leaned over and licked the mating gland on my neck as Nox sucked harder on my clit. I shattered, screaming my release as light danced behind my eyes.

Any lingering pain in my stomach fled, leaving nothing but warm satisfaction. Ares wrapped his fingers around my waist and lifted me almost completely off him as I shuddered with the aftershocks of my orgasm. I moaned in protest until Nox ran his tongue up the length of Ares' shaft. My eyes widened at the sight of Nox licking my slick off his friend's cock.

"How does she taste?" Ares growled, pushing my hair away from my shoulder as he buried his face in my neck.

Nox glanced up at Ares behind me. "Come see for yourself."

Ares pulled out of me, laying me back gently against the cushions. Nox shifted slightly to make room for Ares next to him, and I looked down at the pair of them through half-open eyelids.

"Feeling better, Love?"

My knees still shook, but instead of tired, I felt more

alive—like I'd just drank an extra-large espresso. I would rather die than say that though. "Shut up."

He knew full well I was feeling better. Ares pushed my legs further apart, his smile practically feline. He pressed the flat of his tongue to my core, right where Nox had just been. I writhed as they took turns tasting, sometimes catching each other's lips.

Ares leaned over and ran his teeth up the shell of Nox's ear. "I want to watch you knot her."

Nox shivered against me, mouth pausing just above my hip bone as he looked up at me. "Are you okay with that, Little Wolf?"

I could feel myself growing wetter just at the idea of it, but the real question was, would that push me over the edge into heat? Was I already too close?

Nox seemed to read my mind. "If that didn't set off a full heat, I think you're good for today."

His tone was joking, but I let out a real sigh of relief. Not only was I not ready for a full heat, but if I went into heat without birth control worked out, we were going to have a whole different level of problems. It was too much to hope I'd just get lucky and not end up pregnant naturally—not with four alphas.

"Yeah," I breathed, sounding breathless and not at all like myself.

Nox moved onto his back, and I climbed into his lap. He stared up at me like I was the only thing that mattered as I lowered myself onto him.

I rocked forward, adjusting to the feel of his piercings inside me. I leaned down, pressing our chests together to capture his bottom lip between my teeth. A growl rumbled through his chest, and he looked up at me with a shockingly vulnerable expression behind his black eyes. "You're perfect."

My stomach swooped. I couldn't pretend this was still about a heat spike—that first orgasm had taken care of that. I probably should have stopped there. My heart beat harder, and this time, I wasn't sure if it was from arousal.

Nox's fingers trailed down my neck, settling around my throat, just brushing my mating gland. I whimpered, rocking harder as Nox grasped my hips to hold me down. He lifted me up and brought me back down hard. This time, I gasped at this completely full, tight feeling as his knot swelled inside me, holding me in place.

Ares knelt on the ground in front of me near Nox's head and pushed my damp hair out of my face. "That's my good girl. You take him so well."

I looked up at him through my lashes. "Come here."

I leaned forward as much as I could while knotted in place and ran my tongue over the head of Ares' cock. He pushed forward past my lips, and I sucked him in until he was hitting the back of my throat.

Nox reached between us and ran the pad of his thumb gently over my oversensitive clit. "Can you come again for me, Little Wolf? I want to feel you milking my knot."

I moaned around Ares' shaft, and he dug his fingers into my hair, urging me on. "Fuck, you're so good, Love."

Nox made soft little circles with his fingers in rhythm with my movements until another orgasm built low in my core. I gasped, my breathing becoming uneven, and he rubbed harder.

Ares' hips jerked, and he came down my throat just as Nox pushed me over the edge, and I clamped around his knot, making him come with me. I slumped forward, coming apart completely.

Ares came to lie behind me, and Nox rolled us to the side so I was once again snuggled between them while we waited for his knot to loosen. My breathing slowed, and my heartbeat fell into sync with theirs as we lay there, not quite asleep but not awake either.

Reality tugged at the back of my brain, trying to force me to think about what this meant. I ignored it. *Ignorance is bliss, after all.*

CHAPTER 13
Rafe

I woke up to the sun shining through the dull, dusty windows of the warehouse and rolled over. Ever since Bliss moved into the other house, nothing had felt right. It was like how quiet and miserable things were for the last four years, except now I had a taste of what things could be like. Now, it was so much worse.

I pushed out of bed, stretching broadly. It was…what the hell day was it?

I was losing track of things. I used to keep track of our schedule based on shipments and how much work we needed to get done. Now, without the blocker rotation, blood donations, and constant calls from the guys down at the docks, I had no fucking idea what I was doing. If we could've hung out with Bliss all the time, that would be one thing—I would be completely happy with that, but clearly, she wasn't ready. I was going to have to find something to do with myself fast, or I'd lose my mind. I wasn't good at doing nothing.

I grabbed my phone off the nightstand. There were at least a dozen texts from various members of Alpha Lupi. They didn't want me to find something else to do with my time. I locked the screen again, ignoring the texts.

I showered quickly and jogged down the hall to the kitchen, forcing myself to pass the closed door to the nest without going inside. I was already an online shopping trip away from being completely pathetic; I didn't need to make it official.

Killian looked up at me from where he sat at the far end of the kitchen table and didn't bother to swallow the half-chewed bite of toast in his mouth before speaking. "Morning."

I raised an eyebrow. "What are you still doing here?"

"I'm about to leave." He jerked his head toward the door as if I needed a reminder. "Nox is there now."

I looked around. I widened my eyes in surprise. "Is Ares with him?"

Killian shook his head. "Don't think so. Down in the gym."

"Makes sense."

Nox and Ares had smelled so strongly of sex and sweat when I swapped shifts with them yesterday, there was no doubt what had gone down. It would have surprised me if he were back at the house with Nox again today—not because they wouldn't have jumped at the opportunity, but because I couldn't picture Bliss being willing to go for round two without at least a conversation with all of us first.

I couldn't say I wasn't a little jealous—not of them being with her, but that I hadn't broken down that barrier with her yet. Maybe jealous was the wrong word. Sad.

"I'm going down there," I said, eying the door to the gym.

"'Kay, cool." Killian took another bite of toast, washing it down with what looked like half a milkshake. "I'll catch you guys later."

I shook my head as he sauntered out. He'd been in a much better mood lately—less court jester. It was a good look.

Did I seem different too? I didn't think so.

I took the stairs down to the lower level two at a time. The room was practically empty, and my footsteps echoed against the concrete floor, mingling with the sounds of Ares' heavy breathing as he bounced on his toes in the sparring ring, taking short jabs at the air.

I leaned against the ropes of the ring. "You didn't want to wait and spar with Bliss?"

He stilled, pulled out one wireless earbud, and looked down at me. "What did you say?"

"You're sparring alone. You didn't wait to work out with Bliss."

"Sparring with Bliss isn't a workout. I barely move because all I'm thinking about is not hurting her."

There was half a lie in that statement, but I ignored the scent of it. I got the feeling he didn't mean it to be a lie—the obvious half-truth was what anyone would be thinking while carrying Bliss around in painted-on leggings.

"I'll take over if you want."

"You can help next time if you want. Maybe we'll try surprise attacks."

I was sure he could smell my mingled surprise and excitement—mostly that he was actually fucking talking to me. "Sure."

"Did you need something?"

I cast my gaze around for why I'd come down here in the first place. "Wondering if you had an opinion on what to do about the Alpha Lupi old-timers. They won't fucking leave me alone. I woke up to at least a dozen texts, and that's a good day."

We mostly kept the gang members we'd inherited responsibility for at arm's length, giving them jobs that kept them far away from the warehouse, but now that we'd dismantled our operation without warning, they weren't happy, and they were making it obvious.

Ares furrowed his brow, looking more annoyed than concerned. "Kill them."

"We can't kill them. We're still dealing with the last person you killed."

"Then I don't care."

I took a breath through my nose. "Right. I should have expected that."

He smirked, turning away from me again. "Glad to help."

I bounced against the ropes. For whatever fucked-up guilt Ares had about leading our friend group when we were kids, it was so fucking obvious that he never would have made a good leader in the long term. He wasn't patient, even-tempered, or levelheaded; he was just dominant.

Not that I was the perfect leader, but at least I wasn't the embodiment of chaos.

My phone buzzed in my pocket, and I pulled it out, swiping open the screen to read the text.

Dr. Lewinsky: I'm outside.

I frowned down at the message, reading it again. What

the fuck? "Lewinsky is here."

Ares looked back at me. "Why?"

"Don't know."

"Why didn't he just knock?"

"Again, I don't know. I'm going upstairs."

Ares pulled out his other headphone and reached for a bottle of water on the ground. "I'll be there in a second. I'm going to take a thirty-second shower."

I debated telling him to stay here—the doctor was fucking terrified of him—but what the hell, that might be helpful. "Sure."

Dr. Lewinsky was a fifty-something beta who dressed and acted like he was thirty. His hair was dyed about the same shade of brown as Killian, and his spray tan reminded me of a nectarine. He was motivated by two things: money and protection.

He stood on our front steps, glancing around like he was afraid he was being followed. I looked around too. I didn't smell anything.

"I can't stay long," Lewinsky said.

"What are you doing here? How'd it go with Flora's mom?"

"Fine." He nodded absently. "Try these." He reached into his pocket and shoved a bag in my hand, then looked around again.

"Are you looking for someone?" I asked suspiciously.

The doctor frowned. "I was going to call you this morning to say I was coming, but I could swear my house is being watched."

A shiver traveled up my spine. Then again, the doctor was kind of a lunatic. Smart, but nuts—that's why he worked for us and not a real hospital or research facility. "You're sure."

"No," he said conspiratorially, "but can't be too careful, right?"

I shrugged. "I guess. How'd you get here?"

He gave me an odd look. "Drove. Why?"

I stared down my nose at him. He couldn't be that concerned if he'd taken his normal car. "Never mind. I'll call you once we test them."

I closed the door on the doctor and held the bag of blockers up to the light. They looked about the same as the last ones to me, but that meant nothing.

"What did he want?" Ares asked, appearing in the doorway to the kitchen, shaking water out of his hair.

I held up the bag. "Feel like taking a drive over to the other house?"

———

Thirty minutes later, we jogged out of the warehouse and toward the garage on the opposite end of the parking lot. The sky was growing cloudy—darker than it had been only a short while ago, and the breeze smelled like a storm was blowing in from the east, earthy and salty at the same time.

The plastic baggy the doctor had handed me burned a hole in my jeans pocket.

If they worked, Bliss would be ecstatic. That idea alone almost eclipsed my worries—my entire life, my every other thought had been about making her happy, and most of the ones in between were about keeping her safe. The blockers would do both.

I furrowed my brow. "Do you ever feel like we should have realized Bliss was an omega sooner?"

"What?" Ares looked back, walking two steps ahead of me. His eyes narrowed in confusion, obviously not following my train of thought.

"Never mind. Just thinking."

I stuffed my hand in my pocket, fumbling with the bag. I was…ninety percent excited? The other ten percent knew if they worked, she might leave for good. That had been her goal from the moment she arrived—get blockers so she could leave us again.

I wouldn't stop her if that's what she wanted, but it wouldn't hurt any less.

Ares walked around to the passenger-side door of the van and waited for me to unlock the car. As I crossed the lot, the hair on the back of my neck stood up. I paused, breathing in deeply and scenting the air.

Something smelled…off. "Do you—"

Ares stiffened, and I didn't finish my question. A black sedan rolled into the lot, followed by a police-issue SUV. The SUV stopped, cutting off the main entrance.

Ares and I glanced at each other. What now?

"This has got to be about the other day," he muttered out of the corner of his mouth.

I squinted at the cars. I had missed the confrontation with DuPont, but I had to agree. "Don't fucking say anything."

"Will it matter?" He laughed harshly. "If they're here, looks like she came through on her threat."

"I—" I didn't get to finish my thought.

The sedan turned on its sirens as though we couldn't clearly see it idling toward us. That buzzed at the back of my brain—a power move they didn't need to make, just trying to set us off.

"Don't move," a male voice said over the car loudspeaker.

I glanced between myself and Ares—both firmly planted where we'd been standing this entire time. "What does it look like we're doing?"

The loudspeaker crackled, and I rolled my eyes. I hated cops. You couldn't grow up in the system and have any love for authority, especially the government.

The car stopped, and the driver got out. This was a different group than the detective who'd come by with the first arrest. This guy was nearly as tall as us and wearing a riot vest over his uniform. He flashed a badge that read Police at me too quick to read and took a step forward.

His partner got out of the passenger side—a tall woman with two guns strapped to her belt and a Taser in her right hand. I eyed the Taser warily. She looked more than ready to use it.

"Are you…" The male officer glanced at a yellow piece of paper in his hand. "Ar-ies Moore." He stumbled over the pronunciation, and I prayed Ares wouldn't say anything stupid. "You need to come with me."

"Why?" Ares barked. "I thought we covered this. You guys didn't have enough evidence."

The second officer ignored him and stepped forward, raising her Taser in front of her like a sword. My eyes widened. "Shut the fuck up," I snapped at Ares.

He wasn't listening. "Don't you have to read me my rights or some shit?"

"This isn't TV, kid. Your bail has been revoked. You

need to come with us now, or you'll have resisting arrest and a couple of assault charges to add to your rap sheet."

The other officer pulled out a sheet of paper like a very long traffic ticket. "This is a warrant explaining the bail." He passed it to me.

I looked down at it, but the words swam together. I couldn't think straight. "What the fuck?" I barked as they shoved Ares' head into the back seat. "Where are you taking him?"

"Booking," the female officer said flatly.

"Yeah, where's that?" I stepped forward unconsciously. "You need to—"

"Hey!" The woman wasn't an alpha, but she barked right back at me. Her reddish-brown ponytail bounced with the force of her indignation, and her mouth practically disappeared. "You do not want to get any closer to me, or I'll arrest you too." She rolled her eyes. "Fucking alphas."

Fucking cops. I balled my hands into fists and took a step back. "Look, I don't know what you want me to do here. Where are you going?"

She gave me a once-over that was half-annoyed, half-pitying. "You can't come with us, anyway. This guy your pack mate or just a friend?"

"Pack mate."

"Fine. So that's legally like a spouse. I'd call a lawyer. You'll need one."

I rubbed the skin between my eyes as they all drove away, leaving me standing alone in the parking lot like a fucking idiot. I couldn't decide if I should call a lawyer first, go tell Bliss, Nox, and Killian, or try and find out where Ares was going. My head spun.

I sat down on the curb before I realized what I was doing. "Fuck," I said out loud to no one.

I wasn't good at this shit—any of this. I'd become in charge by default, but lately, everything I did felt wrong. I was leading them all straight into oncoming traffic.

I debated with myself—would Bliss want to hear the news immediately, or would she want answers? Should I get as much information as I could so that I was coming to her with all the facts?

My phone buzzed, making my decision for me.

Killian: Dude what the fuck

Killian: What's going on?

Killian: Bliss said someone is hurt

My phone rang. Nox was calling. I sent it to voicemail.

Shit. I needed to pull it together. I couldn't have a meltdown right now—they needed consistency.

I shot off a quick group text.

Me: No one is physically hurt. Ares got arrested, but is fine. I am getting more information and will be at the house in 20 minutes.

Next, I called the lawyer. Our lawyer was a pretentious alpha in his mid-sixties named Jason Homer. I always got the feeling he didn't exactly like me but tolerated me because we wrote him checks on time. We rarely actually saw Homer because so far he'd settled everything I'd ever needed him for out of court, which was exactly why I liked him. I knew nothing about court except what I'd seen on TV and didn't want to change that. I said as much to the lawyer.

"This isn't a traffic ticket, kid," he said when I explained my goal of just making this go away. "There's going to be a trial. Period."

I ground my teeth. "Isn't there some law that protects alphas who defend their omegas?"

"Yes, but this isn't so cut-and-dry. They're not mated."

"But they're bonded."

"And that will be hard to prove. I'm working on it," Mr. Homer said, his voice filled with so much forced calm it set my teeth on edge.

"Where the hell is he, anyway?"

"He's probably at the local police station right now if they haven't transferred him yet. I'll go down there and see him. Ultimately, he's going to be taken in front of the Assembly."

I waited for him to elaborate. If you waited long enough, people tended to fill silence on their own, and I wasn't in the mood to talk.

Mr. Homer sighed. "You know what that means, right?"

"What do you think?" I snapped. The bastard was lucky he wasn't standing in front of me—I was ready to punch someone, and I needed him conscious. "Do you think they teach high-school-dropout foster kids political science? What am I paying you for? Give me the fucking CliffsNotes."

"Er, right. Sorry." He sounded flustered. "In Winston v. California in 1998, the Supreme Court decided that alphas and omegas couldn't be tried by a jury of betas. They're not peers."

"Uh-huh." I ran my hand over the back of my neck, staring up at the sky. If he didn't speed this up, I was going to lose my shit.

"The Assembly is comprised of one elected representative from each state. Mostly alphas, for obvious reasons, but there are a few omegas on the court too."

I blinked, suddenly putting something together. "Wait. Is Headmistress Omega DuPont on the court?"

The lawyer scoffed. "Kid, do you ever watch the news?"

"No," I said without a hint of humor in my voice.

"Omega DuPont is the first female chief justice. It was a huge win for the Sigma party."

He'd lost my attention again. I didn't give a fuck about political parties, but I did care that DuPont was the head of the court that would decide Ares' verdict. "So we're fucked," I said flatly. "I don't suppose Nero is on the court too."

"Alpha Nero is the representative from New York. Everyone knows that. He—"

"Yeah, yeah," I cut him off. "Whose side are you on, anyway?"

"Rafe." He pulled out the first name, clearly playing the "we're friends" card. "I'm on your side, but you need to understand how serious this is. They have a video. I can't argue that Ares didn't kill that man or take the omega."

"Bliss," I snapped. "Her name is Bliss."

"Okay. And where is Bliss now?"

I paused. "Why?"

"Jesus Christ," he huffed, exasperated, and I heard a door open in the background and the sound of traffic as he evidently walked outside. "The best defense would be for Bliss to say she was there willingly. I'll do some research. I'm getting in the car now and heading over there. I'll touch base after I talk to Ares."

He hung up without saying goodbye, and I stared down at my dark cell phone, unsure what had just happened.

Bliss telling the court she had been there willingly sounded reasonable, but there was so much at stake there. For one thing, she'd have to show up in person, and that was practically impossible. For another, like Mr. Homer said, proving a bond was going to be hard. It wasn't exactly a visible thing.

I stood up from the curb and strode over to the SUV, climbing into the driver's seat. I patted my pocket as I sat down, making sure the blockers I'd stuffed in there earlier were still there—all I needed was to lose those in all this chaos.

Gritting my teeth, I peeled out of the parking lot and headed off toward Bliss and the others. Dread sank into my stomach. I remembered how physically painful it had been four years ago when we'd tried to all go our separate ways after losing Bliss. The longer that Ares was kept away from us, the worse off he'd be. The worse off we'd all be.

CHAPTER 14
Bliss

"You sure you can't just leave him in there? He was kind of a dick." Flora leaned against the bathroom doorframe, brown hair bouncy around her shoulders as she talked animatedly.

A laugh bubbled up in my chest, releasing some of the tension I'd been holding. I knew with a bone-deep assuredness that this was the right thing to do. I just wasn't quite as sure if it was a smart thing to do. "Hmmm. He's too pretty to go to jail."

Her smirk turned mischievous. "You never know, he may like it."

A barely audible growl formed in the back of my throat at the image of Ares "liking" anything with anyone else.

Flora hopped back a step. "Easy there, killer. I was just kidding. At least you got your color back."

My reflection showed a cool pink flush creeping up my neck, overtaking the ghostly white that was there a moment before. I relaxed my fingers, opening my fist slowly, and ignored the sting from where my nails had dug into my palms.

I met her warm gaze, and she shrugged. "You looked a little lost there for a second. Thought the idea of having to share one of your guys would bring you back."

I rolled my eyes hard and got back to pulling my hair into a high bun. I'd gotten caught up in the details of our plan that were shaky at best. I didn't realize I'd completely zoned out while doing it. "I wasn't lost. I was thinking."

Her warm hand wrapped around my arm, turning me toward her. "This is going to work. It better. You can't leave me alone with these idiots. They'll be so whiny if you don't come back." Her words were playful, but her voice was strained. She couldn't come with me for obvious reasons. One, everyone thought she was dead, and two, we only had enough of the new formula blockers for me. If everything worked out, it would get both Ares out and provide Flora the freedom she needed.

I smiled, doing my best to reassure her, even though I wasn't sure. "The place will be full of people. Once I say what I have to say, there's no way they're going to let Nero take me." My stomach dipped, knowing I didn't know what exactly that would be.

Rafe had paced around the living room a few nights ago while explaining the charges Ares was up for, the Assembly, and our only chance of getting him out of there. Me.

The guys had spent the entire night debating back and forth whether it was safe enough for me to go. All the while, I'd been heating with rage that they were going to once again try to make a decision about my life for me instead of with me. I had a plan, not that anyone would let me speak.

Killian and Rafe had gotten into a heated argument, where Rafe thought every alpha would attack me, and Killian thought they could cover me in a cloak. I almost laughed at that. Because nothing says inconspicuous like someone walking into a court wearing something out of *Harry Potter*.

Nox was the one who asked me what I thought, and a little thrill had run up my spine at the way all three of them watched me, waiting. I'd held my hand out and asked for the blockers Rafe mentioned getting that morning. None of them had looked particularly happy about the idea, but I swallowed a pill, and within ten minutes, the mood shifted. Killian didn't meet my eyes when he told me it worked, and the bond strained between us with unknown feelings, the scent of dead flowers filling my nose. They brushed it off and moped because apparently I no longer smelled like them.

"Just be careful, okay?" Flora's seriousness had me coming back to the present.

"I promise."

There was a knock on the wall beside Flora, and she swung back away from Rafe. "Shit."

"Sorry, I didn't mean to startle you. Can I talk to Bliss for a minute?" Rafe towered over Flora's petite frame, and my heart hurt as fear flashed through her eyes before she hid it away. I wasn't sure the effects of what happened to her would ever let her feel truly comfortable around alphas. Even mine.

I chose not to think too long about the word "mine." That was a discussion for another day. Hopefully soon.

"Just remember, kids. No hickeys before going to the Assembly." Flora blew out a kiss with her parting words and vanished down the hall.

I blushed down to my toes, but Rafe just took her place in the doorway. His arm propped up against the wood trim, and his head tilted to the side as he watched me get ready. I thought for sure he was there to talk me out of going, but after a few minutes, it was clear he wasn't going to say anything. At first, the quietness felt off, and I had to fight the urge to fill the void, but the longer he stood there, the calmer I became until I could go back to getting ready.

"You look beautiful."

I paused, mouth open, about to apply my mascara. Warmth filled my veins, pumping through my heart as his words settled in my stomach, chasing away the last of my nerves. I smirked up at him. "Not going to try to stop me?"

"Never again." He brought a garment bag in front of him he must have tucked away behind his back. The zipper was open, revealing a deep purple knee-length dress that had a sash around the middle. The cut was simple, making it both feminine and professional. "When did you get the time to buy this?"

"I made time." Rafe stepped forward and slid his fingers across my jaw. His near-black hair slid forward, and I pushed it back, revealing his deep eyes with lashes so thick it looked like he wore eyeliner.

"Thank you." There was a crack in my voice. I wasn't just thanking him for the dress. I knew it was killing him to let me do this. It was a risk he would never have told me to take. His chest pressed against mine, and his hand squeezed the back of my neck until I tilted my head back.

"Can I kiss you, Bliss?" He was so close his breath fanned over my lips, and a tingle ran down my neck.

This was different from yesterday in the clearing. It wasn't the overwhelming need from another heat spike. Kissing him would be all me, and I desperately wanted to. He searched my gaze, and a herd of wild horses couldn't stop me from closing the distance. We groaned when my lips connected with his, tentative at first but quickly turning desperate. Even though I was confident, the idea of being separated from them had me pulling him closer. My fingers roamed over his face, memorizing every contour. He kissed me like a claim, a possessive growl escaping him when he finally released me. "This better work, Peanut."

The drive to the Assembly was quiet. Wes went with Flora to her parents, which left Rafe to drive, while Nox and Killian sat like bookends on either side of me in the back seat. Nox drew small circles on the sensitive skin just below where the hem of my skirt had pulled up, and Killian twisted my hair. The feeling was so nostalgic I had to fight a sigh from escaping my lips. I leaned my head against Nox's shoulder, his warmth seeping through my side while I breathed in their familiar scents.

Now that we knew how to create side-effect-free blockers, we were going to have to have a long talk about how we were going to move forward. Rafe's gaze met mine through the rearview mirror, and his brows pulled together. If I didn't know for a fact that it wasn't possible, I'd have thought he read my mind.

We pulled into the back parking lot of a building that looked like it could've been built in the 1800s. Carved details etched into the stone walls gave it an almost cathedral feeling. It was darker out here than I thought it would be, with only three light posts illuminating the area.

Rafe looked back. "We have to do this fast. There is most likely an alarm for the back door."

"No shit," Nox replied, jumping out of his side of the van.

Killian helped lift me out, and then Rafe jumped out, shutting his door quietly. There was no one back here, but the nature of our plan made it feel clandestine.

When we got to the door, Nox pulled out a small kit from his pocket, with thin metal blades that he used to pick the lock. It groaned when it swung open, and we all looked around.

"Since when did you know how to pick a lock?" I asked.

Nox smirked, the light reflecting off his glasses. "Since always."

I rolled my eyes. Just another secret in a million secrets, but I didn't let it weigh on me. They'd proven more than enough they wouldn't keep any more going forward, and I would hold them to that. Rafe went through the entry first and signaled back to us that it was clear. The hallway was bright enough. I had to blink several times to regain my sight. It was a pale cream color with a red carpet you'd find in old hotels, and most importantly, it was empty.

We rushed down the hall toward the humming noise only created by a large crowd. We didn't know the floor plan and had taken a few wrong turns already. The Assembly must have been already getting ready to start the proceedings. I picked up my pace. Being late wasn't an option.

Rafe stopped abruptly, and I slammed into his back with a sharp cry. Ouch. "What's wrong with you?"

He didn't look back at me, eyes forward, and Nox and Killian flanked my sides. A tall, slender beta stepped to the left until I could see her fully. Sarah stood still, a gun raised and pointed directly at Rafe's chest. My heart pounded in my ears as my lungs burned with my held breath.

"Let her go." Sarah's voice was firm with the authority that the Institute had trained into her. She'd been the one to pick me up that night four years ago. Her gaze darted quickly over me, and she glanced back to Rafe. "Are you okay, Bliss?"

My breath rushed out of me. Of course, she thought they were hurting me. She clearly drank the omegas-love-to-be-auctioned-off Kool-Aid. I was undecided if that made me understand her position more or less. I stepped in front of Rafe, dodging out of his reach so he wouldn't be able to tuck me behind him.

Sarah's eyes went wide. "What are you doing?"

"I don't have time to explain. You have to let us through, and you'll understand everything in a few minutes." My words came out in a plea.

"You don't have to stay with them." Sarah's voice was low, like she was talking to a wounded animal.

Frustration burned through my patience, and I yelled, "I don't want to leave them. I want you to let me through. Come with us, and listen for once in your life."

She sucked in a harsh breath, taking a step back, and lowered her gun.

I walked past, not taking my sight off her. "Ten

minutes. You can wait ten minutes to get your answers. Now, show us how to get to the Assembly."

She looked at us, then down the hall, and nodded. "Okay, yeah, but this better be good."

I smiled. "Oh, it will be."

CHAPTER 15

Ares

I sat on the concrete floor of my cell, staring at the white-painted brick of the opposite wall. It was the same sort of drunk-tank-style lockup facility they'd held me in a few weeks ago. This time, I didn't think I'd be getting out anytime soon.

My next stop was probably county jail or maybe state prison? I hated myself for not doing more research when I had the chance. There was that self-destructive streak Bliss kept mentioning, glaring me in the face. Not that knowing where I'd be heading next would make things any easier, but it would at least make me feel less crazy. As it was, I was about to crawl out of my skin.

Footsteps sounded down the hall, but I ignored them. Every few minutes, an officer walked by to check on me. I had no idea what they were checking for—it wasn't like I could do anything in here. I had no weapons, no cellmate—they'd even taken my belt and jacket. What the fuck was I going to do with a jacket?

The footsteps stopped in front of my cell, and I looked up without interest. "You've got a visitor."

Keys jingled, and a key turned in the lock. My heart leapt.

It was probably one of the guys—most likely Rafe. Part of me almost hoped it was Bliss, but a larger part knew it wasn't and was glad of that. The guys would have her on lockdown now, and that was exactly how it should be.

In the last few hours, I hadn't felt much of anything from Bliss. The bond had been growing steadily stronger again, and her flashes of emotion were more frequent and vivid until today, suddenly, they stopped. I hoped that just meant her blockers worked and not the more paranoid thought that she'd shut me off completely. Either way, there wasn't anything I could do from in here.

I stumbled to my feet, slipping on my socks—they'd taken my shoes for some fucking reason, as though I would have time to hide a weapon in one before my surprise arrest—and followed the guard into the hall, the fluorescent lights flickering and casting long shadows against the walls.

The police officer was an alpha, so he wasn't bothering with a riot vest or ear protection. I sized him up—he was fairly dominant, like on a scale from bunny rabbit to wolf, this guy would be a Doberman. A small part of me—okay, a large part—wanted to bark at him, just to prove I was a wolf, but I'd probably just end up with a literal bullet to the chest. Not worth it.

See, I have some self-restraint.

We stopped outside a door with a glass window, and the officer opened it slowly. "You've got thirty minutes."

I stepped inside, expecting to see one of the guys, and

deflated a little when our lawyer, Mr. Homer, looked up at me. He sat on one side of a metal interrogation table, a briefcase in front of him and a half-drunk cup of coffee in hand. He stood, holding out his other hand for me to shake. "How's it going, Ares?"

I sat down hard in the chair opposite him without shaking his hand. "Awesome. It's like fucking Christmas."

He pursed his lips and sat back down, evidently deciding not to comment. For an alpha, Homer was pretty submissive. He was dominant enough to be aggressive in court, but not so dominant that he scared betas and got into fights—at least, that was my read on him. He smelled sort of mid-level threatening to me, but nowhere near Doberman level. More like a fox.

He gave me a shrewd look. "You seem to have some powerful and determined enemies."

I clenched my jaw. That was one of the truer statements I'd heard in a while. "I know."

"This is going to be a rough run. The Assembly will charge you with the murder for sure and probably some kind of kidnapping."

"I didn't fucking kidnap her."

"Sure, okay, but the only way out of either of those charges is if you really were bonded."

I growled low in my throat at his phrasing. "You don't believe we are?"

"I didn't say that. I just can't prove it. Without the omega there to testify, no one can."

"She can't testify. I don't want her anywhere near this. I'd rather go to prison than let her get near the Institute or Nero again."

Homer clicked his tongue. "That's probably decent

proof in and of itself that you really are bonded, but that's just my opinion. I don't know. I'll see what I can do."

I narrowed my eyes. "You don't think there's much of a chance though, do you?"

He tightened his jaw, deliberating. "I didn't say that. I think there's a slim chance they'll hang themselves on technicalities."

"Fucking perfect," I muttered, gloom washing over me. "Good thing I look great in orange."

———

I rolled over on my thin mattress, somewhere between sleeping and waking.

The dirt road stretched in front of me through the windshield of the old Impala. Someone shouted outside and waved a T-shirt they were using as a flag. I shifted gears, heart pounding, and slammed my foot on the gas.

Footsteps sounded down the hall, the clink of keys threatening to pull me back to reality.

I took a turn too fast and glanced to the right—a mistake. I should have kept looking forward. My eyes connected with the driver next to me as he sideswiped my door, pushing me off course.

My wheels spun, and my stomach bottomed out. I turned the wheel frantically, trying to straighten out, but there was no point.

"Hey!"

I sat up immediately, as though I'd never been asleep at all. It felt like I hadn't been—this place didn't allow any real rest.

I blinked, clearing the memory of the weeks after they

took Bliss from my mind. At least that dream had been mine—I could swear lately I was having her dreams, waking over and over again in the middle of the night from nightmares and memories that didn't make sense or belong to me. It was like the early days of Bliss being at the Institute all over again, when we'd all been separated for a few months. All the while, I could feel her misery, and that was worse than the physical pain of my body literally trying to force me to return to the group.

"Hey! Are you fucking listening to me?" The guard jingled his keys against the bars.

"No," I said honestly. "What did you say?"

"Get up. You need to shower. Your trial is today."

"What day is it?" I asked—it had felt like it was maybe three days since I'd come in. Four? I honestly wasn't sure.

The guard sneered at me. "Worst day of your life, I'd bet."

I laughed genuinely. "Not even fucking close."

Several hours later, I fell into step beside Mr. Homer as he rushed down the empty hall of the courthouse. He looked sideways at me, and I tensed. "Remember to let me do the talking."

"Got it," I grumbled.

"I'm fucking serious, kid."

I raised my eyebrows. He must be serious—he didn't seem like the type to swear for emphasis. "I fucking get it," I said sardonically.

We stopped outside a heavy oak wood door, and Mr. Homer turned to face me. His brows pulled low, and his mouth became a thin line. "I hope you do. This is already a losing case, and I don't like losing. Don't make this worse by getting yourself thrown out of the courtroom."

He pulled the door open, and we stepped inside the cavernous room. I kept my eyes on the floor—gold-and-blue carpet—avoiding looking up at anything that was going on around me. It was impossible to avoid the scent though. There had to be sixty, maybe seventy people in here.

"Let's go," Mr. Homer said quietly, and I followed him toward a bench at the center of the room, finally looking up as we sat down.

It didn't look like any courtroom I'd seen on TV or in a movie. Instead of one raised dais with a single judge, there were rows of bleacher-like seats in a semicircle around one-half of the room. Fifty or so people—mostly men—sat facing me. They sat almost completely still, most of their expressions blank, some curious, some angry.

In the front row, only slightly raised off the floor, Headmistress Omega DuPont sat in the center of a nearly empty row. To her left stood an armed guard—clearly only there for her protection, and on her right sat a blonde woman, her face half obscured by the screen of her laptop. I squinted at her. She was familiar.

At the very top of the rows of seats, there was a row of reporters with cameras pointed down over the entire room. My gaze zeroed in on them—since when were cameras allowed in courtrooms?

I leaned over to ask my lawyer, but he shot me a look. Right. No talking.

Instead, I refocused on the crowd of people behind DuPont. The Assembly, obviously. Somehow, when Mr.

Homer described them in one of our pretrial meetings, I hadn't pictured it so literally.

I scanned their faces. There were only three women, including DuPont. A tan, dark-haired woman with a plaque reading "Arizona" in front of her and a very tiny elderly woman from Maine who looked like she must be nearing 100.

Aside from them, there were a few alphas I sort of recognized—maybe from TV, maybe because they'd been at the auction, it was hard to tell—and at the end of the second bench… My blood boiled, my heartbeat kicking up.

My lawyer reached out, putting a hand on my arm as though he sensed danger. He probably did—or at least, he could smell my sudden rage.

"Stop," Homer hissed out of the corner of his mouth.

I ignored him. There was no way to stop. No way to sit in the same room as Nero and remain calm. Nero knew it too. He was sitting at the end of the bench, smirking at me like he'd already won. In some ways, he had—this case was a formality. I knew I was fucked.

The headmistress had made that completely clear when she'd shown up the other day, and if I'd understood how the Assembly worked, I would have realized what she'd meant.

The only thing keeping me sane was that Nero still didn't have Bliss. She was safe at home with the rest of the pack. I didn't give a fuck what happened to me as long as she was far away from here, where he couldn't find her.

DuPont cleared her throat, and the woman taking notes snapped to attention. "Sarah, are you ready?"

The blonde nodded, and I realized why she looked familiar. It was the woman who'd been with the headmistress the other day. The same woman who'd picked up Bliss from that gas station parking lot years ago. Who the hell was she?

"Excellent," DuPont said, speaking loud enough that the entire room noticed. In the back, the cameras swiveled to face her. "Sarah?" DuPont prompted.

"Right, sorry." She clicked around for a moment on her laptop, then stood, lifting the computer to chest level to read from the screen.

"Sentencing Number 0089372." Her voice was monotone, as though she were reading without actually processing what she was saying. "Assembly vs. Ares, Constantine Moore, Alpha. The Assembly charges the accused, Moore, Alpha, with the following offenses." She said all of this in one breath and paused to breathe before continuing. "One: Theft of an asset greater than or equal to forty million United States dollars. Two: Possession of an unregistered omega over the age of twenty-one. Three: Murder in the second degree."

"Thank you, Sarah," DuPont said pleasantly.

I gaped. What the ever-loving fuck was going on? I leaned over to my dickhead lawyer. "That is not what you said they were going to do."

"Quiet," he muttered out of the corner of his mouth.

I breathed heavily, playing back what Sarah said as she sat back down. Had I caught that right?

Murder. Fine. I'd expected that—that was the whole reason I was here. It was the rest that tripped me up.

"Is the defense ready?" DuPont asked.

"Yes, Madam Chair," Homer muttered, still not taking his hand off my arm. He didn't need to leave it there. I was too stunned to say anything else.

"Good. We are now in session." I expected her to bang one of those judge hammers or something, but she didn't. Maybe that was only for regular courts. Instead, she looked down at a piece of paper.

"Ares Constantine Moore." She read out my full name again, and I wondered if by the end of this, it would start to lose meaning to me. "Do you understand the charges that brought you here before the Assembly today?"

I didn't say anything, and she looked up at me, obviously expecting a response. I glanced at Mr. Homer, and he nodded. I reached over and grabbed his little microphone, pulling it toward me. "No."

My lawyer audibly groaned.

DuPont narrowed her eyes, and a couple of people behind her muttered, turning to each other. DuPont shuffled her papers, and Sarah typed furiously fast notes.

"You don't understand?" DuPont asked again pointedly.

"No," I repeated.

"What don't you understand?"

"You said theft of an asset."

"That's correct." DuPont's eyes narrowed even further.

"Yeah, and that's the part I don't understand. That sounds like a fucking car or something."

I'd expected them to cry kidnapping, and we would say it wasn't kidnapping—it was a rescue. What the fuck was theft of an asset? They were acting like Bliss wasn't even a person. How could there be omegas in this room and they didn't even react?

Mr. Homer kicked me so hard under the table my chair scooted a few inches to the left. "What my client means to say is the phrasing is a little over his head, Madam Chair. I apologize for the profanity."

I sneered and opened my mouth again, but DuPont cut me off. "Sarah, please strike the last minutes from the record. Mr. Homer, the charges refer to the value that Omega Nero's mate insured her at, as is common with all omegas. We will move on from this, unless there is anything else?"

I could have gone on about this indefinitely, but clearly, there was no fucking point. I noticed that the cameramen and a couple of the reporters at the top of the stands were now facing me instead of DuPont. Interesting. Did they always do that?

"Wait a minute," a huge alpha in the third row boomed into his microphone.

I turned to him, unable to ignore his loud voice. He was dark-haired and had shoulders so large the men on either side of him were having a hard time moving their arms.

"The chair recognizes the representative from Nevada," DuPont said quickly.

The man was already speaking over her. "This is about Omega Nero? Can the representative from New York be in this hearing?" The man glared over at Nero, and I immediately decided that of all the people in the Assembly, Nevada and I would probably get along alright.

"The chair recognizes the representative from New York."

My eyes snapped up as Nero rose from his seat on the bench and leaned into a microphone I'd only just noticed in front of him. All the representatives had one next to their little plaque declaring their state. I glanced around for my microphone—no dice.

"Thank you, Madam Chair," Nero said, barely concealed glee in his voice. "I will of course refrain from the vote as a courtesy to the Assembly, but I think the evidence will speak for itself. My personal opinion has no bearing on this matter."

My lip curled, and I noticed the alpha from Nevada mirrored my expression.

"If we might move on," DuPont said, "I'd like to finish reading the facts of this case."

She appeared flustered now, as though we were already off to a rocky start. I smiled. I hoped it only got worse for her from here.

"Ares Constantine Moore." She used my full name again, this time saying it with such force it was like she was trying to assert dominance over the entire room. I raised my eyebrows. Some omega that woman was. "On the evening of the Agora Ceremony, did you knowingly enter the home of Alpha Nero and leave with his omega?"

"No," I said into the microphone.

The court erupted into whispers.

"Order," DuPont demanded, and everyone fell silent. "No, you did not come into possession of Mr. Nero's property?"

"No."

She blinked at me, evidently stunned. There was no need to make anyone swear to tell the truth in this kind of setting; everyone would know immediately if I so much as told a half-truth, and I wasn't lying.

"Why do you think Mr. Nero believes you did, then?" she said finally.

Mr. Homer cut across me. "Madam Chair, the question calls for speculation. The accused already answered the original question. We respectfully ask that the chair moves on."

She didn't move on; she simply rephrased the question. "Alpha Moore, were you in possession of the omega when you murdered Alpha Carver?"

"Allegedly," my lawyer interrupted, leaning over to speak into the microphone.

DuPont again didn't rephrase, just stared at me, waiting for me to answer.

"No."

She blinked at me. "You were seen on camera."

"I was not in possession of an omega."

Her lip curled, and I watched the proverbial light bulb go on over her head. "Is it the phrasing of the question that you object to?"

"No." I was tempted to leave it there and make them pull every answer out of me word by word but added, "It's the damn caveman ideology."

Sarah looked up at me for a moment, her fingers stalling on her keyboard. DuPont looked over at her sharply. "Sarah, please retract the last page from the record. We'll start again."

I raised an eyebrow. Was that a thing? I wasn't an expert, but could they do that?

Mr. Homer stiffened. "Madam Chair, why—"

DuPont spoke over him. "Ares Constantine Moore," she started again, "did you enter Alpha Julian Nero's house on the evening of the Agora Ceremony?"

I ground my teeth. This clearly wasn't going the way DuPont wanted, and she was going to redirect until it did. I looked for a way around that question and couldn't find one. "Yes."

DuPont's face split into a genuine smile that sent shivers down the back of my neck. "Why did you enter the house? Be specific."

My eye twitched. "He had her drugged. He was going to fucking rape her. I could feel her terror. We all could." I took a deep breath. "I literally couldn't stay out of that house if I wanted to. It's physically impossible."

The room erupted in chaos, whispers and voices rising above each other to speak. DuPont's face drained of blood, and by contrast, Nero turned a dangerous shade of red.

"Order!" DuPont yelled.

Nothing happened. My gaze fell on the alpha from Nevada, whose booming voice rose above the others, yelling something at Nero across the room. I looked for the two omegas, Arizona and Maine, but neither was tall enough to be seen through the chaos of everyone else. The scent of anger, anxiety, curiosity, and, oddly, excitement rose in the air, adding to the confusion.

DuPont reached around and grabbed someone's microphone and banged it against the head of her own, causing it to screech. Everyone stopped talking immediately, alarmed at the sudden sound. "Quiet," she said primly, sitting back down. "Please be seated."

My eyes snapped to the cameras at the top of the room—suddenly, the source of the excitement in the air was obvious.

DuPont straightened her papers in front of her. "Where was I?"

"You're saying you could feel your omega? From a distance?" The tiny elderly omega from Maine leaned forward to speak into her microphone without waiting for DuPont to finish.

I cleared my throat. "Um, yes."

"What do you mean?" her voice warbled. "Be specific."

I could swear she winked when she said the last bit, like she was making fun of DuPont. "I mean I could feel her emotions." *How can I be more specific than that?*

"So you're saying you're bound?" the ancient omega prompted, seeming almost agitated with me like I was slow on the uptake. "Correct? And presumably not just you, but your whole pack?

"Yes." I nodded. "To both."

"That's impossible," Nero spat, so obviously livid he was shaking. "They'd never met. And even if they had, the omegas are kept on blockers while at the Institute. Isn't that right, Headmistress DuPont?"

"Yes." DuPont looked annoyed that he'd called her headmistress in this setting but let it go. "Omega Nero was with us from the time she was seventeen. This is nonsense cooked up to plead a mating defense."

"They did know each other though."

I looked up in shock as Sarah, the court scribe, spoke up. She snapped her mouth shut and looked back down, sinking low behind her computer screen like she was embarrassed by her own outburst.

DuPont glared daggers. "You are not a member of this Assembly. If you cannot be quiet, I will have you removed." She swiveled back to me and took a deep breath, clearly trying to compose herself before continuing.

"Hang on, I want to know what she said," yelled Nevada.

Arizona cleared her throat. "Seconded. I yield my time to…" She fumbled for Sarah's title and ultimately went with her name. "Sarah."

All eyes fell on Sarah. In the back of the room, the cameramen shuffled, trying to get her in view. My heart pounded against my ribs, and I glanced over at Mr. Homer. Was this normal? Was it even legal?

"Um," Sarah stuttered, her face going bright red. "No, it's just they grew up together. I remember because he was one of the alphas who was there when I picked up Bliss. I mean, Omega Nero, four years ago. I didn't know they were scent bound."

"Isn't that an oversight?" North Dakota wondered out loud. "Should we be allowing that to happen?"

"The Institute is not on trial here," DuPont said shrilly.

Maine laughed and made no effort to hide it. "Maybe we should do that next?"

DuPont shot her a look. "This has all been very interesting, but I must insist we move on. The way I see it, even if what you're saying about the bond is true"—she gave me a look like she doubted it—"we can't prove it without seeing Omega Nero. If she is not here to prove the bond, we must assume you are guilty of the theft."

"That's bullshit," I snapped, even as my heart sank.

Sarah stopped typing. She glanced toward the door I'd entered through, then to me. Her eyes went wide, and she quietly rose from her seat. *What the fuck?* She took off through the exit, but everyone was too distracted by the accusation to notice.

DuPont's lip curled. "I wasn't finished. If you can't prove your bond, we also have no choice but to find you guilty of the murder of Alpha Carver. So, while the theatrics have provided the Assembly with gossip for the next decade, you are no better off than when you walked in."

I ground my teeth but kept my mouth shut. She was looking for a reaction, and I wasn't going to give her one.

"Now," she added, "the only thing left to do is find the omega and return her to her rightful mate."

Fuck it. She was going to get a reaction.

I opened my mouth, but before I could say anything, a blissfully familiar voice rang across the room.

"I'm right here."

CHAPTER 16
Bliss

My voice echoed around the Assembly hall, and blood rushed through my ears as the weight of sixty sets of eyes pressed on me.

"Go ahead," Sarah whispered from somewhere to my left.

I moved as if on autopilot, taking several steps toward the center of the terrifyingly large room.

The seats where the Assembly sat reminded me of the colosseum-style classrooms of the Institute, down to the dark wood benches and the warm overhead lighting. A hysterical laugh bubbled up in my throat, born of nerves at the idea of all the classes I'd sat through of alphas and omegas rutting through heat cycles. I prayed today we weren't as fucked.

The line of cameras at the top of the tiered seats all swiveled to face me. I squinted toward them, unable to make out anyone in particular. I'd been betting on media coverage of this—Assembly trials were filmed in some capacity—but there were more cameras than I'd expected.

"Stop!" Three armed guards started toward me, hands on their holstered guns. "You can't come in here."

I sucked in a breath, and rage flooded through the bond. Three growls rumbled until the space went silent. Rafe and Killian flanked my sides while Nox covered my back. The guards froze, taking a small step back.

"What is going on here?" DuPont yelled from her place at the front of the Assembly.

"Keep walking," Sarah said, so low only the guys and I could hear.

I kept my eyes fixed on the table where Ares and his lawyer sat, facing the mob of punishing eyes. Ares ran his fingers through his white-blond hair, his pale blue eyes fixated on me. They went from wide to soft, then narrowed in a matter of seconds before he turned his glare at Rafe, who now stood at my right. Oh, he was pissed.

"What the hell are you thinking?" Ares hissed, not bothering to keep his voice low.

I rolled my eyes, searching for patience for overprotective alphas. "We're going to save your ass."

Somewhere in the crowd, a female voice chuckled, and my chest swelled with inexplicable hope.

I came to a halt behind the microphone propped to the right of the defense table, and Rafe, Killian, and Nox circled me, making sure no one could get too close. The microphone was presumably meant for witness testimonies in a normal trial. Anger leapt in my stomach before I could quell it. They wouldn't have allowed witnesses in this sham of a trial. Well, I wasn't going to let them get away with that.

I took a deep breath, looking out over the crowd. I'd never felt so vulnerable, crushed under the judgment of the gazes. Yet, at the same time, I'd never been so seen. There was a bang, and I flinched as Nero slammed his fist into his desk.

"Fucking get her. She's fucking mine. I own her—"

"Enough," Headmistress Omega DuPont's voice cut him off. "Omega Nero, good to see you again, although I wish it were under better circumstances." Her smile didn't meet her eyes, and my stomach flipped in disgust. I hated her. She gestured toward where Nero stood, so tense I could almost scent his rage from here. "I'm sure you'll be happy to be reunited with your mate."

I raised my chin, unwilling to bend to her. "Don't call me that. My name is Bliss. Omega Bliss, if you insist on being formal. I think you and I both know that reunion will not happen. Not once everyone here understands what you've been doing."

The headmistress stood from her chair, her voice coming out crisp. "You were selected for your mate at the Agora, just like every other omega. You're a perfect match."

Laughter burst out of my chest, but it was strained. "Selected or sold? Nero just admitted he owns me. Tell me, Omega DuPont, do you think the world will want to hear about your little auction?" My eyes flicked up to the cameras, and Omega DuPont followed the direction of my gaze. "Why don't you tell everyone how you steal omegas as children, drug them for most of their adolescence, then literally sell them to the highest bidder?"

A gasp rippled through the room, but for every shocked face, there was one next to them glaring with unsurprised resignation. My blood ran cold, and I leaned back into Nox's hand, his fingers trailing my spine, giving me strength to press on. "Look around you." My voice trembled slightly. "How many people here already know about the auction because they purchased a little omega of their own?"

Now the gasps were louder, genuine shock at being called out on their own hypocrisy and crimes.

"The omegas are happy at the Institute." The headmistress glanced around, giving a reassuring smile to the crowd.

My stomach churned, and I resisted the urge to throw up. "Are they happy? Or are they just drugged? What I could never understand, Headmistress, was why omegas needed blockers in the Institute. You could have easily kept alphas away."

The headmistress glared down at me. "Omega Nero, you are out of order. You will follow proper protocol, or you will be removed from the room."

"I'd like to hear what Omega Bliss has to say." The tiny elderly omega from Maine spoke into her microphone. Despite her age, her gaze was sharp and steady on mine. The way her eyes saddened made me wonder if it had always been like this.

I searched the eyes of the Assembly. "I think The Institute needs the omegas to be pliable. They drug us to the point where we can't think or worry about what's happening until it's too late." I glared up at the headmistress. "Does it make it easier to cash in on them that way? A drugged omega is a quiet omega? We all know once an omega has been mated, she loses her autonomy to her mate, so you just have to get her safely to him."

"What are you basing this accusation on?" asked a beady-eyed alpha from Pennsylvania.

My eyes welled with frustrated tears. "Because it happened to me. They were supposed to protect me, but they sold me. Sold countless other omegas who are now mated without consent. What would you call that?"

A balding man in his forties with the sign reading "Delaware" in front of him leaned forward, his head tilted as he asked his question. "I'm sorry that happened to you, but omegas can't be free to roam before they're mated. They'll be scent bound to the first alpha they run into. And it would be chaos."

"Would it be chaos though? And so what if it was? I was scent bound to my pack at seventeen, and I was happy. It was the Institute who took that away from me. Do you know how painful it is? It's like having a piece of your soul ripped out." The crowd grew louder, but my words broke through. "You're all so sure that you know best for what an omega needs, you refuse to even ask us. I'd have given absolutely anything to stay with my pack back then, and I'd do it again now."

"Packs are an outdated concept," someone yelled from the back of the room.

"No, what's outdated is how he thinks he owns me. Like a broodmare." I pointed my finger toward where Nero stood glaring at me, fist clenched at his side. "Don't I get a say in this? Shouldn't every omega get to decide who they mate with?"

I took a deep breath and looked through the crowd. All eyes were on me, waiting on bated breath for what I had to say next. "The fact that you are charging Ares, my bonded, because he 'kidnapped' me is laughable. *Representative*

Nero jabbed a needle in my neck the second he got me home from the Agora, bringing my heat on instantly. I'd only met him once before that. Tell me. Was there a choice for me? Is that your definition of consent?"

Headmistress Omega DuPont tried to break in, but the representative from Nevada cut her off. "Let her speak."

I gave him a grateful smile and continued. "Ares is innocent. We've been bound since I was seventeen. Based on your own laws, when the alpha attacked me in that bathroom, he had every right to protect me."

The elderly omega from Maine gave me a soft look. "You were scent bound naturally. Didn't that take away your ability to choose?"

"I don't regret scent bonding them for a single second. They were my choice long before I knew I was an omega."

Rafe's fingers grazed mine, and warmth flooded the bond. I met Ares' gaze. "I love them, and even though they can be absolute idiots sometimes, it's my decision, not the Assembly's and not the Institute's. All I want is for omegas to have a choice."

The cameras in the back of the room moved, creaking, as the reporters jostled for a better view of us. My heart pounded—I hoped that no matter what happened, the footage of this found the right audience.

The representative from Maine stood, but she was so tiny that for a moment, I didn't realize she had moved at all. "In light of the new evidence, I move to dismiss this case."

"Omega Levi, you can't do that," DuPont snapped.

"Shut up, Zinnia," Maine barked, and I blinked. I'd never heard an omega literally bark before—was that even possible?

DuPont coughed, obviously flustered. "I—"

Maine straightened her collar and pushed her tiny silver glasses up her pointy nose. "I've been enjoying my semi-retirement, but I'm clearly going to have to come back to the school."

Nevada stood in the row behind Maine, towering over her. "I second the motion to dismiss and move to start an investigation into the accusations on the Institute."

"What?" Nero demanded. "This is absurd."

"All those in favor, say aye," Maine spoke over him, her smile smug.

Whoever that omega was, I wanted to be her when I grew up.

The room filled with the sound of the assembled chairs' agreement, no one daring to be caught opposing while the cameras watched.

Sarah approached us, and a low growl rumbled from Rafe. "That's close enough."

She froze for a second, shaking her head before saying, "I'm sorry. I should have known what they were doing."

I stepped around where he'd taken a defensive stance in front of me. "Yes, you should have."

She swallowed hard and looked at the floor. "Listen, for what it's worth, I'm really sorry. If it's not too late, I'd like to help."

"Why should we trust you?" Nox growled low, and Sarah took an instinctive step back.

I stepped into his side, and he wrapped his arm around my shoulder and looked down at me. "Let's see where she takes us. Turns out I'm in a forgiving mood today."

His smile took over his face, the right side slightly higher than the left. "Thank fucking god for that."

CHAPTER 17
Bliss

Sarah took us to an isolated hall in the back of the Assembly building. "I'm going to leave you here," she said, glancing over her shoulder. "Your mate should be through processing in a minute."

"Thanks," I told her earnestly. "For everything."

"No problem. Seriously. I'm sorry it came to this." She looked over her shoulder again as the door to the assembly room opened. "I have to run. I need to go talk to Omega Levi."

"Who?"

"The representative from Maine. I need to see if I can keep my job." She grimaced. "Bye!"

She darted away, and I stared down the long hall ahead of us. The plain gray-painted walls and tiled floor made it look sterile compared to the timeless look of the rest of the building. I rubbed my hands over my face like I'd seen the boys do a hundred times, then pushed them into my hair, dislodging my ponytail. It felt like we'd been out here forever instead of less than an hour.

My nails dug into my scalp, and I let out a frustrated growl. The sweet lemon vanilla scent of Killian filled my lungs as he pressed his chest into my back and trailed his fingers up my arms, entwining our fingers and pulling them down to wrap around my middle. I leaned my head back, letting his warmth encompass me, and relaxed when he purred.

He ran his nose from my shoulder up the column of my neck, his teeth grazing my ear. "Your anxiety is filling the bond, B. I can help you with that."

A shiver ran through me, heat flooding between my thighs, and I rolled my head, exposing my neck to him instinctively. His purr grew until it was vibrating against my spine, the calming effect shifting to something darker.

Two deep breaths, followed by low growls, had a whimper tumbling from my mouth.

"Kill, you were supposed to calm her." Rafe went to push Killian away, but I glared up at him. "We can't do this here."

"I'm fine."

Rafe's already pitch-black eyes hooded as he searched my face, no doubt flushed from Killian's attention. He raised his hand and grazed his thumb over my cheek. "You're going to be a hell of a lot more than fine as soon as we get you home."

I whined, and if I hadn't been on blockers, I knew that my scent would overpower the hall.

Rafe growled and pressed a kiss to my forehead. "If Ares doesn't hurry the fuck up, we are going to leave without him."

I smiled at that, knowing that he was just as anxious as I was to get Ares back.

Nox stepped out of the steel door that housed the police department, his hand coming up to scrape across his shaved head before he looked toward us and smiled. The bond pulsed with a content feeling as he took up the space to my right. "Few more minutes and he'll be out."

They'd effectively surrounded me on three sides. All they needed was Ares, and I'd be fully encased in my alphas. I made an indistinct sound, and their groans traveled straight to my core. We had to get out of here fast, or I was going to lose my flipping mind. Luckily, the blockers I'd taken to come here today were still holding down the fort, and I wasn't at risk of going into heat. We had a lot to sort out together, and I wanted to be fully conscious when it happened.

I jumped as the door slammed shut, and a pissed-off Ares took up the space at my remaining free side. By the way he looked, I'd have thought he wanted to strangle me, if it wasn't for the convoluted mess of emotions he was sending down the bond. "What the hell were you thinking, Love?"

A laugh bubbled up in my throat, and I couldn't help my grin. "Of course you're mad. All I did was save you from a life in prison."

His pale blue eyes bored into mine. "I'd spend my life in prison if it kept you safe."

I rolled my eyes. "There's that self-sabotaging streak we were talking about. I'll remember that for the next time I want to confess my undying love for you all in front of a crowd of people."

Their growls filled the space, and their breath heated

my skin. They were so close. Ares leaned in and ran his tongue over my bottom lip before gently biting it. "Oh, we're going to talk about that, Love."

I squirmed, no doubt blushing, and my guys purred for me. "Okay."

Nox pulled my hand away from where Killian still held it against my stomach, intertwined our fingers, and led me toward an exit.

"You stupid fucking bitch. Do you have any idea how much I paid for you?" Nero's voice had fear shooting through me, and Nox put a steadying hand on my waist when I stumbled backward.

Ares, Rafe, and Killian formed a wall between us.

"Back the fuck off, asshole," Rafe barked, and Nero took a step backward, unable to fight against the command. Seeing Nero fall into line eased my fear, and I wanted to see the look on Nero's face while my alphas dominated him. I lifted on my toes, and Ares glared back at me, a clear "stay back" written on his face. I pouted, tucking behind him.

Nox's barely there chuckle brushed against my neck. "You're always looking for trouble, Little Wolf." He kissed the sensitive spot just below my ear. "I'm starting to think you've done a much better job of protecting us than we've done protecting you."

A laugh broke through my lips. "You think?"

I went to step in front of the guys, but they closed the gap between them. I spoke over their shoulder instead. "Just give it up, Nero. After today, there's no world that you get to keep me now and everyone doesn't know it's against my will. Maybe try asking Headmistress DuPont for a refund."

"Fucking bitch."

Four menacing growls met him, and I swore the temperature of the room dipped. Nero looked from me to them, then put up his hands and walked backward. "I was trying to elevate your life, but I can see you're where you belong now with low-life criminals."

It was my turn to growl, and Nox banded his arms around my middle before I could go after Nero. I made a disgruntled grunt, and he laughed.

"I'll let you kill him next time, Little Wolf. Let's get you home now, okay? It's been a long day, and I for one can't wait to show you how grateful we are for you in all the ways we know how." His words drifted along my neck until the soft lobe of my ear was between his teeth, and warmth flooded through me.

I took in a deep, raspy breath. "Okay."

Rafe looked back at us the second Nero turned the corner out of sight, his thick lashes covering most of his dark gaze. "Let's go home."

―――

Ares' fingers clenched against my thighs as he readjusted me sideways on his lap in the back seat of our van. Nox and Rafe were in the front and didn't look too happy about it. I wasn't positive, but I was fairly certain Rafe was going well above the speed limit in a rush to get home.

Ares hadn't said a word since we left the Assembly building, just tucked me tight against him. I swore I felt him try to smell me, and he huffed out a breath. My blockers made it nearly impossible to smell anything more than a subtle hint of my scent, no stronger than a beta would put off.

Killian's hand drifted up and down my calf, a lopsided grin on his face. "So, are we going to talk about it?"

I met his honey-brown eyes with a small smile of my own, knowing full well what he had in mind. "Talk about what?"

His fingers traced the sensitive skin just behind my knees, and I squirmed. Ares grunted, shifting below me, but not before I felt his growing hardness. I raised a brow at him. "Okay, Ares, why don't you start."

He stared at me for several moments until my breath caught in my chest. "You said you love us. That you choose us. Was that just to get me off the hook?"

Rafe looked through the rearview mirror, and Nox turned in the passenger seat to see my reaction.

"You realize I only had to say the 'we were bonded when I was seventeen' bit to get the charges dropped, right?"

Relief and hunger filled the bond so strong I had to suck in a breath. Ares purred underneath me, kissing my temple. "We love you too, always have. I wish it would have played out differently, but I'll always be grateful we have you now."

Warmth filled my chest as I met my other three alphas' gazes. The truth of Ares' words was written on their faces.

"I knew you'd forgive us. Never doubted it." Killian squeezed my legs and worked his way down to my foot, where he took off my shoes and worked his firm hands over the arch of my feet.

Ares licked and nipped a trail up my neck. "I can't

fucking wait to sink my teeth into you. I've been dying to claim you as my mate since I was seventeen."

I moaned and tilted my neck, exposing it fully. Ares took full advantage, sucking hard enough to leave a mark, while Killian skated his hands up my dress just shy of where I needed them most.

"Enough of fucking that." Rafe's voice cut through the moment. "I drove through you fucking her once already, and we nearly died several times. You're going to have to wait until we get home."

Killian pouted, but Ares lifted me off his lap and buckled me in the seat between them. I whined, and Ares pressed his forehead against mine. "Be a good girl, and we'll have you coming so hard, you'll be begging for mercy."

Jesus. My skin burned as fire licked through me, thinking of all the ways he could make good on that promise.

Nox grunted, giving Rafe's shoulder a squeeze as he drove. "Hurry the fuck up."

It surprised me when we pulled up to the warehouse. "Why are we here?"

Nox looked over his shoulder. "Unless you want to get fucked in front of Flora and Wes for the next several hours, this was the best place."

The amount of possessiveness that rained through the bond, even in its lessened state, had me guessing they'd kill Wes by the end for even being in the proximity. "Gotcha."

Rafe opened the van's rear door seconds after he parked and stared down with wild, hungry eyes. My fingers lifted to sweep back the hair falling over his face, but he grabbed my hand with a growl and bit the mating gland on my wrist lightly. I choked back a moan as a shiver ran down my spine, and heat bloomed under my skin. It wasn't possible to mate outside of my heat, but it didn't stop how good it felt when his teeth grazed my skin.

The corner of his mouth teased a smile, and he ran his tongue along the spot. "The second you go into heat, I'm sinking my teeth into every one of your mating glands. You chose us in front of the world, Peanut. There's no taking it back."

My eyes widened, heat pooling between my legs as I imagined what it would be like to go into heat and have all four of them bite me simultaneously.

Rafe chuckled, and I squealed as his hands circled my waist, lifting me off Ares's lap and over his shoulder. My dress flipped up, exposing my ass completely. Rafe carried me through the warehouse toward our apartment, his fingers digging into my upper thigh. I shifted, trying to force them higher. When he didn't budge, a small frustrated grunt escaped me. "Put me down. I can walk."

His hand came down hard on my ass in a sharp spank, and I keened, the mix of pleasure and pain temporarily short-circuiting my brain. Rafe rubbed the stinging skin with his flat palm, and I squirmed, nearly knocking myself down. He placed a kiss against the side of my leg, and a low growl vibrated his words. "Did you like that?"

Killian smiled at me as he followed us up the stairs, his honey-brown gaze near black with need.

I grinned. "Yes." I pushed it further, wiggling on his shoulder, and he tightened his grip to stop from dropping me. Another sharp crack had my thighs soaked.

"Stay still." His hand smoothed over the hot skin.

I had half a mind to do it again, but the second we got into the warehouse, Rafe flipped me off his shoulder and pinned me to the living room wall. His mouth was soft and warm as he took his time kissing me, an "I love you" and "I'm sorry" all wrapped into one. I dug my fingers into his hair, pulling him down to deepen the kiss. He groaned against my mouth and lifted me under my thighs until my legs wrapped around him, and he dropped his head to the curve of my neck. "You are so fucking perfect, Peanut."

My breath caught in my lungs, and I tilted, rubbing my core over the feel of his hard cock. My body craved friction, and fire licked up my spine. I moved against him, using the wall as leverage, and dug my fingers into his hair, needing him to help me. "Rafe."

"Fuck, I know." He licked a trail up my neck, and my head fell to the side, giving him even more access. I was lost to him and barely noticed when he stepped back from the wall, deepening the kiss, his fingers digging into the curve of my ass to lift me higher. I whimpered and rubbed myself over him. Even with the blockers suppressing my heat, I needed more.

He stepped forward, and I expected to feel the cool wall, but a hard chest burned into my back in its place. I gasped, craning back, and Killian leaned in, biting my bottom lip. "You look so good right now, B." His tongue trailed along the seam of my lips, and I sucked it into my mouth. He grunted, rocking his hard cock against me. I gasped, heat burning through me as I realized he was naked, his cock bare against my exposed thigh.

"Why are we wearing so many clothes?" I asked Rafe, dazed.

He laughed, stripping before dropping to his knees. Killian held me firm to his chest but let my toes rest on the ground.

Rafe lifted off my dress and placed a kiss over my panties, his hot breath seeping through the thin material. I moaned, a shiver running through me in anticipation. His fingers dragged the thin fabric down my calves painfully slow, and he kissed a path along the way.

Ares and Nox growled, watching us from a few feet away, both of their shirts off and their pants undone. I swallowed hard at the fervent promise in their gazes, and a shiver ran through me. I shifted in anticipation. No one was touching me, and I desperately needed it.

Killian held one of my legs, balancing me on one foot, and spread me for them. Need filled the bond as Rafe sat back on his haunches and licked his lips. "You are so fucking stunning." He ran his fingers over me, spreading my wet slick. "You're dripping for us."

I dropped my head back onto Killian's chest but never took my eyes off Ares and Nox, who were now standing directly behind Rafe. I wanted all of them, and I wanted them now. "Come here."

Rafe gave me a knowing look. "Do you want to feel us, Bliss? Do you want Killian to bury himself deep inside you? Have his knot split you open while I devour this sweet pussy of yours?" He ran a finger through my slit.

I cried out my moan, nodding, and pushed my hips back into Killian.

"Say please." Rafe bit the inside of my thigh, just out of reach of my mating gland, and frustration built with my need.

"What?" My gaze snapped to his, and Killian's chuckle rumbled through my back.

Rafe trailed his tongue up my thigh but stopped inches away from where I wanted him. "Say please, Bliss."

I watched him, debating if I should wait him out. They were just as likely as I was to break. Killian shifted his hips, and his cock grazed over my entrance. My eyes rolled back, and I choked on my breath. "Please. Please."

Killian groaned and sunk himself fully into me with one thrust. He stilled, letting me adjust to his larger size. Rafe's eyes hooded, staring at where Killian and I connected. "You're stretched so good for him." Killian's hips jerked, and he grunted.

Nox stepped to my right side, his fingers guiding my gaze to his. "Tell us what you want, Bliss."

I squirmed, searching for friction. "Fuck me."

Killian licked my neck, biting my ear. "Gladly."

He pulled back and slammed into me, setting a punishing pace that had my eyes rolling back. Ares' and Nox's hot mouths surrounded my nipples at the same time as Rafe's tongue flattened on my clit. I jerked against them, a moan breaking through my lips.

Killian's fingers dug into my hips as his pace picked up. "So fucking wet." His breath choppy against my neck, and he made low, needy noises peppered with near-incoherent phrases. "Ours." Tension built in my lower back, and warmth pooled between my legs. Rafe's mouth closed over my clit, sucking hard, and an almost painful pleasure grew with each punishing stroke of Killian's cock. I dug my fingers into Rafe's hair and dragged him harder against me.

Nox licked up my neck and breathed against my ear. "Does Rafe look good on his knees like that?"

I looked down, meeting Rafe's black, hooded gaze as he licked over my clit. I bit my lip and nodded.

Ares' teeth sank into my earlobe with a growl. "Want to watch Nox fuck him for you?"

A moan pulled from my mouth, and my head fell back, nearly coming at the idea of it. I loved that they wanted each other. That we were together fully as a pack. My voice came out all breath. "Yes."

There was something extremely sexy about the leader of our pack submitting. Rafe and Killian groaned when Nox wrapped his hand around the base of Killian's cock, soaking his hand in my slick before moving behind Rafe. He dropped his pants and boxers, exposing his pierced cock, and prepared himself and Rafe with my slick before meeting my eyes and thrusting into his ass. Rafe's groan vibrated against my clit, and Killian lifted my leg higher to give him more access. He sucked on my clit before dipping lower to run his tongue along where Killian and I were combined, then met my eyes. "You taste so fucking good."

He went back to devouring me, and one of my hands sank into his hair, the other wrapping around Ares' cock, currently grinding against my hip. I tightened my fingers and clenched my pussy, drawing groans from both of them. Nox's muscles rippled as he slammed himself into Rafe, his gaze still intent on me. Nox leaned down and bit Rafe's neck hard. Rafe groaned and bit my clit, my orgasm shattering me into a million pieces. Nox collapsed against Rafe's back with his release, licking the mark he'd left on Rafe's neck. Alphas couldn't mate each other, but the mark screamed they were pack, that they belonged together.

I squeezed around Killian, and his rhythm faltered as he shifted back slightly, denying me his knot before filling me with his cum. I twisted and glared back at him, ignoring the flutter in my heart at the sight of his lopsided smile.

"What the hell, Kill?" Did I sound needy? Yes. Did I care? No. Not with them.

His chest vibrated against my back. "Bliss, I will knot you a million times over. Fill you up with cum until you're round with our child, but I thought you'd want to play with the rest of us before being locked in place."

His words swirled around my head, and I was lucky he was holding me because I went limp in his arms. *Child. Children.* I flushed warm, the heat burning under my skin. I liked the sound of that. Four growls filled the space, drawing my attention. Their eyes were all nearly black, their pupils blown wide with hunger. They liked that too.

I smirked. "I guess that's fine."

Killian's satisfaction trailed down the bond as he slowly lowered my legs down in front of where Rafe still kneeled in front of me.

Ares grazed his fingers up my belly, over the peak of my breast, and gently circled my neck. "What do you want, Bliss?"

I couldn't think coherently enough to put it into words. I wanted more. I needed all of them. All over me. Covering, touching, licking, fucking. I wanted to feel their hands, fingers, tongues, and cocks. I wanted to be devoured and lose myself to them. My slick dripped down my legs, and Rafe groaned.

"Fuck, you smell so good, Bliss." He ran his tongue

over my core, lapping up my wetness. "Taste so fucking good."

Ares growled and tightened his grip on my neck. "Where do you want us? Here or the nest?"

Even with the blockers, my internal instincts perked up on the word *nest*. I looked down the hall to the room they filled with pillows and dim lighting. They'd created it before they knew they'd even get me back. How many times had they walked past it and felt the pain of our distance? Suddenly, all I wanted was for us to get to use it.

"Nest, please."

Ares lifted me from Killian, his one hand under my legs, his other banded behind my back. "Such a good girl, using your manners."

My omega instincts kicked up, an absolute glutton for praise, and I snuggled into his chest.

"I'm going to get water." Killian headed to the kitchen while Nox trotted down the hall into the nest first, and Rafe trailed behind us.

Ares leaned down, capturing my mouth in a slow, languid kiss. Warmth filled me, and a sense of rightness took over. My feelings must have broadcast through the bond because his kiss went from sweet to hungry until I was panting, barely registering being lowered to the cushions. Rafe's powerful arms gripped my hips and pulled me between his legs, my back pressed against his chest.

Ares bit his lower lip, his normally silver gaze completely black as it traveled over my curves. My stomach rolled several times in this position, and I went to cover myself with an arm.

Ares growled, stilling my movement. "You are so fucking perfect, Love. Never cover yourself from us."

I swallowed hard. I wasn't particularly self-conscious, but that didn't mean I didn't love to hear how much they wanted me. I lifted my breast and let my knees fall open, giving him a full view of my wet slick. "Better?"

He growled, stripping off the rest of his clothes, and dropped to his knees, looking like he was almost praying to me. "You have no idea what you do to me."

My skin felt like it might burn from within if someone didn't touch me.

Nox took up the spot on my right, and his fingers entwined with mine. "Relax. We'll take care of you."

It was hard to relax when lust was a living, writhing thing, demanding to be fed. I was starving for them. Nox captured my lips, a low purr emanating from his chest, and his tongue filled my mouth with slow, consuming kisses punctuated by sharp bites. He pulled back, and I lifted to chase him, only to be dragged back by Rafe's enormous hands, flipping me to straddle him.

His cock teased my entrance, and I made a sharp whining sound against Nox's mouth. "Open for him, Little Wolf."

My body obeyed, going limp in his arms, and my head lolled forward as Rafe's cock split me open with every inch he buried inside me. The feeling of fullness momentarily overwhelmed my senses until he rocked into me from below. Ares leaned forward, sucking and biting a trail over my neck. "Tell me what you want, Love."

"I want all of you. I want to be a pack."

Killian dropped to his knees beside us and captured my mouth, thrusting his tongue to match the rhythm of Rafe's hips. "Fuck, babe. We want that too. That's all we've ever wanted."

He sucked hard on my neck just below my ear, no doubt marking me for others to see. By the end of tonight, there would be no doubt we belonged to each other. I slowed my pace, grinding down on Rafe, and he squeezed my hips, tugging me tighter against him.

Nox fisted his hand in Killian's curls, yanking him forward and capturing his mouth in a deep kiss. Killian growled, his hand digging into Nox's jaw as he pulled him closer. Fuck, they were hot.

Nox broke free and licked a line up Killian's neck, then bit down hard, a red, angry mark left in his place when he pulled away.

"You like that, Love. Do you like seeing us mark each other?"

"Yes."

Ares' naked chest pressed against my back, and he guided me forward until I was chest to chest with Rafe and pressed his soaked fingers to my ass. I sucked in a breath as he slid one, then two inside. When I rocked back, he replaced them with the head of his cock. "You're going to take both of our knots, Love."

I keened and jerked back, pressing against him as he slowly filled me from behind, letting me adjust. My fist clenched against Rafe's shoulders. I could barely breathe. I was so full.

My slick soaked all three of us as they rocked into me, all noise lost to pleasured grunts and moans. I ground my hips down, rubbing my clit over Rafe with each thrust until I could feel my orgasm build. My toes curled, and my hands clenched so close to the edge.

Ares's hand buried into the back of my hair, tugging until a hint of pain mixed with the pleasure. "You're going to come around our cocks." His hand came down on my ass in a hard slap that had my orgasm breaking me open. I lay lax between them, and they slowed their thrusts. Killian and Nox entwined their fingers into mine, kissing my neck and whispering incoherent words against my skin. I looked up, and Rafe captured my mouth in a slow, languid kiss. My sensitive skin tingled as their hands and mouths covered every inch of me, and my heart squeezed at the sweetness of it all.

I rolled my hips, and Ares and Rafe groaned, their pace barely increasing. We ground against each other, chasing an agonizingly slow release. My eyes widened as Ares pushed deeper inside me until I fit his entire knot, and Rafe buried himself inside me. My release was instant, the pressure and stretch overcoming my senses as they followed with their own release.

Tears filled my eyes as overwhelming emotions flooded me. I hated I was on blockers and couldn't feel the bond as strong. I knew I would be glowing.

"I love you, Little Wolf."

I bit back a sob, and my smile wobbled. "I love you too. All of you." I was exhausted, and everything finally felt right, surrounded by my pack.

CHAPTER 18
Nox

F*uck, she's beautiful.*
I threaded Bliss' lavender hair through my fingers, listening to her slow breathing. I woke an hour ago with her tangled around me, one arm thrown over my chest, her leg between mine, and her head resting over my heart. I'd barely moved in fear of waking her.

Relief, love, and gratitude filled me when she stood in front of the world and chose us. We would spend the rest of our lives proving to her she wouldn't regret it.

The guys had slipped out this morning one at a time, the scent of their jealousy filling the air as they looked at how Bliss was wrapped around me. I'd smirked at the sight of their bodies covered in marks from teeth and bruises from kisses. We'd spent the night worshiping Bliss, only sleeping for short bursts of time when she needed to rest.

My body hummed, the memory of slow, languid kisses during post-orgasm high as we each took her throughout the night, mixed in with thoughts of us taking each other, teeth marking us as pack. We'd broken apart from each other the night we'd let her go four years ago, and she brought us back together, slowly mending the bond we'd shattered by our own stupidity.

Bliss's fingers trailed over my forearm as she slowly came to, playing connect the dots on my Orion constellation tattoo. She tilted her head, looking up at me with a soft smile. "When did you get this?"

"A long time ago." I'd gotten it after a drunken bender a little over a week after that awful night. I couldn't even look at the stars without my chest feeling like it was shredding itself apart. The tattoo served as a constant reminder of what we did and what I'd lost.

She hummed and stretched out like a cat, the sheet dipping below her breasts. They were covered in bite marks from last night's activities, and the sight appeased my possessiveness.

She scanned my face, placing a gentle kiss on my chest. "I hate feeling you less. I guess I grew used to it."

"Me too." I met her violet eyes and slid a wayward strand of hair behind her ear. My bond hated the new blockers that tried to cut her off from us. On the one hand, it was exactly what we needed; on the other, it was like I was missing a piece of myself. The shadow of a missing limb.

I leaned down and took her mouth in a patient kiss, infusing it with as much feeling as I could, only pulling away when the mood shifted to something hotter. Her body would need a break after everything we'd done to her.

I trailed my fingers over her stomach in slow circles

before meeting her gaze, my voice coming out unsure. "What do you think about coming off blockers?"

She tilted her head, trailing her finger over my ear, tracing the piercings there. "That will put me into heat."

I couldn't help my lopsided smirk, but an underlying feeling of trepidation had my heart speeding. "That's the point. I want to mate you, Little Wolf. I want to feel the bond solidify to a point that it can never break."

She searched my gaze and placed a chaste kiss on my lips, her eyes bright. "Okay."

I pulled her higher until she perched on her forearms above me. "Okay?"

She captured my mouth in a hard, possessive kiss, teeth grazing my lower lip. "I want to mate you too."

Fuck, that sounds good.

I trailed my fingers down her back and gripped her ass, immediately letting her go when she made a small pained sound. "Shit, I'm sorry." I rolled her off me, unable to fight against the instinct to check her for injuries. My heart finally slowed when nothing obvious appeared.

Her body vibrated with the chuckle she was trying to hold back, but her laugh broke out anyway. "Relax. I'm just sore from last night."

"Shit, okay." I got up from bed, carrying her with me. Her arms wrapped around my neck, my arms below her knees and supporting her back.

She laughed as I kicked off the sheets still tangled around her and nearly fell.

I glared down at her and nipped her bottom lip. "Don't laugh at your alpha." Fuck, I liked the sound of that, and from the flush that covered her skin, she did too.

"Yes, Alpha."

I groaned, fighting the urge to take her against the wall, burying my knot so deep inside her she'd feel me for days. Her lips tipped up in a devious grin. She knew exactly what she was doing. I kissed her forehead, a low rumble in my chest. "Be good. You're too sore for what I want to do to you."

"What if I like that idea?" she asked.

The scent of honey filled the air, and I stumbled, clenching my teeth. She was going to be the death of me. "Watch it, Little Wolf. I'll make you pay for this later."

Determined to take care of her, I carried her to the bathroom and placed her on the vanity, where she sat with a small smile, watching me warm up the shower. "Are you going to bathe me now?"

I slid my hands up her thighs to grip her hips. There was nothing I wanted to do more than take care of her. I dropped my forehead to hers. "Are you okay with that?"

"Sounds wonderful." She gave me a swift kiss and went to hop off the counter. I lifted her in my arms until her legs wrapped around me.

"Not a chance." Before stepping under the water, I checked the temperature. I slowly lowered her legs down to the ground but kept one arm firmly banded around her middle. I dipped my head, lips grazing her ear, and smiled at the shiver that rolled through her. "Let me take care of you."

She went limp in my arms, tilting her head back. "Yes, Alpha."

My dick twitched against her, and I groaned, dropping my head to her shoulder, taking several breaths to get ahold of myself. Sex could wait.

I lathered the shampoo, then conditioner through her

hair, eating up her contented sounds as I massaged her scalp. Once I'd rinsed the last of it out, I soaped a cloth and delicately cleaned her body, taking extra care with anywhere she was sore.

"Feel better?" she said, smiling when I wrapped her in a big fluffy white towel.

My instincts finally settled, I realized I'd been a little over-the-top. "Yes, but I will never stop wanting to take care of you."

She hummed, walking back to the nest and calling over her shoulder. "I like the sound of that."

I leaned on the doorframe, watching her get dressed, and smiled when she pulled on my white button-up shirt from last night. It hung on her like a dress.

I pulled her toward me and rolled up the sleeves until they were above her elbows. "They're going to be jealous that you smell like me."

She scrunched up her nose, making a cute face. "We can take turns."

It was my turn to feel jealous. I'd have her smelling like me every day if it was my choice. I kissed her hard, telling her as much, but broke away when her stomach growled.

"Hungry, Little Wolf?"

"Starving."

I sat on one of the island stools, pulling her onto my lap, not quite ready to let her go. Ares sat beside us, pulling her legs over his lap, sliding his hand up the outside of her thigh. I tugged her closer to me, and he let out a low growl.

"Share."

I immediately loosened my grip. "Just be careful. She's sore."

Ares' gaze flashed to Bliss, his hand stilling. "Is that right? Were we too rough with you?"

"What's gotten into you guys? I'm fine. I'm stronger than I look." Her smile split her face.

Killian swooped down, stealing a kiss until he left Bliss dazed. "Never doubted it."

"I can hear your stomach from here." Rafe slid a plate full of pancakes toward her.

I slipped her onto her own stool, and she tucked into her food while we carried on the conversation around her.

"We need to head to the lab today and sort out how we're going to handle making the new blockers." I took a sip of my black coffee, waiting to see if anyone else had any ideas.

Rafe rubbed his palms over his eyes. "That isn't the problem. We have the production ability. We already proved that, but how are we going to get enough omegas? Especially because they have to have just come out of heat."

"Could we ship the blood?" Ares asked.

I took my glasses off and ran a hand over my shaved head. "We can ask Dr. Lewinsky, but my guess is no. He's always processed ours immediately."

Bliss set her utensils on her plate with a small click. "Do you have the resources to open another location? Maybe one on the East Coast, close to the Institute?"

Fuck, I love her. I smirked down. "Yeah, we do."

The drive to the lab was short. Ares held Bliss in his lap on one cot, her feet dangling in the air between his legs as she explained her idea to Dr. Lewinsky.

The doctor nodded, looking impressed. "It could work, but we'll have to go down there. There's no way we can set that up remotely."

"Sounds like a road trip." Killian slapped his hand against Rafe's back where he stood watching Bliss.

"I'm assuming you'll want to come too?" Rafe asked Bliss, already knowing the answer.

"Yup."

I placed my hands on a nearby steel table. "Well, we'll have to do it fast before Bliss goes into heat."

All eyes snapped to me, then to her. She shrugged. "I have enough for a few days, but I don't want to take any after." She bit her lip, looking to me with a little insecure smile. I'd do everything I could to wipe that look off her face permanently.

Rafe's eyes narrowed. "Why?"

She turned her smile on the pack. "Because I want to solidify our mate bond."

CHAPTER 19

Bliss

Two days later, I packed for our trip to the West Coast, an excited slash nervous energy riding my senses. Something big had shifted, and this felt like the first step toward a new future for omegas.

Killian opened my dresser drawer, pulling out a matching deep purple bra and pantie set. "Bring this one, B. I'm going to enjoy taking it off you." His voice rumbled through me, and a warm flush ran up my neck. I hadn't spent a night since the trial without at least one of them crawling into my bed.

"Give me that." I ripped the lingerie from his hands, digging out a few more matching sets before tucking them into the divided space at the top of my suitcase.

I placed neatly folded dresses into the corner of my ridiculously large suitcase. As someone who'd grown up with barely anything, then went to an institute where we had regulated clothing, the amount of clothes I had now was shocking. I'd given up on stopping the guys from buying me things.

Each one of them purchased something slightly different. I realized they'd color-coded me to their freaking eye color: Rafe black, Nox green, Ares pale blue. Thank God Killian stayed out of that, instead preferring to hide my sweaters and leave his own in their place. Not that I really minded. The way his sweater hung nearly below my knees made me feel like I was constantly cocooned by him.

The man himself was now sitting further up on my bed, his back leaning against the headboard and a slow smile on his face. He'd come in here and made me pack no less than three of his sweaters that he must have rolled around on because they each smelled exactly like him.

I swore it had become a competition to see who could scent on me first. They even stooped low enough to continuously switch out my bodywash to ones that smelled like them. For how immature it all was, I couldn't help the happy, bubbly feeling in my stomach. We'd fallen into a routine that was almost domestic. The guys worked on growing the business to support the new production of side-effect-free blockers while I connected with other omegas, figuring out different ways we could help them, including working out a hotline that omegas currently in duress could call and receive the help they needed.

Flora's parents helped her come out of hiding, sticking to the story of her alpha trying to murder her and that she'd escaped to her parents for safety. It was an easy sell that she was too afraid to come forward, and no one dared to question her after finding out how she got mated in the first place.

I could only hope everything went that smoothly. Anxiety crawled under my skin, thinking about what would happen if our plans didn't work out. What if none of the omegas showed up to donate and we couldn't make enough blockers? What if alphas protested against their right to buy their mate? My heart beat faster in my chest as I thought about the possible fight ahead of us.

Killian's arms wrapped around my waist, pulling me against a warm chest, and a calmness settled my nerves. He kissed the top of my head. "Breathe, B. It's all going to work out."

I tilted my head back so my chin rested on his chest, and my gaze met his. "How do you know?"

He smirked and rubbed slow, soothing circles over my lower back. "Because we won't stop fighting until it does."

I let out a breath and pulled back, feeling lighter knowing I had my pack. I tugged through my bottom drawer, looking for the extra-soft leggings Rafe had bought me. When my fingers brushed against something solid, I moved the exercise pants out of the way.

I pulled back the gift box Rafe had left me, and my stomach dropped. "Shit." My gaze snapped to Killian's.

Killian wore a mischievous grin. "I wondered what happened to that. Rafe's been moping for weeks that he hasn't seen it on you."

My brows pulled together. "I forgot."

"I'm sure he'll be happy to know you didn't toss it."

I pulled the black ribbon and opened the deep purple box, revealing a silver charm bracelet. There were charms that marked unique events of our childhood. I ran my thumb over a pair of ballet slippers. I used to watch their practices through the window since there was no way we could afford to let me join. Rafe had caught me one day and spent the afternoon spinning me around, practicing pirouettes with me. There was a small bike, no doubt representing the one they'd gifted me on my tenth birthday, then laughed when I could never get the hang of riding it. There were at least ten other charms, all equally important.

My heart swelled in my chest, and tears stung my eyes, looking up at where Killian watched me. "I screwed up, didn't I?"

He shrugged. "Yup."

I gave him a quick wave, already heading for the door to track down Rafe.

I rushed into Rafe's room, my breath catching at the sight of him bent over his own suitcase. His gaze trailed over me, no doubt checking for why I was so panicked, before landing on my wrist where I'd attached the bracelet.

A slow smile lifted the corner of his mouth, and he pushed his hair off his face. "I was wondering about that."

"I'm so sorry. I didn't throw it out, I just forgot I tucked it away in my dresser."

One of his brows rose in question, amusement trickling down the bond. "But you thought about it. Tossing it, I mean."

I could feel my cheeks flush red. "Only for a second."

He closed the distance between us in three large strides, taking my wrist in his hand and tracing the bracelet. "It looks stunning on you."

My eyes welled, and Rafe caught a stray tear with his thumb before it could roll down my cheek. "Thank you. It's perfect."

I lifted onto my toes, crushing my mouth to his, wanting to show him just how much I appreciated it.

———

We jogged through the airport, catching curious looks from everyone we passed. In many ways, it was similar to the only other time I'd been on a plane—most of the betas milling around the terminals had never seen an omega before and were not shy about staring. This time though, I stared right back, making direct eye contact until they looked away out of sheer awkwardness.

"Do we have to run?" Flora asked, her breath coming out in pants. "Our flight isn't for ages."

"They start boarding in five minutes," Wes told her, shifting her suitcase to his other arm. He threw her a wink. "Want me to carry you?"

She scoffed. "Ugh. No." She straightened and walked faster, as if to prove she could.

He laughed, and I assumed he knew that would be her reply. Wes's smug grin lingered, but Flora didn't seem to care that he was playing her like a violin—it was still working.

"What is the deal there?" Killian asked me, too quietly for Wes to hear.

I shrugged. "I don't know. None of our business."

"Come on," Killian barked a laugh. "Everything is your business."

I shot him a playful glare. "That isn't true. I have matured, and I'm not prying."

"In other words, she's watching from the sidelines for plausible deniability." Rafe came up beside me and threaded his fingers through mine. "It's okay, Peanut. You don't have to pretend."

I huffed. "I'm not nosey. I just care a lot about my friends."

Killian kissed me on the top of my head. "We know, baby."

"Ladies and gentlemen, on behalf of the captain, we would like to welcome you aboard this afternoon. At this time, please make sure your seat backs and tray tables are in their upright and locked position—"

Ares leaned over me and reached for my tray table, flipping it up. I raised my eyebrows at him. "I can do it."

"Did you turn your phone off?"

I furrowed my brows. "I'm not even sure I remembered to bring it. Who do I need to call when you guys are always with me?"

I glanced around at literally everyone I liked in the world sitting around me and smiled. We were seated in first class with almost no one else around us—one of the few perks of the airline being so excited that two omegas were flying with them. Ares sat directly next to me beside the window, and Nox was to my right across the aisle, already reading a book on his Kindle. In front of him sat Wes and Flora, and in front of me and Ares, Killian and Rafe kept accidentally elbowing each other, unable to find enough space for their shoulders even in the giant first-class seats.

"If you are seated next to an emergency exit, please familiarize yourself with the instruction card located in the seat back in front of you."

"What the fuck does that mean?" Ares sat up straighter, and his pale eyes flashed with panic.

I put a hand on his arm. "Calm down, you're fine."

"I'm fine, but what if you're not fine? This is fucking stupid. We should have driven."

"I am also fine," I said patiently. "Why are you suddenly eighty years old?"

He frowned. "I like my feet on the ground."

I softened. "I didn't know you were afraid of flying."

"I'm not afraid of flying." He scowled and didn't continue.

In fairness, it wasn't like we'd been jet-setting around since we were kids. My first time on a plane was when I'd been sent to the Institute, and the whole experience was a little fuzzy. I'd assumed at the time it was because I was so devastated, but in retrospect, maybe it was because I'd taken blockers for the first time, and they weren't the ones made from the hormones of my bond. "This will only be my third time flying." I paused. "No, wait, I also went in Nero's helicopter."

"Fucker," Ares muttered. "He would have a helicopter."

"I want a helicopter." Killian turned around in the seat in front of us, his curls bouncing.

"No," Nox yelled from across the aisle at the same time as Rafe said, "I'll look into it."

I sighed and sunk back into my seat. Things finally felt settled.

We were making real progress with the blocker project. Flora was getting better every day. The guys and I had no more secrets between us, and soon I'd have time to go back into heat and we'd solidify our bond. Things were almost too good. I didn't trust it.

The flight attendant disappeared to take her seat, and the plane started to rattle as we moved into position at the end of the runway. Ares stiffened beside me and turned, if possible, even paler than he already was. I rubbed the center of my chest, frowning. "I'm trying to bask in my moment here, and your anxiety is giving me anxiety."

His lips tipped up like he wanted to laugh but couldn't quite get there. "Sorry, Love." He ran his hand up and down my knee absently.

I flagged down one of the flight attendants not making the announcements and whispered a quick request. What felt like thirty seconds later, she was back, handing me a plastic cup with ice and a couple of mini liquor bottles.

"Thanks." I smiled up at her.

"No problem." She beamed. "Can, I, uh…" She blushed.

I blinked, confused. "Sorry, what was that?"

"No, it's just I've been watching your whole story on social media." She looked at Ares and then quickly back at me when he scowled at her. She giggled nervously. "I was just wondering if I could take your picture?"

"Oh, um." I stumbled over my words, taken aback. "Sure."

She pulled out her phone and snapped a quick photo, angling to try and get everyone in it. Out of the corner of my eye, I spotted Killian leaning into the aisle to be more visible, even as Nox tried to hide.

"Thanks," the flight attendant said breathlessly. "Good luck with everything. Hashtag ignorance isn't bliss."

I blinked. "What?"

"Hashtag…I have no idea why I said that out loud."

"Me neither," Ares said flatly, and I didn't have to look at him to know he was rolling his eyes.

I swatted him on the arm. "Stop it." I turned back to the woman. "Please ignore him. Rudeness is his love language, but he's having a particularly bad moment."

"It's fine," she squeaked.

"What did you mean, hashtag…whatever you just said."

"Oh, it's all over the place. Your speech is on the news and all over social media, and people are talking about freeing the omegas. Look up #ignoranceisntbliss or #blissfulrebellion. Trust me. Thanks for the picture."

My heart pounded, and my chest swelled with combined excitement and nerves. People were talking about this. About us. That was everything I'd wanted, but the reality was nerve-racking.

"Damn, you're famous," Flora said as the flight attendant disappeared.

I smiled but didn't have much time to reply as I sank back in my seat, my mind racing. At that moment, the plane straightened out and trundled forward down the center of the runway. Ares' fingers clamped around my leg.

"You good?" I asked.

"Perfect," he muttered.

I wrinkled my nose. "Maybe we should focus on distraction?"

The front wheels lifted off the ground, and Ares gritted his teeth. "What did you have in mind?"

The corner of my mouth tipped up, and I nudged his untouched drink toward him. "Um, there are movies?" I flicked on the screen on the back of Killian's seat. "How do you feel about superheroes?"

"Thrilled."

"Okay, moving on from that." I sucked on my lip. "Documentary?"

We hit some turbulence as the plane climbed higher and higher into the air, and Ares' fingers slid higher up my thigh, dancing dangerously close to the thin fabric of my panties.

I reached for my jacket and quickly threw it over my lap. "What are you doing?" I hissed, so quietly only he could hear.

"Focusing on distraction."

I gasped, and my eyes widened. "That wasn't what I meant." I glanced around. "Weren't you listening just now? We're practically famous. People will notice."

"Sounds hot."

I made a noise in the back of my throat, somewhere between a laugh and a scoff. "Come on."

"There's no one around but the pack, Love." His fingers moved higher, middle finger brushing against the fabric of my thin cotton panties. "Do you want me to stop?"

His fingers stroked back and forth again, and I shivered, shaking my head. I bit back a moan as he ran two fingers up the outside of my panties, the fabric growing wet under his touch.

He slid the fabric to the side, and goose bumps erupted on my skin as a shiver traveled through my entire body.

I whimpered, and Ares coughed to cover the sound. Ares laughed quietly in my ear. "You need to be quiet, Love. Can you do that for me?"

I nodded, even as my thighs shook, and I had no idea if I would be able to keep that promise.

He ran the tip of one finger lightly over my clit. Too lightly. Just enough to make me want to writhe and beg for more, but I couldn't—not here.

Ares leaned over and buried his face in my neck. To the outside observer, it might have looked like he was sleeping, but under my jacket, he kept running his fingers over me so softly I wanted to scream.

"Do you want more, Love?" he said against my ear, so quietly I had to think for a moment to process what he'd said.

I nodded and shifted my hips forward in my seat to emphasize my point.

The plane dipped low, bouncing through some more turbulence, and Ares pressed the heel of his hand hard against my clit. He thrust two fingers inside me, and I bit the inside of my cheek to keep from crying out.

His fingers moved inside me, fast and unrelenting, and my breaths became uneven.

I glanced across the aisle and met Nox's gaze. His eyes were heated with lust, his Kindle slack in his hand like he'd completely forgotten what he was doing.

My body shattered, fire licking up my stomach as I squeezed my eyes shut in an effort not to cry out. Spots danced behind my eyelids, and it felt like the plane had suddenly dropped a thousand feet.

When I opened my eyes again, Nox's eyes were still heated, but his mouth was thin, like he was trying and failing to look annoyed. "Asshole," he muttered without conviction. "Now everyone is suddenly going to be afraid of flying."

CHAPTER 20
Bliss

"Okay, you're all set!" I said brightly, handing the omega a manilla envelope across the folding table between us. "You can head into lecture hall three."

She ran her thumb across her name stamped along the top. "Thanks so much." She beamed and glanced toward the hallway to our right. "Um, remind me, which way is three? I don't remember a ton about going here for, uh, obvious reasons."

I winced. "That way. Third door on the left."

"Thanks."

I looked down at the clipboard on my table, then up to my laptop screen, comparing my lists. That was twenty-nine check-ins I'd done for names ending in *M* through *S*, and it was only 3:00 p.m. We were way ahead of schedule.

We'd all traveled to California because it was the easiest central location to set up a blood drive for the omegas. The guys were considering opening a lab near the

Institute to start providing blockers directly to the school—this time with my full help and support. At the moment, Killian, Nox, and Ares were out looking at a building for a possible new lab, while Rafe and Wes were here at the Institute with me and Flora.

Feeling the looming presence of the omega still standing in front of my table, I glanced back up. "Oops, sorry, did you have another question?"

She flushed, and her brown eyes crinkled at the corners. "Can my mate come with me?"

I scanned her basic info on my sign-in sheet. Omega Reading had been Magnolia Wright when she attended the Institute seven years ago. She was twenty-eight and mated to an alpha Navy officer, who had accompanied her today rather than sending a bodyguard. My eyes darted across the entrance hall of the Institute, where we'd set up our sign-in tables.

The designated alpha area was next to the door, behind a huge plastic barrier. About twelve alphas milled around, some chatting, some staring into space or playing on their phones. Rafe leaned against the barrier, watching me, and waved when I looked up, his dark eyes flashing. To his left stood a hulking blonde man in a military uniform, scratching his chin over his scent-blocking mask.

I turned back to Magnolia. Her mate looked nice enough, and coming with her to donate to the blocker project spoke volumes about their relationship. Still, I was trying to keep things orderly. "Sorry. We need to keep all the alphas behind the scent screen." I gestured to the plastic barrier. "I understand he's your mate, but there are unmated bodyguards here today, and not every student has started taking the new blockers yet. I need to make sure there are no exceptions for everyone's safety."

Magnolia smiled. "Okay, I gotcha. Thank you for doing all this. I just wanted to tell you I saw your speech on the news, and it was amazing."

"Oh, thanks." I felt the back of my neck heat. "It wasn't really a speech. It was just kind of…well, you know."

"I'm obsessed. You should write a book or something."

I laughed. "Thanks."

She picked up her folder and left, and I let out a sigh, relaxing back in my chair.

"You're doing great."

I swiveled around and grinned when I saw Sarah descending the wide stone staircase that led to the upstairs classrooms. She looked less austere today and more her age, her hair down and a casual blouse over jeans instead of the sharp suits she'd worn around DuPont. I smiled as she approached. "Hey. How are you?"

"I just checked in with the physicians. They've seen nearly forty omegas today, far better than I expected."

I raised my eyebrows. That was better than I expected too. Considering how few registered omegas there were in the country, that was nearly five percent.

I glanced over at the sign-in table next to me, where Flora was stamping the manilla folder of a middle-aged omega in a blue dress. I swallowed down the emotion that nearly rose in my throat. I'd thought coming back to the Institute would upset her, but it was the opposite. She was doing better, channeling all her energy into the blocker initiative and helping to give a lifeline to other victims.

Like she felt me watching her, she looked up and gave me a small smile. Behind her, a huge shadow loomed. The omega taking the folder glanced up at Wes and raised an eyebrow. Down my bond, I felt a hint of amusement and looked up to see Rafe watching the whole thing across the room from behind the alpha divider. He caught my eye and smirked.

"How's it been going at the school?" I asked Sarah while I waited for the next omega to come up to the table. "I see you got to keep your job."

She laughed. "Yeah. And it's been great. Different. I haven't had to do any retrievals since DuPont left, but I don't think they'll be as bad now. I should show you the new protocol packet and get your notes."

"Sure." I nodded enthusiastically. "How is Representative Levi doing?"

After the trial, the representative from Maine had held firm on her threat to oust Omega DuPont and had quickly helped to take back the school. Officially, DuPont had taken a leave of absence to spend more time with her mate and family—who I'd never heard her mention. Unofficially, Representative Levi had threatened to call for a special investigation and the appointment of an oversight committee.

"Good," Sarah said. "At least I think so. You should ask the girls. Their opinion matters more."

I raised my eyebrows. "I'd love to, but I don't think I've seen a single student since we got here."

Sarah frowned and glanced around. "I'm sure we could go ask the headmistress."

I deliberated, looking toward the door. There weren't any omegas waiting outside to be checked in. "Okay. Hang on, I'll be right back."

My eyes collided again with Rafe's across the room,

and he beckoned me to come over. I smiled and jogged over. "Hey," I said when I reached the plastic barrier.

"Hey!" He grinned behind his mask, his voice a little muffled. "How's it going out there?"

"Good, I think. I'm just coming to tell you I'm going to go see the headmistress."

He frowned. "Where?"

I swiveled around, pointing vaguely down the hall. "Uh, I don't know. Her office is that way."

"What are we doing?" Flora called across the hall from her folding table, and her chair scraped on the hardwood floor as she stood up.

"Going on a field trip."

"Nice. I'm coming."

Rafe's brow furrowed, but his eyes darted to Sarah, down the hall, and then back to me. I could practically see him fighting his instinct to tell me I wasn't allowed to go anywhere alone, with the rationale that the Institute was full of omegas on their own with better security than we probably had at the warehouse. "Sure," he said finally. "Have fun."

I grinned, and my eyes darted meaningfully to the other alphas behind the screen. "You too."

He rolled his eyes. "No promises."

Flora and I joined Sarah at the base of the stairs and headed down the hallway that I'd walked countless times on the way to and from classes. Our feet echoed off the floor and vaulted ceilings, and it was all I could do not to shuffle my feet out of habit. I stomped a little louder than I usually had, just to make a point. Flora gave me a knowing look and banged her elbow "accidentally" into a wall sconce as we passed, sending one of the dimly lit bulbs clattering to the floor.

"There's been a huge uptick in casual vandalism since the girls came off blockers," Sarah said.

I pursed my lips, trying not to laugh. "I think the headmistress might just want to let that one go."

"The headmistress quite agrees."

I jumped and turned around, coming face-to-face with a pair of large hazel eyes magnified behind silver wire glasses. "Hi!" I said, inching backward. "Representative Levi, I didn't hear you coming."

"Small feet," the headmistress said, nodding down at her tiny toes peeking out from under a floor-length skirt. "You can call me Headmistress Omega Levi while we're here, Bliss. Or just Delilah, if you like. As for the destruction of the school, I agree with you. It's just things, and when the girls have gotten over this wave of anger, I'm thinking of setting up some intramural sports. Maybe student government."

"Delilah," I said, testing it on my tongue. It sounded weirdly informal. "I think that sounds great."

"Yes, well, I know it seems to you like this place was always horrible, but it really wasn't. The Institute has been around a lot longer than the Assembly, and I'm old enough that I remember how things used to be."

"Can we talk to some of the girls?" I asked eagerly.

It wasn't that I didn't trust Representative Levi did—far more than DuPont—but I didn't go here anymore.

"Of course." The headmistress wafted down the hall, and we followed. She really did walk quietly, though fast for someone so old.

We stopped in front of the door to a lecture hall I

remembered well. Flora and I eyed each other and looked down, hiding laughter.

"One moment," the headmistress said. "I'll go in and get some of the girls."

She slipped into the classroom, and I leaned against the wall to wait. "It really does seem better," I said, meeting Flora's gaze.

"Yeah." She picked at her nails. "We'll see."

Sarah tapped her foot, the sound echoing down the long hallway. I looked over at her. "Anxious?"

"Huh?" she said.

I nodded to her foot.

Wait, no. She wasn't moving.

I spun around, looking for the source of the footsteps.

Then everything went dark.

CHAPTER 21
Bliss

My head pounded as if my brain were expanding, beating itself against the inside of my skull and trying to escape. I moaned, and all that came out was a hoarse, animalistic rasp that tasted of metal and stomach acid. Confusion warred with pain, and I cracked an eye open.

My stomach seized, and my skin seemed to alight with sudden sharp awareness. I blinked furiously, trying to clear my watery eyes, dread coursing through me. There was nothing to see—complete and utter darkness. *What? Where am I?*

My entire life, I'd suffered from nightmares. The worst part about nightmares wasn't the actual images in my brain. It was the feeling of helplessness. The panic kept at bay during the day that crept in at night. About half the time, I knew I was dreaming, but that didn't help. It didn't save me from the horror or the inability to move or scream.

Was I dreaming now? Was this just a new, more vivid terror? Would I know?

I strained my eyes and tried to determine what was real. My head swam, and I pressed a hand to my pounding forehead, whimpering as pain shot through my temples. My blood ran cold. Dreams weren't tactile.

I gasped, a rattling breath tearing at my throat, and I squeezed my eyes shut again. How was it so dark? How did I get here?

The scent was like metal and oil, overpowering everything else and making it hard to think. My breath came too fast and too shallow, even as I tried to fight it. I needed to breathe, calm down, or I would hyperventilate. Easier said than done.

I pressed both palms flat against the ground and took another deep breath through my nose, willing myself to stay grounded. Literally. The world tilted and rocked, as though it were shifting under me.

No, wait. The ground was actually shifting. I was moving.

I opened my eyes again, though it hardly mattered, and ran my fingers along the ground. Not ground—floor, I realized, the heavy smell of industrial steel clicking into place in my brain.

My eyes zeroed in on a sliver of light. I tried to focus. A square—no, a door. I almost shouted, like I'd hit the winning answer on a game show. This was a truck.

My heart immediately sank again.

Knowing that didn't help me. In fact, that knowledge was almost worse. Where the hell was I going? And more importantly, who was driving?

I forced myself to sit up, hands sliding further along the floor, fumbling in the darkness.

"Ah!" I reeled back, surprised, as my fingers met clammy skin.

If I had a shred of doubt left, now I knew for sure I wasn't dreaming.

My heart pounded, so loud it was like a metronome. Who was that? Were they dead? I couldn't focus. Couldn't pick out a scent. Couldn't breathe or remember or think—

"Mmmm." The body made a sound.

I sighed, almost a strangled sob. I wasn't sure if I was relieved or just overwhelmed.

I reached out again, feeling in the darkness. "Hey." My voice was wobbly. "Are you…" I wanted to say, "Are you okay?" But "Who are you?" also came to mind.

The other person shifted against the floor. "What happened?"

"Oh my God." I choked, relief and panic flooding me with equal measure. I recognized the voice. "Sarah."

I crawled over to Sarah where she lay crumpled on the floor and ran my hands along her arms in the dark, feeling for injury.

"Bliss?" she croaked, voice foggy with confusion. "Where are we?"

"I don't know." I searched my memory for how we got here—wherever here was—and came up empty. "We were at the Institute, and…" I broke off as a fresh wave of terror shot through me. "Flora."

I took another breath through my nose, this time scenting the air for my friend's distinctive floral scent. My stomach dropped when I could make it out.

"Where are you going?"

I ignored Sarah and crawled along the side of the truck, fanning out my hands, my knees scraping on the metal ridges of the floor and the sharp edging near the wall. "Flora," I hissed, unsure if we should make noise.

Sarah shuffled around behind me, her clothes scraping against the floor as she sat up. "Is she here?"

"Somewhere…" I crawled faster. How big was this damn truck? "Flora, wake up. Come on, you—"

I broke off as my fingers brushed long tendrils of hair, and the odd sensation of relief and panic hit me at once. She was here, but if she hadn't heard me looking…

I knelt next to her and squinted in the dark, trying to angle to see anything but the tiny amount of light coming through the sliver in the cargo door. I pressed my head to her chest, and relief filled me, like inflating a balloon. "She's breathing."

"Thank God."

My own pounding head and the foul taste in my mouth told me she was probably knocked out but alive. For now.

I felt Sarah's presence at my back and would have jumped if not for her slow approach. "Should we try and wake her up?"

I deliberated. I didn't really know, and we might do more harm than good. I didn't answer, stalling.

I wished we could see our surroundings better or had any way of knowing how long we'd been here. I sniffed the air nervously, checking for anyone else. Sarah's soapy smell and Flora's floral were by far the strongest, but there was also metal, blood, and stale beer. "We're alone in here, but I don't know for how long."

"The last thing I remember is touring the Institute."

"Same."

"So we were probably taken from there," Sarah reasoned, and I felt her shift around. She pushed to her feet, stumbling a little with the motion of the truck. "We need a strategy. Can you smell anything?"

I rattled off the list of scents in the room. "That doesn't tell me who took us, though, or where we're going."

Sarah hummed, thinking, and I heard the snap of bone as she presumably cracked her knuckles. "Try to wake up Flora. I'm just going to try something."

I still wasn't sure if I should mess with an unconscious person, but I was pretty sure we weren't knocked out by a head injury, and we didn't have a lot of options.

I gently patted my friend's cheek, whispering in her ear as Sarah's footsteps echoed around the inside of the truck. Every so often, she would mutter something random, and her voice rang out, changing in volume as she moved. Finally, Flora groaned in the back of her throat, groggy and not fully present.

"Okay," Sarah said, her voice coming closer. "It's a moving van or some kind of semitruck. Maybe nine yards long, give or take the difference of my feet, and there's nothing in here but us."

I raised my eyebrows, impressed, then realized she couldn't see me. "How do you know?"

"You hear the echo?" She stamped her foot. "If there was anything in here, it would muffle the noise. Also, I didn't bump into anything walking across it."

"Fair enough, but how does that help us?"

"Because this kind of truck has a detached cab. Whoever is driving can't hear us back here at all. Also, we haven't taken any turns or changed speeds since we woke up, which means we're on a highway."

"Shit. I always want to get kidnapped with you."

I whipped my head around at the sound of Flora's sarcastic voice and almost laughed. Or would have if the situation weren't so serious. "How are you feeling?"

"Like I took a load of chloroform to the face."

"Is that what it was?" My mouth dropped open.

Flora sat up and made a noise like she might throw up. "Wild guess?"

I grimaced. She had a point. I wouldn't have been surprised if that was how they got us.

I rubbed my temples. "Okay, so we're on a highway. How does that info help us? Even if we can get that door open, we're going to fall out into the road and die on impact."

Sarah sighed, deflating a little. "If we go through a toll or something, that would be a good time to open the doors, but otherwise, yeah. We don't have a lot of good options."

"What about your pack, Bliss?" Flora asked. Her voice was still a little off but quickly gaining steam. "Can't they feel you?"

I cocked my head to the side, putting a hand to my chest absently. Depending on how long ago we were taken, the guys had to already be looking for me.

I reached down the bond, searching for them, and met only hollow rage and frustration. Closing my eyes tight, I focused harder, willing them to feel me. My body buzzed, adrenaline tingling in my fingers, warming my middle. The intensity of the anger hit me all at once, nearly crippling me, and I doubled over.

"Bliss." Sarah put her hand on my back. "What happened?"

I gasped. "I think…" I coughed and tried again. Damn, that connection was not to be played with. "I think I've been offline, and they weren't sure what that meant."

"They thought you were dead?" Flora sounded horrified, and I recalled the pain she'd gone through when her mate died, even though she'd despised him.

"No, they just can't find us and couldn't feel me."

"So now that they can feel you, will they come get you?"

"I'm sure they're already trying, but it's not GPS." I pressed my hands to my eyes. "We're going to have to hope they find some other way."

Sarah hummed, thinking. "That's not good enough. They'll have to stop eventually, either because we get where we're going or for gas."

"Okay," I said quickly, my heart racing. A plan was good—that at least felt like we were doing something.

"There's only one door, so they'll have to come in that way," Flora supplied. "Right?"

"Yeah." Sarah smacked her lips like she was thinking. "I think there's only enough seats in the truck for two, maybe three people?"

"What if there's more people on the other side?" I asked.

"If we're outnumbered, or it's all alphas, we're fucked anyway," Sarah said. "But if it's betas, and there's only one or two, we might be able to rush them."

I bit my lip. "So instead of waiting by the doors, we make them come inside to get us and try to slip past them?"

"Basically, yeah."

Flora didn't look convinced. "It might work if they're not expecting it, unless they just shoot us."

"They won't," I said. "No one kidnaps omegas to just kill them."

I took their silence as combined agreement and horror.

I straightened my shoulders. It wasn't a great plan, but I didn't have a better one. I could kind of see the logic. If it was our only plan, I was damn well going to act like it was going to work. "Come on." I reached down and helped pull Flora up. "Let's move back from the doors."

We settled down in the center of the truck to wait, and I closed my eyes, swaying back and forth with the motion of the road. I refocused on the emotions roiling in my chest—anger, determination, love.

A tiny kernel of hope swelled, and I prayed that wherever they were, the guys were working on a better plan than us.

What felt like an hour later, the truck finally slowed down, taking a few turns before rolling to a slow stop.

My breath sped up, and my heart raced. I gripped Flora's hand tightly next to me as we waited for the doors to open.

"Remember to wait," Sarah said for probably the tenth time.

She was a planner, clearly controlling her own fear by having an escape strategy. That said, she had been security for the Institute; she probably knew better than us how to get out of something like this.

The scent of industrial grease, gasoline, and sweat

mingled with gunpowder hit me as the door opened. Two dark figures stood framed against the light of the entrance, looking in on us.

"Here they are," one gruff male voice said.

Beta, my mind screamed, connecting both the pitch of the voice and the stature of the speaker to the scent.

"Get ready," Sarah muttered so low that no beta could hear. "Wait until they move out of the way."

My heart pounded, and I forced myself to breathe evenly, counting to ten in my head.

"There's only supposed to be two," the other man said —also a beta. "What the fuck happened?"

"I don't know, man. I just grabbed all of them."

The larger of the two swung his leg up onto the truck bed, coming closer to inspect us. Sarah's breathing picked up, almost excited, as the scent of her adrenaline spiked. "Okay. Three, two…"

The man took two steps into the truck and squinted. "Fuck, Joey. That one isn't an omega."

So fast I almost didn't see his hand move, he reached into his belt and pulled out a gun. The thwup of the silencer sounded, and something wet and sticky splattered my face.

I froze. Sound stopped, and silence pressed in on my eardrums before being replaced by a distant roar. Sarah's body slumped to the floor beside me, blood and brain matter leaking from the fragmented hole in the back of her skull.

I screamed.

CHAPTER 22
Killian

"Do you think she'll want to move out here?" Nox asked, storing a box on one of the many metal shelves lining our new lab. He hung his vest on one of the plastic waiting room chairs and rolled his crisp dress shirt sleeves up. Sweat dripped down his neck, catching on his collarbone—

"Kill, quit checking me out, and answer the question."

My gaze snapped up to meet his crinkled eyes behind black-rimmed glasses. "Honestly, I don't really care. If she wants to move here, then that's where we'll go."

He tilted his head. "Yeah, true enough."

Ares slammed a large box on one of the steel medical tables, and Dr. Lewinsky winced. "Hurry the fuck up. I want to get to the Institute sooner than later. I don't like leaving her like this."

"She's with Rafe, man. She's not alone." I tugged on the bond, so much fainter with her on blockers, and was met with dead air. I paused for a second, trying to feel her, but

Nox and Ares were arguing about something. "Shut up. Everyone shut the fuck up." I took a deep breath, searching through the bond, but nothing. Panic ran under my skin, and the hairs on my arms stood up. "Fuck. Can you feel her?"

The scent of cranberries and hot ginger burned my nose. Ares threw a box across the room, and the sound of shattering glass cut through the air when it collided with the wall.

"Where the fuck is she?" He shook his head, his gaze unfocused, and dug his fingers into his white-blond hair. "I can't feel her."

"Fuck. Quiet, I'm calling Rafe." Nox's bark sent a shiver down my spine. He hit the call button on his phone and brought it to his ear. "What the fuck, Rafe?"

I couldn't hear what was being said on the other end, but before I could say anything, Ares had already pulled it out of Nox's hand and put it on speaker. "Rafe, where's our girl?" Ares' voice came out hard and a touch unhinged.

"She was just here. Then the bond went silent." His words were breathy, and the sound of running feet on the tile floor was clear through the speaker.

Nox, Ares, and I stayed quiet, listening to what was happening on the other end of the phone.

A distant "Hey! You can't come through here. It's omegas only."

"Fuck off."

"Stay where you are, or I'll Taser you." Whoever that was, their voice shook, no doubt terrified of a pissed-off Rafe.

Rafe growled low. "I fucking dare you." His ragged

breath came through the line. "Listen, something's wrong with my omega. As soon as I know she's safe, I'll head back to the alpha side. Now, fuck off, or I'll knock you out."

"I'm sorry, sir, but I can't do that. I promised Omega Bliss I'd keep the omegas and alphas separate." Fuck, the guy was just trying to do his job.

"Sit down and don't move." Rafe's bark came out strong, and there was no more resistance as the sound of his running feet continued. The guard was no doubt pissed, but it was better than the alternative. We'd have to get them those fancy earpieces the police betas wore. Rafe's breath grew louder with each second.

"What the fuck is happening, Rafe." Ares sounded raw as he glared down at Nox's phone as if it personally offended him.

A female voice cut through the speaker. "Alpha Farral, I saw what happened." Her voice broke around the vowels, and a coldness closed in on me.

"What do you mean, what happened?" Rafe's voice was harsh but controlled, obviously not wanting to terrorize whoever he was speaking to.

There was a sob, quickly cut off. "Someone took them. They put something over their faces, and they all went limp."

My heart rate slowed with each word, and ice filled my veins as my emotions shut down with each pulse.

"Who was taken?" Ares growled, heat practically radiating off him with his anger.

"Flora, Sarah, and…Bliss."

A man's voice came through and the sound of a struggle. "I caught a beta outside. Looks like they left him behind."

The world went silent as the ice took me fully under. Nothing but a cold, menacing calm remained.

———

By the time we got to the Institute, Rafe already had the captured beta tied to a chair, his face covered in blood from the split in his eyebrow and lip, and his chin tipped up with defiance. Wes stood behind him, guarding the door, and nodded to us as we entered—his jaw was tight, his face a mask of rage.

A small thrill ran through me, and a growl rumbled my chest as I took in the hostage. The beta's eyes went round, and the cockiness he'd been holding on to vanished as he watched us walk in.

Ares, Nox, and I crowded closer, forming a semicircle with Rafe facing the beta.

"Where is she?" I didn't bother to hold back my bark.

"Listen, I'm just the lookout. They paid me a few bucks. I don't know anything." The beta looked away from me, his eyes pleading with the others. *Good luck with that.*

"Where did they take her?" Ares leaned over, his hot rage scenting the air.

The guy shook on the chair, struggling against his binds. "I don't know. Could be anywhere."

This asshole mustn't have known we could scent his lie. I stepped closer, and Ares looked me over, clearly seeing the state I was in, and got out of my way. I crouched down and cut one of the beta's hands free. He went to grab me, but my bark had him under my control.

"Undo your pants and take your dick out."

The beta's fear stank, and his hands trembled, unable to fight against me.

Nox put his hand on my back. "The hell are you doing?"

I shook him off me, a low snarl his only warning. He pulled back, but I could scent his worry. It had been a long time since I'd lost myself in the cold void I'd buried inside me. The beta's dick lay limp outside his pants, and he tried to cover it with his free hand.

A sneer tipped up the side of my mouth, and I grabbed the knife I'd brought from the lab and handed it to him. His brows furrowed, and he didn't take it.

"Take the fucking knife."

His hand instantly wrapped around the handle, the sharp blade nicking my finger, and blood pooled on my thumb. I couldn't feel it—I couldn't feel anything when I leaned closer, fully in striking distance. The beta was frozen in place like a deer in headlights.

My voice was low and menacing, full of promise. "It's up to you, beta. I can either make you cut off your own dick and sit back and enjoy while you eat it. Or you can tell me where they took them."

The beta sucked in a breath. "What? Jesus, I already told you I don't know."

"I was hoping you'd go that route. You'll confess anyway, but I'm going to like this part." My bark came out clear and firm. "Cut. It. Off."

His hand shook as the blade touched the base of his dick, red blood against his pale skin. "Wait. No—"

"Stop," I barked, and he slumped into his chair, chest heaving.

Nox glanced my way, then to the beta. "I'd hurry the fuck up if I were you."

"There's a group of low-powered alphas that help move betas. They were excited about how much the job paid to pick up two omegas. They have a few locations. I only know the one. It's a warehouse in Barstow. You can't miss it. It's on the corner of Westview and Vimy."

A hint of warmth sliced through the ice. We'd get her back. "Is that all you know?"

The beta nodded, "Yes. I swear."

Truth.

I grabbed the knife from his hand and split his neck, stepping to the side to avoid the stream of blood. His eyes were wide on mine, then went blank.

I turned to Ares, Rafe, Nox, and Wes. "Let's go."

They stepped further away from me, then followed to the rented truck.

———

My heart rate spiked moments before Bliss' bond crashed back into my gut like a punch, cracking through the cold shell I'd wrapped myself in. My relief at feeling her was quickly replaced with anger as her fear felt like a knife.

Ares' fist slammed into the dashboard where he sat in the front seat beside Wes, who was now glancing at us, brows furrowed, before returning to the road. He'd been just as much of a wreck as the rest of us, and I knew Flora was responsible for that. If I didn't know it was impossible for a beta to mate an omega, I'd have sworn they were.

"What the fuck is happening? You know I can't feel shit," Wes asked.

A growl ripped from my chest, echoed by Nox, Rafe, and Ares as the feeling of helplessness sank in. My instincts screamed to get to her, and the hour we'd been stuck in the truck felt like torture. Nox's fingers entwined with mine, pulling them on his lap, his thumb drawing slow circles over my palm like I'd seen him do with Bliss a million times. His piercing green eyes met mine. "We are getting her back, Killian. Just breathe."

I took three large breaths through my nose, letting the fact that his words didn't smell like a lie calm me. We would get her back, then tie her to the fucking bed while we filled her until she was round with our kids, then do it over and over again. The image had my dick twitching, and a hint of honey wafted off me.

"What the hell are you thinking about?" Rafe growled from the other side of Nox.

I shrugged, leaning into Nox's reassurance. "What are we going to do to her once we get her back?"

Rafe gave me a sharp look, then rubbed his palm over his eyes. "You're fucking crazy."

I spun the knife in my hand, still coated in beta blood. "Just wait 'til you see what I do to the guys that took her."

The tires screeched, and I slid into Nox's side with a grunt as Wes took a hard right into a warehouse parking lot. There was a giant U-Haul sign on the top of the building. It only took a second for the five of us to rush into the building, the glass door nearly shattering at the force of Ares opening it. A short beta walked into the open bay. He couldn't be over eighteen, and the bitter smell of cranberries filled the air.

"Um, can I help you guys—"

Rafe had him lifted by his collar and pinned to the wall before he could finish. "Where the fuck are they?"

The beta trembled, his eyes wide on Rafe. "Who?"

"Where the fuck are the omegas?" Ares' bark echoed through the warehouse.

"I don't know, man. I've never met an omega."

My stomach dropped out. He wasn't lying. I tilted my head back and took deep breaths before I ripped the kid apart for just being here.

Nox pulled Rafe back, letting the beta's feet land solid on the ground. "Are you able to track a truck for us?"

The kid looked between us, fear still pungent. "Depends if you know what truck it is."

"We know where it came from."

"Okay...yeah. Okay, I can check the GPS and find it." He pointed toward a desk a few feet away, and Rafe and Nox moved back, letting the kid go behind the counter. He typed on the computer, then asked for the information. After Nox gave the clerk the Institute's address, his hand tightened on the computer mouse, and he looked up. "I found it."

My shoulders loosened, some of the tension letting go. "Where?"

The beta snapped up straight and rattled off the address. "135 East County Parkway, Henderson, Nevada."

Fuck.

CHAPTER 23
Bliss

My stomach roiled, and I vomited all over the floor of the truck.

"What the fuck!" The big beta grabbed my arm, wrenching me forward toward the mouth of the truck. "What's wrong with you?"

There was blood on my face, on my arms, all over the floor. The sound of the silencer pounded in my head: *Thwup, Thwup, Thwup.*

I stumbled a little, stepping into the puddle of blood leaking across the floor, and another scream rose in my throat. My screams came out as sobs, and I choked, my stomach twisting again.

The man holding me by the bicep gave me a rough shake. "Shut the fuck up."

"Shhhh," Flora said behind me, her voice an urgent hiss. She rubbed my back, half soothing, half warning. "Come on, you're okay. *You're okay.*" The last bit sounded like a demand and a plea at once.

I met her eyes—haunted and practically vacant. "Stay alive."

"Dude, careful with the omegas," the other beta yelled.

My gaze zeroed in on him. He wore a backward baseball cap that would have looked more at home on a teenager than a man in his forties and a T-shirt with a casino logo and a screen printing of the Las Vegas Strip.

He overpronounced the word "Dude," drawing it into two syllables, and my brain latched onto that one innocuous thing as something to focus on. Something other than the body at my feet or the screaming still going on in my head.

Careful with the omegas. Does that mean he isn't going to kill us?

They had just proven they had no problem getting rid of people or—I swallowed—things that didn't benefit them anymore. This was not a good time to play hero—I needed to follow the rules and stay alive.

"Alright, get your ass in gear." The one holding on to my arm let go of me and shoved me forward toward his friend. "No more drama."

I nodded and walked out of the truck, knowing that Flora was doing the same behind me.

Thwup, Thwup. Thwup. My footsteps echoed across the floor. *Thwup, Thwup, Thwup.* My heart pounded in my ears. *Stay alive.*

It was barely brighter outside the truck than in. The betas marched us over to a metal bench, like the kind inside a subway, and forced us to sit down. The taller of the two men, the one who had shot Sarah, pulled a handful of zip ties out of the pocket of his black jeans.

He looked at the bench, then at us, then shrugged.

Running the ties through the back of the iron slats, he cuffed one to me and one to Flora, then stepped back to admire his handiwork. I stared at him, trying to memorize his face in case it was relevant. He looked a bit like a very average-looking Chris Pratt. The other guy—Joey—had no celebrity look-alike I could think of but reminded me of a pointy-faced goat.

As he stepped back, I got a better view of our surroundings. We had stopped in the center of what looked like some kind of old, abandoned parking garage. The scent in the air was damp, like mildew and street sewage mixed with construction materials. There were old, faded lines of parking spaces on the pavement, and the concrete ceiling was low but not so low that the truck couldn't fit inside. To our right was the door to a fire exit—with my luck, probably locked, and some broken ticket machines.

Judging from the "Exit this way" and "Keep right" painted on the walls with corresponding arrows, we were underground, though likely by only one level. Maybe two.

I ran through all of this very fast—trying to mimic the deductive reasoning Sarah had displayed in the truck. Without my nose—by far my best asset—working quite right, I was missing some of my best clues, but even a normal beta would have been able to smell the scent of sweat coming off gun-happy Chris Pratt and the gunpowder on his hands.

The other man—goat-faced Joey—had no obvious scent, but his Nevada T-shirt might be a clue. Could I assume that meant we had left California, or was it a coincidence?

Bad Chris's eyes darted over me, and I shivered,

revolted by the obvious desire in his gaze. He wasn't an alpha, but he could still be a creep, and he was still obviously dangerous. His eyes moved from me to Flora, and my vision blurred, anger overtaking my discomfort.

"Hey!" I said a little too loudly and nearly winced. Now I was going against my own instincts to sit down, shut up, and stay alive.

He focused on me, and suddenly, I came up short. Questions like "Who are you?" and "What's happening?" were pointless. It was obvious what was happening, and he wouldn't tell me who he was or who hired him.

"My mates will fucking kill you," I settled on. "Do you understand what you've gotten yourself into? Your only option now is to run and hope you get a good head start."

He blinked at me, then looked up at Joey. They burst out laughing.

My stomach rolled. *Awesome.*

"Your mate is the one that called us, girlie."

My stomach jolted—more in confusion than anything else—and for a moment, I blinked at him. "What—" Then, I got it. "Nero."

I couldn't believe that wasn't my first thought. Except maybe that Nero tended to do things the bureaucratic way and had no reason to take Sarah or Flora.

My stomach roiled again at the thought of Sarah simply being in the wrong place at the wrong time.

"Your mate is coming to pick you up," Bad Chris said. "What do you think, Joey? Maybe he'll let us keep this one."

He reached out to touch Flora, but goat-faced Joey swatted him away before he could. "Fuck off, dude. We should sell her, and if you touch her, I don't think they're worth as much."

I ground my teeth. *So close, Joey. Why couldn't you stop talking before the suggestion of trafficking?*

Bad Chris thumbed the gun in his belt and glanced at me as though thinking about asking the rules and then thought better of it. "I'll google it."

I ground my teeth, rage coursing through me—that was good. Rage was a more useful emotion than anything else right now. If only I wasn't on blockers; I could have really used an adrenaline boost from my guys right now to supplement that rage.

The betas turned away from us. "Did you call him yet?" Bad Chris asked.

"Yeah. On his way."

I leaned over to Flora, trying to keep my voice low enough that their inferior beta hearing wouldn't pick it up. "Nero will probably only want me, so maybe I can distract him."

"Don't be stupid. I wouldn't let you do that," she hissed out of the corner of her mouth.

I bit my lip. I wouldn't let her do that either, and therein lay our biggest problem. I was more likely to try and protect Flora than I was to protect myself, and she was undoubtedly the same. That was a shitty catch-22.

"The guys will find me eventually," I said, and I was certain of that.

Now, more than ever, I knew they would always find me. Still, they weren't superheroes, and they could always be too late.

"What does Nero want?" I asked.

Flora shot me a look. "Don't. You're going to get yourself killed."

I frowned apologetically, even as the sound of the silencer rang in my head again, reminding me that she was completely serious.

"Listen to your friend," the Chris Pratt guy said. "We didn't sign up to listen to you whine."

I mulled that over. That sounded like he was just hired muscle—or lack of muscle in this case. A random, unaffiliated guy who wouldn't be traced back to Nero. Probably paid well, but also likely not loyal to him.

"Hey," I tried one more time. "You know Nero isn't going to let you leave here."

The betas glanced back at me. "Shut up, girl."

I bit my lip but kept going. They couldn't kill us before Nero got back…probably. "He's not going to want witnesses. I'm all over the news, you know, and her mate is a congressman. He hired you because no one knows who you are. You think he doesn't have staff who would have done this for him? He wants no record."

I was so glad that betas couldn't smell lies.

The men looked at each other, then back at me.

Bad Chris sneered, but his eyes betrayed a hint of doubt. "Don't waste your breath, bitch. We're not listening to you."

"I don't know, dude," said Joey. He pulled his friend a few feet away so they could chat.

A little further. Come on. If they walked far enough out of sight, maybe I could get started on trying to figure out these zip ties. They stepped just beyond the edge of the truck, and I went to work immediately.

"Lean forward," I told Flora.

"One step ahead of you."

She was running her ties up and down against the metal bars of the bench. I imitated her.

"Look at the truck," Flora hissed, and she worked her ties against the metal bars.

I did, and I had to swallow down the lump in my throat at the shadowed figure still visible inside.

Thwup. Thwup. Thwup. "What is it?"

"Those things have trackers, right? Or at least check-in points?"

It took me a moment to figure out what she meant, and then I caught sight of the logo on the side of the rental moving company. We looked at each other. "Maybe."

I leaned forward further, and the ties cut into the skin of my wrists. Tears pricked at the edges of my vision, and I beat it back. I didn't have time to cry.

Flora's ties snapped, and she let out a breath that was almost a sob. She turned to me, her dark hair clinging to the wet streaks on her cheeks. "Here. Let me help."

The door to the emergency exit banged open, and Flora jumped, returning her hands behind her back. I braced myself at the same time as my stupid heart leapt, hoping to see the guys. Dread landed in my stomach as Nero stepped into my line of sight, his gaze trained directly on me.

"What, no gasp of shock? You used to have the most entertaining reactions."

I gritted my teeth, refusing to react. Anything I did would just give me away. He'd smell my fear, anger, and loathing, and I didn't want him to have any of it. He didn't deserve the satisfaction.

He looked less put together than he had the other times I'd seen him, like he was unraveling at the seams. His blond hair was dirty, stringy, and sticking up in odd places. His clothing was unironed, and he had a suit coat thrown on over a T-shirt, like he'd worn half an outfit. Somehow, this felt like it couldn't all be about me. But then again, who was I to judge the bruised ego of a crazy person?

He stepped up and stood directly in front of me, running one finger down my cheek. He stopped at my chin and tilted my face up so I was forced to meet his cold eyes. "How was your day, honey?" he said, voice full of sarcastic malice.

I reeled back and spit in his face. "Fuck yourself."

Time slowed as Nero's face split into a mask of rage. He raised his hand to wipe my saliva off his cheek. "Bitch. When are you going to learn your place?"

Just as I expected, he raised the same hand and brought it down across my face, hard enough that my head whipped to the right. Involuntary tears rose in my eyes, but I didn't resist, letting all my weight flop to the side. My already weakened zip ties snapped with the force of the motion. I gritted my teeth against the pain and kept my hands behind my back, pretending nothing had happened. *Worth it.*

"When are you going to learn I'm never going to belong to you?" I said with as much venom as I could muster.

He bent so we were on the same eye level and smiled, genuinely this time—or genuine for him. He wrapped his fingers around my throat. "But that's where you're wrong. You do belong to me in every way that counts, and now I need you to help me retract some vicious lies you told that are creating problems for me."

I stared at him. Was he insane? "Why would I ever help you?"

His smile grew wider. "Because I don't think you want anyone to find out your friend killed her mate, do you?"

I gasped—one of those entertaining reactions that Nero had been hoping for, I supposed—and he laughed. I didn't care. Flora and I looked at each other, and I knew we were thinking the same thing. How did he find out?

With Flora miraculously turning up alive, there probably would have been suspicious questions, but her parents had been all over it. Lawyers, publicists, friends in the government, I didn't even know. Sometimes I forgot that Flora was rich and that her father was the kind of alpha who had an omega mate because he was important and not because he gamed the system. Regardless, Nero shouldn't have known—unless he didn't know and he was guessing. Had our reactions just told him?

The sound of Flora's mate tumbling down the stairs combined in my head with the silencer of the gun, the locking of a door, and the pounding of my heart. *Thud. Click. Thwup.*

I needed to breathe.

"Hey, man," Joey greeted Nero loudly, striding over.

Nero stepped back from me and turned his nose up at Joey—literally. "What is that stench of blood?"

"Oh," he laughed. "No big. We just had an extra on board."

Nero glanced at the truck, and his face twisted in rage. For a moment, I thought it was about Sarah, but—

"You fucking imbecile. What is this?"

"Um, a truck?"

Nero blinked at him in a way that conveyed so much violence it was oddly poetic. "Is it your truck?"

"No. Our truck is at the shop, see, 'cause my cousin had this thing, and then—" He broke off, seeming to realize he was in very real danger. *Good job, Joey.*

Nero looked in the truck, then back to us and to the two betas, now evidently thinking. A growl bubbled up in his throat. Bad Chris seemed to shrink, no longer so cocky with a bigger dog in the room.

"You have created quite a problem for me, boys," Nero said in a tone that promised murder.

Joey glanced at me, and I wondered if he was thinking about what I said. Nero would kill him. I gave him a tiny nod as if to say, *You should run, or better yet, shoot this asshole.* It was a lot of words for a nod, but I hoped he was listening.

The doors opened again, and I looked up, my heart pounding double time, hope filling me.

But no one stood there.

I blinked in confusion at the empty space beyond the door. We all turned to stare.

Another crash echoed through the parking garage, rattling off the walls and through the cavernous space. A car careened inside, stopping just behind the truck, and all the doors flew open, revealing my alphas.

A bullet flew through the air, hitting the large Chris Pratt beta, the one who had killed Sarah, right in the neck. Blood sprayed everywhere, again splattering my arms, but this time, I didn't vomit. I watched him topple to the pavement in a pool of his own blood. *Good riddance.*

Nero and Joey turned in unison to see the pack and Wes all getting out of the car, seemingly before it had come to a complete halt. Flora and I took the opportunity of their turned backs to jump to our feet.

The sound of me standing behind him had Nero spinning to look at me. His face twisted again, rage and mania flashing across his features.

My eyes darted to the beta's dead body, zeroing in on the gun in his belt. My adrenaline spiked, and I was sprinting around the bench and toward the gun before I knew what I was doing.

"Stop!" Nero reached for me, his fingers grazing my hair.

"Bliss!" Flora tried to get between us, shoving him back with all her strength.

Nero growled and swatted her like a fly, her entire body flying backward. She bounced off the bench with a sickening crunch that could only be her skull and slumped to the pavement as my lungs seized, panic overtaking me. Wes' incoherent scream reverberated through the garage, the echo as sickening as the sound of the crunch. *Thud. Click. Thwup. Crunch.*

The beta's arms came around me where I'd frozen to watch Flora.

"I've got her," Joey yelled in nervous triumph as he held me in front of him a foot or so off the ground. "If you shoot me, I'll shoot her."

"Don't fucking touch her," someone yelled. Ares or maybe Rafe—their voice was distorted by the echoes of the garage and the ringing in my ears.

I stared out at the scene in front of me, my head a mess of sound. The guys carried guns but seemed reluctant to keep shooting at this range in case they hit us by mistake. Wes held Flora, and she blinked up at him, a little dazed.

I breathed again, trying to find focus in all the chaos. I imagined for a moment I could hear the breathing of my pack beside me, though they were too far away. No echoes. Just their breathing and my own heart.

"He's not going to let you leave, especially after that truck," I said so only Joey could hear. "Stay alive."

And then, I let my body go limp, just like I'd practiced a thousand times.

Joey dropped me. I crashed to the ground, my knees slamming into the pavement, and I yelped but kept moving, crawling toward the puddle of blood and the body with the gun. My breath came in fast, erratic pants.

Out of the corner of my eye, Joey backed up, making a break for the door.

"Fucking cunt, get back here," Nero screamed, tearing after me.

I reached the body and fumbled for the gun just as he came up behind me. His fingertips grazed the back of my head, but I turned around, pointing the gun at his face. Our eyes connected at the last second, and I breathed a sigh of relief before pulling the trigger.

Thwup.

CHAPTER 24
Wes

I shifted my weight in the uncomfortable hospital chair, knocking over two mostly empty coffee cups with my elbow. *Shit.*

I looked over to the cot three feet away, where Flora was still deep asleep. She didn't move as the cups clattered to the floor. I sighed in relief.

Flora had pulled the thin blanket over her shoulders and curled onto her side, facing me. A small bandage wrapped around her head was the only thing indicating she was injured. Well, other than being laid out in a hospital.

The room was specifically designed for omegas. There was a special ventilation system, a guard on duty, and no other occupant. Other than that, it looked like a typical sterile patient room. The nurse had turned off the overhead fluorescent lights, saying something about how they would aggravate Flora's concussion.

She looked peaceful, her even breathing easing some of

the tension crawling up my skin. Fucking Christ, it had been close. I swore I felt my fucking heart stop when she collapsed.

Nothing in my life had prepared me to see her limp like that, and the pause between me reaching her and her next breath felt like a lifetime. Her lashes had dropped over her eyes, near black with over dilated pupils. The only thing that stopped me from losing it was her tight grip on my hand, tethering me to her.

The door opened slowly, and Flora turned away when the light cast over her face. A low rumble formed in my chest but quickly cut off as Bliss walked in, a nurse walking close behind her.

Bliss held two coffees from the cafeteria downstairs. She handed one to me and propped her back on the door. "How is she?"

I lifted the cup, and the bitter taste filled my mouth. "Same as she was an hour ago. She hasn't woken."

The nurse nodded as though I were talking to her. "That's to be expected. I'll check her vitals now."

She bustled over to Flora's monitor while reading something on a clipboard. I nodded to Bliss as if to say, *Well, there you go.*

The middle-aged doctor had already assured us it was a mild concussion. Flora staying the night was an extra precaution because she was an omega, and the hospital was more than happy to accommodate. That didn't stop me and Bliss from watching over her.

Bliss rubbed her hands over her face. She looked exhausted. It was a sheer miracle the guys had let her stay this long. Although there was a fat chance they'd ever say no to her again. The power of four alphas in the palm of one small omega. I would think that was a bad idea if it wasn't clear she was just as much in love with them as they were with her.

"I can stay with her. You should get some rest." Her nose scrunched up, and her voice was light. "Maybe a shower."

There was no fucking way I was leaving this room without Flora. I held up my cup. "Thanks for the coffee, but I'm good."

Bliss smiled at me, then glared at the window as if she could see the guys through the closed blinds. She let out an exasperated huff, pressing her palm below her ribs and rolling her eyes. "I'm being summoned."

I raised an eyebrow. "Can you really do that?"

"No. Not literally, but they're making their displeasure impossible to ignore. I feel like my skin is trying to walk away without me."

"Huh," I said. What the hell did you say to that? It was creepy how they could "feel" each other like that.

"That might not be empathetic bond transference you're feeling," the nurse said as she checked something off on Flora's clipboard and leaned over to press an electric thermometer to her forehead.

Bliss cocked her head to the side. "Excuse me?"

The nurse pushed her hair behind her ears and looked up. "Did you say you feel like you're being summoned? Is that common?"

Bliss hesitated. "Well, no, but—"

The thermometer beeped, and the nurse pulled it back from Flora's face. She gave a satisfied nod. "No fever. Your friend is a very normal 101.3 degrees. Care to check yours?"

I blinked and quietly slid my phone out of my jeans pocket to google "average body temperature."

"Um, I guess," Bliss said awkwardly.

The nurse finished with Flora's chart and crossed the room, coming to stand in front of Bliss. She changed the cover on the top of the electric thermometer wand and ran the thing along Bliss's forehead. It beeped.

"Ah, see? That's what I thought. You're already at 104.7."

"What?" Bliss squeaked, grabbing for the thermometer to look. "What does that mean?"

"It means you'll be heading into your cycle within the next day or two."

Bliss flushed, and I looked away, doing my best to blend into the wall.

"Listen, I guess I do need to run." She looked out the window again. "Call me the second she wakes up, okay?"

"Will do."

"I'm serious." She squared her shoulders, all traces of exhaustion or discomfort vanishing. "I don't want her to wake up here alone."

The "or else" was heavily implied.

Annoyance crawled up my skin. There wasn't a world where I'd let that happen. Hadn't I just said I wasn't leaving? "I swear I'll be here. And I'll call you. Or she can if she wants."

Bliss made her way to the door—I guess she was satisfied—but then she stopped and glanced back at me. "I don't know exactly what's going on between you two. You've somehow wiggled your way to being important to her."

I choked on my laugh. "Accurate."

Bliss' gaze softened as she looked at her best friend, still asleep. "She's just been through so much. I...she can't break."

I gritted my teeth against the growl threatening to escape. "She's stronger than you're giving her credit for."

Bliss smiled, wiping a tear away from her cheek, and sniffled. "I know she's strong. I just wish she'd stop having to be."

My jaw clenched, and I squeezed my hot coffee a little too hard, the scalding drink spilling over onto my hand. I quickly put the cup down. "If I have a say in the matter—which from now on, I fucking do." Bliss raised an eyebrow at that statement, but I ignored it. "Flora will never be in this kind of situation again."

"I'm happy she found you," Bliss said finally, a small smile crossing her face. "Not that I think this is settled or that she'll make it easy."

"Good," I said without a trace of sarcasm. "I like a challenge."

Bliss laughed and gave me a look that clearly said I had no idea what I was getting myself into. I glared until she shut the door behind her, muffling the sound.

Rubbing fabric and the cot creaking brought my attention back to Flora. She touched her hand to her head. "Bliss?"

Shit.

"Bliss just left. Do you want me to go get her?" Every fiber of my fucking being hated the idea of leaving even for a second, but I waited for her reply.

Her deep brown gaze met mine. "Wes?" Her brows pinched together, and then a flash of panic crossed her face.

"You're safe." I cupped the side of her jaw, making sure she could see the seriousness in my eyes. "Bliss and the guys are safe. Nero was...taken care of... For the most part, everything turned out okay."

I wasn't sure what to say about the girl who was taken with them and got killed in the van. Things hadn't turned out one hundred percent okay, and I had no way of knowing how much that death would impact Flora or Bliss. I didn't know the other girl or how they knew her. I did know that I was selfishly grateful that our whole group had come out miraculously unscathed.

If that made me a bad person, fine. I was willing to lead the parade of sinners into hell on Judgment Day, as long as my girl would be right there beside me, twirling a flaming baton.

All the tension drained from Flora, and she leaned against my hand. "Well, that's good, then."

Her response was a little too bubbly. "Still a little woozy from your concussion, aren't you?"

"Hmm. A little."

"Alright, get some rest. You'll be going home in the morning." I went to lift off the bed, but her hand clenched in mine.

"Don't go."

"Never dream of it. I'm just sitting in that chair right there." I pointed to the chair in the corner. Half of me wanted to crawl onto the cot with her, but the smarter half knew now was not the time.

She glanced at the chair, then back at me. "Okay." Her eyelids were drooping before she finished the word, and I watched until her breathing grew deep in sleep.

"I'm glad to see that Omega Flora has so many caring

friends." A slender lady who had to be at least as old as written language entered the room. She wore a black sweater, and her hair was piled on top of her head.

"Sorry, who are you?"

She gave me a look that made me feel like she was looking through me. "I'm the headmistress of the Institute."

I relaxed a bit, remembering that Flora said Bliss liked this woman. Representative something or other. "Does Bliss know you're here?"

"Of course." She raised one brow while simultaneously looking down her nose at me. "You do not think they will let just anyone in here, do you?"

I shrugged. "They let me in."

She gave me another quick assessing look, and her eyes turned soft. "It's quite clear *you* are not just anyone. You love her, correct?"

I flinched back. "I don't—"

"Save your lies for your priest and your mother, dear. I'm an omega. I'm sure you know we can scent lies, and I'm trying to help you."

I did, and it was annoying as all hell. "I don't have a priest," I said acidly. "I've got a hell of a bartender."

"Well, by all means, go on and try lying to him. Bartenders also have a shockingly strong ability to smell bullshit."

When her gaze met mine again, there was pity in them. She was old and spindly but somehow terrifying. She also somehow made the word "bullshit" sound proper, which was astounding.

I leaned back, not sure what to make of her. "I'm not sure what you're getting at." *Or why you're here.*

"You're a beta," she said. "It's clear you love her, and from the scent in here, it would appear she may feel the same." Warmth flooded my chest, and my heart pounded in my ears. I could barely make out her next words. "The question is, will you do what's right for her?"

My voice rumbled with a growl. "Of course I will."

Her eyes searched over me. "Enough to step back?"

"What?" I flinched, her question coming out of nowhere.

"She's an omega. She needs an alpha. Preferably a pack. You can't be that for her, no matter what."

My stomach plummeted. I didn't need to be able to smell a lie to know what she said was true. That I would never be enough for Flora. "I—"

"Just think about it, dear. Sometimes we have to sacrifice for the ones we care most about." She gave me a sad smile and walked out.

I bared my teeth. I didn't care what everyone else thought; I fucking hated that lady.

Who the fuck was she to throw out suggestions like that? Like I hadn't run that same problem through my head a million fucking times. The thing was, no one would care for her the way I did. Even the idea of leaving her, no matter how selfless the reason, felt like someone was trying to cut through my chest with a dull knife.

It felt like my eyes had just closed when the door opened wide. *Again.* Rage sifted through me at this latest interruption. *Alright. Visitation time is fucking over.*

"Wes?" said a voice from the doorway.

Clear gray eyes met mine, and I choked on my next breath. Fuck. Memories flooded back as I took in the doctor standing in front of me.

I stared, my chest burning with the need to take my next breath, but I was frozen on the spot. His hand dropped to his sides, the clipboard nearly forgotten. He wore the half mask all the professional alphas wore around omegas, but it didn't stop me from recognizing him.

How could I forget?

He checked me over, as if making sure there wasn't any other reason I was in this hospital room. His fist clenched at his side. He took a step toward me but stopped. "I didn't think I'd see you again."

I narrowed my gaze. After several moments of silence, he huffed out a breath, turning his back to me, and checked on Flora.

The second he faced away, air rushed from my lungs, and my chest heaved with my next inhale. He was here. *He was here.*

The doctor's voice was low. "Okay, Flora. I just need to check your eyes. This is going to be bright but only for a second."

She nodded, her gaze round on him. Soft. I hadn't seen her look at anyone like that, especially not an alpha. He flashed a light in her eyes quickly.

"You are looking good, Flora. I'll be back in the morning, and you should be free to go." The doctor paused at the door, eyes on me, but let it close behind him after several more moments of me not acknowledging him. I let out my breath. I wasn't ready to deal with that.

Flora sat partially up and looked around the room until she found me. "Wes." She sucked in a breath. "I thought you left. I heard what the woman said." Her voice broke.

I rushed to her, running my thumb along her cheekbone. "Never."

CHAPTER 25
Bliss

It turned out the nurse was wrong.

I didn't have a few days. I had a few hours.

By the time we got back to the Institute, it felt like my temperature had already risen another degree or so.

As soon as we had escaped the garage in Nevada, I'd spent a long time going over everything with Headmistress Levi and some police officers she insisted were unbiased. They agreed that I shot Nero in self-defense, and the Assembly wasn't going to press charges.

The Assembly might have had some help reaching that conclusion.

They had a strong interest in keeping me out of jail and a new chairwoman, who I was strongly considering naming my firstborn after, given everything she'd done for us.

In fact, the headmistress came through for me one more time, offering up the Institute's designated heat suite, since I wouldn't be able to fly home in time.

Two things surprised me about the heat suite at the Institute: first, in the entire time I'd lived here, I'd never realized it existed, and second, it never occurred to me that the Institute would need a heat suite.

While there weren't a ton of omega staff members, there were more than anywhere else in the country, and all the staff lived on campus. It seemed reasonable that there was someplace designed for emergencies.

What *didn't* surprise me was the design of the room—or rooms, as it were.

It was like a large hotel suite with a bedroom, combined living room and kitchen, and a bathroom that was the same size as the living room. The bedroom had no windows and a ceiling that was so low, I suspected all the guys would have to duck—a suspicion that was confirmed as soon as Rafe tried to step inside. He grimaced.

"We'll make do," I said bracingly.

"I should be comforting you, not the other way around," He stepped into me and ran his hands over my arms. "I'm sorry we can't go home in time. Familiarity is important, right? It's not just about a small space. It's being at home."

I smiled—that sounded like something out of one of Nox's books. "You guys are my home. I'm just as happy here as I would be back at the warehouse or even in a fort made of damp cushions and old crates."

He grinned at the memory, and the scent of his happiness was infectious. He pulled me in and kissed the top of my head. "Do you still want to go through with the mating?" he asked after a moment.

I stepped back to judge his expression, but there wasn't

a hint of hesitation there. The question was purely for my benefit. "More than anything."

The feeling of relief and excitement hit me down the bond, stronger than if it was only coming from Rafe. I wondered if actual mating would make picking out lines of communication more clear or if there would be no change. I glanced behind me to see who was listening to us.

All three of the other guys were lingering less than six feet away, clearly listening. Killian sat on the sofa facing the TV, but it wasn't on. Nox was staring at his phone, but his eyes weren't moving—he wasn't reading. And Ares was leaning against the counter, staring at me, not bothering to pretend he wasn't eavesdropping.

As I glanced at him, he raised a pale eyebrow at me. "So, who gets to go first?"

I furrowed my brows in response. "Um…I hadn't thought about it. Is that a decision I need to make?"

"Yes," Ares and Killian said at the same time as Rafe and Nox said, "No."

"I'm breaking the tie and saying no." I crossed the room and sat on the couch next to Killian, promptly reaching for a magazine on the table to fan myself with. "Rock paper scissors for it."

My fan had no effect since the climate in this room was similar to the surface of Venus.

"Speaking of decisions," Rafe said, stepping forward.

I glanced up at him, and at that moment, a bead of sweat dripped down the side of my face, landing on the cover of my magazine. "Can we turn down the temperature in here?"

"No, actually, the AC doesn't go any lower," Nox said

apologetically. He eyed me closely. "You are probably only a few hours away, if that."

I leaned against Killian, who was closest, and sighed. "I know."

"Right," Rafe said, his tone brisk. "So we should just talk about something really quick."

"What?"

His expression was more uncomfortable than I'd seen in a while—maybe ever. "Peanut, you're not on birth control."

Glancing around at the others, I had a strong feeling Rafe had been nominated by the rest of the group to be the one to bring this up to me and probably couldn't come up with a good enough reason why he shouldn't have to do it. Unbidden, my brain conjured up how everyone else would have started this conversation:

"So, I've been tracking your ovulation, and you smell different, Little Wolf."

"Fuck, I can't wait to knot and breed you, Love. Would you like that?"

"Hey, babe? I like kids. Do you like kids? Well, you're gonna."

I shook my head to clear it. Oh my God, I was officially losing it because all of that sounded pretty good to me, and it was all in my head.

"Bliss," Rafe said, a little louder.

I blinked. "Sorry. Heat...I'm getting spacy."

Rafe exchanged a glance with Ares, who pushed off the counter where he'd been leaning. "Do you understand what that means, Love?"

This was one of those rare moments that I had to keep in mind that sometimes biology won out. There wasn't an alpha on the planet who didn't have a thing about breeding, even if my guys were clearly doing their best not to show any reaction in case I didn't want to be knotted without birth control.

"I understand. It's bound to happen sooner or later, right?" Sooner being the more likely option. Nine times out of ten, omegas didn't get pregnant in their first heat, but every time after that…well, that was what a heat was for. Even if I did go on birth control, it wasn't as effective for omegas…and with four alphas. I looked around at them with wide eyes. "I think we all know this is a done deal anyway."

The scent in the room shifted, immediately going from salty anticipation to honey-scented excitement. I wished I could be quite as ready to go as they were, except I was about to strip off my dress and have the rest of this conversation naked—and not for sexy reasons. It was so damn hot.

Nox eyed me, wiping sweat out of the crease between my boobs. He leaned around Rafe to peer into the bathroom in the next room over. "What if you went and took a cold bath?"

I weighed that suggestion. "Alright."

Ares opened the refrigerator and peered inside. "There's nothing to eat. Literally nothing." He held open the empty fridge for us to see. "If we're going to be here for a week, we should do a store run right now."

I frowned. I didn't want any of them to go anywhere, but logically, I realized that was unreasonable. And he was right—now would be the time to go. "Get me Chocolate Peanut Butter Split."

"You got it, Love."

"Bathroom" wasn't quite the right word for the room that contained the bath. *Bathhouse? Spa?*

The floor was mostly tiled, except for a row of wooden sauna-style benches along half of one wall. A huge sunken tub the size of a commercial hot tub, like I'd seen on reality dating shows and teen dramas growing up, was set into the floor. Across from that was a shower large enough to easily fit ten people. Against the wall stood a massage table, and there were enough creams, oils, and lube to last several lifetimes.

It dawned on me that there was no reason for the most recent administration to have created a heat room with enough space for a pack—maybe this was leftover from the distant past that Headmistress Levi had referenced.

I turned on the bath and stripped out of my clothing, looking over myself in the mirror. My hair was mostly blonde again, only the palest hint of lavender remaining. I fingered a strand, trying to decide what to do with it. Maybe I'd really commit and go indigo next.

When the bath filled, I dumped in a handful of salts and some bubbles from the table of various products and dipped a toe in the water. I hissed at the temperature—too hot. Yet, I didn't care. I was too impatient to wait for it to cool down.

It probably wasn't even that hot. It was me that was running a crazy fever, and anything other than an ice bath would make me feel like a boiled lobster.

I put one foot in completely, then the other, wincing as my skin acclimated to the temperature and I was able to sink fully beneath the surface. Despite the heat, the scalding hot water eased my tired muscles, and I relaxed, lying back against the porcelain edge of the tub.

The door creaked open, and Killian's lemon-and-vanilla scent invaded the bathroom, made more intense by the steam. "How's it going in here?"

"It's going," I replied, cracking an eye open.

"You want company?"

"Sure."

My body wasn't yet demanding to be touched every second, but I was close. Even now, as he got closer, walking around the edge of the tile floor to stand near the foot of the massage table, my pulse slowed. I only now realized I'd been on edge since leaving the living room.

Killian didn't bother to hide his wandering gaze, darting to my naked body under the water, barely covered by my lackluster attempt at bubbles. He smirked, his eyes heating, and I clenched my legs together.

"Is it only you still here?" That seemed odd.

"No. Rafe will be here in a—" He broke off as Rafe stepped into the room.

"Nox went with Ares," Rafe said. "They'll be right back."

As he came in, my pulse thrummed, my body reacting

Once again, my chest panged. My body didn't want the pack separated, and I voiced that thought.

"You must be really close to heat," Rafe said thoughtfully.

I nodded in agreement. If we hadn't already been warned by the doctors and by my scent, my mood and the fact that I felt like Icarus would all be dead giveaways.

Even more than that, my hormones were riding me harder now that my brain had begun to relax.

"Come here, baby." Killian beckoned me to the other side of the tub near the faucet. He grabbed shampoo and conditioner off the table and was squirting some into his palm.

I swam the couple of feet across the hot tub and settled in front of Killian. "Are you coming in?"

He flashed his dimples. "Not for this. Face the other way."

I turned my back to him and let out an embarrassingly loud moan when he ran his fingers through my hair, massaging the shampoo into my scalp. He massaged along my temples, lathering the shampoo until the floral aroma filled my nose and some of my stress melted away. "Mmmm."

"Better?"

"So much."

He poured water over the back of my head, washing away the suds, then started running a conditioner through the lengths of my hair. My chest warmed, my entire body feeling like it was floating.

I opened my eyes just a little and caught Rafe's gaze. He was watching us with an expression that danced on the line between desire and tranquility. That need to get close surged, doubling and rebounding on me until I felt like I could combust.

"Come in with me," I said in a tone that came out as almost a moan. I gestured to the tub, which no longer felt too hot—just the simple act of being touched was regulating my body.

I needed to be near them, but soon, I knew that wouldn't be enough.

"Not yet, Peanut," Rafe said, sounding a bit pained.

"We can't start yet, and if either of us gets in that tub with you, there's no turning back."

My eyes narrowed in confusion. "What are you talking about?"

"He means *we* can't start yet," Killian said, rinsing my hair out again. "We said we'd wait for the others to get back. That doesn't mean we can't make you feel good."

I whimpered, and I reached back and palmed his hard cock through his jeans. "I'd feel good with you inside me."

"Fucking Christ, you're going to kill me." He took a step back and put the shampoo back on the table.

I craned my neck around to watch, just in time to see him grab a bottle of lotion instead. "Come up here, baby." He nodded to the massage table.

Rafe walked around to the edge of the bath and lifted me out as if I weighed nothing, not caring his clothes immediately got drenched all the way down the front. He put me down on the white sheet covering the table, and his dark eyes flashed as they raked over me. "Lie down."

"If you're trying not to accelerate things, isn't this the opposite of that?" I asked as I rolled onto my stomach. "Not that I'm complaining."

Killian passed Rafe the lotion, and he slid his hands easily up the backs of my calves to my thighs, the lotion mixing with the water still clinging to my skin. He rubbed the heel of his hand back and forth over the backs of my thighs, maintaining firm, even pressure. I moaned as he ran over the tight, tired muscles, no doubt sore from being tied to the chair.

"I think you're right. If you keep moaning like that, this will be a short massage," Killian joked.

I chuckled, even as my stomach leapt with excitement

and heat licked up my belly. "I don't know if that sounds like a threat or a promise."

"It's both."

Killian positioned himself at my head, and then a second set of hands landed on my skin, running up the length of my back and over my arms in firm, even strokes. The scent of vanilla washed over me, and I sighed in contentment.

Strong yet gentle fingers trailed over my bare ass and back down. "Are you feeling better, Peanut?"

"I don't feel like I'm boiling alive," I said, intentionally not answering the question. "Better" was relative. I was less uncomfortable, but now I felt like I was going to combust in a whole new way.

Rafe ran his hands over my ass again, moving up and circling my lower back. A shiver traveled over my entire body, and I squirmed, part of me loving the relaxation, part of me wishing he would linger just a bit lower. Move his fingers just inches down and reach where I really wanted him. Instead, he moved higher, kneading my shoulders and occasionally brushing Killian's hands.

Rafe let his hands trail lower, running along my lower back and over my butt cheeks. I arched my back and moaned into the towel folded under my face. "Please. I need you to touch me."

Rafe chuckled quietly so low I almost didn't catch it. "Look, I think she wants more."

"Yes," I whimpered into the towel under my head. "More."

"More than this, baby." There was humor in Killian's voice as he kept working his fingers into the tense places in my upper back.

Rafe ran his palms over my thighs, his fingers getting tantalizingly close to my throbbing core. On the third pass, when I was practically trembling, my moan turned into a growl—they were teasing me, working me up while we waited for Nox and Ares to get back. "No more teasing."

Rafe nudged my thighs wider and finally cupped me from behind, stroking softly and teasing my entrance with the tips of his fingers. "There you go, beautiful. Fuck, you're so wet already."

I moaned and arched up into him and spread my legs even further.

Killian leaned over me, folding himself in half, his chin resting on my spine. I felt the vibration of his words as he spoke to Rafe. "Let me taste."

Rafe parted me, running his fingers back over my entrance, and I heard the telltale sound of sucking as he offered his fingers to Killian.

Damn. "I can't," I whined. "I can't take it."

"We know," Killian said.

And maybe he did know, if he was feeling anything like the crazed need I was down the bond. I wasn't out of my mind—I knew where I was and who I was with this time, but it was like if I didn't get closer to my alphas now, I was going to crack apart.

"Turn over, baby," Killian whispered near my head. "I want to see your pretty tits."

I obeyed without question, rolling over onto my back. Killian stood directly behind my head, looming over me, and I blinked up into his honey-brown eyes. I bit my lip, and a jolt of excitement shot to my belly as I watched him swallow thickly at the sight of my naked body laid out in front of him like a buffet.

His large hands landed on my shoulders, then slid lightly down my collarbones to my breasts. I trembled as he gently massaged, running his thumbs over my almost painfully hard nipples.

You just wanted to see them? I thought. "How about taste them?"

Killian laughed. "Fuck yes."

Oh, did I say that out loud?

"My heat is coming on," I said, my distress obvious. "My head's all…" I trailed off, distracted by Killian's wandering fingers and talented tongue as he bent and sucked one breast into his mouth, his hand gliding over the other. His tongue circled my tight nipple, and a jolt of pleasure shot through me so strong I thought I might ignite.

"We know, Peanut." Rafe stood at the base of the table between my slightly parted legs, eyes hooded as he watched us. "You're doing perfect."

I whimpered, and my voice sounded foreign. "What if I don't remember anything?"

"It probably won't be like that this time."

"But if it is, I want all of you. I need all of you before it gets to be too much." My voice already sounded needy and not completely like myself.

Killian lifted his head from my chest, and I moaned at the lack of contact. His curls brushed my cheek as he straightened slightly. "Pace yourself, baby. It's a marathon. Ares and Nox will be back in a minute."

"Where—" I could feel myself getting worked up, my hormones going all wonky. Where was the rest of my pack?

"Shhh," Rafe soothed. He glided his fingers over my

entrance again, this time taking advantage of the better angle and circling my clit with one delicate finger. "It's okay. You don't need to worry about anything right now. Just let us take care of you."

He pushed two fingers back inside me while at the same time massaging my clit with his thumb.

"More." I bucked against his hand, helpless against the intensity of the sensations coursing through me.

Killian leaned over and resumed his meticulous licking over my nipples, and it was torture. Slow, sweet, torture because they knew what I really wanted. How long did I have to wait before someone put their cock in me?

Rafe added a second and third finger and resumed his slow, steady fucking of me with his hand.

"More," I begged.

Rafe curled his fingers and stroked deep inside as my hips rose off the table. He bent and replaced the fingers of his other hand with his tongue, lapping at my clit with almost indecent enthusiasm.

Killian released my nipple and moved to capture my mouth in a hungry kiss. "Are you ready to come for us, baby?"

"Yes," I moaned. My voice was needy and foreign, the last...however long we'd been in here having completely pushed me over the edge. And still, this wasn't enough. I needed to be filled. Mated. "I want to feel you inside me. Please. I need it."

Rafe stopped licking me and raised his head. "Fuck." He stood, and I watched him glance at Killian over my naked body. "I tried. I can't do it." I lost my breath for half a second until he grabbed me by the thighs, hauling me to the end of the table. "Fuck Ares and Nox. They're taking too long."

Rafe lined up the head of his cock, and I screamed my approval, teetering over the edge as he thrust into me in one stroke.

I wrapped my legs around his waist instinctively, squeezing tight as I rode out my first orgasm, and waves of pleasure rippled through my entire body. I whimpered as he pulled back out and thrust into me again, moving the table forward several inches.

Killian came around to the side of the table and undid his own jeans, kicking them off. My mouth watered at the sight of his cock, hard bobbing right next to my mouth. I smiled and turned my face to the side to take Killian in against my tongue as Rafe pumped into me.

His knot knocked against my clit with each stroke, and almost instantly, I was close to coming again, my body beginning to shudder. "Mmmmm."

Rafe pushed my hair away from my face as I continued to suck. "I need to feel your tight little pussy around my knot."

I whimpered and nodded. He could have asked me to do anything, and I would have done it in that moment. Can I knot you? *Yes, please.* I'm going to jump off that bridge, want to come? *Sir, yes, sir.*

Killian moaned as my tongue swirled his shaft. I reached over to stroke his knot as his shaft choked me, and involuntary tears poured down my face, landing in my hair where it fanned out across the table.

"Shit." Killian pulled back from my mouth abruptly. "You need to stop, baby, or I'm going to come."

Rafe chuckled at his friend's expense but reached

down and cupped my face, drawing my attention. He stroked my hair and smiled down at me, then bent and sucked on my bottom lip for a moment, and I opened my mouth for him, sweeping my tongue against his before he moved to my neck. In one movement, he lifted me and flipped our positions so he was lying on the end of the massage table, his legs hanging over the end, with me draped over him. My knees were planted on the surface of the table on either side of Rafe's hips, my chest pressed to his.

He drew his tongue over my mating gland in a long, slow lick, and I shuddered, quaking against him. A heat started to build in my lower stomach.

I ground down hard on his knot as it swelled inside me, locking us together. He pulled me closer, brushing his lips against mine. His black eyes scanned my face. "You ready, Bliss?"

My heart ricochet in my chest, the thrumming of my pulse in my ears. I'd been waiting for years for this moment. I kissed him, long and slow, pouring my emotions into him, and breathed against his mouth. "Yes."

He swore loudly, and I felt his hot cum inside just before he sunk his teeth into my neck. I sucked in a breath, and the world went silent, the explosive mating bond snapped into place.

A warmth and a sense of completeness filled me. I shattered, clenching around his knot as stars burst behind my eyelids.

"Holy fuck," Rafe said after a minute, his pupils blown so wide his entire eyes appeared jet black.

"Yeah," I agreed, though I had no idea what aspect of the experience he was referring to.

"Damn," Killian's voice sounded right behind me, his tone as shell-shocked as I felt.

I twisted to see where Killian was standing—where he had been while Rafe was finally mating me—and jostled Rafe's knot, still locked inside me. We both moaned at the abrupt movement.

Killian laughed and moved so close I could feel him against my back.

He stood flush with the end of the table, knees bumping against Rafe's. He ran a hand along my spine, gently guiding me back to a lying down position, and pressed his hard cock into my ass.

I knew what he was thinking before he even voiced it.

"Yes. Please," I moaned.

Killian petted my head, running his fingers through my still-damp hair. "You're such a good omega." He reached for one of the many lubes on the table of bath products and rubbed some over my tight entrance. He pressed the head of his cock up against me, and I gasped, needing a moment to adjust.

Rafe held me tight to his chest, even though it was impossible for me to move even if I wanted to. "I've got you, beautiful."

Killian pressed in another inch, and I whimpered, growing hotter at the sight of the obvious lust on Rafe's face, watching Killian fuck me. I braced myself against Rafe, breathing heavily as Killian pounded into us. I rocked forward a little, loving the tightness and the complete feeling of them filling me. "Yes, please. More."

Killian reached over and pushed my hair to the side and ran his tongue over the spot where Rafe had just marked me. I bared my neck, expecting another bite.

Instead, Killian rubbed his nose against the spot, scenting himself all over it, purring.

He leaned over my shoulder and grabbed Rafe's hair, pulling him up to meet his mouth in a sloppy, bruising kiss, and Rafe twitched inside me.

"This is wild," Killian said, pulling away and speaking against Rafe's surprised mouth and the shell of my ear sandwiched tight between them. "I can feel you now too. Almost like with Bliss."

"Really?" I asked, so shocked I momentarily forgot that this wasn't the best time to be having this conversation—while I was pressed between two of my alphas on the massage table, both buried deep inside me.

"I can't feel anything new." Rafe sounded almost panicked.

Killian seemed totally at ease. "No one else has created the bond yet. You'll see. It's like we used to be just getting one channel, but you just jumped on the conference call."

"I don't think that makes sense," I pointed out.

"I don't care. It feels fucking amazing. You're still the main planet, but now you have a satellite."

I blinked at him, surprised. It was funny. That was how I used to think about my relationship with the pack. Like I was the satellite to their world. Instead, maybe there could be one planet with four moons.

I leaned over, bringing my entire body flush against Rafe, and Killian groaned as he followed me over, bracing his hands on either side of us. I bared my neck to him. "So, what are you waiting for?"

Killian ran his hot tongue in teasing circles over my glands that made me shutter. The act of mating itself seemed to send me over the edge, but there was also the incredible fullness between my thighs, the gentle pressure Killian was putting on my clit with his free hand, and the muscles of Rafe's hard chest rubbing against my sensitive nipples.

As Killian sunk his teeth into my neck, I went practically limp in between them, fully exhausted from pleasure.

I was pretty sure it was Nox who lifted me off the table in a boneless heap and carried me to the bedroom.

"You're back," I said sleepily.

"Rest, Little Wolf. You'll need it."

When I woke up next, I was on fire.

The darkness of the room was disorienting. I had no sense of time or space, only them around me. I moaned and cried, needy incoherent sounds I didn't recognize.

Nox knelt beside me and held my wrists, pressing me gently back into the mattress. He bent his head and kissed along my collarbone, and I whimpered. "Don't cry, Little Wolf. We're going to take care of you. Always."

Killian pushed my thighs apart, and I gasped as his fingers grazed over the mating glands there. "Shhh, baby. I've got you."

As he slid inside me, I lifted my hips, meeting him stroke for stroke. "Please."

The fresh scent of a summer's night filled my mouth and nose, and Ares knelt on the bed opposite Nox. I turned to him, reaching, and he bent down to capture my mouth. Heat and desire rippled through me, and I writhed, grinding my hips against Killian.

I propped myself up on my hands, leaning as far back as I could while Killian was still thrusting in and out of me, and took the base of Ares' shaft in my fist. He hissed and grasped the top of my head, instinctively steadying me.

I licked up his shaft, sucking and nibbling. Killian leaned forward and matched my speed as he licked up the other side.

Ares made a sound that was somewhere between a hiss and a moan. His other hand landed on Killian, and he clearly didn't know who to look at. Killian and I met in the middle, our lips pressing together over the tip of Ares' cock.

No thoughts permeated my consciousness, only scents and colors and sensation. Flashes of white and red behind my eyes, honey and spice in the air, and that line between pleasure and the burning pain coursing through my whole body.

Rafe's dark eyes watched me over Nox's shoulder, hot and filled with hunger. He reached one hand around and thumbed my clit and at the same time grazed his teeth over Nox's neck.

I keened, the need inside of me building. My mating glands throbbed, and my body still felt somehow empty. I needed more. "Please, Alpha," I said to everyone and no one in particular. "I need you to fill me."

The scent in the air was hard to distinguish, though my nose, like everything else, seemed on high alert. The honey taste of sex in the air eclipsed everything.

At least I felt more or less lucid. *Would I know if I wasn't?*

I reached out blindly in the darkness to my right and left, and my fingers wrapped around someone's bicep. I tugged, pulling whoever it was even closer.

Ares rolled over in bed next to me, clearly half-asleep. "Hey, Love."

He wore only black boxer briefs, and his tattooed muscles were on full display, somehow looking larger and more lickable to me than they usually did.

Did I mean lickable... I racked my brain for another word. *No, that was* exactly *what I meant. Maybe I'm not totally normal.*

My pulse thrummed, and my body felt cold and hot at the same time. Empty. I needed to be touched. I reached out in what I hoped was a subtle, normal way and put one hand on his chest.

Two hands. Two hands were better.

I peered down into his pale eyes, which appeared eerily white in the darkness. "You're here."

"Yeah." He blinked up at me. "I'd never miss this." He paused and made a face. "Twice. I'd never miss it twice."

"But you were gone."

"Just at the store." He leaned over to the bedside table, careful not to jostle me, and grabbed an empty carton of Peanut Butter ice cream. "This is what I gave you last time we talked about this."

My eyes widened. "Oh, shit."

He laughed. "Yeah. It's been about twenty-four hours. Not that bad."

"Wait." I sat back a little and brought the fingers of my right hand to my neck. "Did—"

"No. We've been waiting for you to seem lucid. Those lucky pricks snuck in just under the wire, but you were asleep when Nox and I got back." He glanced at something behind me. "Traitorous fuckers were supposed to wait for us."

I turned to realize that Rafe was asleep right behind me, and Nox was on his other side. As I looked on, Nox threw an arm around Rafe in their sleep, and they angled into each other.

I cast my gaze around and realized that Killian was behind Ares; I just hadn't seen him at first because of the dim light. "I couldn't wait."

"I know, Love. I'm playing with you."

I shifted, trying to get closer again. Ares reached out and pulled me down until I was lying in the crook of his arm, half my body next to him, the other half draped on top of his. My skin hummed contentedly everywhere we touched.

"Right," I said, picking up on the last bit of the conversation I could remember. "How am I doing now?"

"With what?"

"Do I seem lucid to you?"

He thought about it, one hand running up and down my bare back. "6.5 out of 10."

I scoffed, offended. "Why so bad?"

"Because I know you're okay right now, but in five minutes, it will be 'Knot me, Alpha. Come inside me and breed me, Alpha.' Not that I'm complaining."

I choked, caught somewhere between laughing and moaning. I knew he was joking, but the words themselves sent a pulsing awareness right to my core, like a ticking clock. "I don't know about that."

He gave me a face that seemed to say, *"We'll see."*

"Bend over, Love."

I pressed my hands to the headboard and looked back to check on his reaction. "How's this?"

He smacked my ass, then bent to kiss the spot with the stinging handprint. "That's perfect. You're such a good omega,"

Ares nudged my entrance with the head of his cock, running it back and forth over me until I was mewling, trying to drive my ass backward to impale myself on him.

"Fill me," I whimpered. "Please. I want to feel you coming inside me."

"Fuck, you're beautiful," he said in a quiet, soothing voice I'd only ever heard him use with me.

Then he pressed into me, filling me entirely as his huge body crowded me, making me feel safe, small, and protected. I moaned and stretched around his huge shaft.

Ares lapped at my neck, sucking and biting along my glands and sending little sparks through me every time his teeth grazed my flesh. He gave my pebbled skin a long, sensuous lick, and I trembled, sounds tumbling from my mouth with complete abandon.

He reached around and wrapped the hand not holding on to my hip around my throat on one side and pulled me up, harder, as he fucked me as rough and as intensely as I'd seen him do anything.

"Please, Ares," I begged, almost crying now. "I need it. I need you to knot me."

He slammed into me again, nipping at my ear. "What

did I tell you?" he whispered, the dark humor evident in his tone. "Didn't I promise you that soon you would be all about begging your alpha to breed you?"

I panted, and my voice was shaky as my entire body rocked against the headboard. "I didn't say a-alpha," I told him. "I asked you. I want you to come inside me. I want your knot."

"Fuck," he practically screamed but not as though he were mad. More like he was in disbelief.

He pulled out of me and moved to lie on his back, yanking me down on top of him. Sitting up so we were chest to chest, he pressed his face into the crook of my neck. "I love you, Bliss. You're perfect."

The combination of the words and his teeth sinking into my flesh set something off in me I couldn't describe, a fullness that was almost painful in its intensity. I cried out, clenching around him. His knot swelled, locking me in place, and I slumped forward, feeling his heart beating fast under my cheek.

"Fucking crazy," he said against my hair.

"The bonds?" I asked, suddenly remembering.

"Yeah."

I glanced over to my left, spotting Nox's green eyes open in the darkness, watching us. Not asleep, just not playing this round. He smirked at me. "We always knew you bonded us all to each other. This makes sense."

I held my arms out, wordlessly asking him to come over to us, and he inched closer around a dozing Rafe. Nox's eyes flew to my neck, and an unmistakable look of longing passed over them. He dipped his head and nuzzled my neck, scenting himself all over the existing bonds.

"Did you lose rock paper scissors?" I quipped, feeling much more myself now that the latest heat wave had been taken care of. Later, I'd ask Nox if he'd read about this—if it usually came in waves and if last time the drugs had been the biggest factor in my total blackout.

"We didn't play," Nox said. "We were going to go by age, but..." He trailed off—or maybe I fell asleep.

"It doesn't matter what order you went in," I tried to say as I was dozing off.

Soon, I'd have all of them.

Rafe lay on his back, gripping my thighs with both hands as I straddled his face. He licked up and down in long, slow strokes and circled the tip of his tongue over my clit until I was gasping for air.

Nox took the opportunity of my distraction to capture my mouth in a long kiss. I moaned and opened for him, my tongue darting in to taste him before sucking on his top lip. He turned his head, and I moved my mouth to his neck, running my tongue along his glands. He growled low in his throat, the vibration making me shudder with anticipation.

Ares appeared beside Nox, capturing his chin in a harsh grip and reclaiming his freed lips in a dominant kiss that had my eyes going wide and heat traveling to my core.

Large hands—Killian's—slid down my hips, pulling me back slightly against his hard cock as Rafe continued to press open-mouthed kisses to my clit. My eyes rolled back into my head.

Rafe reached up and ran his fingers over my entrance, and I moaned as he dipped them in just slightly. "Look at you, dripping. How many knots have you already taken?"

"Not enough."

"That's right, little omega. It's never enough." He shoved his fingers further inside me, to the point that it was so overly tight I almost fell apart. "I'm going to just shove all that back up there. Don't want you to lose it and ruin all our hard work."

I shuddered, arching my back, a soft purr bubbling up in my chest.

It seemed as though I was close to the end of my heat. At least, it seemed that way to me—time was a little hard to keep track of.

I reached out for Nox again and pulled him away from Ares. They'd all knotted me countless times, but my respectful, red-haired overthinker hadn't bitten me yet, waiting for when I would be the most lucid I could possibly be. At this rate, he might end up missing it.

I leaned over and licked his neck again, palming his cock at the same time, and he growled. "Bliss—"

My name was left hanging, like a devotion.

"I need you. Please mate me."

He kissed me again, softly this time, and lay on his back. I sunk down, impaling myself on his thick shaft. "Mmm."

He looked up at me with hooded eyes. "Fuck, I will never get used to this."

I understood what he meant. I hoped we'd all be together forever, and I would still be amazed and excited that they'd chosen me. That it would still feel like I was the luckiest beta girl in the world, who somehow ended up part of this pack of alphas.

Nox grasped my hips and lifted me, bouncing me up and down a few times. I whimpered and bent my head to the side, presenting my neck.

He raised up on one hand, his eyes dark, and ran his tongue over my mating glands in hot, slow strokes.

I bucked my hips, already too sensitive from Rafe's gentling licking and soft nibbles. "Now. I need it," I begged. "I can't—"

He sunk his teeth in, and a wave of pleasure washed over me that I felt everywhere. My back arched, and I throbbed deep inside. His knot swelled, and I ached, clenching around him.

My breath was uneven, my whole body suddenly hyperaware of all my bonded mates around me. *All of them. Finally mine.*

I glowed, feeling all the emotions around me. Everything they felt for me, had always felt for me, was suddenly clear, and my chest seized. Knowing somehow this would be the end of my heat, I glanced around. "I need all of you. Together."

They rearranged themselves without words, like maybe they'd found some kind of equilibrium too.

Coming up behind me, Killian grazed his teeth over my shoulder blade, and a new shiver rocked my body. "You're so beautiful." He pushed me down flat against Nox until my sensitive nipples rubbed along his chest. "Ready, baby?"

"Always." My lip tipped up at the corner, and I shivered, rocking back and forth to expel some of the tension. "Yes."

I braced my palms on Nox's shoulders, and the pressure started to build as Killian inched his way inside me. Nox moaned as Killian pumped in and out of me a few times, situating himself before stopping, like he was waiting for everyone else.

Rafe knelt in front of me, over Nox's head, fisting his cock. Without question, I leaned forward and took his head in my mouth, swallowing as much of his length as I could. Nox cocked an eyebrow at me and moved his head up to take one of Rafe's balls into his mouth.

"Fuck." Rafe jerked forward and braced a hand on the top of Killian's head.

Killian trembled against my back, and at first, I thought he was laughing at Rafe. "Holy shit." His voice was barely in control as Ares pressed into him from behind, pushing him deeper into me.

My body spasmed, the complete fullness second only to the completely right feeling filling me now that I had my whole pack in every sense.

Soon, my body began to quake again, my final orgasm rocking through me, and I slumped between them, completely spent.

Sometime later, I lay in the center of the bed in a tangle of limbs and twisted sheets. I stared up at the ceiling, one hand on my stomach, listening to the quiet breathing of my mates. I smiled—the scent in the air seemed to have changed.

Rolling over, I pressed my face into the pillow and went back to sleep. This really was bliss.

Epilogue
1 YEAR LATER

"Why wasn't there cake when we were at the Institute?" Flora spoke around a mouthful of food and moaned as she licked the icing off her fingers.

She glanced to the side, where a grumpy-looking Wes leaned against the wall of the Institute gymnasium. He eyed her in a way that made me think I should be the one to leave even though we were in a crowded room, then looked away. Flora huffed beside me.

"Still not giving in?" I asked, stuffing another guide pamphlet into one of the takeaway bags.

"Males are idiots," she grumbled, filling her own bag, then putting it in the basket a little harder than necessary.

I glanced over to where Killian and Rafe laughed at something the group of alphas said. My chest warmed, and a barrage of squishy emotions bubbled in my stomach. Their eyes met mine, and their heads tilted simultaneously, bringing a grin to my mouth.

Our pack had done a lot of healing in the last year, and

we'd all grown closer because of it. I gave them a quick wink before returning to my work. "I don't know. They aren't all bad."

Flora rolled her eyes, making an exasperated sound. "Says the omega with four alphas so head over heels for you, they're practically upside down." I turned my face, trying to hide my grin, but she caught it. "Don't say it."

I widened my eyes, all innocence. "I said nothing."

The only person in the way of Flora's own happy ending right now was Flora, and we all knew it.

She huffed. "Whatever."

I turned back to look at the stage. "Let's wrap this up. The last speaker is nearly done, and I'm starving."

This was our second Omega Awakening Event, and we were already planning a third. It turned out now that the Institute had stopped snatching omegas from their families and instead provided them with the option of side-effect-free blockers, the omegas who'd gone into hiding started to come out.

Each of these events had several speakers who were omegas that didn't go to the Institute. What life and mating could be like when there was no interference.

We also had speakers from omegas who matched happily from the Institute and wouldn't change it for the world. This event was all about giving unmated omegas options and information. Some would still go to the Institute while others would choose to stay with their parents, but either way, it would be their decision.

Strong arms wrapped around my middle, the scent of lemon vanilla filling my nose, and I sank against Killian's warm chest. He kissed the top of my head. "I agree with Flora. Let's go."

"I can't just leave."

"Sure you can." Rafe stuffed the last of the packets, placing them into the basket. "Let one of the other organizers do something for a change." He ran fingers along my arm, and my skin pebbled in their wake. The sweet scent of honey filled my nose.

"Okay, lovebirds. I'll finish up. Don't need the impressionable young omegas seeing that."

I rolled my eyes, going to insist we stay and help, but stopped when Killian nipped my ear, whispering, "Come on. I want to see the twins before nap time."

My chest warmed. I would never get over how much my alphas loved our kids. One of them always whined to go home if we were away for more than a few hours. I wouldn't lie. I loved it.

"You sure, Flora?" I asked, Rafe already pulling me toward the car.

She laughed, blowing me a kiss. "Yes. Get out of here."

It was only a twenty-minute drive from the Institute to the home we'd purchased in California. We still stayed in New York, but I wanted to stay connected to the changes happening at the Institute. I wouldn't say I didn't trust them to change their ways, but I also couldn't say the Institute had a great track record.

I sat in the passenger side beside Rafe, my eyes catching on the large wooden sign as we turned onto our property. Blissful Pack Orangerie.

I'd been shocked the first time Rafe brought me here. I thought it was a fancy date night, only for the rest of my alphas to appear and say they'd bought it with the additional revenue the new blocker formula brought in. I wanted to be mad that he'd made such a big decision without me, but it became extremely apparent that the place was perfect.

The driveway was lined with orange trees, and I rolled down my window to smell the sweet scent of new blossoms. A happy hum trailed down the bond, and Rafe reached over, squeezing my thigh.

We pulled into the roundabout drive. The house was enormous, with ten bedrooms and eleven baths, designed in a Mission Revival style. It had red clay tile roofing with low-pitch slopes and a white stucco exterior. The doors and windows were arched, giving it a Spanish old-world look that was the epitome of welcoming.

Rafe parked, and I was barely out of the car before Nox and Ares stepped out of the front double doors, each one holding a bubbling blond-haired, violet-eyed baby. Everyone said they looked just like me, but I could see a little of each of my alphas in them.

Killian moved past me, quickly taking Orion from Ares' arm, and love pummeled through the bond as she looked up and smiled at him. Rafe picked up Oliver, rocking gently so he would fall back to sleep.

"How was the event?" Nox pulled me into his arms and kissed my forehead.

I snuggled into his chest, breathing in his smooth sandalwood scent. "Really good. I think it's going to work."

Ares pressed his chest against my back, sandwiching me between them, kissing a line up the curve of my neck. "We never doubted you, Love."

"I'm thinking of doing some kind of academic scholarship next. I don't know. I need to talk to Delilah."

Rafe pretended to roll his eyes, but I could feel his

pride and excitement. "If you keep hanging out with her, she's going to convince you to join the Assembly."

I grinned. "Don't tempt me."

My heart sang as the perfectness of this moment sank in.

In all my years at the group home, then the Institute, only in my wildest dreams had I hoped for this.

Epilogue
4 YEARS LATER

"You look nice," Flora said, taking baby Delilah from me when she walked through the front door of the warehouse.

Delilah's grubby one-year-old fingers tugged on Flora's hair. She made a small squeak sound and shifted her like an expert, switching out her dark brown locks for a rubber giraffe toy. My fingers lifted to twirl my lavender hair before I remembered I'd had it swept up into a chignon.

"Thanks. Nox and Killian ran interference with the littles, and Ares and Rafe took Orion and Oliver to get ice cream so I'd have time to get ready." You'd think four would be more than enough, but the guys were already fighting about names for the next ones.

At some point, I was going to have to break their hearts and cut them off.

"Are you excited about tonight? First Agora since ours?" Flora asked hesitantly.

A twinge of nerves flirted in my stomach. "I'm not sure I'll be 'excited' for the Agora. No matter what changes."

Her gaze softened knowingly, and she eyed my deep green dress. "Nox pick that out for you?"

I rolled my eyes. I gave up long ago on trying to discourage them. Changing the subject, I said, "I really appreciate you coming over here. I know you had plans to visit your parents."

"Are you kidding? I'd never miss a chance to spend time with my nieces and nephews." She kissed the baby's cheek for emphasis. "Plus, just think how happy my pack will be when I get home." She smirked and winked at me, causing me to roll my eyes.

"Well, I appreciate it." I turned toward the disaster that was my living room, strongly considering calling tonight off and crashing on the couch.

Doors creaked shut down the hall, and Rafe, Ares, Nox, and Killian joined us. I sucked in a breath, and heat warmed my skin as I took them in. They were all in black tailored suits, crisp white shirts, and slender ties. I had a feeling Nox had played a large part in picking out what everyone wore tonight.

"Like what you see, B?" Killian chuckled, and I narrowed my eyes in a playful glare. I might have felt embarrassed for ogling them if all four of their hot gazes weren't focused on me. Honey scent filled the air, and Flora cleared her throat.

"Alright, lovebirds. Out you go." Flora shooed us toward the door.

"Wait. Okay, Orion, Oliver, and Theo are already in bed. Now—" I pointed at the sleepy-eyed baby snuggled into Flora's shoulder. "There's a bottle for her ready in the fridge. Just drop it into the warmer, and it'll be good to go. You may need to lie with her, but it shouldn't take too long after that for her to fall asleep."

Flora laughed. "I know what I'm doing now. Quit stalling and get out."

Rafe placed his coat jacket around my shoulders and kissed my forehead. "Come on, Peanut. Before she changes her mind."

———

Killian wrapped an arm around my shoulder, and Ares entwined our fingers as our limo inched toward the front of the gala. The eight tall columns holding up the arches of the museum were lit with bright purple, and people were already crowding up the red-carpeted stairs. A small shudder ran down my spine as I took in the building that looked like it was from Ancient Greece.

"Look at me, Peanut." My gaze flashed back to Rafe, who leaned forward, elbows resting on his knees in the seat facing me. "We're going to walk in there and see all the amazing things you've accomplished."

I huffed out a laugh. "You make it sound like I did this on my own—"

Nox raised a brow. "I'm going to cut you off there before we get into a long debate about how we all know you are amazing, and you seem to be in deep denial of all the good *you* have caused."

The car pulled up further, and a male in a black suit went to open the door. Ares held it shut. "You ready?"

My four alphas watched me, ready to turn around and abandon our plans if I so much as hinted at it. I felt down our bond and was met with nothing but pride and love. I didn't think I could ever come back here, but it turned out I could do anything with them.

The walk up the red carpet was blinding. Reporters shouted my name, looking to get a sound bite. My alphas formed a barricade around me until we crossed through one of the giant arched doorways. My heart thrummed in my chest as we walked into the large open space used for the Agora.

"Excuse me, just squeaking through." An omega and her mate walked past us to take their spot in one of the many rows of seating. By the time everyone settled, there wouldn't be an empty spot in the house. When the Institute board decided to bring back the Agora Ceremony, we made a conscious choice to make it the polar opposite of what it was.

A part of that was inviting the graduates' families. The decor had to be switched up to accommodate—row seating instead of tables, and the stage was significantly smaller now that it didn't house glass cages. A tremble ran through me with the memory, and Nox's fingers grazed down my back and tucked me to his side. "I've got you, Little Wolf."

I leaned against him, soaking in his strength. "I can't say I like it here."

"Same," Killian rumbled behind me.

My mentor, Delilah, tottered into the center of the stage, wearing a royal blue gown with long lace sleeves. She was so tiny that for a moment, most people didn't seem to see her over the tops of their programs, but when she reached the microphone, her voice was unmistakably loud. "If you could all please be seated, the ceremony is about to start."

We took our seats in the back row, Nox going in first, then Killian. I followed close behind him, and Ares and Rafe took up the last two seats. The Institute had offered spots at the front, but I honestly did not feel the need to be that close to the action. Plus, there was some relief knowing I could sneak away if I felt too uncomfortable.

The lights dimmed, and a gentle hush fell on the crowd.

"Good evening, and welcome to the annual Agora," said Delilah. "My name is Headmistress Omega Levi, and I will be leading tonight's ceremony. We are so happy to have you all here to help celebrate this momentous occasion."

Anxiousness started to crawl under my skin. Knowing it was a completely different ceremony didn't make this part any less nerve-racking.

"Tonight is a moment to recognize the achievements of our youth. We're here today to witness the graduates from the Omega Institute and celebrate their futures. The omegas receiving their diplomas tonight have…"

"Well, this is going to be boring." Killian rested his head on my shoulder. His breath tickled my neck, and he rubbed my knuckles until my fist slowly uncurled.

He trailed his fingers up my green satin-covered thigh, and I swatted his hand. "Killian."

"What? I'm just saying. There are better ways to pass the time."

I rolled my eyes, and amusement flooded the bond,

washing away the last sense of trepidation I was holding on to. Distracted, I missed most of the speech.

"Welcome the graduating class." The room erupted in cheers, drowning out her words as the back doors opened.

Twenty or so omegas stood, heads held high, and practically floated with excitement as they moved down the center aisle toward the stage. Their emotions wafted off them in fresh citrus, sweet flowers, and mint.

Relief flooded me, and Ares squeezed me to his side. They were happy. They were all so freaking happy.

The omegas lined up on one end of the stage, waiting for Delilah to call them up.

"This year's recipient of the Sarah Miller Memorial Award for Outstanding Achievement in Academics, Omega Eden Mendes." A curvy omega with bouncy deep brown hair practically ran up to the stage and stood in front of the headmistress.

"Omega Mendes, we present to you this diploma in Mechanical Engineering. You have earned this diploma through hard work and dedication, showing enthusiasm over the past four years. Congratulations." The headmistress handed Omega Mendes her diploma and stumbled back as the young omega hugged her. A smile split over my face as the crowd laughed. It was all so different from what the Agora had represented before.

Ares kissed my temple. "You did this. All of these omegas will have better lives because of you. Our daughters will have better lives because of you. You are amazing, Love."

Killian squeezed my thigh, much higher than he should've been. "Lucky for you, you're stuck with us forever now."

Peace settled over me, and I leaned into his side. I was finally happy right where I was, and there wasn't anything I'd change about it. "I love you guys."

Warmth flooded the bond, and I knew from now on, everything would be okay.

Continue

Hey! If you liked this book and want to help support indie authors, the best way to do that is by leaving a review. Just a few sentences makes a tremendous difference.

Want more from the authors?
The Gentlemen Series
On Amazon
Read Now
Need someone to share theories with?
Join Kate King & Jessa Wilder Reader Gang
Facebook Group
JOIN NOW

Follow Us

Join Our Facebook Group:
    Kate King & Jessa Wilder Reader Gang
    TikTok:
    Jessawilderauthor
    Katekingauthor
    Instagram:
    @kateking_jessawilder
    Get all the latest news first by signing up to Kate and Jessa's mailing list.
    Katekingjessawilder.com
    Website:
    Katekingjessawilder.com

Acknowledgement

While we're here, there's a few people we need to thank:

Thank you to our husbands who have supported us through six published books in one year!

Thank you to Emily, for reading the roughest of drafts, giving the best advice, and the third cog in our wheel.

Thank you to Cait for all the groveling advice.

Thank you to Nicole for joining our team on short notice and reading along with our writing process.

Thank you to our PA Kayleigh for being our mom and looking out for us.

Thank you to our editor, Sandra and our ad manager, Melissa.

Shout out to all our ARC readers. We couldn't have done this without you.

About the Authors

Kate King: Kate King is an author, coffee addict, and avid reader from Boston, Massachusetts. She lives in a converted church with her husband and two cats, and often writes in cemeteries.

In addition to romance, she writes YA thrillers with a magical twist and wants to publish thirty books before turning thirty.

Jessa Wilder: Jessa Wilder is a Canadian author of steamy contemporary and unconventional romance. When not writing, you can find her chasing around her seven-year-old son, walking her dog in the woods, and devouring Kindle Unlimited books.

Printed in Great Britain
by Amazon